USERLANDS

USERLANDS
NEW FICTION FROM THE BLOGGING UNDERGROUND

EDITED BY
DENNIS COOPER

AKASHIC BOOKS
NEW YORK

This collection is comprised of works of fiction. All names, characters, places, and incidents are the products of the authors' imaginations. Where names of actual dead persons have been used, these are fictional renderings and are not meant to bear any resemblance to actual persons bearing the same name.

Published by Akashic Books
©2007 Dennis Cooper

ISBN-13: 978-1-933354-15-6
Library of Congress Control Number: 2006923118
All rights reserved

First printing

Little House on the Bowery
c/o Akashic Books
PO Box 1456
New York, NY 10009
info@akashicbooks.com
www.akashicbooks.com

Also from Dennis Cooper's
Little House on the Bowery series

Artificial Light
by James Greer

Wide Eyed
by Trinie Dalton

Godlike
by Richard Hell

The Fall of Heartless Horse
by Martha Kinney

Grag Bag
by Derek McCormack

Headless
by Benjamin Weissman

Victims
by Travis Jeppesen

Table of Contents

11	**Dennis Cooper**	
	This Is Not an Isolated Incident: An Introduction	
14	**Mark Edmund Doten**	
	Five Versions of a Story about Trains	
19	**Garrison Taylor**	
	Fantastic, Made of Plastic	
29	**Zac German**	
	letting me out first part	
33	**Bett Williams**	
	Crossroad Blues	
39	**Joshua Dalton**	
	I Don't Know What This Means	
43	**Jeff Jackson**	
	Three Untitled Stories about Smoking	
52	**Marc Andreottola**	
	Red Tape	
59	**Nick Hudson**	
	Oh Joy	
70	**Sean Pajot**	
	Zombie Nightmare #7	
73	**Angela Tavares**	
	Fast Ones	
87	**Jose Alvarado Lopez**	
	Fake Animals	
95	**David Saä Viccenzo Estornell**	
	The Confined of the Saint-Sépulcre Convent	
105	**Mike Kitchell**	
	When I Was Young, I Always Had the Same Nightmare	

109	**NICK CACIOPPO**	
	Lycanthropy Wife	
113	**JAMES CHAMPAGNE**	
	Kali Yuga	
138	**MARK GLUTH**	
	The Late Work of Margaret Kroftis	
145	**EDDIE BEVERAGE**	
	from *Return to Zero*	
153	**M.A.D.**	
	Fencetown	
161	**JACK DICKSON**	
	Mine	
171	**JOSEPH MARCURE**	
	Dear Sybellus	
182	**CODY CARVEL**	
	The Before and the Plastic Dinosaurs	
192	**MELISSA MUSSER**	
	Saliva	
204	**CALLUM JAMES**	
	The Bedside Table	
210	**CHARLIE QUIROZ**	
	Out of Control	
215	**JOSH FEOLA**	
	Command Psychology	
	The Unknown Becoming Louder and Louder	
218	**ROBERT SIEK**	
	Sixteen	
232	**STEVEN T. HANLEY**	
	Something about Jenna Hayes	

238	**CHRIS VON STEINER**	
	Switch	
241	**JACK SHAMAMA**	
	Spatial Devices Can Take Any Form	
255	**NICHOLAS MESSING**	
	You're in My Blood Now	
257	**NICHOLAS RHOADES**	
	Klonopin	
267	**T.P. KENDALL**	
	My Venn Diagram	
271	**PATRICK DEWITT**	
	from *Ablutions*	
277	**MIKE KASCEL**	
	Five Glimpses into Armageddon	
288	**JUSTIN TAYLOR**	
	Estrellas y Rascacielos	
296	**STANYA KAHN**	
	Hell	
303	**JAGO PALLABAZZER**	
	you weird people	
307	**AARON NIELSEN**	
	Breakfast in the Toy District	
313	**FRANKIE P**	
	Patrick	
321	**WILL FABRO**	
	Duels	
329	**MATTHEW WILLIAMS**	
	my body's work	
364	**About the Contributors**	

THIS IS NOT AN ISOLATED INCIDENT
AN INTRODUCTION
by Dennis Cooper

Twenty months ago, I started a blog. At the beginning, it was my stab in the dark variation on a zillion other blogs: some fiction and poetry, snapshots, a little autobiography, a little porn, lots of links to recommended sites. After a few posts, strangers started adding their comments: They liked my books and thought it was cool I had this forum. It seemed natural to add postscripts to my entries with return comments: thanks, who are you, what do you do? Most of the time, I didn't need to ask. I clicked on their screen names and found their own blogs and sites, most of which were not unlike mine. I don't suppose I was too surprised that most of those commenting were writers of fiction. I was a little surprised and grateful that, almost without exception, they were very good, interesting writers. I didn't need to clutter my blog with polite thank you notes. Instead, my responses were as genuinely enthusiastic and querulous about their writing as theirs had been about mine.

Six months later, the blog had become something I hadn't anticipated. People who knew my books had gradually found the blog. Discovering that it was a place where I not only made myself accessible but seemed as curious about the people posting as they were about me, they'd joined the handful of early visitors to the site, propulsively sharing their own writing, art, music, and so on with me and their fellow regulars. The blog was now getting an average of forty to sixty comments a day from people in far-flung towns and cities across the U.S., Europe, the U.K., and Asia. The comments section had become something of a virtual workshop full of supportive yet sharp discussions about the writing by the people posting there. While I still used the blog as a creative outlet and playground for my own ideas, it seemed to me that my creations were less the point than the lure that brought newcomers into the growing artistic community that had formed in the backstage of the blog's main page. Quite excitingly, I was not really an artist using a blog to gather and entertain his fans but rather like a kind of magnet for artists who were, in many cases, as talented as I but with fewer opportunities to exhibit their creations to the world.

Early in 2006, I got the idea to contextualize this singular, thrilling, and hugely diverse community of writers in an anthology. It's not exactly a revelation to say that book publishing in the United States is in a gentrified, conservative, and economics-driven state. The contemporary fiction known to the majority of book buyers and reviews readers is a highly filtered thing composed for the most part of authors carefully selected from the graduating classes of the university writing programs that have formed a kind of official advisory board to the large American publishing houses. To read that allotted fiction and look no further, it would be easy to believe contemporary English-language fiction has become a far less adventurous medium than music or art or film or other forms that continue to welcome the young and unique and bold. *Userlands* offers one alternative to the status quo, one unobstructed view of contemporary fiction at its real, unbridled, vigorous, percolating best.

This is an anthology of nothing but fiction alive with passion and belief and possibility. Its authors range in age from mid-teens to middle age. There are writers here who have never published before. There are published writers whose books' lack of monetary success have cut off their access to the reading public. There are writers who have graduated from writing programs but whose fiction is nonetheless too abnormal to make the major publishers' cut. There are writers of great sophistication and nerve, writers who have personal truths they need to express in fiction as forcefully as possible, writers whose first language is not English but who see it as the right stage for their creations. Etc. This is an anthology that intends to energize existing fans of contemporary fiction and inspire newcomers. I hope readers who look to fiction for the fresh and original will find some new favorites among the multitude of voices gathered here. I hope writers who might doubt the possibility that their own unusual fiction could find a rightful audience will read *Userlands* and think again.

Not that long ago, I started a blog in a fumbling, self-conscious way, and today that one unremarkable blog gives you this big, wild collection of forty-one distinct and gifted writers whose efforts prove that fiction remains a youthful, boundary-breaking genre with an entirely unpredictable future. This is not an isolated incident.

Dennis Cooper
Los Angeles
December 2006

FIVE VERSIONS OF A STORY ABOUT TRAINS
by Mark Edmund Doten

1.

For many years I directed the fall production. My son never cared for it. Something more than annoyance, something closer to rage. Would I have said so back then? I was a single father, young, often at a loss. This morning, the light breaking through the trees to the empty street, I found myself at the window turning over memories of Danny's childhood. The programs, for instance. I wondered if it was true that he'd shredded his copy at every performance I ever brought him to. We always sat side by side, I could easily have put a stop to it; and after it had happened once or twice, withheld them until we got home. What I remember, though, is sitting by helplessly while Danny bit his lip and with small quick movements tore off strip after strip of paper, one year's in green, the next orange, then red, then blue, a dozen colors fluttering through the darkness to our feet.

We were generally happy, I don't want to give the wrong impression. Weeks at a time went by when he wouldn't tolerate any separation, at night tossing his sleeping bag on the floor of my room, in the morning pouring my coffee. While I was sorting the laundry he would sit knees tucked to chin in an empty basket and narrate an episode in the life of Marmaduke, a character of his own invention, a fighter-pilot black lab, my son and I together in the shadowed cool of the basement, his hands stretching up to my own, head tipping back as he let loose an array of barks and sputters and siren-like cries. But he didn't care for my work. That is a fact. And this antipathy is the only excuse I can offer for how terribly I misjudged his intentions that October afternoon.

I was entering the rehearsal hall to begin auditions. This year was of great importance, as I'd just been notified that we were being considered for a production on the trains. Impossible to turn on the TV without clicking past an update on the movements of the sleek silver double-deckers fanning out though the highlands, vanishing into the underground networks of New York, Saint Paul, and San Diego, only to be spotted again the following day at some far-off town on the margins of the prairie, just a general store and a post office on a dusty white road. There they halted for minutes or hours, to this day we are not sure why, an endless chain of cars slung out and glinting in the noon sun.

That the trains were sleek, that they were silver or glinting, are not questions that have been resolved with absolute certainty.

2.

1) The trains were something new.
2) Even today we don't know what to make of them.
3) We know exactly what to make of them. Trains are trains.
4) They rumbled through the cities with a calamitous din, an earthquake on wheels, disrupting the work of hospitals, penitentiaries, food chains, morgues.

5) An exaggeration. They were no worse than your average train.
6) Held aloft by magnets, the only hint of their passage was the cloud of leaves and gravel whipped up in their wake.
7) It could not have been magnets. They ran on the old rails.
8) They cut the air like eels.
9) And no one saw a whirl of leaves.
10) Head cupped in hand, you listened. Spread on your mattresses at night. The trains were on the move, not a light to mark them by.
11) They shot past in absolute silence, parting the air without disturbing it.
12) Who knows when the train passes?
13) Only the one it strikes.
14) But they never struck a soul.
15) They were never here.
16) Or were, but our people didn't realize it.
17) Or always had been, so our people forgot.
18) They knew. Good manners forbade discussion. But of course we knew.
19) It was all we could talk about. Even back then. Yes, we talked about it. Yes, even then.
20) They came on the rails our forefathers laid down.
21) They cut through mountains, the prairies.
22) One day they disappeared.
23) Who are you to question the business of our trains?

3.

If every fingernail conceals a letter, a letter not to be tweezed out until the post-mortem, then how are we to know, Paul, what anagrams we might have set ablaze?

Dangling between two poles, caught up in a sudden gust, our streetlight swings—red, yellow, green; should we now mention that you, the best of us, are not here to see it? Measuring our words against what you would have wanted, when you want nothing? They found you in a boxcar. The owls are restless.

Disaster singes every hair. All we ask is an end to pain. Surely not happiness—just an end. But see?—already the pain is fading. And yet we cry out—we must—that it still aches, that these are not ordinary lives, we, who are out of gasoline.

Abandoning the diner, the roadhouse, the Old Prairie Motel, assembling as we haven't for years, our flashlights race through the forest, stealing back what the night has hidden. A face swims out of the darkness and turns, catching light. Only one of us, lost, looping back across the trail. Well, what does that matter, which of us is above suspicion? We search the face. We ourselves are searched. Unmoored by the mechanics of grief, gauging the distance between the expected and the felt, we can almost bring ourselves to believe your killer a stranger, his train gone, rails torn up in its wake, ties heaped and torched. But the night, your mouth, is closing around us.

Friend, I have too many letters now. This is the way things burn.

4.

1) I have built my train.
2) There is a man who wishes to destroy it.
3) I am searching for his train.
4) It is somewhere in these hills.
5) I will destroy it.

5.

. . . before the break, I feel compelled to address an ugly rumor. One hates to dignify it, but such lies left unchallenged can leave even the most loyal of us casting about, as it were, for solid ground. So: Let us put it to rest.

It's so simple. Go to your window. Draw back the curtain, just an inch and no more. In the street you'll see any number of them. They're playing tag or hopscotch, skipping rope, chasing each other into the alley. There are not as many as you had hoped, but at least you recognize a few of them. Or feel that you might someday come to recognize them, should the sun fall more cleanly on their faces, should they finally arrive, this handful of unknowns, to crouch on the sidewalk and accept the clean evening light. And though there is no sign of them yet, there is at least the lone child stumbling forward, chin raised to hide his confusion, his tears. And even if you can't see him, and his face grows dimmer by the year, there is nothing left but to stand at your window, staring without reserve, and become a creature of waiting, your eyes, without opening further, growing more open, so that when he turns down your block, when he comes kicking and tripping and laughing at these leaves that have never stopped falling, your eyes will have burned to pure intensity, like headlights on an empty road. It has been some time since we've seen our children, but we are waiting by our windows and when we do—I swear it—we will put this rumor to rest.

FANTASTIC, MADE OF PLASTIC
by Garrison Taylor

Kate blows her boyfriend with the hope he'll stop crying.

It's actually sort of working but the embarrassment's acute, particularly for Dug, who is barely seventeen and shaking now as he burrows further into a crumpled cave of pillows.

"That feels killer," is all he can say in a voice jagged with phlegm, much of its rancid Georgian accent tastefully filtered through down feathers.

This really gets Kate going.

She hums softly as her head bobs, lifts a trembling hand to caress Dug's pale and bony chest. Its surface is slick, hairless, shimmering beneath a thin sheen of tears.

Ted tells Saul his latest dream.

It's bleak, recurring, and about the only one he has now. Ted's expecting more and is eager to talk. Saul knows he's the only guy at school Ted can tell "things" to, which is well past frightening. Regardless, Saul's ass remains glued to the floor of a darkened bedroom.

He imagines the pitiable air conditioner, a creaky window unit, as being somehow spiritually kaput. He's hoping Ted will get hot soon and take his shirt off, or at least get them high.

* * *

Dug prays for sleep, a simple plea mouthed gently against a coal-black comforter.

Kate ignores him as she types beside the bed, her freckled face stewing in a modern blend of light. There is something very close to a powder that glows now from her ancient, sputtering laptop. It settles in clumps upon two high and hollow cheeks, a fleeting symmetry secured only in the blush of a flashing alarm clock.

To view Kate in such a manner is to unquestionably reach the borderline of something. And yet still, at the age of twenty-six, she is obscenely unaware of this.

"Hey, Dug," she suddenly calls out, his name tossed carelessly.

The kid isn't answering her.

"Hey, Dug," she throws again. "You really smell like ass tonight. You know that, man?"

Still nothing.

"Down there," Kate continues, unfazed, chubby fingers still rapping at the keys.

"I mean, behind there, too . . . obviously."

She laughs, uncomfortably, mortified for the both of them.

Without opening his eyes, Dug hurriedly slides his underwear back on beneath the covers.

"Uh oh," he says quietly before plunging into the sheets again, steadily sinking and almost certainly gone.

Reclined in a corner, Saul's eyes start to drift.

This is his mistake while studying the giant movie poster near a rank tangle of bed. Some dumb Chinese action bullshit. Dark sunglasses reflecting off-screen explosions.

The film is obscure enough. He'll give Ted that. But it's not *unknown* in the way that Saul thinks is sexy, so he

simply rolls his eyes. Ted sees this, or at least Saul sees him see this. The result is Ted's hard, instructive silence.
    Saul always cringes when squirting tepid apologies. He does this now.
    Ted only sighs, begins again.

From: KissMeKate@yahoo.com
To: AgentCooper21@hotmail.com
Subject: RE: a dream is a nightmare
Date: Fri 28 June 2005 23:32:22

Saul,
A little rusty, but here she blows:

Otto Rank, who was once a student of Freud, reinterpreted the Oedipus Complex as being about power, rather than sex.

In Rank's scheme, the child's struggle is that he wants total control over the world. Even though he wants it to be an extension of his will, he becomes increasingly aware over time that he is an individual and doesn't even have command over his own mother or body. Basically, he discovers all the things in life he has no control over but wishes he did.

Such a lack of control seems to be a key theme in Ted's dream. I can definitely see a hypersensitive "straight" guy like him having recurring nightmares because he lacks the power to have what he wants in the world (which is probably you, if you really think about it).

And didn't you once say that Ted was incredibly afraid of losing his mind? Take GREAT note of this, Saul, for self-control is obviously an important virtue to him. Although he believes in freedom, he's simply terrified of abandon.

Above all, I consider this to be the most pressing obstacle to your plan. You've really got to work around it if you truly want to fuck him.

Good luck,
Kate

>From: AgentCooper21@hotmail.com
>To: KissMeKate@yahoo.com
>Subject: a dream is a nightmare
>Date: Fri 28 June 2005 23:01:33
>
>Miss Kate,
>What follows is neither an apology nor a request for one . . .
>
>First things first, a tiny bit of gloating, cuz I'm in Ted's BEDROOM right now and he wants me to stay over and there's weed, and if it's ever gonna happen it'll be tonight, right?
>
>Presently, he's just plopped in front of his faggish Xbox, but the way he's sitting keeps making his t-shirt ride up on his back a little so that from his computer I am definitely catching some covert butt crack.
>
>Now if I could only just get him to clamp up about this stupid nightmare he keeps having. He's been harping on about it all night long, for so many hours that I actually mentioned how I knew this TA from an old psych class who could help him interpret all this shit. Dig it out of his head, you know? He was super interested right away, even after I told him that I hated your guts and that the feeling was probably mutual by this point.
>

>He sensed almost immediately that we'd fucked. I could tell because he NEARLY didn't push the matter, and then he started chewing on the tips of his hair like he sometimes does whenever he's feeling small and useless (the kind of thing that just kills me about him).

>

>Anyway, below I've included Ted's personal description of the nightmare, cut and pasted from his very own blog (which I rarely read cuz it somehow only makes him less attractive to me). Please have a look at it for him . . . as if you even had a choice. Thanks in advance:

>

>"Hey, guys. It's Ted again. I'm wide-awake and out of Tylenol PM so it looks like I'm pretty much finished with slumber for the night. I had that nightmare again, so, yeah, okay, I'll finally describe it for you now. Pull up a chair, haha . . . So it starts out in the neighborhood I used to live in as a kid, back before my stepdad keeled over and my mom said we needed less closet space. I'm, like, ten years old or thereabouts and I'm walking down the sidewalk with my best friend Oliver. We're heading to my house cause my mom's making hot dogs or snow cones or some bullshit. When we get there, the house is locked and no one answers as we ring the doorbell. Oliver tells me that my mom is probably inside taking a massive dump, and that the ventilation fan in the bathroom must be too loud for her to hear us. I nod in agreement, and that's when I catch my first glimpse of the gray car. It's kind of long and boxlike and it hardly makes a sound as it glides to a stop before my mailbox. A big smiling woman steps out and waves us over. She is total trash, and she's asking Oliver and me for directions to her mother's house. Before I even know what's happening, the woman is opening the door to the backseat and Oliver is climbing in. He tells me that we'll show her the way, cause it's near a Hardee's and he wants a Frisco burger. I want to stop him, but for some reason I'm unable to speak. Instead, I just follow him into the

backseat, and that's when things really start getting clichéd. The trashy woman suddenly locks the doors as she climbs behind the wheel, turning to us and scowling that we will never see our parents again. The car speeds off and I start screaming as I grab for Oliver. This is when I notice that I am alone in the backseat. Oliver has inexplicably vanished, and with this discovery I feel the largest swell of despair I have ever experienced. I immediately hit the floor and start calling out for my parents to help me. A few moments later, there is this beautiful relief once I realize that I'm only dreaming . . . then ultimate dread again as I find that I can do nothing to wake myself up. I huddle and cry for what seems like hours, and I'm not kidding you. Eventually, though, I start to wake in this real slow way that somehow feels like dying."

Dug's splotchy skin drains white at the news of Kate's birth defect.

Earlier, when she had grabbed at his gaunt hand, he had all but moaned. Now, he's just inhaling sharply as she guides his fingers over the delicate peak of her right love handle.

"There," Kate says to him, stopping softly as she presses down. "Right . . . there."

"I don't get it," Dug says warily.

He moves closer to her on the bed, produces an audible swallow of spit before nuzzling half-naked against her bare and flabby back.

"And this whole time," she says, "those fuckers thought they were looking at my kidney."

"Oh yeah?"

"And I'm a real freak, Dug."

"You're beautiful."

"But I'm not dying."

"Thank God."

"I should've never done what I did to you tonight."

"I liked it."

"You were so not ready for that."

"Who cares?"

"Were you scared?"

"I don't think so."

"You just can't ever, ever cry around me, okay?"

"I didn't mean to."

"They thought there was this mass. Can you believe that?"

"Doctors are weird."

"And I've just been thinking about it every single minute, every fucking second. I've been touching my back and wondering . . . and it was just . . ."

"You're fine now."

". . . my lower colon."

"Huh?"

"This whole time. The mass."

"What about it?"

"It was always just shit."

"What do you mean?"

"On the X-ray."

"Shit?"

"In the wrong place. My colon . . . in the wrong place."

"Really?"

"Born that way."

"Fuck."

"It happens."

"When did you find out?"

"Yesterday."

"Why didn't you tell me before?"

"You're gonna have to leave now, honey."

As small children—and this is pure coincidence, for their

paths would not cross until early college—both Ted and Saul used to watch *Small Wonder*, a short-lived sitcom of inadvertent eeriness.

Each episode had followed the plucky Lawson family and their absurd attempts at harboring Vicki, a robotic little girl. This adorable dead-eyed android had each day worn the same red dress and frilly white apron. She'd been prone to sudden and peculiar body contortions, random steam-type leakages (mostly from the ears), and always spoke awkwardly in this unmistakable synthetic parlance.

It was perplexing to both Ted and Saul that all Lawson family outsiders (i.e., the apparently not-nosy-enough neighbors and their extroverted children who were most likely *not* robots) had forever failed to take notice of such glaring abnormalities.

Had they simply just not cared, or was there a darker, more menacing force thrashing somewhere in the unseen exteriors?

Could the Lawson family actually have been the brutal gag of their entire neighborhood, each member meticulously placated by all and deprived of a pity inarguably due to them?

Was it foolish to even bring pity up at all?

Such odd but honest inquiries are the gist of the current conversation, and Saul—who is keeping his erection a secret while joining Ted upon the floor—is surprised at how much he remembers (like the name *Vicki*, which *he* recalled first, no matter what Ted says).

Kate's mind leaps miles at the fading sound of Dug's rusty BMX.

The boy, once a janitor at her university, had remained

far too long in the apartment's cramped and cavernous bathroom, purging his pizza into the coarse toilet in this super-dramatic way that even he seemed to ignore. Such vain attempts and disorders had been losing intricacy for weeks now, and Kate, having already grown bored with them, is welcoming eagerly Dug's reluctant, moping exodus.

Watching him pedal away in the dark now, she is aware of a newfound lack of interest (is thankful for it, even) and so quickly makes a mental note to have her phone number changed on Monday.

To crush any future doubt, Kate supplies a lean smile to seal this sincerity.

Ted says he's hot and takes his shirt off.

This subtle shift is a prince of gestures, knocking loose a bit of string meant to shield a tan angular face from a heap of muck-blond strands. Ted is soon shaking free a violent, shaggy haircut. Unconsciously, and for these sporadic four-second intervals, his shoulders are jutting inward.

Nearby, Saul sits watching, wordlessly, undeniably present. He eyes the modest muscles on Ted's upper arms as the guy methodically wraps a thin black cord around a bulky video game control pad. Obviously, he is no longer thinking of Kate's response to his awkward e-mail, or that he'd deleted it before even deciding to withhold from Ted its contents. In fact, he thinks of nothing now as he dutifully takes the final hit from a neglected glass pipe.

A full, barren minute then passes by before Saul enacts a sudden lunge against his unsuspecting friend, coming harshly and from behind, each of his broad and meaty arms locking tightly about the guy's bare torso. At first, Ted is all laughs, amused at the supposed game, but then Saul just keeps on squeezing harder . . . then harder still.

Ted is quick to note the rapid change, but appears strangely resigned as both he and Saul fall profoundly back upon the bedroom's dusty carpeting. His green eyes slam shut once Saul's damp breath begins to form curls at the back of his neck. He is anxious, grateful, fully relishing a blank slate.

As for Saul, there isn't much left.

He's just like everybody else . . . acting first and for himself . . . holding close what he wishes held him.

letting me out first part
by Zac German

sonia and the deck and the sun is like something real uh regular. i'm wearing all white and it's real weird like i'm sleeping. i haven't slept once since i've been out here. girls come in to open the door, by the time i say the words "stick around" they've uh. it's no use.

i don't know what i want. coming out here was the End, it was what i wanted. so now i'm out here with all these toys and uh. there are all sorts of things but they're just not really what i. whitehouse didn't respond to the invite, but dennis cooper did. i thought "great!" but he's boring as shit. brian eno and somehow lou reed and kanye west all got out here. it's the most boring group ever.

nobody smokes or sleeps or anything. i think just about every album ever is here but people keep saying they haven't heard of things, like prurient and uh uh the first odb album. i dunno. that kid sean wears a no new york shirt and i dunno. it's hard to say if there's a drug problem? here: roe v. wade gets overturned so we hit the road. david geffen lets me use this huge yacht (i'm not sure if he's here) and all these famous (to me) people are out here making it work. it seems though like nothing's changed, or something. people are always (i'm sort of the captain, but the captain doesn't listen to me) coming in my office or quarters or whatever to let me know things. pig destroyer, another one no one says they've heard of, even dc who i thought liked them a lot. daniel johnston is here and is so boring. and a lot of my friends, whatever, are here. everybody drinks and the beastie boys aren't here but people talk about them like they are, cos everyone's so close with them now, right?

me and this girl sonia are sleeping together, i never use her name or anything but she's pale with blond hair dyed black to look like what it is. she's pretty smart (unhappy), and with the situation is getting paler by the. by the pool we are for the first time, some old bullshit's playing and martin amis is definitely high and steve buschemi is frowning at us. everything is immaculate—right? she turns toward me and the patches of black are amazing. she tells me: "is this ending?" i never wrote that or planned it or anything, just listed all my heroes from when i was younger. i thought that'd be the future, and i'd make whatever comes next. i tell her "uh, well, something will. is. don't act like there is something." i think we're all high. the unicorns haven't come up for a long time. nobody mentions how bad they feel.

i don't know if anyone from punk is here. on the one hand i haven't really seen any but on the other i hadn't seen anyone from blur until this morning damon albaurn ate breakfast with me. he asked about what we were using in the pool or something and i directed his query. i start to feel that a lot of people aren't aware that kathy acker and charles bukowski are dead.

the boat's big and we set off from somewhere in massachusetts (not boston, obv.). i ask the captain how far out we are, or something, and he gets uh i dunno if he speaks english? he's old but doesn't wear it well?

i have sonia walk with me. we both have a small wardrobe but very good. she wears colors without irony because she doesn't know that emptiness is closer to black than to color? i'm real glad to learn that she doesn't believe in anything (science) either, that's what made us go together most of all. we're both something like twenty here and have spent the last five years listening to dipset and guided by voices and drinking massive amounts of alcohol by ourselves or with kids we couldn't stand (good friends though, mind you. we're not casual, we just lie constantly). we both hope we're the least ironic people we know. we mean everything! we're both vegan but we don't talk about it. we burn ourselves sometimes and have the other look at it. she does noise but mostly production for talentless mc's (she loves it when they talk about weed, she grew up in the suburbs of wilmington, delaware, maybe?) who think she's hot and things like that. she has helped me believe that people are attracted to me.

it's good because she has never been with anyone either, just worn lots of clothes or none or something and never bought cigarettes or magazines or anything. we both manage to stay wherever and well and i think it's love? we both like rainer maria rilke and phillies blunts. we're so cold old o.

we shoot down a helicopter and something's definitely getting better. kanye west and rhymefest and common maybe do a show and we smoke weed outside. apparently she has a connect? we both think it's real funny and are wearing scratchy jackets. we make plans to see ikue mori when we get back to new york and i go back to my room.

the next day (ben stiller and matt groening are here, silver jews are here) i have breakfast with jay-z and tell him how much of an influence he'd been on me. he acts happy to hear that and we both chew slowly. he asks if i write for pitchforkmedia and i tell him i've done some reviews. he says, "yeah, i think i saw them, i was going to say something earlier but" our eyes lock and it's i dunno. it's good because you can ask for the check here which is a social thing that uh i was worried about, but uh adam carolla and i think black dice but not wolf eyes or the other way around? and trent reznor and a lot of people who remember working with andy warhol. thurston moore's brother's here and a lot of people that don't remember the vienna actionists (i've only asked a lot of people so maybe some people do? it's hard to keep this up). i've made a lot of money on this.

CROSSROAD BLUES
by Bett Williams

Driving to Freddie's, it was slow going, rush-hour traffic in all the lanes. Driving back it was late. I pushed the gas pedal down and turned the music up loud. The freeway was a ribbon suspended in black.

I got off two exits early and drove the surface streets with the windows down because of the jasmine. A friend of his friend said, "Night jasmine blooms in even the shittiest neighborhoods in L.A. It smells like come-stained sheets." I quote people. It's a problem, I've been told. Like I can't mean anything on my own.

But let's say I might know something. Let's try for a minute, beginning with a crossroad. Fairfax and 3rd is fine. Or a high-tech intersection in Lakewood presided over by a Jack in the Box. Any crossroad will do. In fact, it's enough to just say the word. It always begins with a road. The first road is a road in Africa. It rises up through history, turns from dust into a snake, and hides in the music. That's how the road gets in us. Possessed, we drive the roads endlessly, listening to the music, snakes going in and out, using up all the gas until it's gone. Yes, there is a gone. Then the snakes go back to dust and the music back into the drums made of skin and sometimes bone.

Freddie's car had 650,000 miles on her, but he doesn't drive her as much as he used to. At what mile mark does an IT become a HER? Does the HER within the IT precede the miles, spinning them from her center like a spider?

My girlfriend said to me, *Don't you ever write about me, and don't think I don't mean it.* I'm not afraid of anything anymore. I'll respect that, but girlfriends don't belong on the road anyway, so she's just making it easier.

To be kind, I will say I believe she really did love me. To be truthful, I will also say she was my enemy. In my private realm, she tried to steal the files she deemed dangerous and replace them with replicas—without my permission and without discussion. She succeeded at this for a while. She used my deepest realizations against me. Other than that, I guess you could say she was perfect. It took five years for me to remember she was my enemy—to know what an enemy is.

When the bar closed, Freddie gave me a ride to my car. My skin was a warm blanket of blood and booze. I could have slept in it. Freddie was going on about the railroad again. He turned the engine off. I waited for a break in conversation to say I had to go, but none came.

"Let's drive to Canada," I blurted.

"Why Canada?"

"I don't know. It's far."

"There's all kinds of far," he said, staring at me. He stared at me like he would never stare at me again. Because he had to try just once. After all, he was a man.

But I am a man too, sort of, so I met him back with my handy distorted guitar sound. I engaged my fragments, my other floating bodies, pulled them down like puppet balloons on a string, my family of twisted genders ready for the show. We both had to do a bit of work, but there we were. I softened my eyes. That was how my real man came out anyway. Vulnerability is an old trick.

"What do you really want to do? I mean *really*?" he said.

Anything opened up and it was a circle I could see and feel. After some thinking, there was only one thing that seemed right. I reached up with both my hands, clasped them around his neck, and pulled his head down. I sunk my teeth into the soft part of the back of his head. He let out a teenage cry. Drama being necessary, I dragged my front teeth up around the ridge near his ear. He squeezed my leg till it hurt. I dug my fist into his hair and pulled. We sat there in the silence like that for a long time, me holding his head hard against my chest. Freddie sprung up at an agreed-upon moment and bit my chin. It was only fair. Then he bit the back of my head too. He bit harder than I did.

"Don't leave any bruises, okay?"

"I do good work," he said.

"Did you have sex with him?" she asked.

"No," I said. "I bit his head. He bit my head."

I regretted it right away—the truth angle. Shouldn't have started, but those were the facts. What was really happening was I was using him to get to the next place, which was something she really needed to worry about.

We drove 123 miles before talking much. His car hit the 700,000-mile mark in Flagstaff. Freddie had made his car a tape in advance for the occasion.

We ate lunch at a diner. A young man of about twenty waited on us.

"You would never have seen that fifteen years ago," Freddie said. I didn't know what he was talking about at first, then he gestured to the man.

"Yeah, real men wear aprons, Freddie."

"No, I mean a man of his age would never be working in a place like this. There were other jobs for him. Now the jobs are gone. Towns like this are dying because the road is over."

The road is over.

I bought a fifth of vodka in a liquor store next door. I knew Freddie wouldn't let me drink it in the car, so I took it into the bathroom and chugged the equivalent of a half-pint. He was waiting for me outside.

"Don't look at me like that, Freddie. I'm already looking at me like that."

"That doesn't go in the car."

"I know."

"It doesn't go in the trunk either."

"It's not illegal."

He simply nodded again. "I know you paid a lot for that bottle. I can wait while you finish it. We could get a room. For a few DAYS."

While he was talking, I was drinking. I managed to get the bottle lower by a third. I walked it over to the curb and set it down carefully.

"Why'd you break up with her?"

"For giving me a surprise birthday party at Hollywood Billiards because she really wanted to catch the tail end of the Raiders game playing on the TVs there."

"Unforgivable. How long ago was that?"

"Five years ago."

"You know how to hold a grudge."

"I left her then, in my heart. I've just been hanging around since then."

"That's not nice."

"I know."

"One thing about you and Angela, you two were never very good on the phone."

I was zoned out, looking at the mesas and thinking about Angela.

"I'm not a fucking TAXI DRIVER!" he said, loud

enough to startle me into a straight posture. "I need you WITH me."

"Fine. Sorry. I'm here."

"What did she say on your machine?"

"She said I wanted my cake and eat it too."

"What is THAT supposed to mean? What the hell is a CAKE for if you can't EAT it? You BUY cake and then you EAT it and then you go to the store and buy MORE CAKE. HOW IN THE HELL ARE BAKERS SUPPOSED TO STAY IN BUSINESS IF PEOPLE DON'T EAT CAKE?!!"

"I have to pee," I said.

"You're kidding."

"Sorry."

He pulled off, rather fiercely.

"You think that my having to take a piss means I'm not in cahoots with the road, don't you? Just because I had to pee at the last exit, you think it's bad luck, maybe personal. Everything on the road is a sign, isn't it, Freddie?"

"Yes, actually, I do think that."

"I need to pee again. Sorry."

"Again?"

I nodded yes.

"It's a weird thing. This will sound strange but women who travel with me have said that they end up having to pee more than usual. I have no idea what that means."

"It means you think you have a magical cock."

He might as well have dragged me into the Denny's by my shirt collar. I didn't sit down but was "sat down" by him.

"What's eating you?" he said.

"I keep thinking about Angela. The way she used to eat her little health food breakfast, it makes—"

"Listen, I'm sorry about you and your girlfriend, who you didn't love anyway. Who would have given you CANCER. I'm sorry. But we're on the road now."

"You don't have a crush on me, do you?" I said. I was out of control. I wanted a swirl of a fight. I wanted my face on the concrete, a gone farther than already gone. "Cause it's really important that we be just friends," I said—well, actually, slurred.

He got up and walked outside in a gesture that required no beats. I saw him through the '50s glass, smoking a cigarette. *$2.50 eggs and bacon special* painted on the window bleeding over his head. The waitress came around.

"Coffee?"

"Yeah."

She gave me that sympathetic feminine look. Like, *Sorry your boyfriend's an asshole*. I would have tried to hit on her but it would have taken language not available to that particular room.

He came back and sat in front of me.

"Listen, we're on a road. Do you understand what that means?"

He leaned back. I'd never seen a man in a cheap restaurant wearing so clean a shirt. I wondered then how he transported it so that it had no wrinkles.

I DON'T KNOW WHAT THIS MEANS
by Joshua Dalton

We're at school when the meteor shower hits, big fiery chunks of sky that pelt the roof and leave craters in the plaster. Josh and I are the only ones who aren't screaming—we're sitting on the windowsill for a better view of the scorched fields and wrecked cars.

They make us go on to third period because *it's important that no one panic,* only our biology teacher has fled and a janitor's been rushed in to babysit us. Stacey Farmer says she saw on the *700 Club* how it's the end of the world, and any day now Jesus is coming back to rescue the believers. I remind her she's too fat for even God to lift to the clouds, but she pretends she didn't hear me.

Bobby Fisher switches the janitor's portable radio from Mexican pop to the tail end of a news report—*and more on the possible causes of this catastrophe after this word from our sponsors . . .*

Josh and I head back to the supply room to get high. *Hey,* he says, trying to pass off a cough as clearing his throat, *hey, Brian, since the world is ending and all, I wanted to tell you that I just*

zone out because I know what he's going to say. He loves me, blah, he always has, blah, I'm the Ross to his Rachel and so on, but I'm too bored for these reheated sentiments. Josh has an utterly forgettable face, ten pounds too many, barely an ass, and a marginal dick; all forgivable, I guess, if only he weren't so dull.

and I just want you to know that it's okay if you don't, like, feel the same way or whatever, but I was hoping that we could just be close, you know, and

I pull the joint from his fingers, take a deep drag, try to mask my boredom with this as discomfort, as if I can tell the difference anymore. He doesn't get it and thinks I'm about to get emotional or something, so he starts to wrap his pale arms around me in an attempt at a hug. At first I'm just pushing him off me, but then, when he falls, landing with a pleasant smack, I can't help but kick him a little for being so goddamn needy. He starts clutching himself and whimpering and someone pounds on the door, asking if we're in here fucking. *This isn't a Motel 6, you faggots*, and I just sigh because the moment's ruined.

The "woods" by my house are usually little more than a few trees drowning in an assortment of puddles, but it's been dry enough lately to turn the area into cracked dirt, ruptured by the occasional anorexic tree. It's not even winter, but all the leaves have fallen, and I grind them into the dirt with every step I take. I still have my lighter and I start with a young sapling, the only living thing I can find, blacken its buds. It's slow to catch but finally does and ignites the leaf scraps around it and fumes black, black smoke. I inhale, cough and gag, inhale more. Over the crackle of the spreading fire I can still hear the sizzle and pop of hot meteor frying the ground only a few yards away.

The screen door slams behind me and I'm barely inside before Mother catches on and calls me into Caitlin's room. Caitlin's strapped to the bedposts with some of Dad's old belts and the gauze in her mouth is flecked with blood and hair. Mother's scrouched in the corner over Nostradamus, patting his head and putting Neosporin on his lips. Caitlin bit the dog again, Mother explains. She leaned in to kiss him, scratched behind his ears, and playfully tugged his thumping tail, but then lunged forward and tore at his face. This is why we can never keep pets.

Caitlin's eyes are coated with nonchalance from whatever medicinal mix drink Mother poured down her throat, but they try to widen as I approach her, removing bloody dog fur from the corner of her mouth. She squirms under the pressure of the belts for a moment but then gives up, like she always does.

Josh knocks on my window that night while I'm masturbating. I ask him to go away but he enunciates overly well and demands to see me. I can tell he's been reading that self-help book again. I finish quickly, imagining Clint Willis from second period slamming into my ass, and drag on my boxers as I crawl across the bed to unlatch the window.

Josh's feet slip on the decorative wheelbarrow parked in the bushes outside my window as he climbs, and he crashes head first into the crack between my bed and the wall. He comically brushes himself off, adjusts his pants, rubs his bruised eye. He musters up whatever hatred he can and glares at me.

Alarms go off in the distance. Another shower is coming, and the cheap metal grafted onto everyone's roofs will only hold for so long.

I don't know why I put up with this, he says. *I just care about you so much, and you just don't get it.*

Sorry, Josh. I lost my temper. You know I care about you. I have to keep him on a short leash or he'll stop giving me his weed.

I just don't get what's so wrong with me, he says. *I mean, I know*

I'm not "hot," or whatever, but surely you're not that shallow. And you mean so much to me. I just feel like my life is on pause when I'm away from you, like I'm just treading water. I really think that if you could just let yourself feel for once . . . I mean, I really think

The first of the meteors hits, triggering car alarms and howling animals. Caitlin cackles from the other room, delighting in the loud noises and, I think, the destruction. I interrupt Josh's speech to ask if he wants to get high and he agrees like he always does, but not even pot can erase my boredom this time. Meteors shred the clouds.

THREE UNTITLED STORIES ABOUT SMOKING
by Jeff Jackson

To find out what a tobacconist is thinking, follow this simple rule: Do not try to make out his features behind the veils of smoke, but examine the manner in which he takes a drag.
—Thomas De Quincey

[ONE].

They're lost in each other and the afternoon is half over before the man thinks to check the time. Both hands on his watch point to the door. He quickly starts gathering clothes, straightening the bed, stuffing the remains of their lunch into a special garbage bag. "Don't give me that face," he says to his lover, "we're late." As he hurries them out of his apartment, she cuts her hand on the jagged bolt of the lock. A dark line springs up along her knuckles. It remains frozen there for a moment and they both think it's only a scratch until the blood begins to flow.

They stand over the bathroom sink, hold her hand underwater, press toilet paper against the cut, but nothing stops the bleeding. "We don't have time for this," the man mutters, throwing away one red-soaked bandage after another. Despite the pain, the woman doesn't complain. The man is impressed at how she remains so calm. He gently caresses her cheek to reassure her. For a moment, he thinks he might love her. She turns away from his touch and continues to stare at her hand.

"So much blood," she says, "for such a little cut."

That night, after the man has fallen asleep, his wife wanders around their tiny studio apartment. So as not to disturb him, she sits on the toilet to light up a cigarette. She idly flips through a fashion magazine while trying to blow smoke rings. She ashes in the garbage can and notices the bandages caked with rust-colored blood. *It must have been a terrible cut*, the wife thinks. *Why didn't he tell me?* She crawls into bed and runs her fingers gently along his face, neck, and hands. She searches but finds nothing, wondering how the wound could have healed so quickly.

[TWO].

It's a stupid thing to do and he does it. He crawls out on the roof carrying a grocery bag with his model airplane collection in one hand and a red can of gasoline in the other. He surveys the yard below. Not smart enough to be worried about falling. There's nobody underneath and he smiles. It's hard to know what he's thinking. Probably just enjoys how the shingles feel warm and scratchy beneath his bare feet.

He rummages through the bag. The idea is to set the planes on fire, then launch them off the roof. See how far they fly before disintegrating into flames. Ha ha ha. But right now the kid seems more fascinated by the plastic pilots. He plucks them from their cockpits and dips them into the gasoline.

He holds the little men at arm's length and one after another gives them a light. They're instantly ablaze and he watches as their faces melt. For one quick instant, their features contort as if they're in unspeakable agony, their whole bodies twisting into a single scream. But the moment passes and everything melts and becomes blank and they're just smooth lumps of plastic threatening to burn his fingers.

Back to the planes. The kid examines the models—Messerschmitts, Spitfires, Harrier Sea Hawks, other names he probably doesn't know. To look at him, it's hard to imagine how he ever assembled these things. Sorting the parts, fitting pieces together just so, applying minuscule dollops of glue, painting insignias, applying decals. The hours of painstaking effort. No way he could have made them himself. Some parent must have helped.

The kid scans the yard. Still nobody. His eleven-year-old face is perfectly smooth, unscarred by any mark of intelligence. He's scrawny and shirtless. His tousled crew cut ends in a long rat's tail that he flicks back and forth across his back. A few more splashes of gasoline. That should do it. He lights the wing of the aircraft and gives it a heave.

The plane does half a loop-de-loop then plummets into a shrub. Nothing happens. Then the bush bursts into flame. The boy hardly takes notice and prepares the next plane. One with another exotic and unrecognized name, but nice, with two gunner turrets near the tail. He gives it a harder throw, almost losing his balance, but it doesn't go much farther than the first one. Becomes a smoldering black stain on the grass.

Frank appears down below, gawking first at the burning bush and then up at the kid. "Get down," he says. "This instant."

A flaming plane lands at his feet and starts to singe the lawn. Frank stamps it out, curses, and marches away. The kid blinks a few times, then hoists the gasoline can and prepares the next plane, the one he probably can't tell is a Messerschmitt even with its German-looking decals and folded-up wings.

Before the next launch, Frank reappears with a can of tennis balls and starts hurling them at the kid. "Off the roof!" he shouts. "You're in a world of trouble!" The first two balls miss wide right, ricocheting off the roof and back into the yard.

This gets the kid's attention. He sneers at Frank. "You're a lousy drunk," he says, but not so very loud.

The third tennis ball hits the kid square in his skinny rib cage, like a mallet hitting a xylophone, but without the appropriate sound effect. The kid winces and drops the plane, still unlit. It skids down the roof and sticks tail first in the gutter.

Frank stares up at the kid's unreadable face. The boy's expression is as impassive as a goat's, his eyes glazed and hardened. No way to tell if he's gotten the message yet. No way to tell anything, really.

The kid kicks the gasoline can off the roof, sending it flying end over end. But something must have gotten through to him, because he doesn't wait to see if the can hits Frank. Instead, he climbs back inside the house via the nearest window.

Quietly. He tries hard not to make noise. The room is dark. The shades pulled tight as usual. Old magazines are piled in the corners, mostly cooking and detective titles, some of them bound in twine. Everything is perfectly still, except for the soft rattle of the air conditioner and the humming pulse of the respirator.

Only now does the kid notice the sharp tang of the gasoline on his hands. It burns his nostrils, but he doesn't mind because it masks that other scent. This room always smells like fermenting dishrags. In fact, the whole house is starting to smell. It's from her. His mother, who lies there on the bed, attached to the respirator, never moving.

The kid perches on the sewing bench at the end of the bed and stares at her. She can't communicate, but it's kind of peaceful just to look at her, watch her breathing so regularly. The kid finds himself here often. Traces of sunlight filter through the blue curtains and give everything a peaceful glow.

His twin sister enters without a word. She takes her place on the bench next to him and they watch their mother's chest rise and fall, the respirator machine steadily working away. The mother's eyes are closed and her features are smooth, not unlike the plastic pilots after a bit of fire. They don't linger on her face. "Frank is pissed at me again," the boy says.

His twin shrugs.

"She hasn't got much longer," the boy says.

Neither of them say anything after that for several minutes. The sister plays with her flip-flops. The kids' bare shoulders twitch from the chill. They both stay seated.

"We'll wash her tomorrow," the sister says eventually, as if she's just made some momentous decision. She pulls a pack of cigarettes from the top of her cutoff shorts.

He reaches for one but she slaps his hand. "Don't be stupid," she says. "You're soaked in gasoline."

The boy smiles sheepishly. He puts his hands behind his back and sticks out his jaw. His twin lights a cigarette and places it between his lips. She lets him take a long drag, then exhale. Another long drag, exhale. They sit side by side at the foot of the bed, both hopelessly scrawny, their features almost identical. She continues to help him smoke the cigarette and it's impossible to know whether or not they realize that the rhythm of their breathing is slowly becoming synchronized with the machine.

[THREE].

It's a humiliating scene and our man in apartment B75 immediately regrets coming downstairs. The cops have the super in handcuffs. He kicks, shouts, struggles to shake himself loose. Two officers easily manhandle the super's wiry frame and push him through the front door. This isn't our man's thing, but he can't bring himself to look away either.

The other residents of the Midland are also packed around the edges of the courtyard. It's a hot Saturday morning and they're out here in bathrobes, shorts, and tank tops, half-shaven and hair askew. The word rippling through the crowd is that the super beat his wife. That's her standing by the curb, the pixieish young thing in the blue track suit, sobbing.

Our man can't quite believe it. He's always thought the super was a nice guy. A lanky Pole with bushy black hair and eyebrows, probably in his forties, but with the goofy sense of humor and loping walk of someone much younger. Maybe he misjudged him. Our man looks to see if there are any marks on the wife. Her face is red, but it's hard to tell what's crying and what isn't.

As the police parade the super across the front lawn, he calls out to his wife in Polish. Nobody can tell whether he's cursing her or begging for help. One of the cops shakes him like a sandy beach blanket, then folds him into the back of a squad car. He'll be booked at the station for resisting arrest, at the very least. The wife leaves in another police car. And just like that the scene is over.

The residents linger on the lawn for several minutes, neighbors consulting neighbors about the intricacies of the situation. Not everyone is surprised. Peggy, a retired woman who lives on the ground floor and knows the history of every rusted pipe and rattling radiator in the building, claims to have seen the super raise his hand to his wife in the past. "Plus, they've got all those kids," she says.

Our man knows what she means. The apartments in the Midland aren't huge and the super and his wife squeeze themselves and five children into three modest rooms. Four incessantly squawking kids under the age of seven, plus a sixteen-year-old who's probably the product of a previous marriage. The super and his family live two floors below our man and it's not uncommon for moments of their daily lives to unfold at top volume. Multiple children crying. The wife yelling, "I'm losing my mind!" Arguments over the super's incessant chain-smoking, the wife's refusal to help with even the simplest chores around the building, his flirting with the new girl on the second floor. Actually, that's a guess. They argue in Polish, so none of the residents know what they're saying, though the shrill tones translate clearly enough. At night, the super unwinds on the fire escape and our man can often smell the smoke from the super's cigarettes as it wafts through the bathroom window.

The conclave on the lawn winds down with people wondering how the scene will play out when the super returns. More violence, more screams, more police cars skidding to a halt in front of the building? Nobody believes the drama has reached its last act. "Whatever happens," Peggy predicts, "it won't be pretty."

A break in the action. The residents of the Midland tune in the ballgame, cart baskets of laundry down the elevator, crank the air-conditioning, and make idle plans for the evening ahead. Our man stares out the window of his top-floor apartment, trying to lose himself in the impressive vistas—the rooftops of surrounding buildings, the traffic patterns shaped by interlocking streets, the spires of four churches that form compass points in a sea of trees, the radio towers nestled in the surrounding hillside. It's usually a calming view, but today our man isn't really looking. He's only killing time, waiting for news.

Word spreads quickly when it finally comes. The super's wife has returned. Naturally, Peggy has all the details. The wife arrived alone and didn't speak to anyone. She coolly entered the building, walked past the elevator, and climbed the five flights of stairs to her apartment, then snapped the deadbolt shut behind her. Everyone now figures the super can't be far behind. Residents by the entrance peel back their curtains and steal glances out their windows, hoping to be the first to catch a glimpse.

But the super is nowhere to be found. For the next few days, the building is unusually subdued. Garbage piles up in the basement. The laundry room is closed. Nobody complains. The residents are more concerned about sightings of the super's wife, her black hair pulled back in a tight ponytail, shepherding her brood through the hallways. The super's sixteen-year-old son is seen on the front lawn, operating the sprinklers and hosing down the yellowing grass and flowers, trying to revive them from the unrelenting summer heat.

Speculations continue. Our man tries to sort through the tangle of rumors. There's a story that the super remains locked up for aggravated assault because his wife refuses to post bail. Peggy claims the wife has a two-by-four ready to nail across the apartment door to prevent him from returning. Some wonder if the crazy Pole believes the beatings are justified by an Old World code of conduct. Others speculate his wife is simply having a nervous breakdown. And threaded throughout all the conversations there's the unspoken belief the super might not return home at all.

The week winds down. Gray clouds hover on the horizon as thunderstorms begin to erupt over the town. The downpours last all day, but the sprinklers in front of the Midland are never turned off. They revolve against the wind and spray into the air until the courtyard lawn resembles a rice paddy, the water spilling over and submerging the sidewalks.

Late that night, after the rain has stopped, our man in apartment B75 gets up to take a leak. The unmistakable scent of cigarette smoke filters through his bathroom window. For a minute he stands transfixed, inhaling the acrid fumes. He wonders how long the super has been back. He can picture the scene below and it gives him a chill. The super lurking in the dark, perched on the fire escape, brooding over his next move. Figuring how to make amends with his wife or fuming about how to get the bitch back good. How to keep a low profile when interacting with the tenants, whether to play it off like a big misunderstanding or act like it's none of their business anyway. The silence is enormous. Our man can practically hear the super thinking down there. The smoke has that reflective tinge.

But what our man doesn't see is a pixieish woman with a ponytail leaning out the window. She works her way through her husband's last pack of cigarettes. Every time she takes a drag, a red glow is visible. It's like those blinking lights on the radio towers in the far hills—both patterns are too random to decode. When she's done, the woman rubs the last cigarette out on her forearm. She grits her teeth but doesn't utter a sound. It's just a burn, a small angry sore, another black-blue mark to add to her collection.

RED TAPE
by Marc Andreottola

I first asked if it were possible and the nurse responded, "Yes." She put my trousers, belt, and tee into a drawer, then locked it. "You have lost an idea of yourself." She poured some tap water into a cup. I sat, dumbfounded, checking the corners of my fingernails. "You just need to take it easy," she said, overfilling the vase with the tap water. I watched her closely. All I could think about was how far I had gone into another world, just to keep in touch with a guy.

All the nurses in the House were strange amalgamations of perky and curt personalities; quiet, but prone to explosions. They were direct, but also condescending. There was always some hint in their voice that they were listening but not listening. I heard one whisper something about me not knowing something one day. I would try to figure out what it was I thought they thought I didn't know. My leg hung in a sling over my bed where I was recuperating until I could go outside again. You'll have to imagine these days. I'm not very good at capturing them. Outside, very near, you could hear the caws of gulls. And when I asked about outside, and the wind and the waves, they shared looks between themselves—not that there was something I didn't know, but something I couldn't even possess. Things were hopeless for me for a very long while, not just during this time. And they knew it, from reports. I'd have to restrain myself to get out. But I greeted them with a gentle smile still, like a kid afraid of his teachers. I saw it in the mirror once, an afraid-looking smile that cut across my face from ear to ear like a bent jigsaw. I would stare blankly out that window then. Only other windows and brick. That other half of the complex. The glare of the sun sometimes. Just a square of sky, really.

Every day the nurses would draw blood on the hour and connect me to an IV. They had both my arms in slings by now. I just had the one leg left. The accident took it all out of me, except for that one leg and a cage of ribs. They'd feed saline solution into my arm so I would not get dehydrated. To top it off, they put me through all the monotonous surveys you could think of. They wanted to know what mood I was in every hour, hour after hour, what I remembered, if I felt like getting up or not. It was embarrassing sometimes. Where'd the blood go? I don't even know! It went to someplace where they made the reports, and the reports always came back to the hands of the nurses, and I could get a feeling for what those reports were saying based on how the nurses talked to me. I saw patterns sometimes.

One day, one nurse, Shauna, exploded at me for not having folded my clothes. I looked around. My belt? My trousers? Shauna opened the closet and pointed at the rack, where I saw my outfit folded in a tidy square. The lines were perfect. "I already did it for you!" she snapped. Shauna stomped across the room, throwing open the window. "I need some air!" I never knew it opened. I watched Shauna like a zoo animal for those brief moments she wasn't by my side. I'd be fine when the gentle breeze cooled her pink, hot skin. But for the time being something got to her. Then she started up again, watching the sky. She seemed to have a conviction that I had taken something away from her. But she wouldn't dare say anything. No one ever says anything. But some people do speak to themselves, like Shauna. She was really just speaking to herself at the window there. Then she got to screaming and said I would just "take and take and take."

The next day another nurse came in. Her name was Alexi. She stood at the door and said we'd have to go to a different room to take the IV today. We walked down the hall for the first time, and Alexi took my hand. Or we rolled down that hall, actually. Alexi pushed me. I pulled my IV cart along. It swerved to the right a little bit with that floppy bag I kept thinking might crash and pop. The room I entered looked identical to my own. Things were white. But then I saw something different and incredibly close, almost simultaneously. Instead of a bed there was a table; instead of sheets, outstretched on beds of lettuce lay two cooked lobsters.

Alexi informed me that everything was all right. She explained that we were having a special meal as "a treat" for how "well behaved" I had been lately. I objected, saying that I could hardly stomach the stench of fish, let alone break apart and devour an entire lobster. Alexi got mad just then. She stormed out, screeching about "all the trouble" she had gone through to find those lobsters and how "ungrateful" and "picky" I was. But I was used to it. I was thinking where out there did she trap and find lobsters, really thinking of the color of the sky and what was beyond those bricks, to be honest.

After she left the room, I looked at the lobsters head on. They seemed kind of loose in their shells. I ripped one open. You could see, without its shell, a slimy, insignificant puss-filled sack, with long black eyes bulging and dragging behind it. I had been so careful not to tear it up. Then I felt sort of remorseful about it all. It reminded me of the accident again. The fire-siren red shell at least gave the lobster presence in the world. I put that back on. Alexi returned. I asked her why people did not like the tastes and smells of certain things. She just sighed and put the lobsters in two plastic bags.

The next week was a difficult one. They told me to stay in my room. I noticed one day that the floors were not very busy. You could only hear the sounds of janitors drifting in and out to collect linens. I was wondering why it was that at all hours some light was on, there was a shimmer on the bricks. The room above. I could see a faint shimmer on the bricks. I watched the light melt into the coming dawn, seeing faint shadows play against the wall with strange, hasty movements.

Then, of course, soon after seeing the shadows I left my room. When I reached the elevator down the hall, I got nervous. I heard footsteps coming from somewhere. There was only one corner where the sharp footsteps could be coming from, like a thin horse approaching. The signal said the elevator was on this floor. It didn't open. What the hell was going on? I decided I'd have to find an excuse for my being out of my room when those footsteps found me. I resolved that I had a great accident, a spill, and would call a nurse for towels. I turned the corner to face those footsteps. There was no one there. There was just another long hallway. But I still heard the footsteps when I hushed my breath. I looked again. Maybe there was a hallway I hadn't noticed. There was no place I could see where those footsteps could feasibly be coming from. It could be the vents, I told myself. Or it could be my head, I said out loud.

When I looked at the intercom inside the elevator, I started thinking again. Perhaps the sound was just the elevator passing floors. I told my heart to stop beating, but it beat twice as loudly. When the elevator swung open, I was somewhere else. It was alluring and exotic. Several gorgeous women sauntering around in slinky red dresses, coned red hats, ruby jewels, and charred eyes. It was the party. They were all in monochrome, and serene. I got nauseous, just staring that way you see in cartoons, with my mouth hanging open. The elevator door began to close.

But I stopped it from closing—to see more. The women here were so colorful, humorous, and delicious. Their mannerisms and way of talking were out of date, sure, but they had a way about them. They were characteristic of something. They were showy. They were raunchy, but harnessed. They could be crass, but smooth. Their mouths didn't match their outfits. I was tickled by some sort of smoky ease they had, maybe their warmth. Of course they saw me there and invited me over. I walked over. One of them offered me cookies. It was suddenly cold again.

I tried to pull back. I watched them dance to some strange songs. Their crimson beads leapt from side to side, harnassed by their necks, and the fabrics they wore beat violently as they threw up their arms to dance. We enjoyed ourselves that night. One was named Tammy, another Phyllis, another Dana, another Sarah. I'm forgetting one. But anyway, we laughed and talked. I felt a part of them, very cozy in a way, and I spoke up, leaning forward on my toes.

For several minutes they let me speak, and then Dana interrupted, redirecting the conversation. "Phil," she said loudly, "what is it that is wrong with your teeth?" The several women were drawn in by Dana's tone and changed positions on the couch.

Phyllis took her teeth out. Something was happening, something was set up, some horrible meaning predicted for me as I saw the wide horseshoe-size dentures Phyllis pulled from her mouth. I didn't want to make it strange, but it did happen this way. I asked Phyllis where she got her teeth. She got very upset and ignored my question. There seemed to be a very weighty issue ahead of her, something I said which she might address. Or maybe I was being rude, coming in here like this—"Young man," she exclaimed, "where did you get your own?" The ladies laughed.

I did not understand Phyllis's question, going back into the elevator. And when I reached my floor the hallways were still, vacant, and empty. Walking further I realized that the center of the floor had a red line that bisected the entire hallway. This red line led straight into a room, my room, as well as the other identical empty rooms or ones with their doors locked shut and with clothes hanging on hooks outside. I was happy to return there. James would have thought that newfound red line was as funny as I did.

(Which brings me to the accident again. James, I should have never said all the stuff I did. From now on I'll send the letters to your office and not your home. As a lobster delivery man, I should have just left your package at your doorstep. I couldn't help, though, talking to your wife and your young daughter. She is beautiful and the perfect spitting image of her father. I still have the small crayon drawing she drew for me while your wife called the police. I can't believe it happened to me, though. You have to understand that after all these years, I really just stored you in a box somewhere. Seeing you for real was too much for me, James. But yes, I'm making the same mistakes again. I just wanted to send this thank you letter for escorting me to the proper place. I always go through the wrong door, don't I? I'm glad you took me here, and I hope you'll keep in touch. You know I wish I could tell you everything. I didn't mean to give the wrong impression. When we were younger. By telling you all that. James, please forgive me. I don't feel the same way anymore. You mean nothing to me.)

OH JOY
by Nick Hudson

My dad talked to me for the first time in forever over breakfast. I would have preferred him not to. I'm still drunk. Oh Joy. He wants me to get a job:

"I want you to get a job."

I can't do that. My head would erupt if I sacrificed any more time for other people. I go through this fucking holocaust every day where I coast through school getting exponentially bored, all the while risking contamination by my fellow students' stupidity. I need my time in the evening to gather the fragments and put myself back together before I go to school the next day, like applying makeup to a corpse for an open-coffin funeral. I need the money but I really can't get a job. People think I'm lazy but my mind is not a vacant cubicle. It's occupied with other things. Predominantly, seesawing between wanting to kill myself and wanting to kill everyone else. My dad's the only person I can't stand up to and typically the person I most want to confront. I can moan at him. I always euphemize. He can't do directness. So I talk around the issue. He laughs it off. Sure, he's easy to discuss stupid trivia with, but when it comes to anything tangible he's useless. He gets defensive. Like when he has a go at me about anything and I try to stay cool; this syncopated thumping claws at my chest. When I try and arrange the words of my defense, the sentence caves in like a rope bridge and I deliver this queasy mangled shite in a girlie submissive voice. The sort of voice you don't intend anyone to hear. I don't know why he's intimidating but I fucking hate it and one day I'm gonna explode and confront him with more than idiot shallow words and a self-imposed bedroom exile. He's a self-righteous fucker and if you try and explain this to him, he goes AWOL:

"Shut up Alexis don't start psychoanalyzing me I don't need a loada gob from your skinny ass I've got enough to think about you don't fucking know me as well as you think you do so stop being a goddamn adolescent brat and get over yourself I've got enough to worry about without your melodramatic shitstorms every time I ask you to do something I don't need your shit you know how your mother cries whenever I tell her what you're like and how you make me so angry and how you promised to do more around the house once she started working nights and haven't lifted a finger to help anyone but yourself to notes shaved here and there from my wallet like I don't notice any less-forgiving parent would've shopped you to the police by now but I haven't because I kept hoping you might pull yourself together and do something I can be proud of so we don't have to keep moving house to erase your spiteful destructive little kiddie episodes from our family history and preserve our reputation so your mum who's already unstable has to be ripped out of her scarce little comfort zone and inserted into some new and frightening environment where she has to go through trust trials and confidence crises just to even arrange a job interview did we ever have this trouble with your sister whose sublime perfection radiates from her every pore like scales on an angelfish whose schoolwork was never less than diligent and whose attitude exudes a selfless optimism and generosity of spirit and then we get you injurious snivelling trash being basically a nasty bastard a spineless little turd an irresponsible degenerate self-aggrandizing waste of mine and your mother's time do you ever see your sister behaving like an attention-craving raw cyst on the good name of this family rotten misanthropic empty emotionless lazy facile intolerant fucking antisocial crybaby the world doesn't owe you shit take more pride in your appearance you scruffy unkempt stinking turdbag faggot wretch brush your teeth more often you killed our dog because you didn't walk it often enough you lied you said you'd walked him when you hadn't so he died prematurely I don't like to have to tell you this but you need to wake up to your manifold failings as a person sonny I'm doing this because I love you and I wouldn't be a good father if I didn't say it like it is I'm doing you a favor so nobody in the real world if you make it that far ever has to tell you this I'm saving you the embarrassment of a public shaming even though that's precisely what an inaccessible little prick like you needs to be pried open and have the forceps of compassion probe about inside your diseased insides and rearrange your skewed moral axis into anything resembling a human being if only you were more like your sister then we might get an invite to your mother's parents for Christmas instead of being shunned and disowned because they can't stomach the notion that they might actually share genes with a turgid dicksore like you why can't you use your sister as an example where did we go wrong I get mad and your mum starts crying so I get angrier and then your sister walks by to say goodnight and flashes me that sweet smile to remind me that all of this anguish and expenditure wasn't a complete waste of time and resources why aren't you more like your sister if only we'd . . ."

Or some such bullshit. Maybe if I didn't feel like a phantom pregnancy that, to everyone's stunned dismay, followed through, I might be as generically uninteresting as my sister.

I was an only child once. Until I was six. Then my sister barged her irrelevant way into the cosmos and what little identity I'd forged at that point got raped, upended. I'd gotten happily accustomed to not sharing. I've rediscovered the art recently. But for those six glorious years I enjoyed the attention of both parents, high as they were on the residual euphoria that peaks with a honeymoon and slowly dries up through the years. When I was five they found me a babysitter. Joy.

Joy said: You can't build on the sunset.

I said: I want some ice cream.

Joy wasn't a great babysitter. She was a sadistic, evil bastard of a fifteen-year-old cuntsplash. It's little wonder I don't like girls much.

Joy said: We're going to watch the "Thriller" video.

I said: I don't want to, it looks scary.

Joy said: If you don't I'll tell your parents you pissed yourself.

I said: Fine, if you feel like that I'll watch the damn movie you manipulative bitch.

Joy said: Like, you so wished you said that.

I said: Actually, no, given the opportunity, I'd like to have said, "If you tell them anything like that, I'll tell them you habitually pushed me down the stairs and fed me drugs pretending it was lemonade and threatened me with even nastier things if I told my parents."

Joy said: But, er, then you'd be right. I did.

And she did. I'd be right. My parents would deposit me in her care, head off to their opulent soirée, get shit-faced, throw buns at other guests, turn up stinking and gooey at about half-eleven; Joy would appear in doting, compassionate babysitter mode, return a roughed-up, slightly dopey kid to them. They'd be too drunk to attribute the dopeyness to anything other than his being an active go-getter of a child and it being way past his bedtime. I'd lie awake all night panicking about the gravity of her threats—should I squeal? What if she tells my mummy that I got my penis out and started playing with it? Mummy would be really disappointed. I never did like disappointing her. In fact, my dick still never gets much exposure. Joy could resurface at any moment to manifest the threat. By the morning, I'd have paranoiacally weighed up the situation from every angle and invariably decided that I wouldn't squeal this one time, but if she does it again, I'm definitely telling Mummy. And that's final. As final as perpetual deferment of the truth could ever get. And here I am now, documenting it in some hermetic little prose piece. Next time, next time . . . You won't get away with this, you evil bitch. But she has.

"Alexander, do something ridiculously humiliating/potentially frightening/utterly beyond your post-toddler grasp of the world/or I'll tell Mummy you broke my mum's limited-edition floral plate." The plate dangles from her stumpy pig-fingers.

"No, I don't want to. That's a bad thing to do."

"Oh, go on. Don't be such a goodie-goodie. Don't be so fucking safe."

"It's bad to swear. I don't want to. I like cats. I don't want to hurt her. Put the plate down."

"Okay, well, in which case, you're a very brave boy for

saying no. That's the right thing to do. So come with me upstairs and I'll give you a present." The plate is back on the wall. The cat darts for the garden.

"Oh. Okay." Greed fuels our ascent. Hers, for my pain and her sick gratification. Mine, for a phantom present.

"So where's my present?'"

"Sit down up here, cover your eyes, and I'll go and get it." It's a tall flight of stairs.

Hey, this is cool. If I were made of paper instead of meat, bone, skin, and hair, I'd leap off here and flutter slowly to the ground with all the grace of a swan's feather. Peace. Freedom. Joy. Where is she? The anxious voice of greed. Oh there she is.

"Ready? One, two, three . . ."

Then I'm crying. Crumpled, upside-down, my head forcibly tucked into the concave of my collar bone. I wasn't engineered to be naturally arranged this way. If I were made of paper, Joy would have just performed the most gruesome origami on me. Being tiny, it took about four revolutions of my pretty lean body to arrive at the floor. By which time, my limbs had undergone so many fucked-up contortions that I felt like one huge, amorphous double-joint. Jolts of hurt ripping through my slim, under-padded kid body. About two-thirds down, my head scraped along the bannister railings, rebounding like a scale plundered across the bars of a xylophone by an over-zealous player. Disoriented, the only sense I can rationalize is my hearing, which picks up Joy laughing at the top of the stairs. This hurts at least as much as my journey down them, and my crying escalates. Inappropriate choice of words perhaps. My babysitter joins me, cradles me into a nervous calm. Maybe she's not that bad. Perhaps it was an accident. She was laughing because she's so in love with the giants of slapstick. I've just performed one of the famous slapstick routines. Now she feels bad for laughing when I'm clearly experiencing profound discomfort. I think my nose is bleeding. Maybe it's just snot from crying so much. Either way, she wipes, takes my hand, and maneuvers me into the kitchen.

"Oh, you poor little dear!" Still laughing, with a hollow, forced self-consciousness at this point.

"Let's fix you a drink. You're a very brave boy. And a very good boy for not telling your mummy about this."

Only now do I appreciate how to unravel such loaded rhetoric. Oh, that's a good idea. I won't tell Mummy. Wait a minute. I've been duped.

"Which you can't. It'll be our secret—Mummy already knows you're a brave little soldier. Don't want her thinking you're a fearless trooper who knows no humility and has no understanding of danger, do we? Let me fix you a drink. You deserve some lemonade after those nasty stairs sucked you down them. It was like being swallowed by a big hungry giant, wasn't it? And now the giant's poo-pooed you out of his bottom and you're safe. And you can go home knowing you're a hero, and the only one who ever survived being eaten by the big wooden giant. But you mustn't—would you like a straw?—you mustn't tell anyone about your victory against the evil giant because nobody will believe you. Everyone knows that nobody can be eaten by the giant and come out in one smiling piece like you have. There you go. Drink it all down. So it'll be our secret, what a brave little man you are."

"Okay."

"And you'll never tell anyone, will you?"

Yes. "No."

"Good boy." She ruffles my hair. Her behavioral contraditions are really fucking with me. Her inconsistencies are probably accountable for the fact that I still trust approximately no one; and for my assumption that any authority figure is covertly plotting to destroy me. All because I wouldn't tie a sparkler to a cat's tail. Actually, I hate cats too now, which may be tenuously postdated.

"Drink it all up."

"It tastes funny."

"Well, it's from the same bottle you had last time."

"Well, it tastes funny."

"Don't be so ungrateful. Your mum and dad said I wasn't supposed to give you any sugary drinks at all, so drink up and shut up."

"Okay." Like she's giving me something; like she's turning me against my parents by allowing me to gorge on the decadent fancies they so explicitly prohibited. Joy is wonderful.

I feel dizzy. I feel sick. Why was that lemonade all powdery at the bottom?

"Well, you drank it. It can't have been that bad."

"It tasted really . . ." Bitter, I sensed, but couldn't articulate.

"Hahaghhaha." Fifteen, and she's already got a smoker's cough.

"Joy . . ." I'm swaying on my stool, trying to steady myself on the kitchen work top . . . "What was that drink?"

"Ha. Alka Seltzer."

"What?" My vision is obscuring, like I'm viewing the world from the bottom of an industrial kitchen sink.

"Alka Seltzer."

"What's Alka Salka?"

"Alka *Seltzer*. It's a drink grown-ups have to stop them feeling. It's nicer than lemonade, isn't it?"

"I feel sick. I feel dizzy."

"Oh, that's just from the fall. That'll pass soon. You're being such a brave boy. Do you want some more drink?"

"Okay. What if I'm sick?"

"Oh, you won't be. What you need is plenty of drink to wash the bruises off those bones. You'll be good as new tomorrow." I'd seen my mum make gravy by crumbling a stock cube into a pan and adding water. Joy did something similar with a white capsule to make Alka Seltzer. There couldn't be anything wrong with it if it's made like gravy. I used to find myself absorbed in the sound of my mum stirring the gravy sauce pan with a metal spoon, a rhythmic, muffled, modulating *chrring* as every figure-eight circuit brought us closer to lumpless gravy and a big dinner. This new drink just emits a big fizz, like if a snake could foam with rabies when you startled it.

"There you go."

"Thanks, Joy. You're really nice." I downed this one in two gulps.

"Oh, you think so?" A slutty smile, I later decide.

"Yeah, well, you look after me when Mummy and Daddy are having playtime."

"Well, they give me some money for it. But I like you too. Do you really like me?"

I hiccup a giggle. Then I belch, and giggle again. "Yeah!"

"Well, do you know what girls and boys do when they like each other?"

"Play Transformers?"

"Sometimes they do. But Transformers is kids stuff. Do you know what brave grown-up boys and girls do when they like each other?"

"Can I have another drink?" She's spun my stool around.

"Look at this. Put your hand here."

So over the next few weeks I develop a taste for Alka Seltzer. The third time I fall, and beyond, I'm fairly convinced she pushed me. Sometimes, twice in one night. Then I feel dizzy and sick and she gives me some Alka Seltzer for being a brave little soldier. And because I'm a big strong boy, the aching subsides really quickly. After a few weeks I start to feel sick for longer, though, even at home, so I ask my mum for some Alka Seltzer. She wants to know how I learned about Alka Seltzer.

My parents no longer give Joy any money. I'm back on regular lemonade. I use the stairs very tentatively. One evening I saw a Gremlin on the landing window sill and freaked out. My new babysitter's name is Chelsea. I tell her it sounds like a dog's home. This endears me to her. My mum's gone to the freezer to fetch the sausages. I sneak myself a stock cube from the cupboard and chew it up. It's really strong.

I was six then. At six years and ten months my sister arrived. I'm no longer an only child. At seven years and three months I push my sister down the stairs. I hate her. At eight years and four months, my auntie and her boyfriend come and stay with us. He's young, muscular, wears a sleeveless vest, is called Simon, beats her up. I have a real taste for strong flavors these days. And that's another reason I can't get a job. Because I'm still drunk. I'm no longer an only child. I'm still only a child, though, only, longer.

Ode to Joy:

Joy is now a junkie single mother. I'm so sorry. I hope for the kid's sake she lives in a bungalow.

Joy says: I want you to get a job.

Joy Jr. says: But I'm only seven.

Joy says: Don't answer back. You're the reason I'm in this fucking state.

Joy Jr. says: So the cycle of abuse perpetuates.

Joy says: What did you say?

Joy Jr. says nothing. So the cycle of abuse perpetuates.

ZOMBIE NIGHTMARE #7
by Sean Pajot

New Poem: *From deep inside the silver skull an expressway emerges . . . It forks twenty times until that original thought has been sufficiently abstracted to have no specific purpose, perhaps aesthetic. Really, just a gleaming latticework of lost minds, another "monumental" layer obscuring the spookiest landscape ever conjured by a soul squelched to a puddle of evil.*

    I wrote that locked in a treehouse without windows. It's painted black, inside and out. It's nestled in the top of a tree like a secret nest for fuck-ups. Most importantly, the tree was burning.

Kip was already drunk. I was already high. He said he thought tonight was better than Halloween for Trick or Treat. I agreed.

    We threw on our costumes. He: a pedestrian. Me: a killer clown.

    Hours later, we had wandered into a neighborhood I didn't recognize and I noticed we had nothing to carry the candy, if we ever found it. Kip suggested pockets. Those weren't big enough.

    So we emptied trash bags onto front lawns. From inside houses there were threats of calling cops to which we replied with human shit, B&E, and bags of other people's stuff we would never use. Except the pills. There's the treat. Down the hatch.

Finally we found someone feeling festive . . .

Short story: We stumbled into some weird guy's garage. He asked a few creepy questions that we refused to answer, ping-ponging goofy looks instead. He pulled out two fifty-dollar bills. We got serious, knew immediately what he wanted. I imagined the two of us flopped face-down into bags of freshly raked leaves, our belts undone, the weird guy disappearing into our asses like a werewolf feasting on a twin kill.

I smashed in his sick smile with the stick-end of a shovel nearby. Kip pocketed both crumpled bloody bills. There's the trick. Up the ass.

I don't remember how but we ended up in my backyard, in the tree, winding toilet paper through its branches, soaking its leaves in gasoline. A match seemed the next logical step.

Inside the black box I was slumped in a desk chair with an overturned Ouija board for a seat. That was the detail we had originally considered occult.

The chair was the only furniture in there. It was designed for channeling ghosts. Hence, the "atmosphere." And in order to accomplish this sorcerer's work you could either write or masturbate. I was always ambidextrous. Therefore, double duty.

I can't imagine what we looked like crashing through that inferno, unconscious before hitting the ground . . .

I asked Kip if he was okay. He laughed. Then I saw that piece of bone escaping from his knee. He blacked out laughing, screaming. I rolled onto my back, my own busted leg lagging behind.

Fire hopscotched from tree to tree. For some reason, I expected it to fizzle somewhere along the way. But it kept spreading. From power lines to the roof of my house; there were flames eating out the upstairs bathroom. At first I thought the house was empty. The lights were out, no TV. Then I understood: My family was sleeping . . . *Ding-dong* . . . uhh, dead.

Old poem: *Fuck me while shooting free throws.*

FAST ONES
by Angela Tavares

A day like this is reserved for old movies on television and doing all your laundry. A day like this means staying in your pajamas until it's bedtime again and, during the twelve-hour downpour, checking the bathroom window for flooding. I am not wearing a bra under my sweatshirt or underwear beneath my jeans. I am not wearing deodorant.

The rain dissipates into a light gray mist and, leaving my apartment, I want only two things: a half-gallon of milk from the store on the corner and my shoes to not be soaked through by the time I get back.

But Kate is coming up the walkway with a handful of flowers and I have to look twice. I am not ready for this moment.

She says my name. She says, "Julia, hey," and I squeeze my keys tight in my hand. "I know that this is a weird time, but I just wanted to do this." As she gets closer to me I can smell something sweet. I don't know if it's Kate or the flowers, loose in her hand, not wrapped like something she had bought from a florist. She could have ripped them up from the front lawn of my apartment building and cut them with her pocket knife for all I know, for all I care.

She looks like she is late, or that there is something she forgot that she rushed out the door to do. She wears a cotton cardigan sweater with the sleeves pushed up her forearms, a white shirt that does not disguise the darker bra beneath it. Her black canvas sneakers are two-tone after walking through the puddles instead of navigating around them. She says, "Don't feel like you have to invite me in, but I'd like to take you somewhere."

When I smile, she looks down and lets out a laugh that is only a quick burst of air. Then she points at me, says, "We could go for coffee and pancakes."

Inside her car, the seats are cool from the air-conditioning. She stares at the blue light of the clock in her dashboard and says, "Look at the time."

I am moving the flowers in my hand, picking up the stems of each so that I can look at them individually. I only recognize the black-eyed Susans. I don't know the names of the others. They have white and purple blooms, some leaving petals on my legs. Kate motions toward the space behind her seat and says, "You can put them back there on the floor." When I look there is a plastic milk jug with its spout cut off, half filled with water. Supporting it on its sides are textbooks and a dirty blue sweatshirt.

The streets hiss with the sound of water beneath her tires. The rain forms small streams that run along the sidewalks, carrying brush and flattened cigarette packs toward the street drains. We pass the new café that is in direct competition with the one in the center of the city where Kate works. This café is part of a regional chain, the insides designed in bold modern colors. The lights, shaped like silver spaceships, hang from high ceilings. Kate says, "I know that they're open late, but I refuse to bring you there." We are in the right-hand lane, ready to take the highway on-ramp headed north toward Boston. "If I were to bring you in for soup, and then we were to visit the Roxbury shop for the exact same soup, they would taste identical. You wouldn't be able to tell me which cup was from that store, and which one was from the store in Roxbury." Kate is watching her sideview mirror, and I am watching Kate. I have never seen her with her hair down, dark and longer than I would have imagined. I am used to seeing Kate only one way, in the café, hair up in a loose bun, a white apron on. "We make things from scratch. Sometimes our soup is too salty, or maybe it needs more pepper. But there's room for error. That place," Kate says, switching off her directional and looking back at me, "is soulless."

I say, "You are a model employee."

Kate brings me to an all-night restaurant on a highway rest stop. It is one of the few places left where she can smoke, she tells me. The woman who seats us is dressed like the other waitresses in black and red, and she has a cough that rattles in her chest. There are only two tables being used in the smoking area, one by a loud but small group of teenagers. None of them can sit still, it seems. There is constant bouncing in the booth. There is constant laughter. An older man sits alone at a table parallel to the teenagers. He has one hand on his coffee mug and the other on a cigarette resting in an ashtray. He watches the kids with a calm face and doesn't look over at us when we take our seats.

On the other side of the restaurant, there are no non-smokers. The maintenance crew shampoos the carpets.

With Kate across the table from me, I order a coffee and the fruit cup. When she orders chocolate chip pancakes, I instantly wish I had ordered a caramel sundae like I had wanted.

Before our food arrives, Kate blows smoky clouds over

my head and I tell her about where I work, the place where I go after she sees me every morning in line at the café. "I do illustrations of cartoon-like people in influencing and negotiating situations. I design brochures and presentations. In blue and gray only," I tell her. "Our corporate colors. Sometimes I get to add black and purple, but those are under very rare and special circumstances."

She has been smiling at me evenly, amused, with slightly parted lips and only a hint of teeth, since the moment I started talking. I want to stretch across the table, put both of my hands on her cheeks while I kiss those lips closed, and say, *Stop*.

Kate smokes her last cigarette when she tells me about her husband. She says it nonchalantly, "I met him when I was seventeen," and my eyes instantly fall to her hands. She notices, holds them out in front of her, fingers extended and her cigarette hanging from the corner of her mouth, it bouncing up and down when she says, "We don't wear rings."

Her story begins on her twentieth birthday when she married her husband, a nineteen-year-old sophomore at the community college, at City Hall during the height of a snowstorm. "It was just him and me," Kate says. "I wore a sweatshirt and my ski jacket. I don't remember what he was wearing."

Three months before their wedding her husband had been diagnosed with lymphoma or melanoma or another type of cancer. My ears are buzzing, so I miss the fine details. "He was my first time," she says. "I would have done anything."

The following twenty months brought with it surgeries and chemotherapies, then a full remission. Seven weeks was all it took for their first pregnancy to end in miscarriage. "If there is a God and He ever looked down on me kindly, He did it then," she says.

I am squeezing my hands together in my lap beneath the table. I am not thinking. I am listening.

Four years to the marriage and her husband now builds houses in towns that I could never afford to live in. He works for his father, who will soon retire and leave the business to him and his brother. "I love his mother more than anything," she says, and smiles wide at me.

I am thinking, *What am I thinking?*

Together they have moved from an old starter home to a larger older home, and now into the largest house that he has ever built, that she has ever seen, ever been in. "Really," she says, "he has done amazing things for my credit score."

The house has three empty bedrooms, a kitchen with skylights. It sits off a cul-de-sac. She tells me that at night he sleeps on the sofa, and on other nights when she's at school late and he gets to bed first, she sleeps on the recliner in front of the television. When she's too tired, she will climb into bed with him, their legs snapping back to their sides when they accidentally touch under the sheets.

When the waitress comes to clear our table, Kate sits back in the booth and looks smaller than I remember. Watching me, she says, "Tell me more about you, Julia. More than the blues and the grays."

I lean slightly over the table, moving closer to her, until she does the same. I say, "Right now, I think that I am by far the most confused person that you will ever meet."

Kate's dress is small and red, low-cut with spaghetti

straps. She tells me that she's been to a cousin's wedding, but the dress doesn't seem like one you would wear to a cousin's wedding. For the first ten minutes after she arrives, it captures my full attention.

She comes to my apartment on Saturday nights now, too, not just Tuesdays and Thursdays after her late classes. Last Tuesday I told her to take my parking spot outside of my building since I didn't have a car to fill it, and then she wouldn't have to spend so much money at the parking garage across the street when she takes the subway into school.

We sit in lawn chairs on my balcony, sharing bottles of beer that she says she took with her from the barbeque reception. She wrapped eight bottles in her jacket, she tells me, then waved goodbye to her cousin the bride and her new groom. She says she didn't feel guilty when, accidentally brushing her bundle against her leg, they clanked together.

We watch the windows of the apartment building that sits across the quiet dead-end street below us. She has her feet up on the railing, her legs exposed up to her thighs where her dress rests in a wrinkled bunch. How much of Kate could I see if I was in one of the windows staring back at us?

She says, "I'm certain that I can trust you with this."

Kate tells me about Marianne. She tells me that technically Marianne is her niece, but having been raised together and only nine years apart they are more like sisters. She tells me about her wild oldest sister, Marianne's mom, who went out late on school nights. There would be a call the next morning from a neighbor, and then, peering down from a window, her sister could be found passed out in the rose bushes. She tells me that

Marianne hates her mother, who moved to California days before Marianne's first birthday. She hates her mother so ferociously, Kate tells me, because she doesn't know her father, and therefore has no one else to hate.

I ask Kate what she thinks of Marianne's mom, her sister, and she says, "I was jealous that she got away." Then she adds, "But it's Marianne who's important to me here, and I think you can help."

Kate tells me a story that her mother had told Marianne and her. She told them that when women are unhappy with their lives, they rarely take it out on the things that they love. They rarely smash up their houses, punch holes in the walls, like men do. They rarely slam doors so hard that family portraits fall from the walls. They never smash jadeite vases, passed on through generations, against kitchen floors, because women know how long it takes to build a home. They know firsthand the energy that goes into keeping a family together. When women are unhappy with their lives, she told them, they simply pack a bag and go, leaving behind what they've built for so long for another woman to reshape and build on. They pack a bag and find another place to unpack it. They start all over again.

To Kate I mention the woman in Texas who drowned her five children in her tub, one after the other. She had to chase the oldest one throughout the house, I say. She tips a beer bottle my way and replies, "She told this story before women got as unhappy as they get today. She told this story before women got desperate."

When Kate gets up to leave, my head is heavy from drinking. The way she moves in front of me in her red dress reminds me of bonfires. She presses her lips against mine and they are wet and forceful. When she moves away, she doesn't smile. She says, "I wanted that to be more perfect."

Marianne plays striker for my college alma mater, and she is one of the fast ones. In three steps she's already past the last defender, with an arm's length between them. She moves well on the ball, makes perfect through passes to the right wing when she's looking left. On corner kicks she doesn't enter the mix in the front of the goal, too short to win the ball in the air, but she stands just inside the 18' and hopes for it to ricochet her way. She is unmarked, the only short-haired blonde on a field of ponytailed brunettes. Her teammates in purple have bronzed skin from three-hour practices and summertime double sessions, their thighs wide with muscle. Marianne is slight, her skin white as my sheets, her cheeks red from sprinting upfield and then jogging back to the center circle.

On a throw-in she stumbles toward the sideline like she has been taken hostage. A defender pushes from behind with a fist full of her shirt and another pressed into the center of her back. Marianne looks at me then, takes her eyes off the ball for the first time during the match. Up close I can see the hardness in her legs, the sinew of muscle and faint brown freckles. Quick breaths come from between her parted lips, and I step back from where I'm standing with the crowd, as if somehow in her way.

Minutes after the final whistle, I stand alone in the dimming sunlight, my hands in my pockets. I regret now having dressed so casually. Brown corduroys wearing thin at the knees, zip-up black sweatshirt with a band's logo screen-printed in white across the chest. I don't even listen to this band anymore. My jean jacket I wouldn't have left at home.

"You didn't really have to come to the match," Marianne says, suddenly at my right, both hands on the strap of her duffel bag that weighs down her shoulder. I realize that she must have picked me out with help from Kate's careful description. I wanted to ask her, *What was it, exactly?* The way I slouch? Or how I shift my weight on my feet? To find Marianne, I had it easier, her shirt number printed in the photocopied leaflet handed out at the gate.

"Have you been here for the whole game?" she asks, and I work hard to keep my eyes on her face, away from her bloodied right knee, away from the damp, dark V that has formed on her jersey, stretching from her neckline to her breasts.

"The whole game," I say. Her blond hair is dark from sweating, the skin under her eyes wrinkled from too much sun. I want to say, *Tell me how she sees me.*

"Do you still want to meet at the restaurant across the street?"

"Yeah, let's do that."

I walk with her, and she leads me toward the exit gates. She says, "I'm just going to shower and change in the locker room, then I'll be right over." She stares at the backs of her teammates walking single file into the clubhouse, shin guards in their hands, socks rolled down to their ankles.

I touch the inside of her forearm with my fingers and she looks at me. "Marianne, you were great today," I say.

She gives me a practiced, tired smile and answers, "Thanks." I wonder if she's having trouble remembering my name.

* * *

Eighty-five minutes and I think she's bailed. I can't blame her, and at quarter past I will pay for my beer. I will say goodnight to the waiter who has been watching the empty seat at my table from the station where he places other tables' orders, looking at me occasionally with a tight smile that says, *Whoops!*

Without the duffel bag I would never recognize her. She looks blonder in the dark of the restaurant than she did in the sun on the field. "Swedish blonde," my dad would say, "Not Irish blonde," like my mom and me, a somehow inferior shade of yellow. She scans the room until she finds me by the window, then turns back toward the hostess who nods her on. She comes at me wearing a black turtleneck sweater and gray wool pants, shoes that look new and expensive. I zip up my sweatshirt, not remembering if the shirt I'm wearing underneath it is the one with the small holes at the collar.

When she puts her bag down between her chair and the window, her hair falls in front of her eyes. It is cropped close in the back, but on top there are longer yellow pieces that fall from a darker, combed part. When she sits, she moves the strands to the side of her face with pinched fingers, like turning the page of a book.

"Sorry," Marianne says. "That took a lot longer than I thought." She is out of breath, from running in a crosswalk with a flashing warning signal, maybe. The cars at the red light inching forward, intimidating her into a sprint.

The waiter heads our way and I push the menu toward her. "You should order a drink," I say.

He stands between Marianne and me, his hands behind his back. When she looks up at him, I can see what I think is a light application of pink lipstick. "Just water," she says.

The waiter looks at me and winks. He takes my empty beer bottle and says, "Another." It's not a question. I smile, don't stop him.

I am alone with Marianne. I like the way her hands, resting on the table, look half-swallowed by the cuffs of her sweater. I like her thin ringless fingers, the pink beneath her short nails. She sighs, and I move my eyes up to her face. "Please don't think that this is typical. Kate talks about you a lot. I guess I was just interested." Beneath the table, I bring my legs together, then cross them at the knee, sitting up straight in my seat. "Well, I'm happy we could meet."

"I hope she didn't pressure you too much."

"No," I say.

"In my head," she runs a thin finger over the sugar packets standing upright in their dish, "I've been repeating things that I shouldn't say to you tonight, so that I don't forget. But now I'm having trouble thinking of the things that I wanted to say."

"Kate's worried about you," I start. It's coming from out of nowhere, but I want her to be clear on why I'm here. "She thinks you're very lonely."

She moves her hands together as the waiter places a small red napkin in front of her, followed by a glass of water. Clearing her throat, she waits until he's left me with my beer, then asks, "Very lonely? Me or her?"

At that, I sit lower in my chair with my hands in my lap, listening as Marianne tells me things that I already know.

I don't tell Kate that Marianne calls me on nights when she's not here. I can't figure out how Marianne knows that I'm alone. When I answer the phone she greets me only with, "Hi," and then I'm left for a moment to roll through my memory of the female voices in my life until I can find the face that matches. I've gotten quicker now that she calls sometimes two or three times a week.

We talk for hours. When we're ready to say goodnight, I've already changed into my pajamas, and she listens as I brush my teeth, telling me that it sounds like I'm using sandpaper. "You brush too hard. I can tell," she says. "What about your gums?"

Underneath my sheets I fish for lost socks at the foot of my bed and she asks me why I have yet to invite her over. The following Wednesday she is grazing with her fingertips the old tapestry that I use as a tablecloth. She is staring at the books in my bookcase, fingers pressed to her chin. She fits in my small apartment well, like she's lived here longer than me, and I let her walk around unguided. I call out to her that the bedroom is on the left, the pink and blue bathroom on the right. The photograph on the wall is of me and my parents when I was two, taken in the wooded area of a campsite in Florida. In it I am bald and fat, and Marianne tells me that she has never seen me happier. The charcoal drawing was done by me, the legs and feet of an ex-lover hanging over an unmade bed. I can hear her footsteps coming toward me on the hardwood floors, the flicking on and off of light switches.

I am noticing all the wrong things. The back of Marianne's neck, dark with sunburn. Her thin blue shirt fitting snug all the way down to her waist and stretching tight across her breasts. Her pink tongue running quickly along her lips as she listens to me talk. We are sitting close enough together that when she moves her hands to help make her point, she brushes lightly against my arm. When she does this a warmth runs through my insides, starting at my throat and heading down toward my stomach, but not ending there.

Here on my sofa, Marianne is a decision to be made.

Kate is on top of me and I am thinking, *She is stronger and heavier than she looks.*

I am pinned, her hands pressing down on my upper arms, and my first reaction is to laugh. I laugh softly, but loud enough that I know that she can hear me, that she cannot mistake these noises for anything else. On my neck her lips are hot, and behind my knees sweat forms, and I am laughing. "Kate." I say, "Kate, Jesus."

Kate releases her grip on one of my arms and moves her hand beneath my shirt. On my stomach, her fingers are cool, not like her lips. My arm feels light and free without her weight there, but I don't even think about moving it. I don't think about moving it when I feel her hand slide lower, her fingers tugging on my belt buckle. I don't think about moving it when I feel her teeth on the tip of my chin or her breath heavy in my ear, like she has been running for miles, like I have been just out of her reach but finally she has caught up to me. I am only laughing, and Kate is saying, "Too late." She says, "It's too late now."

There are many things that Kate taught me. She taught me exfoliate, cleanse, then moisturize. She taught me low-rise, boot-cut stretch, and that a cheese course is not a cheese class.

Kate taught me how to take a part of your past that you regret, pretend like it never happened, and just move on with your fucking life.

Tonight my parking spot is empty between an old pickup

and my neighbor's tall SUV. Kate's car is normally there to greet me on Thursdays after my walk home from work. Past the corner store, I take a turn onto the quiet side street and it is the first thing I see, the first thing I look for. Then I will wash the dishes in my sink and light a scented candle. I will dust the television screen and change my bed sheets. Small and silver, her car is a color that, Kate tells me, excels at hiding dirt.

Kate is not parked in my spot. She is parked in front of the entryway to my apartment building, her brake lights blazing red. I see her car and stop right where I am, watching her dark silhouette behind the wheel, as motionless as my shadow.

I am thinking, *I know what she is thinking.*

A rush like this is reserved for split-second reactions to the car that has come to a sudden stop in front of you. For phone calls that come too early in the morning or too late at night. A rush like this means your heart is pounding harder in your ears than in your chest. It means your palms are damp and slick.

The sun is setting behind the apartment building whose windows we watch sometimes at night. Through the tall oak trees that frame the streets below, it casts a honey-colored spotlight on Kate and her car, her driver-side window reflecting a still-life snapshot of my neighborhood, clouds full and white in the sky. I stand just behind it, out of her view.

Kate's head is down like she is faking sleep. She has one hand on her lap and moves the other hand from the wheel to lower the window after I rap my knuckles gently on the glass. When she lifts her head to bring her eyes to mine, I want to say, *You don't need to say a word.*

FAKE ANIMALS
by Jose Alvarado Lopez

Danny's fingers lose their grip on the fence; he stumbles back and falls down. A CD player in his backpack makes a crunching sound. The boy who punched him grunts laughter; his friends pass a knife from one hand to the other. Boots and basketball shoes come down, making a scrambled frame around Danny's transparent face.

Marvin catches it, the moment that stoned mask slips off his brother, and the raw confusion underneath. Danny's huge disbelieving eyes pop under awful realizations—like knowing his little brother is watching this. The sun breaks over a stranger's shoulder, and Danny almost shuts his eyes against the brightness of it.

Five kids in baggy thug uniforms cross the street to a waiting car. Marvin doesn't look at their faces. He knows he isn't tough like his brother, so why bother. It sounds just like 5 o'clock outside. Girls are shouting at each other across the high-rise balconies, it's almost quiet. Coming down from a disinterested after-school sky, the wind tells Marvin to go home and turn on the TV or the computer. Danny never came home right after school so he would have heard it differently. But Danny has gone and made things impossible for Marvin.

Kneeling over the body, Marvin feels little more than curiosity. The only reason he'd waited after school was that Danny promised to sneak him into an R-rated zombie movie tonight, but when Danny did show up, an hour late, it was just to say they weren't going anymore. Marvin was about to walk away without saying shit, then it happened.

He closes his eyes and pushes two fingers through the hole stabbed through Danny's jacket, feeling along the edge of a rib, stops, pulls them back, and slides them in beneath it, curving his skinny hand under the sternum until he holds a slimy organ he's guessing is his brother's heart. Marvin can't help but look over at Danny's face while holding it—it's not really his face anymore, everything about him is absent, and what's left looks like it could have been drawn by a child. Danny's fat red tongue makes a cartoonish shape, like it's plush red lining and his mouth is a gift box.

Beside the heart his fingers find something sharp. It feels like a tiny ear or horn, two of them, connected by a muzzle that extends down into a body. With his thumb and forefinger he grabs ahold of it and carefully works it out from the wound where he'd slipped his hand in up to the wrist. It's a four-legged figure, sticky with red blood. He scrapes it along the ground, leaving a rough streak on the concrete, and cleans the blood off its legs and long neck with his shirt. Marvin spits on his thumb and uses it to wipe the face clean. Two tiny sculpted eyes look back above a toothful smile. It is a toy giraffe.

A memory builds slowly around the object; Marvin can almost remember holding it when he was little. His eyes blur forward, open, but looking backwards in time to the oldest, smallest glints of prerecorded history. The sound of wrapping paper tearing, the sound of couch springs jumping, it must have been Christmas. When else would people give Marvin and Danny fake animals to play with? He wishes Danny would get up so he could ask him about it. Maybe he's just making the whole thing up.

A police siren streaks across the schoolyard, it could be going anywhere but he won't chance it. He folds the animal in sheets of math paper and cuts across the soccer field into the woods.

The black creek is stinking and sorry-looking. If he follows it long enough, eventually it leads back home. Marvin watches the scarily thin spiders glide around his wrists on the water surface. A rust-colored thread unwinds from his fingers and is carried away by the current. He kneels at the bank; his knee crushes a pop can in a patch of tough weeds edged like saw blades. Marvin wonders, as he dries his hands on the clean piece of his shirt, if the forest has always been like this, ugly, or if it's been ruined by the trash seeping down from the buildings—knocking them down, smashing the bricks into dust; melting the pipes and burning the leftover furniture might make the land beautiful again, slowly; it would take thousands of years. Marvin guesses that's what recycling is about, and things being biodegradable, like human bodies. He imagines Danny's body going through the phases it'll take to become dirt on a skeleton. How about Danny's anonymous skull, pushing up through the earth like in that zombie movie he was supposed to see. A red snake in his jaw hissing, *I'll take you to the movies.*

Marvin jumps over the spiders, landing on a tiny island made of lumped-together rocks, and crosses to the other side of the creek. From a green hill he can see cars on the road beyond a parking lot and some backyards.

On his back, he looks up at the sky, feels disconnected from it; the wind's not telling him anything he can understand. Even angling his ears in the breeze doesn't help him catch a whisper. It must be confused, thinks

Marvin. That doesn't surprise him, the wind is such a dumb thing; it only cares about going places, and Marvin doesn't want to go anywhere. The only thing he admires about the wind is the way it rattles everything at once, which is a totally inhuman thing to do.

He's letting the ground take its time, pressing rocks and knots of grass into his back until he won't be able to stand it anymore. Then he'll get up and massage the train tracks out of his skin. The road is too loud and jammed with cars, so he'll walk along the quiet streets, where kids pass by on bikes, holding hockey sticks under their arms, gradually choosing turns that will take him somewhere else.

Until he finds a curb to sit down on, and unties the knots in his head. Like how he and Danny looked so different, he figures that one of them had to be adopted. Danny was athletic, even though he smoked and hadn't played a sport since he was ten. Marvin played softball for a while. The other kids could tell right away that it was his mother's idea. Nobody ever gave him shit about it, even when he'd struck out for the third time in a row, probably because Danny was always there at his games. Back when he knew how to keep promises. He'd ride over on his bike, jumping off of it and letting it drop beside the bleachers in one movement. Always clapping his hands and screaming, "Hit it out of the park, Marvin!" as if Marvin could actually do it. Sometimes Danny was all Marvin needed to wait that extra moment it took to see the ball, and although the bat was too heavy for him, somehow he made contact and dropped one over the second baseman's head.

Last year Danny came to every game just like he'd promised. He wasn't sure how, but Marvin could tell

Danny was high. He'd show up at the third inning with his friends, and the group of them would sit around nervously quiet or laughing ridiculously until the sixth or seventh inning when they'd get up and leave without saying goodbye. Marvin didn't hit much that year. He remembers lying in bed after games with the sheets wrapped around his head.

Back then, Marvin wished in daydreams to go out with his brother and do the things he did, so that they wouldn't be such a big deal anymore. That never happened. Marvin thought his first year of high school would be different; it would be Danny's last, but at least they'd spend it together. Danny didn't avoid him, exactly, he said hi in the hallways and let everybody know Marvin was hands-off, but Danny didn't let him go to the park where he and his friends went at lunch. Marvin was too shy to ask why.

Fine, then, he thinks, *you stupid asshole*. Marvin's ass hurts. The pavement is glistening; he walks with his fist out over the road, all the way down to the store.

He's fishing around in the ice-cream fridge, looking for a cheap popsicle, something he can afford. On his way to the counter he spots his best friend David crouched down by the magazines, reading an X-Men comic. Marvin looks at the back of David's T-shirt; slight currents move its fabric whenever a page turns, and round folds at its bottom swing like bells as David shifts his weight from foot to foot. Marvin wants to touch it, he knows exactly how the material will feel; his fingers press it like a memory. They've been best friends since seventh grade, but still, just thinking about it makes his face hurt. The door clatters open, David's mom walks in, Marvin takes a step backwards into the aisle.

"Oh, hi, Marvin, I didn't know you were in here."

David turns, surprised. "You were going to see a movie?"

"Danny didn't show."

"Oh. Mom, I want this comic."

She sets a ten-dollar bill on the counter. "Do you need a ride, Marvin?"

"No."

"Come on," says David, using his arm to motion, as if gathering Marvin toward the door. Marvin shakes his head. David doesn't understand that, and narrows his brow as he heads out. "Okay, see you tomorrow."

Marvin follows a few steps behind, thinking that he'll cry for sure if he gets into their car. He takes his time, watching the toe of each shoe fall step by step into the parking lot, still thinking that he can't catch that ride without bursting, until he's standing behind David's minivan.

The space between him and home is narrowing way too fast. Marvin looks across David's lap at the brightly colored superheroes. He reads the words over and over, trying to connect them to the images, but as soon as he shifts his attention from one to the other, both are lost. His brain can't hold onto either and David isn't waiting long enough to turn the pages. Frustrated, he's choking down on incredibly deep breaths that make him feel as momentarily hollow as an open fist. In the rearview mirror David's mom watches Marvin's eyes become wet and frightened, losing it more with every bump on the road. Marvin tries to blank his mind and shut his eyes, but the ride has only taken a minute, and when he looks around he sees that the car is already idling in front of his house.

"Marvin, I'm going to call your mother when I get home, okay, sweetheart?"

"Okay." Marvin opens the sliding door and drops his legs unsteadily on the lawn.

"Get online and I'll send you the address for those Manson videos I was telling you about."

"Sure."

The minivan pulls away quickly.

Marvin runs to the upstairs bathroom, locks the door, and turns on the tap, he's crying. The boy in the mirror is too skinny, his sharp cheekbones make the lower half of his face look like a withered bear trap. His hair cut looks like nothing. Marvin tried shaving it off with a razor like Danny did, but the back of his head has a weird bump on it that everybody pointed out. On top of that, he wears big, round, thick-rimmed glasses. Behind them his puffy red eyes are making him look like a sissy. He takes the glasses off; that's better, his shot eyes make him look sort of tough.

The sink swirls with water about to overflow. Marvin takes the giraffe out of his pocket, unwraps it, and drops it into the pool. An airy brown cloud spreads out to the edges. In a second, the animal's color transforms to bright banana-skin yellow mottled with brown dots. Marvin grabs it out of the water, turns it around in his hands; his name is etched on the giraffe's stomach.

Danny's face drifts into focus, the way it looked when he fell, kind of like how it looked when Dad beat Danny for beating up on Marvin. Danny hit his head on the sidewalk, hard, and then they killed him. Marvin guesses he sort of closed his eyes for the worst part and listened to the complicated sound. When he looked again, Danny wasn't there anymore.

A streak of vomit hits the mirror and spatters onto the floor mat and the shower curtain. *Fuck.* Leaning into the sink, Marvin can only think of them sneaking up from behind, never giving Danny a chance to run. Puke comes gushing through his mouth, lodging something in his throat. It's hard and sharp and hurts almost as much as it's messing up his breathing. Marvin is on his knees with his hand in his mouth, pushing to make the convulsion strong enough to get it out. The phone rings, his mother runs from the kitchen to the living room. Despite how often Danny comes home at 2 in the morning, she still hasn't learned not to care. A thick strand of saliva runs from Marvin's mouth to the tiles, trickling down with dots of red and orange. The lump moves, and Marvin coughs out a plastic lion.

He cleans it in the sink. Danny's name is etched into the lion, just below its mane, which looks unrealistic, like a ring of petals.

Two towels soak up his mess and get thrown into a garbage bag beneath the sink, along with his shirt and socks. He runs through the hallway into his room. The shelf on his wall is where he keeps his favorite books and, although he doesn't have many, a few old action figures. The lion and the giraffe stand among the collection. Marvin presses them together so that their sides touch.

THE CONFINED OF
THE SAINT-SÉPULCRE CONVENT
by David Saà Viccenzo Estornell

Deep whispered wound, my touch is still willowy.

The holy children bathed their feet in plum brandy. When someone decides that they don't want to know something, they become invincible, they don't crush the prejudices, but become their corpse, flooding the incommensurable becomes the task of what emanates. The soul.

To assimilate the darkness, to throb for it, from it. To shield it from the crudeness of the body, swamped in that myopic problem. A halo of water, mulatto spit. At six, his instincts told him to tie himself to the void, that self-denial was a weakness. He was crossing the doorway and his nausea spawned his conclusions, vomiting threshold and threshold mulatto dogs. The whinnying of the unperceived, and vanity acts in the guts. It carried him along like a silent idol.

To walk gives dignity to the fall, the acid sweat of the slip formed his sutras. Many people live by their intuition. The mist is idiotic, amassing the flesh is difficult and it can die from anonymousness, autolysis.

The valve of an oyster is the result of sixty thousand times its weight in seawater, a true judgment of patience. The obsolete world, the chalice of memories, the liminal humus of the mist, the fetal phonation that gloats at the deceptions that abase you.

The mist's petals continue to flow like pustules. Risking all means to risk everything, rebuilding the medication that links to the outside world. Sometimes I beat the wind of the dreams that someone has stopped dreaming, the belly of those wings. How someone who doesn't know how to cry, cries. I rehearse my happiness a second time, palpitations of dolls with no illnesses, with no decay, no life. The answer is violating children. I chant his smell of armpits and moss, ceded before the plants. Inhaling cigarette butts would be an intimacy, screaming no longer pacifies. The evening lights up what I am thinking.

A storm of effusion from a woman and her nightmares. I fear my undoing. That lichen that kills the remaining guilt. I understood that the consciousness persists until the last litigation. The opacity of things, the errancy of objects so many voices, he suffered creamily. The residues of my mother, her memory smells of apricot and vanilla. She predicted the black holes.

I no longer fight, that is my secret. The white snake returns to its stream, Jesus' carpentry. I drink vinegar soup at his doorway. I am anxious with nerves I can't convey, the affection of a cat. The thirst of not daring to confront your own shadow, to succumb to this response. My lock's cavity, the politeness of the glances and its stenches that groan, the lowness of knowing that doubting breeds alienation. She gnaws her words, fissures, cracks, convexes, the internal changes, the scenes. Now I know, all feeling is shame. Incoherent wind, indecisive, it's always water that reflects, I lost that jewel, your family deceives you, vicars of the home and the sway of the nocturnal butterfly as it castrates. The singing of my flesh, so many energies, so much ink that prays, here and there. She would do it, she sifted the heart with essences of orange blossom, lichens, and my vapors. The mineral feed as it comes into sincere contact with that watery outline. The jewel of being the depth of someone else, your own impulsive vagary.

The touch and its phlegm, we learned to kiss the indubitable fecal dregs of the other, he razed with the sluggish fraction of softness, he suppurated humility in that fight between ribs and my intermittent groans. That skin like a smell that buries the flower of the carob tree, she knew that everything that makes men rested in my uterus. To fertilize the invulnerable, sweaty skin, intact in the ejaculations that hair has made strong, vigor. The taffeta of the eyelashes, the yolk of the tongue, that brutal sea, mists and shadows that thrust themselves in Mother, all women. The breaking out of a body without a palate. To fuck. The order when you are happy, the thickness of the coralline infernos, the impetus of that lax texture. The illation of a bed and his handouts, I have apologized so much. To blame myself for the dead food, me, when I've already accused myself so much.

I have learned things inside here, when you cannot even overshadow yourself, it's because you are living in the dark, blind to yourself. The screams of the body travel the foreseeable paths, nourished, as I now know, not by expectations or experiences, but by their inoculation; the carriers of the body of anguishes. In the register of silences, at intervals I know I'm alive because I am afraid of ceasing.

He explained his tricks to me, like the aged urines, his beverage, which whitened the teeth, his scorn, he tricked me again with his white smile. Him, always reconquering.

I remember his silence, his muteness was the catalyzer

of emotions. I knew that we all need to reduce everything to concepts, to not give way to alchemies.

He showed me everything, how a mother lulls her child, how she kisses the child and measures the child's nationalisms, the scrap of the flesh, a suicidal dream.

Yellow sex, the mouth of autumn, that acrid smell that stains beauty.

The tongues lick each other, my father removed the bones from his moral. His baby does not decide or explain anything. The root of the voice seals the fate of others, he explained to me that *evil* in Hebrew means *the adversary*, the others, your fellow man. A filthy lie, my subduction. She always knew how to contain her internal humiliation, she laminated the sign and joined it to the storms of pollen. The secret, in itself, throbs brutality.

His pustular breath, it hated chatter. He said that a heart should face sideways, if the stream of foam mislays the shackled navels. That was how he bevelled my fears, on an evening without prisoners, a group of us, children, curled ourselves up, glycine, in the butterfly's loams. I grope. I grope. The arrogance of the poppies that pant their suspicion. She conjured the spell. Cast the spell.

I poke in those tendons, deepening myself in the nausea, in that obverse of the other side. The wrapping of the mutilated, from which parietal hole did you come? My teeth fell out; I didn't even notice. Now I know, you don't win by obeying a nightmare, but you can be a person by following it. The courtesy of the guts knows how to churn butterflies with excrements. The doctor speaks, speaks. His austerity opened a peephole. The sickbay, my past. The withering skin of the foals freezes its darkness, they would confuse the day, miles to the east, where the sea still ferments, I know, the crotches of the daughters with the pelage of the community. Arctic air like a pulse and vastness like a porous word, the past dismantles its madness.

She conjured everything, the hair creaked under the touch. The coldness of a spring, the mist wrapped itself up, that child that will be born, now I am born, with needles in the brain. I withhold my feces. I hear the phonemes that my voice drags with it. Fucking. Fucking. Fucking. I have never stopped surrounding myself in that drilled dead daughter, the baby that thought for her, blind. I was born welcome to the morgues. The dizzy sweat surrounded finally convulsive, belated spasm. I had already grown up, collecting her memory, retaining myself in that infancy, through the elaboration of carnal feelings, the previous life of what were the first digestive juices. That was where courage was stirred.

Impossible to lose when you are a butterfly, I could not stand my elemental reflection, I looked at the circles forming in that liquid, the cup of camomile. To mark the breath, quieten that which must be evoked. She was not a monster, just selfish. The softened appetite in the hands of the female, obeying.

I obeyed, I sing out everything that sinks me! I carry that voice in my veins, a memory of the juniper's saliva, its amniotic liquid. She was the one that told me, the impatience and anxiety stops us. That fetid mouth, the retention of feces. The monster of incest is the frosts, the freezing colds that break through. Now, little by little, I unbury myself.

My people, here, they don't cry, and if they do, it is because of the sting. Nobody knows a lot, but these things were respected as much as the families of the drowned were. Speak. Speak.

I suppose it is a secret, just as few people knew that seal spit is sweetish and acidic, and that stinking fat, left over from the broths, which was so frequent there, was often used as wax to polish the wooden façades.

There was only one hymn and it is violet. Abused like the horizon. The crowd is purple, the elders already murmured that the inertia of time did not affect everyone in the same way. There are puddles on the tiles on the floor.

The flesh behaves like the tide, its cycles, the rushes and cracks of the scabs of passion, still hang on the oceanic icebergs, those that wreathe the very innards, through the paunch of paunches.

His reddish pleasure imposed itself, the guarded dessert, the marshes of the female stacked all of the spirits, all of them summoned each other in the night; they would go up to their respective slings and that made the woman fertile, the backbones of the soul were tied to the handles of the brazen flesh, the sexes still hiss at each other. The coast of personal impulses salted the brains. They spoke for me. Here.

To abandon what spills, that stateliness that is inherent to our effect, I taught myself how to kill the lie; in other words, how to swallow death.

His papier-mâché breath, the lilies of the valley, the aroma, they said that my passion was due to them. It's tough to know that all the plans that you scrap, torture their owners, my fruit is no longer the complaint.

I try to find my side with my fingers, that pseudo-bulb where the energy of the plant should concentrate, pressing the intangible, the world already is, in your world, and there, biscuits and aromatic plants were cooked in an oven, the axis was unravelled.

There in your womb I would have marmalade in the tinplate crop of various kittens, discrete and accumulated, I mocked the herons, my quietude before the secondhand dealers that contaminate everything. I am food for kittens, the soft breeze of a blooming time. I am ashamed of my grandfather.

I was embarrassed of mother, her new ways of reifying words. I powdered myself as I did my remote nose, the cocktail of return. He was the smell of the shining, Mother would ask me, omnivorous of the rest of the world, she wanted to know who it would be. The missive of identity, the saliva of the juniper conspired with her fingertips, she considered the maiden grass of the other's pubis. I knew it, the past is not in the blood, like many Bulgarians believed; the past rests in the course of ice. It is not that it takes refuge there; it now destroys everything on the basis of pneumatic-colored processes. When the giant was like that, it was better not to go in.

Old bread soaked in cod liver oil was a rectal cure that he liked a lot. He noticed that his grandchild's wrist became dislocated and, timid as he was with the women, his remedy was the offensive. The rest would have been dishonorable.

The waters are cut, they burst the freezing twilight, hollies, daneworts, gooseberries, and wild blueberries allying themselves in the mouth of the stomach to cancel out the saline smell of pubis that agitated the men each winter. I am hungry.

The struggle of detecting the world, the tolerance to food, my baby is jealous, I can tell. When you enter a house, you never leave. Your sutures stay there. A mute seed.

Gingerbread as a backbone, the meat where I

developed my private mythology. They bit my pus, suctioned the purges. The fate of the food is unknown to me, that outrage of identifications of what is absorbed and what is rejected. I am no longer injured, I am the fragility of knowing that nobody else will immolate themselves to me.

The lachrymal let out tomato pips instead of wasps' oil. The time of the black fires, I retain it. The amber animated the toys to their concrete delirium, subsuming some slopes that created rings of more smoke, where before there was an abyss. The seal meat and cider with natural saffron oil douse the intestines, it is here they said, since time immemorial, that in each person there is at least one ant larva that would come out of the corpse, one day, after a rainy evening. My palate gets dry when I think of those salted rice patties, the plums and pulverized bones, echoes and sleepiness. The darkness formed by my own wild beasts, discarded. I repeat. It is not the guilt that hurts me, it is the remorse. I absolve myself, glottic, complete and mute. Eviscerating is not just the preserve of ants and pits, that bustle, the truth shines through, an intestine can be detuned from the rest of the primary organs. Winter storm, the coast quieted, balancing itself between gusts of wind and the drowning salted resin.

That first scratch is the first proclamation. I am afraid, sometimes I cry for what is to come. I fast and shudder, people don't speak out. I am afraid of the moment that I am no longer affected by things. I submit the punishment of isolation to requiring specific things in that feared sensorial privation.

Far away, the sun shaves the embers, I blow the trade winds. Nothing is real, everything burbles, sometimes memories embed themselves in the lamps of some of the elders from the time when they lived from the red earth, back then when the hay was not sedated. When you love, nothing rejects you, not even the varicose veins, you thirst for them.

I don't have a vulva, nobody loves me, everything creaks and hurts. I am possessed, fragmented of his whispers, they are the putrefaction of the sun. Parsley was a highly valued good, it flooded gravel, crown, the seams of the flu, the common fevers of the cornel, everything fills with shadows of those that, in the stillness, carved the incubation of the evilness of magic. I know that there are sensations that one has never allowed oneself. The whiteness of the air, the subtlety of the perfume, I rub my hands around my groin.

The doctors say that my semantic burden is in my larval halo. The guilt, where I am going. The instinct that you defecate, I injure my spill. Here I am, when my father liked to dig graves in the earth, in the ground, in the basement of the house. I am in danger if I am faithful to the expectorations of another being, that is why I am locked in here, bolted in. He would threaten us, saying that those would be our graves. I stay in the finest strand of the fabric of insolence, it is overwhelming. To touch is everything, that genuflected fetus.

I settled with daughter, everybody tired, the burden of the weariness of more people, the extremities of the dead mother were very narrow. The symmetry, the murmur of the concentration of ebbing tides and the moon, they tainted the young flesh when it was also touched by one of its brothers with the stench of squid, carnations, vanilla, and toothpaste. It was him that told me the last daughters would serve as a spittoon if the father were widowed.

I twist my daughter with excoriations. I want, desire, need to consume myself with her transformation. Every moral has its tears, its cries, each glove needs a hand. Each lash needs its resentment.

That's what loving is.

(Letter found in the S.S., collected from Fêre, undersigned upon receipt by Alphonse de Massary)

WHEN I WAS YOUNG, I ALWAYS HAD THE SAME NIGHTMARE
by Mike Kitchell

I was my neighbor, running on the top of our apartment complex, jumping off and flying to the ground. I always woke up before I hit the pavement—but that's a natural thing, right? I've heard that if you actually hit the bottom, you wake up dead.

It happened when I was six. I really don't have any memories before then. My mother says that nothing really happened before then, and the death of our neighbor, my friend, was such a monumental thing—she's not surprised that I don't remember anything before then. His name was Erik, and he was nine. Three years older than me. He lived in the single-room flat next to ours. He didn't have a kitchen like we did, he didn't have his own room like I did.

He would come over almost every day. We'd eat lunch and talk about how we liked it when it rained. It helped him sleep at night, he told me. It was one of the few things he found comfort in.

We lived on the top floor—the twelfth. The building was sparsely populated; most of the inhabitants had low-income jobs. My mother told me later, when I asked about it, that the electricity would occasionally turn off because of neighbors neglecting their electric bills. A fluke in the building's wiring, I suppose, as our bills were always paid.

When I was young, I always had the same nightmare.

It started out that I'd just wake up in a cold sweat—I couldn't remember what had just taken place in my head, or why my temple was pounding and my shirt was sticking to my back. Sometimes I would wake up screaming; that always alarmed my mother. My screams weren't long and withdrawn like a normal kid's, they were short and intense, like I was gasping for air.

When I was eight years old I was asked by the second grade teacher to draw a memory I had. I started to draw what I had for lunch. The teacher saw me doing this and instructed: "Not like that! A memory is something you remember from a long time ago!"

But I didn't remember anything from a long time ago. I just drew a picture of me and a dog and told the class that I had a dog named Susie when I was four. But I hadn't. I knew absolutely nothing about my life before I moved to the suburbs. I asked my mom what had happened, and she just told me that I wasn't happy. When I got even older, closer to entering the realm of adolescence, she finally told me about Erik. It didn't make a big impression on me, since I didn't even remember who Erik was, but the suicide shocked me as it would shock any twelve-year-old. I didn't understand why anybody would want to kill themselves. Why anybody would want to stop existing.

At only twelve years old, I didn't start asking why I had to do my homework, I started asking why I had to live.

The more I thought about it, the less bizarre it seemed. Mother had told me that Erik was poor and his family situation was fairly painful—it's possible he had been abused, and his mother had a different man in the apartment almost nightly. But still, to commit suicide at only nine years old is a really strange thing.

I turned sixteen and was a sophomore in high school. My grades started to slip, I didn't have any friends, and my mom lost her job. We moved back into the apartment we had lived in before Erik's accident, but of course I didn't recognize anything. I could tell it was really hard for my mom, because she cried the first night we were there. I'm not sure if she was crying because of what had happened, or because of the casual memories that the building recalled. We were on the twelfth floor again.

It was about a week after we moved back into the apartment that I heard my mother come in, excessively drunk, laughing. I heard a man's laugh too. At first I was happy, happy that my mother had finally gotten over the death of my father. But she wasn't. I walked into her room the next morning and there was blood on the sheets. I didn't know what it was from, but it wasn't important. When I got home from school that day she was sitting at our card-table-cum-kitchen-table, crying. I pretended not to notice and walked to my room.

Shutting the door, I hopped into my bed with dirty sheets and closed my eyes. I'd rub my eyes real hard until I'd start to see splotches of color and a sea of deep crimson red. If I twitched my eyes (while they were still shut) the designs would dance. Sometimes I could hear music in my head, the dots and lines choreographed perfectly, spinning and shifting and floating across the underside of my eyelids.

The drunken laughter and bloodied sheets became common. I turned seventeen and nothing really changed. Sometimes while I would be lying in my bed I would think about Erik, think about how strange it had to have been to make that kind of decision. What was he thinking as he jumped? Did he hesitate? Did he change his mind at the last minute?

On my eighteenth birthday, I bought a gun. I never bought any bullets, but I hid it under my bed and slept on it every night while listening to my mom fuck her latest trick in the next room. One night I took the gun to the roof of the complex and threw it off the edge. I watched it fall to the ground and crack into a hundred pieces. Nobody noticed. Nobody even turned a light on and looked outside.

I closed my eyes and started spinning around in place. I would spin and jump, as if somehow I could raise enough momentum to lift myself off the ground and float. That's what I wanted. I wanted to float. Nobody would notice if I failed, if I broke into a hundred pieces. Nobody would turn the light on and look out the window. I climbed onto the edge of the roof and closed my eyes. I started spinning slowly, counting the rotations. When I got to five, I jumped.

When I was young, I always had the same nightmare.

LYCANTHROPY WIFE
by Nick Cacioppo

The teapot began billowing steam, softly. I snapped two of her ten digits at their roots; one completely forward and the other completely back, until the little hooks of bone cracked the skin. She fell halfway to the floor, knees crashed to the tile, wrapping the fingers of her other hand around the wrist of its mutilated twin. The bubbles and pops of the boiling water made the pot whistle-to-scream.

She curled up, back to the black stove door, knees now up and hidden in the brittle, almost paperlike fabric of her black dress, hysterically inhaling and exhaling, the snot lumping in the back of her nose, trickling down to her throat, baptizing her cries with the thick milk of phlegm. I put the olive-green oven mitt over my right hand and picked up the teapot, the glass of its lid completely fogged, beads of condensation dripping along its metal rim.

Her hair was parted down the middle. Dry. Color of hay. I took off the lid and dumped the boiling water where her hair parted, a baritone yet feminine growl coming out of her mouth. "There is some fight in you left," I told her as she made a fetus of herself, praying the atmosphere would sheath over her person as some sort of a faux-uterus . . .

. . . The shaving cream gathers in white clumps in the

thistles of hair below my chin and cheeks, hairs that amass into a follicle chinstrap, unable to connect to the coarse moustache that has been needle-scraping against the pig-fat upper lip, their near constant irritation making the pink swollen, darker, and hard, oozing venom in every pout. Steam arises from the pool of water, pulverized into a toy typhoon by the faucet, spurting out muddy chunks of rust that create liver-spot stars on the yellow porcelain. My face looks inked, like a pen streaked black rain over bland marble, using artificial details to mask the uneventfulness of my features. The reflection and the flesh collide as each of our spit splatters on the mirror, the light green of the mucus like the chalk outline of an insect homicide.

My face stretches in the reflective portions of the mucus that drip down the mirror like heated cheese, liquified into a near white, robbing itself of the vivid dairy that defined it. The skin looks to be clumsily slipping from my skull, the bags around my eyes melting like unfinished Rorschachs on vertical pages. The skeleton looks back, the once indifferent eyes now wide as grappling hooks, their metallic spider legs twitching desperately for concrete to impale.

The jaw opens to unleash a slow olive drab flame, billowing out more like smoke than fire. It comes through the growing cracks in the mirror before quickly vanishing, the skinless nightmare of a blood-thick hallucination now just vapor and memory. The snot-target thins before me as the bog of sink water pushes the last of its dancing gas upwards, its humidity eliminating the shotgun-blast phlegm's brief density. The chrome button resting in the far-up of the sink's deeper end is pushed in, swallowing the corroded metal flakes and pale-oil slick of shaving foam that granted the water the will to congeal into something sick and rich. The lead pipes rumble the paneled walls with orchestral sucking noises, the drain of the sink vocalizing their wind and brass with a brief gurgled belch that caps off their tainted symphony.

Thick diseased vines of sewage-growth followed me on my way back to the bedroom, giving my shadow the illusion of tendrils, as if its host was part octopus. The vines beat me to the door, crawling on the surface of the wood, connecting like fingers sliding into the open spaces of each hand. The door wasn't shut all the way, and the mere weight of my shadow was enough to push the door wide open. The bed is anticipating my return to its womb-comforting cottons, culling my phantom nerves like amputated limbs that twitch with the pains of their former host's mutilation. The plaid comforter, the protective fabric skin of blanket, crumbled and starched sporadically from the protein of last night's masturbation, ejaculates compacting strands of fabric into gelled spikes.

A naked woman is lying on her side, back to me. Ghost-white cells compose the pale organ, shrink-wrapping the skeleton in soul-cold baggage. Her hair goes straight down before the ends split and feather just above her shoulders. Grease-black-ice, like snow aged by months and road. Droplets of sweat sputter down the crease in her back, arrowing to her asshole, where the moisture collected coats her sphincter with an appetizing glaze.

I climb into the bed. I rest my semi-hard cock in the crack of her ass, facing down. She slowly shakes and grinds her ass-cheeks into my cock, massaging it on both sides. The sweat that collected in and around her ass lubricates my cock, allowing it to slip into her ass with ease. The cavity chokes with delicacy, but with enough strength to suck my skin clean off. I could swear I hear faint tears, as if the skin of my back is ripping in half. With every intake/outtake thrust, I can feel the split becoming a divide, exposing red meats whose slime freezes in the open air.

I flip her to her stomach and start thrusting back, as if a vacuum attachment is throwing up garbage it was never meant to swallow. She's up on her knees, pushing me back with her waist, making her ass ripple with waves. I grab her arms and pull them behind her, pressing her wrists close to each other just above the small of her back. Her guts are finally packed with fluids vomited from infected veined sacks.

I go soft inside of her, falling right out of the cavity. I turn her over to her front. Her face looks like it has been streaked with Wite-Out and then Xeroxed. Long black hairs spring out sporadically from her breasts, as if spiders were inching their way out of her chest cavity through pinholes in the skin. Her stomach is toned, details outlined with faint hairs that make it look like the belly of a humanoid-wolf. A set of teeth glowers from her vagina, its lips pulled back, fastened open by hooked wires that coil around each other starting just above her belly button, running up her lycanthropic stomach and through her cleavage, splitting a few inches below her throat and going around into the nape of her neck, where the cords are pulled inside of her by tiny rodents. The abdominal rats take them to her vaginal cavity, where the jaw is wired shut.

I lean over to kiss her and I am sucked in, tongue first, by the wormhole of her face, where I will be dissolved in the stomach acids that broke down the fabric of any universe she has ingested before me.

KALI YUGA
by James Champagne

Whenever I tell people that I work full-time at Barnes & Noble, their first reaction is usually: "Oh! You're so lucky! I wish I could work there!" Well, you know the old saying: Be careful what you wish for. On the surface, it appears to be a nice place: Oak furniture, elegant paintings hanging on the walls, sophisticated classical music playing soothingly in the background, the smell of food and fresh coffee wafting from the Starbucks café, and so forth. But look a little deeper and you will uncover a toxic oasis seething with primordial horrors. The surface impression is a façade, an illusion: Beneath the stodgy professional environment lurks the adumbration of a nightmare made into flesh. If you think I exaggerate, let me tell you this: I've been in retail nearly ten years now. First, I spent seven years working at a supermarket part-time, and more recently working at Barnes & Noble full-time for about two years. Before working at Barnes & Noble I was under the assumption that, with my supermarket experience behind me, I had seen all the shit that retail could throw my way. But that assumption, as I have come to find out, is horribly false.

The following account is a typical shift for me, 3:30 p.m.–12:00 a.m., what we call a closing shift on a Saturday. In this story you will see the crap I have to endure on a daily basis, and the obnoxious encounters I have with people who probably shouldn't be shopping in bookstores, let alone being let loose in public. Some aspects of my story may make you laugh or shake your head in sympathy. Other aspects may chill you to the very core of your soul. However, rest assured, after reading my story, you will never look at a major retail bookstore in quite the same way ever again.

Oh, and before you categorize the following episodes as the rants of a depressed, homicidal lunatic, let me assure you that almost ninety percent of people who work at retail end up with a deep and everlasting hatred of the customers they serve (some of us also end up with pretty serious sociopathic tendencies, but that's another story). If there's one thing that unites retail workers, it is our mutual disgust over the great unwashed mobs we provide service to. With that in mind, I will now begin my narrative, which finds me standing before the front doors of Barnes & Noble at 3:30 p.m. on a cold, dead winter Saturday afternoon.

As I step into the store, I note with some dismay that they're playing the "pop-rock" background music today. In the manager's office is a machine called "Muzak" that controls what background music gets played over the store's speaker system. There are a number of channels to choose from, some playing classical, some playing New Age, most playing conservative "easy listening" adult soft rock. Sadly, this latter station is what they play more often than not. I kind of like the New Age channel, mostly just pleasant bird noises and atmospheric water sound effects, but the customers complain that it makes them have to use the bathroom.

If there is one thing I hate, it's banality. Stuff that takes a middle road, plays it safe, avoids extremes, doesn't want to run the risk of offending anyone. And that's just what this easy listening "rock" music is. Of course, the store doesn't want to scare customers away, so I know they aren't going to start blasting out Merzbow or anything like that, but at the very least, play stuff a little more upbeat! Every now and then I'll hear a song I like, such as Blondie, Dream Academy, Madonna (mostly her ballads, they never play her dance stuff), Gwen Stefani . . . Okay, I will admit I do like Genesis and Phil Collins, but this is probably due to the fact that *American Psycho* is one of my all-time favorite books. If they ever play any '80s music, it's usually not the good stuff like Depeche Mode or Talking Heads or anything New Wave, it's always Elton John or something lame like that. Our poor ears are bombarded by the demonic sounds of sober, depressing, middle-aged men and women strumming acoustic guitars and over-enunciating some of the most terrible "profound" lyrics I've ever heard in my life. There are easily hundreds of horrid songs to choose from as the worst, but here are a few of the ones I especially hate:

Eric Clapton: "Wonderful Tonight"
I've always hated this song . . . Slow and boring, with dull lyrics and an annoying vocal from Clapton. Puts me to sleep.

The 5th Dimension: "(Last Night) I Couldn't Get to Sleep at All"
One of my coworkers *really* hates this song. He says whenever he can't sleep at night he keeps hearing this stupid song in his head, with the horrifying knowledge that he knows the next day at work he'll hear it at the job. It's a pretty bad song, I have to agree.

Joni Mitchell: "Free Man in Paris"
Mitchell has an irritating tendency to slur words at the chorus in this song that really bugs the hell out of me for some reason.

Bob Seger: "In Your Time"
So many of the muzak selections at work feature craggy-voiced older man singers belting out "deep" lyrics. Bob Seger is the epitome of this. God, I hate this song.

James Taylor: "Mexico"
It is a humiliating fact, but James Taylor provided the inspiration for my first name when I was born. Which sucks because I hate his music and this is probably the worst song of his they play at work, from the irritating chorus to the noxious ending, when Taylor starts babbling "quirky" lyrics.

Dobie Gray: "Drift Away"
When that chorus kicks in (*"Oh, give me the beat, boys, and free my soul / I wanna get lost in your rock and roll and drift away"*), I want to start blowing things up.

However, there is one thing worse then all of those songs put together, and that is Rod Stewart's unholy "Great American Songbook" series, which is now up to Volume 4. To be blunt, if there is a Hell and it has a soundtrack, then this is the music they must play there. It's hard to keep a positive outlook on life when you've been exposed to this series—Rod Stewart slurring out covers of some of the most boring "oldies" songs of all time like "These Foolish Things" and "Isn't It Romantic" in his washed-up old smug rocker voice over a backdrop of laid-back lounge music. I'm not joking, it's possibly the most annoying, irritating, downright offensive music I've ever heard in my life, the sound of boredom captured on CD. Rod Stewart is the Devil.

I recall reading a quote from Kurt Cobain once where he said he used to walk around supermarkets with his Walkman on, listening to Half Japanese cassette tapes, wondering how the people around him would deal with that sort of music, how they'd probably melt or jump out of their skin, and how he would blare the music at full volume and imagine it pumping out of the store's speakers. Substitute Diamanda Galás and Throbbing Gristle for Half Japanese and I know exactly how he feels.

I digress. Anyway, I go to the info desk, say hi to a few coworkers along the way, punch in at the time clock at one of the computers there. Then I go into the back room, hang up my coat, and put my dinner in the fridge. After that I put on my name tag and go into the receiving room, where I grab a PDT from the charger station. A PDT is a gray cudgel-shaped electronic device with a small screen and a keypad that is used to scan barcodes on the backs of books. They can be used to receive books, to return books to publishers, and, most importantly, to find out a book's price, how it's selling, where in the store it goes, and so on. I log into the PDT and get to work. Before I get to work, however, I briefly stop by the info booth to check the daily planner (to see when my breaks are: I get three every day, two fifteen-minute ones and a half-hour meal), and to grab a small black portable phone. Technically, the person working info is supposed to answer all the phone calls, but sometimes they get swamped and the people working the floor like me have to help answer them. It's not fun, but it's part of the job.

Before I go on, I should say here that the majority of the customers who shop at Barnes & Noble really, really annoy me. For years I complained about how dumb supermarket customers were, but at least they didn't put on airs and think they were smarter than you: They knew they were dumber than mud. But I swear, so many bookstore customers will talk down to you just because they're shopping in a bookstore. Well, let me tell you this, shopping in a bookstore does not a smart person make! It would be like me going to a sports store and acting like I'm an athlete or something. In any event, after a few years of observing bookstore customers in their natural habitat, I have compiled the following zoology of some of the more repellant types I encounter on a regular basis. After reading this list, you will come to see why I often appreciate the company of animals over people.

Political Assholes
The customers are always right . . . wing. They bitched when the new Bill Clinton biography was at the front of the store (where all the new books go, mind). They bitched when we didn't have *Unfit for Command* in stock (hey, it's not our fault the publisher didn't print enough). They complain we don't have the new Mike Gallagher book *Surrounded by Idiots* or Zell Miller's *A Deficit of Decency* (hey, it's not our problem they sold so poorly at our store that we returned them to the publisher). Just for the record, our particular Barnes & Noble is pretty small, so Current Affairs only fills two bookcases.

One day I did a check and I was surprised we actually had more conservative books than liberal ones. I also noticed that the conservative authors more often than not plaster their faces all over their books (and let me tell you, most of these guys ain't pretty) and seem to rely more on their "loud" personalities and bully talk than anything resembling facts ("jerks," "idiots," and "intellectual morons" seem to be the extent of their vocabulary). You could argue that liberal writers like Al Franken do the same, but I'd argue back that Franken writes comedy books and his face is pretty funny looking. Okay, I will admit I was annoyed by that sanctimonious picture of Michael Moore on that book cover for *Will They Ever Trust Us Again?* where he's holding a little American flag in his cupped hand. I liked Moore a lot better when he was more gadfly than bleeding heart.

But god, I hate political books. I ranted about Michael Savage's latest, *Liberalism Is a Mental Disorder*, in my LJ so I won't go into that here, but what a moron that guy is. He isn't even that funny—his idea of a joke is to call lawyers "the briefcase mafia" and refer to the common man as "the sheeple." Then a page later he'll say how he fights for the common man, but in reality, he's just as bloated and elitist as the Hollywood celebrities he rants against. And his website has links to videos of terrorists beheading civilians . . . You're supposed to be morally outraged, but it just comes off as political pornography. (He puts the letter X all around them, making it seem even more like snuff porn.)

Perverted Old Men
There are some nice older customers, but I'm willing to bet that at least fifty percent of the old guys who shop at our store are pervs. These guys flock to the Sexuality section like cultists shambling to the mothership. Don't buy into that myth that all old men are these wise, morally upright people. Sure, they may go to church on Sunday

morning, but then they go to Barnes & Noble in the afternoon and tell their granddaughters to go play in the Kids section . . . while they flip through the sex books with sweaty, shaking fingers.

If there's one section I hate zoning, it's Sexuality. First off, it's right near "Self-Help," where we stock books by people with last names like "Mountain Dreamer" and, oh god, Sark, a "beacon of light and hope" who lives in a "magical cottage" in San Francisco and writes books about her charming, quirky personality (*"Eat mangos naked!" "Oh, I'm such a free spirit!"*). Or Dr. Dyer and his dime-a-dozen cereal-box platitudes (*"LIVE the Ten Commandments!" "People treat you the way YOU want to be treated." "Live . . . be You . . . enjoy . . . Love." "The freest people are those who know inner peace"*). God, I've seen better inspirational quotes come from Doc in *Mike Tyson's Punch-Out!!*

Second, some of those Sexuality books are just nasty to handle. Either they grow little legs when I'm not looking and dash off to the men's restroom (which is also a popular hangout for slumming art books) or these old guys bring 'em in there, then bring them back when they're done doing whatever it is they do in there (I don't even want to know). I'm not kidding, some of the covers are sticky with god knows what . . . Jeez, Gramps, ever heard of a little invention called the Internet? If you want free porn and cheap thrills, you don't have to drive all the way to the bookstore just to flip through Anne Hooper's *Sex Toys* or *101 Nights of Grrreat Sex* or the *Kama Sutra* (for the more high-brow pervert). Some of these old guys will sit down right in the public flipping through cheerleader magazines or *FHM* or (if they're a little more culturally hip) the Suicide Girls book, practically drooling. Really gross.

Hipsters and Their Girlfriends

I always dread when I see this type walk into the store. It's almost always two girls gravitating to one guy like moons encircling a dorky planet. The guy almost always has either glasses or a Mars Volta afro (or sometimes both) and usually wears intentionally ironic T-shirts like the Ninja Turtles and Steve Urkel or the Spice Girls. These types will come into the store and make snide remarks on how bourgeois everything is, yet they'll still swill our coffee and make a mess of things like anyone else. They put up this front like they're the most individualistic people on earth, but then they go home and listen to Weezer or 311 or Sublime and get high. Dolts. Just as bad as the druggy, doped-up kids who think they're cool because they read skateboard magazines or those how-to-grow-pot books or ninja training manuals. Hipster assholes.

Attention Seekers

I don't tell the customers about all of my little quirks . . . I certainly don't want to be the audience of theirs. Some people must think I'm some kind of living wailing wall or something because they always pick me to unburden every little thing that's on their mind. Like this one guy who wanted a dictionary that had "every word in it." I told him we have dictionaries that have a lot of words, but not every word (after all, new words are made up every day and some fall out of usage). Then this guy goes into a spiel about how he hates when he reads a book and he comes across a word that he can't find in the dictionary. I'm not joking when I say he ranted on about this for five minutes. Geez, buddy, I got enough to do as it is, I don't care. I hope he never tries to read a beat novel or an occult manual; then he'll really be in for a tough time! Then there are those fussy curmudgeon types (usually old men with curly beards and suspenders) who are obsessed with proper grammar. "Oh, so you're obsessed with proper grammar? Wow, you're so cool! Here's a Lynne Truss book, go fuck yourself with it, you irritating freak!"

Annoying Mothers
Mothers, when you go to a bookstore, please, keep your kid in sight at all times . . . We aren't babysitters. Recently we had this mother drop her daughter off in the Kids section, then she went to the café to drink coffee and jaw with other SUV-driving neocon-voting soccer moms about, probably, the Red Hat Society books or the latest episode of *Desperate Housewives*. Naturally, some pervert exposed himself to the kid, and the mother was MAD at US because we weren't watching her kid (I think she threatened to sue us). Rich bitch. And yes, I'm sure, your little "bundle of joy" is the most "charming little thing that ever existed," but, ma'am, the sad truth is your stupid brat broke one of our bookshelves trying to climb it and threw up after attempting to eat a quilt. So many of these pestilent WASPs expect the media to raise their little rats, they're too lazy to set a good example themselves. Parent better, please!

The Totally Ignorant
"I saw you guys had this book on your website. I can't find it in the store."

(Just because one finds a book on the bn.com website does not mean that every Barnes & Noble bookstore has that particular book in stock: Every store has a different selection.)

"I'm looking for a book on (vague, general subject), but I don't know the author. Or the title."

(Need a bit more information than that, dipshit.)

"I'm looking for this book that went out of print in 1949. Can you guys order it?"

(You must be fucking joking, cunt.)

"Why don't you guys have the new *Vanity Fair* with Jennifer Aniston?"

(Because you're just like everyone else, with one exception: You're late.)

Another thing I've observed about all the above is they're almost always white people. White people should not shop in retail stores, especially privileged white people. They waltz in there like they're the Kings of the Earth and you're just some ignorant serf who has to pander to their every whim and desire. I've almost never gotten any trouble from black people. In fact, back when I worked at the supermarket, black people were my favorite customers: They thanked me when I bagged their orders, sometimes they tipped me, and I recall this one guy who even put the heavy items on the conveyer belt first and the soft stuff last so it would be easier for me to put it in the shopping cart. He later told me that he used to work in a supermarket himself so he knew the proper way to put the groceries on the belt so they were easier to bag. I almost never got that kind of help from these rich white assholes who obviously have never worked a shit job in their life. Like this fat bearded motherfucker with curly hair and glasses I once served. This bloated moron watched me put three heavy cartons of milk at the bottom of his cart before he told me, "Oh, by the way, could you bag those for me?" I didn't tell him that one of them was leaking; I hoped it stained the insides of his BMW.

* * *

Anyway, there you have it: a motley crew of spoiled white women, annoying quirky curmudgeons, public perverts, pedophiles, dirty old men, exhibitionists, doped-up kids, hipster poseurs, stupid soccer moms, psychos, right-wing assholes, Groznyan fairy-boy manga geeks with their faux-Tolkien poetry and heavy-handed hand-wringing proselytizing. And that's only just picking at the scab of society.

The biggest rush of customers usually occurs sometime between 12 in the afternoon and 5 o'clock. That's why I don't mind closing the store: I usually get more work done with less irritation. But those rush hours . . . those hours are malodorous. The doors of the store fly open like the gates of Hell and the mob flood in like polluted waters, boiling over the hapless employees like a tidal wave of parasites. I get very little done the first two hours of my shift. Most of my time is spent on customer service, the idiots being drawn to me like brainless remoras, elemental larvae preying on unprotected astral travelers. I don't really know why we pride ourselves on having such a big selection of books, as there are really only ten or so titles we sell on a regular basis: *The Da Vinci Code*, *A Million Little Pieces*, the newest Harry Potter, the latest Oprah Book Club selection, and so forth. The few books we do have that are actually *good* books are usually looked over and sent back to the publishers after a few months of not selling. It's a tragic cycle.

I can tell it's going to be a very long evening from my first customer encounter. Just as I'm about to get to work, I hear a woman clear her throat behind me. I turn around and find myself face-to-face with a fat woman in a dress suit, makeup caked on her face like corpse colors, the perfume of the grave emanating from her corpulent flesh.

She asks me, in a strained, impatient voice, "Do you work here?"

I'm wearing a tag with the words *Barnes & Noble* on it, with my name underneath. Should I say, "No"? Would she believe me? Probably.

"Yes," I say, my voice calm. "How can I help you?"

"I'm looking for the Nonfiction section," she says in that irritating hurried voice, the words wriggling out of her lipsticked mouth like star-venom.

Patiently, I say, "I'm sorry, but we don't have a Nonfiction section, per se. We arrange all of our nonfiction books by subject, like history, computers, and so forth. What subject are you looking for?"

She stares at me, confused, like I'm speaking in some sort of alien tongue. Has this place become the Tower of Babel? Why am I not getting through to this stupid cow?

"I don't know," she sighs impatiently. "Nonfiction."

I stare at her now. I can tell she's mad at me. I don't understand why. I'm being nice to her, offering to help, yet she's giving me nothing to work with. Looking closely at her, I see an ugly woman clad in a tacky dress suit she probably purchased at K-Mart. I look at this disgusting specimen of the human species and I'm appalled she probably thinks she's smarter than I am, have trouble believing that in her eyes I'm not even human, just another annoyance. This woman thinks the whole universe revolves around her majesty, thinks that everything should go her way, that reality should constantly warp and reconfigure around her like quantum magic to accommodate her selfish needs. I'm suddenly reminded of a coworker from my supermarket days, this mother in her forties, a short woman who seemed like a nice person, until that one day when I was bagging at her register and I heard her say to a customer, "I think we should just nuke the Middle East. Sure, a lot of innocent people would probably be killed, but it would solve a lot of America's problems and it would be good for Christianity." This beast said these words of wisdom in a casual, relaxed, utterly sincere voice, and to my horror the customer we were serving was nodding in agreement. I realized that I was witnessing what is known as the "banality of evil." I'll never forget that shift . . . I think a layer of frost formed on my spine that day, listening to those two monsters talk about nuclear annihilation like it was some sort of soap opera plot.

Eventually, I figure out what book the customer before me is asking for. I take her to it and then perform the most important function I can as a bookseller—what our corporate training manuals refer to as the "moment of truth." In reality, it's simply taking the book that the customer wants off the shelf and personally handing it to her, but the manuals portray this simple act as some sort of Wagnerian epic worthy of the praise of the gods. She just takes the book from me, grunts some kind of subterranean "thanks," and walks off.

When business dies down around dinner time, I can actually go about my duties. As a lead of my own zone at Barnes & Noble, my job mainly involves putting out new books (this is referred to as "front list") and, each month, scanning every book in my section and sending certain books that aren't selling back to the publishers (this is called "zoning" or, to be more fancy, "zone maintenance"). The purpose of zoning is two-fold: first, as noted above, certain books are sent back to the publishers, giving me much-needed shelf space, and two, while I do this, I organize the shelf so it looks nice (because customers are notorious for putting books back the wrong way). As you can imagine, after a month the shelves start looking pretty nasty, so it can be a real pain to fix them back up again. It's a never-ending process, like that guy in Hades who pushes the rock up a hill only for it to roll down again, and then he has to repeat the process. That's a good description of my job, actually: almost reaching a state of perfection, but never quite getting there.

My own zone is comprised of the following sections: Games, Humor, Computers, Science & Technology, Nature, Pets, Sports, Study Notes, Study Aids, Reference, Language, Audio Books, Travel, Law, and Weddings. Now, those are some pretty big sections, especially Computers, so it's quite a load to handle. But last month the Zone 4 lead took over Bargain, so as a result some of her Zone 4 sections were divided out amongst the other leads. Lucky me: I got Self-Improvement, Home Reference, and Gardening.

What sucks about the Home Reference section is that two chairs are located in front of it, and customers are drawn to these chairs like flies to shit. These slobs lounge about for an hour or so then get up and either a) leave their books on the floor, or b) shove them in with the Home Ref/Gardening books even though they clearly do NOT go there. Add to the fact that spring's coming, and the section becomes a Dante-esque nightmare to navigate. I've been working at B&N for over a year now, and I've NEVER seen that section clean.

But duty calls, and sooner or later I had to zone that section SOMETIME this month. So I decide to do it tonight. I look at the Baudelaire void before me: three massive bookcases, all loaded with books out of alphabetical order, books in the wrong sections, books that didn't even belong there in the first place, and my knees turn to jelly. Then I sit down and quietly begin going about my task, taking each book off the shelf and scanning it with my trusty PDT, one after the other. I feel like a sculptor trying to slowly turn a mountain into an ocean of pebbles.

I start with Interior Design, Feng Shui, and Lifestyles, arranging them in alphabetical order. Interior Design, in particular, takes awhile. Next I zone the Outdoor Recreation section, followed by Home Ref, Organize/Clean (ironically, one of the messiest shelves in the store), and House Plans. Then I zone Remodel/Renovation, which takes the longest of all because they were totally out of order (unless the letter Y switched places with the letter A when I wasn't looking). These were arranged alphabetically by topic rather than author (for example, *basements*, *bathrooms*, and so on). Finally, I take all the misplaced books from other sections and return them to their proper shelves. Then I walk back over to Home Reference and admire my handiwork. It has taken over five hours, but my task is complete.

And then, right there, for just one moment, in the middle of the sterile consumer squall surrounding me like a storm (a pervert reading a cheerleader magazine and leering at children, customers leaving books all over the floor, nauseating antiseptic muzak and "soft rock" playing over the speakers, in this case Enrique Iglesias over-emoting about how he *"wants to be my hero"*), yes, amongst all this chaos, I have managed to carve, briefly, a monument of order, and for a minute I have managed to transcend my tawdry milieu, and I feel like an angel floating above it all, or maybe some sort of enlightened Eastern sage achieving some type of heightened state in this cathedral of corporate banality. For a minute, I am satisfied.

Sadly, as usual, the second law of Thermodynamics wins again. Exactly one minute after I have created this monolith of perfection, some . . . IDIOT skateboard pothead walks over and pulls out a book from the Organize/Clean section. You know the type: long hair, grungy clothes, think they're hardcore because they read about tattoos, skateboard moves they couldn't do in a million years, and Bob Marley is, like, God? Well, this moron takes this book, goes down to one of the chairs, sits down, flips through it, then puts it back on the shelf . . . in the wrong spot. Then, before my disbelieving eyes, this MONSTER, this Manson, this Hitler takes another book, a big one, off the shelf and sits down. He flips through it a bit, then walks toward the shelf to put it back. Now, this book he just took off is really big and there's a huge spot on the shelf where it once went, so I figure, *Hey, there's no way this Neanderthal can miss this one.* I rationalize that in what must pass for his brain, somewhere amongst all those neural twitchings and chemical spasms, he must have some idea where that book goes; perhaps he may have some dull idea deep down in his basal ganglia (the part of your brain inherited from your marine forefathers), but nooooooo, he goes and puts the book back . . . in GARDENING! A book of fucking house plans . . . in GARDENING! And thus, the harmony is disturbed. But hey, what are you gonna do?

The shift seems to drag on and on like some feeble cripple. I feel trapped in some sort of zombie time mode, the voodoo-meat of my body being dragged down like abstract quicksand by the prosaic situation I find myself in. What happened to me? How did I find myself in this position, my life resembling the lyrics of some lost unrecorded Manic Street Preachers song? Time freezes like an abyss of ice all around me, yet at the same time everything flickers in hallucinatory fast motion, as I bounce from one task to another like some demented toad leapfrogging across vast, imponderable gulfs of infinite non-space. Only I can see the black hole swirling above the heads of the customers like a satanic sun, nourishing their Nosferatu needs with its vampire rays. None of this makes a great deal of sense to me. I think I'm working too hard. Way too hard. I need a vacation.

Now I'm at the info desk for thirty minutes, covering someone else's break. Business seems to have died down, and the store is quiet now. The only downside of this is that with the mad babble of voices removed, I can hear the background muzak all too clearly. There's nothing for me to do right now except wait for a customer to show up looking for help. I drum my fingers on the surface of the info booth, which is shaped like an octagon and can fit about three people, one person per computer. In front of the info booth is the last tier of the Bargain section. This is where they keep bargain books on dictators, serial killers, and game show hosts. One book on serial killers shows a picture of Ian Brady and his girlfriend, Myra Hindley: the Moors murderers. Those infamous mug shots. Right next to it is a blue book called *The Most Evil Women in History*. Same picture of Myra Hindley. I stare at Myra: She stares back. I look away, but her eyes follow me. I look over some of the other covers: Hitler, Stalin, Vlad the Impaler, Son of Sam, Ted Bundy, Charles Manson, Satan . . . They probably all make better company than the sloths I serve on a daily basis.

Suddenly, some kind of seal breaks and I find the info desk surrounded by frantic, impatient customers, and I'm feeling like a lone knight trying to defend a castle under siege. It's at this moment that the phones start screaming like they're being tortured. One guy asks me if we have any books on building submarines. Another guy wants to know if we sell home drink mixers. A woman on the phone wants to know if we have *Hook* on DVD. I spin around, mind multitasking at microprocessor speeds, trying to accommodate everyone, but it's an exercise in futility. They swarm from the cardinal points like giant locusts, and I'm surrounded on all sides, the faces merging and blurring into a mandala of idiots, a circle of stupidity. Myra smiles her cryptic *Mona Lisa* smile at me all the time. I feel like I am being taunted.

And the gauntlet marches on at a funereal pace. Situations occur that, by themselves, are illogical but in this context fit like perfect puzzle pieces: A customer (some teenager) calls and asks, "Do you guys carry *Chicken Soup for the Nazi Soul*?" He probably expects me to act shocked or hang up, but I say, in my most pleasant voice possible, "We don't carry that title, but if you want I can go to a computer and order it for you." He pauses for a moment then hangs up. I wonder if he thought I was being serious? On one of the tables I find a piece of paper with these words on it, hastily written down: HELP I HAVE BEEN TAKEN HOSTAGE BY SOME GUY HE IS TORTURING ME IF YOU HAVE A HEART CALL POLICE. There are a lot of teenagers around so I assume it is someone's idea of a prank. At one point I return some magazines to the Newsstand section, only to hear a deep howl come from behind me. I turn and see an oddly shaped man with gray hair and a crazed face running around, shouting, while another man with curly gray hair and glasses chases after him. The howling man is a retard that the staff refers to as "Slow Stu." The guy chasing him is his caretaker (I assume). Stu always causes trouble, shouting out mindless howls, urinating himself, and rumor is that he's a molester. I know it's not nice to wish ill thoughts on those with mental problems, but most of us secretly can't stand Slow Stu.

I'm feeling rabid tonight, on the edge: The customers are grating my nerves, and I'm feeling the urge to spill blood, to use the PDT in my hand to club their skulls in, or stab them in the eyes with scissors, play Cat's Cradle with their guts. A 2Pac lyric that I heard on a mix tape on the ride in to work has been following me around leech-like all night: *"You're watching the makings of a psychopath."* Patrick Bateman would say my mask of sanity is on the verge of slipping. I have this bizarre need to say unacceptable things to customers like, "The new James Patterson book is with the bestsellers. Oh, by the way, did you know I'm utterly insane?" or, "Would you like to hear about our great membership program? And, hey, did you know I have a fetish for big-breasted Asian girls?" I find nagging questions spinning around the interior of my brain like a washing machine filled with words: Who am I? What is the meaning of life? Am I really making the world a better place by shelving the kids book *Hanukkah, Shmanukkah!*? (The excerpt on the back of the book says, *"'I heard you like to patshke with clocks,' said the little man. 'It so happens that I do, too. I am the Rabbi of Hanukkah Past, and I have arrived to shlep you to hotzeplotz and back so you will see that Hanukkah is nothing to sneeze at.' 'Hanukkah, Shmanukkah,' replied Scroogemacher. 'Probably I ate too much garlic and onions. I'm seeing a little dybbuk at the foot of my bed. You let yourself in, so see yourself out.'"*)

I guess what I'm trying to say here is that in some ways, the store reflects myself. On the surface, it appears to be calm, orderly, laid-back, but in reality it's all just chaos. Likewise, in person I project an atmosphere of calm horizons, an almost stoic, zenlike poker face, but it's just a disguise. Inside, I'm utterly chaotic. I'm just so good at hiding it, it doesn't show, except maybe in the occasional spasms of my eyebrows. What I really want to do sometimes is scream and shout and laugh wildly and just be a total dick to all these pointless morons. But then I'd be lowering myself down to their level. So I try to keep my chaos private, saving it for expression in my art. In some ways, it's the only way to stay sane.

Still, I've seen worse nights. Like that night where the new Harry Potter book came out. That was a bad night.

Picture lines of people stretching all the way to the nearby Wal-Mart, irate customers complaining nonstop to the manager by the door, cop cars continually driving by, fire marshals shutting us down every few minutes, a hysterical teenager escorted outside of the store by the police, some little boy vomiting all over the sidewalk, mosquitoes feasting everywhere, adults walking around in purple wizard robes and pointy hats swearing, the moon gore-red as if it were drenched in witch blood . . . It was Hell. To make matters worse, Wal-Mart, located about two hundred feet to the left of our store, was staying open all night and selling the book for only fifteen dollars (we were charging seventeen). So you had some customers driving by the line and yelling out that you could get the book at Wal-Mart for fifteen dollars, but most customers in our line said, "So what?" and, "Yeah, but Wal-Mart's evil," or, "Fuck off!" At one point I was crowd control, so I tried to look intimidating by crossing my arms over my chest, but I don't think it got the intended effect . . . The cop pulled it off much better, though he had actual muscles and a gun, so that probably helped.

Yeah, as I said, that was a rough night. I ended up giving the Harry Potter baseball hat I got to an old lesbian friend from college. At least there are some cute people shopping in the store tonight. Like that thin hippie chick in the long dress looking at books in the Native American section, or that hot totally kissable emo-punk guy browsing the Poetry section. The young people are better than the adults, most of whom are old and bitter. I hope I never get like that. I have to get out of retail before their bad behavior stains me permanently.

During my final break, I shrug on my winter coat and head outdoors into the freezing winter night. To the west of our store, only about a minute's walk away, is the giant Wal-Mart, the building sweating cancerous corporate vibes. I normally hate shopping there, but I desperately need to buy some blank CDs, so I trudge over tonight. Our stores are split up by a long sidewalk and a road that leads from the parking lot to the backs of all the stores in this particular plaza. Behind these stores is a dark forest that spreads out for miles and miles, as far as the eye can see. As I head toward Wal-Mart with my hands in my pockets, I look out at the forest, which for some reason seems to be calling out to me, murmuring to me in cobwebbed whispers.

At Wal-Mart, I buy a ten-pack of blank CDs. I'm cashed out by a black lesbian dwarf (I guess she must fill all kinds of corporate quotas). Because my break is almost done, I run all the way back, but something funny happens: When I get to the doors that lead into the bookstore, I almost don't slow down, almost keep running. Where I'd run to, I'm not sure: maybe that mysterious forest behind the store. Could I survive in the wilderness? Somehow, I doubt it. It's not a very realistic idea, though it is a romantic one. I suppose I could carve a house out of a tree, but what would I do for food? Hunt animals? I could never do that. Maybe I could trick customers into the woods: drag their expensive sports cars and gas-guzzling BMWs into the forest, and kill them when they come looking for them. Such a life would be harsh and difficult, but I can't help but wonder . . . would it be preferable to the one I'm living now?

I pause at the door, look at a nearby window, which lets me see into the café. I see a hoard of self-satisfied slug-people lounging around wooden tables, slurping down cup after cup of coffee, chowing down on cookies and cakes and brownies, smiling, laughing, yapping nonstop into cell phones, checking the stocks, fiddling around with iPods, typing loudly on laptops, leaving books and magazines and empty cups all over the floor, and I can't help but think that I'm witnessing the end of civilization, the total breakdown of society brought about by a decadent, uncaring, selfish gulag of mindless consumers, the human species plummeting down a reversed epistemic ladder. I'm struck by the sinking feeling that somewhere on the other side of the universe, trillions and trillions of light years away, beyond the Cosmic Light Horizon, the Apocalypse has already commenced, and is slowly creeping toward the Milky Way like a bloated parasite, worming its way to us down the endless black gullet of space.

People are dropping dead like flies in Africa, tsunamis killing people by the thousands, earthquakes, plane crashes, suicide bombers in the Middle East, vaginal mutilations in Sierra Leone, hate crimes, death plagues and bird flus, butchery, the destruction of the ozone layer and the rainforest . . . No one cares. These people are living in a bubble. As long as they have their comfy chairs and their hot coffee and their inane magazines and their vapid bestsellers and people to wait on them hand and foot, they're happy, content to drone away their little fastfood insect McLives. Yet in some way it makes me feel better about myself. In some ways, by being polite and courteous, by not succumbing to the monster inside me like everyone else, I rise above the heaps of human rubbish all around me. I am untouched, virginal, totally pure, like holy snow, while all around me is rudeness, idiocy, and bloodless apathy.

I do go back inside though, and finish the last hour and forty-five minutes before the store closes. As expected, the customers are still their annoying selves: I'm trying to do recovery in the Magazines section (that is, I'm trying to clean up the place), but it's a fucking nightmare, and some annoying teenagers are lounging around making a total mess, leaving empty Styrofoam cups of coffee around the floor, basically acting like uber jackasses. Most of them have long unwashed hair, glasses, and these stupid-looking knit caps, and they're speaking in these annoying, ironic voices. Stoner losers. A flock of high schoolers dressed in black trenchcoats are haunting the Occult section, trying to look all dark and menacing . . . They probably think they're serious because they read Hitler biographies and hoax Necronomicons and maybe they have a de Sade book or two on their coffee tables at home for show, but to me they're laughable. Meanwhile, over in the café, three loud middle-aged dolts (two men, one woman) have begun playing a game of *Scrabble* at one of the tables, even though my manager has just announced over the intercom that the store is closing in ten minutes.

Oblivious, they just keep yapping away and laughing loudly, slurping down their coffee and acting boorish. We close at 11, but soon 11:05 rolls around and the assholes are *still* there. Finally, my manager shows up and tells them to get going, that the store is closed. They try to play dumb, say they thought the store closed at 11:30, but finally my manager gets them out of the store. Then we waste a few minutes cleaning up the mess they made. I'm outraged, red spots dancing before my eyes like blood-drenched snowflakes. I'd love to pry open their mouths and shovel *Scrabble* tiles down their bleating throats. Don't these people know *anything* about good manners?

What more is there to say? About forty minutes after closing, we gather up our stuff, go outside, lock up, say our "goodbyes" and "see you tomorrows" and all that before we head our separate ways. The parking lot is deserted at this hour, as vacant and desolate as a decaying amusement park, and under the skeletal light of the full moon it seems as barren and alien to me as the surface of an asteroid. As I walk toward my car, keys in hand, full of anxiety because I know I have to repeat this whole damn process the next morning, I want so bad for something exotic to happen: a car pulling up in front of me, the man/woman of my dreams at the wheel, and, like a knight in shining armor, s/he'd whisk me away from all this shit and we'd live our lives as porn stars in Tokyo or assassins in London or cannibals on a small island in the South Seas. Alternatively, maybe it could be a spaceship descending from the sky, piloted by a three-eyed, sylph-skinned frog-boy from Venus, escorting me to galaxies and alien dimensions beyond the Milky Way and space and time. Whatever, I don't care. Get me out of here! I can't get used to this lifestyle.

THE LATE WORK OF MARGARET KROFTIS
by Mark Gluth

Margaret's sitting at her writing table, then walking downstairs to put a kettle on. A dog walks in the kitchen behind her and yawns. Outside the window the weather's a film of the seasons changing. Those are geese flying south. Upstairs, she's no longer cold. It's the tea. The dog turns three tight circles and lies down on the rug he's mushed up against the wall. She's working on a piece of fiction. It's autobiographical in a sense. She dies in the end.

    She goes into town to buy groceries. The sidewalks are covered with fallen leaves. They're trying to become a forest floor, she thinks. At the store she buys cans of soup and bread instead of ingredients. On the way back to her car she sees the bay. It looks like it goes on forever. For a moment she imagines the world like that. Just the ocean and the weather.

    After dinner she writes three sentences. They're not worth keeping, she thinks. She lets the dog out one last time, then dries him off because he's soaked. She brushes her teeth, gets in bed. He burrows under the sheets and rests his black head on her feet. In her dream he can see ghosts.

    She goes for a walk down by the water. A plastic bag washes up on the shore and gets caught on a wormy log. She picks it up. It's tangled with seaweed. She leans on her cane and thinks. The rain's suspended between the sky and everything else. The fog smudges the horizon.

Later, back up the path, she smells something. Twenty feet farther she can see in her kitchen window and it's so horrible.

Margaret's in the hotel room insurance put her in. She cries so hard she coughs, lies down on the bed, and makes a fist. She wants to punch herself like a wall.

They let her walk through what's left of her house. The fire gutted most of the ground floor. Upstairs, her books were largely untouched. Likewise her computer. Back downstairs, in the kitchen, her fingers are trembling. She's kneeling in front of the back door. She's memorizing the gouges his claws made in it as he tried to escape.

2.

Last night I had a dream about you. It was horrible. We were walking on a trail that I didn't recognize. You humored me and didn't pull on your lead. We walked through a field and entered a forest. The trees blocked the sun. The trail followed down into a valley. Fog rolled in and I thought of an owl. My foot slipped on loose gravel and we fell into a cave. It'd been hidden by brush. I landed on my ankle and you landed on your head. You yelped and shrieked and I dragged myself across the cold and wet floor. A pool of blood ranged wide around your head. I loosened your collar. I pet your face and smoothed your ears back. I looked into your eyes. They told me that you were scared, strong, sad, wistful, doubtful, confused, brave, and in pain. I told you I loved you. I told you how sorry I was. The words were worthless because whatever hope they came from was unfounded. You tried to bark and instead gasped for breath. Your leg began shaking like you were fighting something, then your whole body. I was overcome. I laid over you so you would feel protected and less scared. I hoped you couldn't tell I was weeping. You became a memory.

3.

Months later
Margaret bites the fingernail on her left pinky. She takes a sip of cold tea, then sets the cup on the saucer and picks up her notebook. She's working on her short story. She tells herself it'll be the last thing she writes. She's working on a short passage about her dog. Including him in the story is the most important thing in the world. In her latest draft she put him on a boat, surrounded by water. There's no way a fire could suffocate him there. But she realizes it's ridiculous. So the boat sinks and the inconceivable happens anyway. She still sobs as she falls asleep at night.

She sets down her pencil and leans back. She rests her eyes for a moment, then dabs at them with her handkerchief. Her hand's numb. It's shaking. She rubs her wrist but that doesn't do anything. She's going to take a nap, she thinks. After that, she'll work on the story a little more.

The officer knocked, got no response, then found the spare key the neighbor talked about. It was on an old necklace, hanging from the rhododendron next to the porch. He walked upstairs and into the bedroom. He called out to the shape under the covers. When he touched her face it was like ice. He closed her eyes and called for an ambulance. While he was waiting he walked into the next room. Beside the computer he found a small stack of papers. He read them.

My Watery Death, by Margaret Kroftis

I was down by the water. Someone said my name, and when I turned around to answer, I saw a boy standing in front of me. He introduced himself and apologized. He said he'd knocked for five minutes before coming around the back. I told him not to worry. He told me that he'd come to ask me to read his story and give him advice about writing. The sky behind him was white but it looked black reflected on the water. He bit his lip. I told him I could have the story read in a couple days and I watched the rain pool on his hood. He handed me the manila envelope he'd been holding and the pool fell past his face and dissolved into the sand. I watched him as he trotted up toward my house and then disappeared behind the garage.

Inside, my footsteps left puddles the shape of continents on old maps. They evaporated while I ate dinner. I read magazines in the bath then, in bed, the boy's story. It was ten loosely organized pages describing an army of demons attacking the earth via a porthole to another dimension. The next morning I wrote down my dream. In it, I was standing in the kitchen looking out the window onto the water. It was dark but I could see that the water was luminescent, like it was lit from within.

A week later the boy arrived in the rain on his bike. Inside, the steam from the kettle scalded my fingers as I made tea. At the table I held some ice cubes wrapped in a tea towel and told the boy that I didn't know anything about horror, that I didn't know if I'd be able to help him with his writing.

He said, "But isn't all writing the same, I mean, in the end?"

The boy told me where to drive. We turned left out of my driveway and headed north. He had me pull over next to a trail head that was overgrown by snowberries. We followed it until we came upon a clearing where the boy climbed a boulder. It was rounded and smooth because eventually it will be nothing. From behind the trees ahead of me I heard the drone of cars driving on the freeway. It reminded me of an overcast sky which reminded me of my childhood.

The boy brought me to the clearing to help explain his writing. He told me he fell asleep here once, laying on the boulder, and when he woke up he had the entire plot for his story in his head. His thought was that I would understand the tone he was going for if I came here. He opened the thermos and poured himself some tea. I had a daydream in which my ears were so sensitive that they could hear it evaporating. He sat on the boulder and cupped his mug in both hands. I walked around the clearing and then scratched at some stinging nettle on my calf.

Then November. Each day mirrored the previous one: breakfast and coffee, then yard work until my energy disappeared. Nap then dinner, then soaking in the tub. Bed. Once a week the boy came and we talked about his writing and the work he was doing.

One night I dreamed that a ship sank in the middle of the ocean and all the passengers drowned except for a dog. The dog swam until his muscles became numb and then began to ache. As the sun set he stopped chasing the birds that he would never catch and tried to move toward the reflection of the moon on the water. His muscles gave up and he stopped swimming. Water coursed down his throat and he was blinded as time and his suffering stopped.

The boy told me he thought he'd never finish his story. I told him I thought that with every book I ever wrote, that it was normal. He smiled, and asked me why I didn't write anymore. I told him I didn't have the time. I realized the boy had read each of my novels but none of my recent press. He didn't seem to know about my retirement, Mastocytosis, anything. As he was about to leave, he asked me if there was something he could do to repay me for my help. I asked him if he had a boat.

I was sitting at the kitchen table reading the boy's story. Several months worth of work had improved it. The demons had been replaced by a vague and malevolent cosmic force that was causing a gradual apocalypse on earth. It was now written as a series of diary entries by a teenage girl, one of the last survivors remaining. In the section I was reading, the narrator was huddled in her bedroom, turning the dial on her clock radio, looking for some signal. It had been night for the past three days and she'd not seen anyone else in two weeks. She found an automated emergency response broadcast, it said that the earth had apparently stopped spinning on its axis. The girl laid down and started crying. She missed her parents but had no hope of ever seeing them again.

The boy paced between the stove and sink as I finished his story. In it, the narrator fell asleep as the world slowly disappeared. She had a dream she was dead and that her ghost was traveling around the earth. I underlined the last sentence: *The trees are like wisps, and I can float through them, but they seem even less there than they were yesterday.* I told him he should be proud of it and he smiled.

After lunch the boy and I walked down to the water and got in his kayak. He rowed us through mist that became drizzle. It beaded on my skirt and clouded my glasses. There was barely any breeze and the air smelled like the sea, and diesel. The boy rowed and I daydreamed that the water was a black hole. I slipped through space and into it.

from RETURN TO ZERO
by Eddie Beverage

Pain is the dead of night stuffed into my ears, nose, and mouth, sticking to everything and filling me up like black cotton candy; gummy strands of regret and emptiness. You go your whole life thinking you understand pain, know pain, feel pain, but you have no idea because pain wears a thousand masks—a chameleon with teeth like a shark. And it can become you. Unless you're prepared to wed yourself to pain, it will always control you. So marry the bitch . . . fuck the bitch. And ditch the morphine condom. Go bareback and take it like a man.

    I used to be good at forgetting. I was a real pro. People fade from memory at a predictable rate with an almost scary mathematical precision. I can measure weeks, months, even years by the state of the decaying image. Skin stretches and tears. Bones disintegrate. Voices are forgotten. But this is different. The image runs interference on my every thought. Crack open my skull and you'll find an entrenched parasite with a poison center that couldn't be burned or flushed out with Vaseline like a tick. All attempts at operation would fail. The thing with roots dug in like a cancer would squeal like a slaughterhouse pig and take the better part of my brain with it if anyone tried to remove it. I figure the wheels of any vehicle traveling at a high rate of speed would have about the same effect, which is why I'm lying in the center of the freeway. It's 4 o'clock in the morning and the events of the last few months keep playing in my head like some perverted snuff film. Shoot the projectionist. Kill the messenger. But there are no fucking cars on the freeway. All I can do is remember.

The crowd at Markie's was more amped up than usual. My band, Heroes Die, rocked that spot at least twice a month and I never really understood what made one night any different than the rest, but sometimes that place shook with a manic energy that I should've bottled and sold. This stuff would make Red Bull look like liquid Valium if only I could figure out how to squeeze all those steel-toed crowd surfers into a can. I couldn't, obviously, it was their essence I needed . . . but I'd never get them to hold still long enough to wring out all that sweat, testosterone, speedy sperm, and teen angst, and it wasn't any good once it hit the floor. Punks were like oranges; they had to be freshly squeezed and drank right away.

    I played lead guitar but there was a bassist trapped somewhere in my body. I wasn't much for solos. Power chords were all fine and good. But most of all, I craved the spaces in between. For me it was all about the rhythm. The staccato stops. When my drummer froze an inch above his toms, my bassist fell away, and I muted my strings, the silence was like a bomb dropped in an elevator shaft and you can't see it, don't know when it's going to hit bottom, explode with flames, and come screaming back up; a contained inferno that sears the hair off your balls. That's where the action is, in the spaces between. The shit. The shiznit, as the homies say. There was always homies at the shows tatted up in wife-beaters and cuffed denim moshing in the pit to punk rock and bumping Jay-Z in the parking lot. They rapped about who was more whack, the Black Eyed Peas or Ja Rule, while the middle-schoolers who invaded the beach like insecurity on a field trip rapped about Britney fucking Spears, who's sold twelve million records worldwide while Heroes Die has sold 124. Except they weren't really records, or "units" like they say in the biz. They were more like live bootlegs. Recorded on those cheap cassette tapes like you buy at Wal-Mart. Copied over and over again on a shitty stereo, stolen no doubt. The irony is that Britney sucks and we rocked. So what the fuck?!

The problem is my generation's a bunch of media sycophants. They embrace popular culture as if it were the axis the world turned on, when it's really their mutant priorities on a metal hot dog spit. Britney's as good a place as any to start my story—though for the record, I don't really trust the whole idea of beginnings and endings. The stories of our lives seem more like a web of yarn stretched between the fingers of God, Buddha, Allah, whatever you like to call it, impossibly intertwined with no beginning or end. But back to Mrs. Spears—

Music hasn't rocked for decades, and without getting into a long diatribe on why it blows, the rock drought, the Sahara of popular music where pre-fab pop stars are plentiful as the sand and twice as expendable, is what led me to pick up a guitar. I started playing in my first band, Sack of Skin, when I was fifteen. Let me just say that this wasn't the oasis that I promised, but as first bands go it's exactly what I needed. We played speed metal fast and sloppy, the kind that makes your parents want to chew glass rather than listen to it. The plan was to record a theme record about a serial castrater. My lead singer Dax had even started work on the cover, which he kept top secret. Rumor was it featured some hairy trucker dyke behind the wheel of a dumptruck full of bloody balls. Yeah, I know. Like I said, it was my first band. It doesn't happen overnight. But I still think "Neutoronomy" is a great fucking song, no matter what anyone says.

Over the next four years, I was in and out of just about every band in the South Bay. Shit happens. Whoever said that deserves a Pulitzer. It's even truer with musicians. We develop habits. Father illegitimate children. Move away. Pawn our instruments. Break bones. Sell out. I could've played with a rock group gigging weekly on the Sunset Strip, but they were the biggest bunch of poseur asshole douche bags I'd ever met. No thanks. I'd rather die in obscurity than live in conformity. So what ends up happening is you have to form your own band. It all feels a little childish, like picking teams in gym class, but you have to invite the best of the best into your circle and hope for the best. There's always plenty of gasoline. Chemistry decides whether you get H_2O or a match. With Heroes Die, we got a flaming log.

Our lead singer Ronny was from Philly, a former skinhead gone straight edge with a melodious growl. Other bands drooled over this guy, but they couldn't lure him away with booze and girls because he didn't give a shit about either. All he wanted to do was torch the house every night, and he finally had the band to do it. Our bassist Steve and drummer Billy were from Orange County; they'd been playing together since they were young kids and jammed so tightly they might as well have been one instrument. Then there was me—Tommy Zahn on lead guitar—zigging and zagging through the spaces in between.

Of course, there's a long history of punk rock in Los

Angeles' South Bay. The LBC. Manhattan Beach. Redondo. Hermosa, which happened to be my turf. There was Becker's Surf and Sport on Pier Avenue where Phil Becker spent forty years shaping boards for the waves set. The Baptist church where legends like Black Flag, the Last, and the Descendents lived and made music in the heyday of the late-'70s. Sweaty beerfests. Bad behavior. *Carne asada* up the ass. I certainly wasn't the first to play a guitar in that town and I wouldn't be the last. History had its place with me, but I didn't worship the players—I didn't shuffle down the sidewalk hoping my boots would absorb some ancient strand of Greg Ginn's spit—musically, I preferred newer bands like the Deviates and 98 Mute.

After the gig at Markie's on the pier that night, I packed up my stuff quietly backstage, rubbed some lavender oil on my wrists, bent one knee to the floor facing the stage, and bowed my head in appreciation. That was my ritual. I preferred to be characterized as terminally inaccessible to antisocial—I wasn't much for hanging out after shows.

Steve and Billy were cool like that though. That was *their* ritual: drinking beers and bullshitting with the fans. There were too many parrots for me. The talk was always about this or that show, this or that band, this or that song; if you hung around long enough and listened real close, everything you heard had already been said by someone else, if not that night then the night before. Just like the world outside. So-called opinionated people mindlessly repeating something they heard on the news or the comments of a smarter friend. Parrots. I had no use for them. My language was music. Words were mostly pointless. No one listened to each other anyway over the roar of the world and the screaming whistles of ego trains.

If there was anything else in the world but art, I hadn't seen it.

"How come you never break your guitar?"

I had just stepped outside and there was this guy standing there, and that's what he said to me. I figured he must have been a regular to ask that. I liked to tease the crowd, whirling my Fender around by the neck, but I never did it. I never broke it.

"Too predictable," I said. Plus I didn't have the money to replace it, but I didn't say that.

He smiled with a sort of sincerity that I wasn't used to. "Good show."

"Thanks."

He didn't look like a regular anymore. Dressed sort of trendy in an old-school polo shirt, denim, and Adidas. Somehow it didn't look trendy on him though. It looked natural, not forced, and his hair was the same way, spiked on top, stylish, depending on who you talked to, but no gel or hairspray. Looking to be several years older than me in his early to mid-twenties, he seemed wildly comfortable in his skin, while I twitched with a sort of nervy feeling. I had nervous problems ever since the accident.

"Take care," I said, slinging my guitar across my back and walking on. I could feel his eyes on my back and it freaked me out. Not like he was trouble or anything, but like he knew something about me that I didn't know. I'd never even seen the guy before. Was he waiting outside for me? Did he know my routine? I needed a Klonopin to chill out—I used to take them after shows to come down from the rush, got 'em from this girl named Tracy I used to date who had a street connection, but I hadn't seen her lately and didn't know how to get in touch.

It was a Monday night and Manhattan Avenue was

dark and lifeless except for the hypnotic alternating red and green traffic lights to which my mind paid no heed. It was always stuck in go, scaling the slippery moss-green rocks of my subconscious or shooting dice with my ego. There was no turning it off. Flames licked my memories and started fires. My grandfather was a war vet with post-traumatic stress. It was like that. I guess you could say I had issues, but who doesn't? Tracy said to me once that faking sanity was like faking an organism. Just pretend like you're having fun. Smile real big and when assholes sling shit at you, grin and throw it back like an ape at the zoo. We're all monkeys, she said. She loved that movie. *Twelve Monkeys*. We used to watch it together all the time and do our Brad Pitt-as-mental-patient impersonations. *You are a total nutcase, completely deranged, delusional, paranoid! Your thought process is all fucked up.* When we got high and too stoned to talk, one of us would always say, *Your information train is jammed, man!!* I didn't get high anymore. After a while, it just made my bad trip worse. But thinking of Tracy still made me smile.

Maybe I should go see her, I thought. I didn't have her number but I knew where she lived. If I kept walking north, I could be there in a day or two; less if I hitched a ride. She lived in Hollywood near the stupid sign that all the tourists come to see. I hated going there. There were just too many people in Los Angeles, millions of them, crawling all over each other. I imagined them all in a pile and one stubborn asshole eating his way out from the bottom to conquer the city. And that would be his prize. Those broken, graffiti-tagged letters that said, *Hollywood.* He would hang it in his bedroom like some college kid vandal with a stop sign and all his friends would think he was the man.

God, I hated that I was so cynical. I had to stop

bumming myself out. It was a great gig. I was alive. I had my guitar. What, me worry? Maybe it was that kid outside the show making me superstitious. That wasn't the right word. Superstitious. I was feeling . . . vulnerable? It didn't make sense. Why would I feel vulnerable around a complete stranger? I might as well have been transparent. He was looking right through me. I shivered even though it wasn't cold.

My street was coming up, so I turned to look to make sure no one was following me. It wasn't just that night. I did it out of habit. There was a BMW idling in the turn lane at the last intersection; the windows were tinted, I couldn't see inside. I didn't see many BMWs in my neighborhood, maybe one for every hundred I saw in Hollywood. When the light changed, it turned left, drove past me. I turned the corner onto my street. The tenants in the adjacent apartment building tossed their garbage out the second-story windows and sometimes hit the dumpster but more often desecrated the pavement. *We're all monkeys.* Pressing my nose against my wrist to block the stench, I took deep drags of the lavender oil as I stepped around the ripped plastic bags filled with decaying food and who knows what else. The street dead-ended and narrowed into an alleyway. I tried my best to keep it clean. Luckily, a Pacific breeze came in off the water and through the far end of the alley to keep the garbage smell where it belonged, which was right under the noses of its owners. A kid at the grocery store around the way hooked me up with fresh boxes every other week. I made jokes about "installing new flooring," like some butch suburban dad.

It wasn't much, but it was all I had.

I was home.

FENCETOWN
by M.A.D.

A sign comes out of the ground on a sharpened wooden post, crookedly sledge-hammered down, big blue faded letters spell out, Fencetown—The Place to Be, *across its face. Small grafitti is scratched all around the white background of its catch phrase:* Fuck U, Traci wuz here, Kevin ("is gay" *added by someone else*), Cummers & Goners '95, '96, '97. *They're messy remembrances that'll go away when they replace this thing again. There's an intersection here too; a square of phone lines overhead, streetlights flickering dim bulbs. We'll go left, for some reason it just seems logical.*

Down a two-lane street; to the right, past a spotty row of houses, a creek appears. A short fence comes after, standing at the top of where the ground descends into a crevice. Then, between the fence and a big house that follows, a gap probably just wide enough for a car to go through takes you into an open, grassy area. The fence runs beside the line of water, but ends when a wooden bridge begins, hovering above the runny stream. Pop cans and bottles ride the weak current, random garbage sunk to the bottom. People crossing from the subdivision on the other side end up on a black path winding through what's left of a forest, trees and tall plants that any way you go turn into civilization within a mile.

The Bridge
A dirty landslide of broken glass leads into the shade beneath a bridge. Two kids scratch their mosquito bites until they draw blood. Jamie, the ugly-faced one, sucks at

his fingers. Above, wheels roll over cracks between two-by-fours, girls' and boys' voices half-muted by the bike's thunder. The spitty blood on the joint's pinched ass looks real sexual, it reminds them of the lipstick smudges left on hot girls' cigarette filters.

Across the stream's banks, dandelions just wait to be blown away, like the spiky heads of punks. Their white fluff floats up across the rusty rail, next to some kid's dandruff, his scabbed fingers combing his girlfriend's hair into a handle. "Listen, bitch, your ass is gonna be in the water if you don't shut up, then I'll come down there and kill, then fill you." She screams like a crazy person, and he pushes her over the side, pumping her once like a hundred-pound weight. He lets go of her dirty mop and watches her drop into the pointy reeds. He throws a pink bike on top of the body, a silver pedal crushes a hole in her head, making her brain accessible.

Jamie's and Brick's shoes are sprayed with muddy splash, a thrashing girl turned into a fucked-up angel right in front of them. The kid rides away and they walk over to the corpse, bloodshot eyes looking completely amazed.

Brick: "Whoa, man."

Jamie: "Yeah, I know."

Jamie's working the dirty cunt with his undersize dick. Brick sticks his in her wide-open mouth, caught in a noiseless scream, her throat's stiff, it seems clogged, and her tongue isn't doing anything. So he jams it in her cooling mind, knowledge crawling all over his cock, extended like the arm of God into her head. He thinks of all the shit she kept in this slime: memories, school stuff, and the faces of teenage idols. He gasps, closes his eyelids, and leaves a gob of come somewhere inside, erasing everything.

They finish up and pull ripped jeans over their wet parts, satisfied. Jamie puts his sneaker on her face, grabs the handlebars, and walks the bike up through a shredded gap in the fence. Two innocent-looking kids disappear down a tar trail.

They went this way, through a few deadend roads that run parallel to each other, intersecting with the path. At the last road, off to the right, a flag's raised behind some house. Old hippies must own it cause there's a peace sign stitched in red on the material's rectangle.

Joe's

A guy in his mid-forties is relaxed on a reclining lawn chair, he has 1960s eyes and hair, an old homemade tattoo blurred in the center of the back of his hand, a cold beer cradled in his palm. He takes a slurp of his drink and looks at a bunch of flowers (weed) lassoed into a narrow rectangle of dirt by a little metal fence.

Joe is a big drug dealer around here. He mostly sells marijuana, but has some others occasionally, like coke, acid, or mushrooms. For his next expected customer, Ezra, he'll always have a bag of dope for her to pump into her skinny arms. She's young with brown hair that hasn't been cut in years. He hears the click of the gate's latch and the creak of her little hand pushing it open. He moves his feet off the chair as she stops in front of him.

"Well, hello."

"Hi." Her voice is a sick whimper.

"You look good, sit down." He has an ugly grin as he takes a thick doobie and a lighter from his tropical shirt pocket. He flicks the mini-metal wheel and ignites a flame, puts the stick of weed between his lips, and stares down into the small fire. Ezra's really dark compared to it.

And the beads of sweat on her neck and arms and face are like little bike reflectors making her look sexy. He passes the joint into her pair of clamped fingers, smoky rings exit his mouth, and he starts to talk again.

"So you need, what, six grams, you said?"

"Umm, yeah, six." Her nose is a chimney.

"How much money ya got?"

"Uh, nothing, zero dollars."

He takes his joint back. "You know what that means, huh?" The little red circle glows beneath his nose and forms a weird triangle with his pupils. Mixed in with his smile, it makes him look evil.

"Yeah." She smiles back. They pass the joint between them for a while. He smashes the stub into an ashtray.

"Come here." He pats his lap, she moves up, he grabs her hips and pulls her blue-jeans-sealed ass into his crotch. They mash lips, he bites her chin, his fingers in her half-open fly scratch around.

"Unh." He feels her moan and breaks their kiss, lowers his shorts, and finishes the job on her pants. The band of his underwear is pulled under his balls. He penetrates an arrowhead of hair.

"Unh." They stop. He lifts her off and lays her down, chest-up on the chair. The skin around the blood in his dick is thrust back and forth with the simulated hole of his hand.

"Swallow." It's an order. Her wide mouth's full of anticipation . . . genetic waste. She shovels it into her stomach with her tongue like some sort of cannibal. A splash of come's below her left eye. Joe thumbs it off her face.

"That's good for you. You should eat more often." The weed and beer have really made his smile grow.

"And you know that's not all. I need twenty bucks, or you can come back tomorrow night and I can make you another nice dinner." She tries to laugh, but is seriously contemplating her options.

"Umm, I don't know, I'll call you." She gets up and he hands her the bag. They kiss goodbye. She leaves. He takes a swig of beer to wash the taste of himself out of his mouth.

We cross a busy road. The trail continues on the other side, running along a way bigger body of water than the last. Everything curves left, then straightens out again. A set of swings appears next to a cage of tennis courts. We keep going until milkweed towers into walls, creepily enclosing the path.

1980

A kid sits between a swing's two chains, twirling himself and turning the metal ropes into a shiny braid. He hops off, dizzy, and stumbles through the sand, the world trying to escape his view. He collapses onto a patch of grass, watching a pulsing red through his eyelids. Silently, a shadow falls over his face and turns him over into darkness. He reopens his beady eyes to a mystery man blocking the light.

"Hello, Daniel."

"Hi." The man's face is bordered by the edges of the sun. Blink, blink—he's blinded trying to make the guy out. He looks away and rests his eyes on the blue creek.

"Why are you just laying there like that?"

"I don't know."

"I thought you were hurt."

"No, I'm okay."

"Good." His features are a black sphere set against a huge, blazing yellow background.

"How do you know my name?" he forgot that he was wearing a T-shirt he decorated at school with glue and glitter that spells his name across its white chest.

"I'm a friend of your dad's, don't you remember?"

"Yeah, but, uh . . . I gotta go back home . . . for dinner."

"Come on, I'll give you a ride, my car's just down there." His hand points in gun-shape toward a rundown gray car sitting in the parking lot made up of little stones.

"Actually, I'm just gonna walk. It's not far."

"Really, it's not a problem. It isn't out of my way, come on." As Daniel tries to pass him, the guy morphs into a minor devil. He tugs the boy onto the ground and drags his lightweight body across the muddy grass to his crappy vehicle. He throws him in the backseat and drives away. A screech of tires is no goodbye.

We turn right onto a sidewalk and come to another intersection. Going straight puts you in a plaza full of convenience and drug stores, fastfood restaurants, and a supermarket. A laundromat is tucked away in a corner, lit up and unlocked twenty-four hours a day, seven days a week. Adolescents take refuge there, and just hang out doing nothing.

The Laundromat
It's hot from all the dryers in the walls, running on quarters the whole day. They make it look like the inside of a submarine. Right now it's abandoned, none of the washing machines are rumbling around, not even any of the local bum kids are haunting the place. But you can see all the dents and chips, things scratched into the walls and tables by random people's knives, names scribbled with anything on whatever will take it.

On the outside of the door, *this place is cursed* is written with a serious purpose. A long time ago, two loser kids made a pact to fuck it up cause their enemies sat around here cracking jokes about them and being jerks. Now they don't even exist to this place, everybody aforementioned.

A table's marked up all across its flat top. It looks like a huge page. *Manny* is drawn into one of its corners darkly. He was a black kid from way back, when there were none here but him, about 1974. He boxed at a local club, and would go to a convenience store after practice to get slushies. Then he would come here, sit down, rest, and drink for a while, then leave. He disappeared after high school. I just mean he left, didn't like this town.

On one of the table's legs, *PELVIS* runs into the ground in deep capital scratches. They were a great local band with "*apocalyptic lyrics hidden in electric clashing of harmonized noise mimicking murder.*" A young groupie worked hard to immortalize them in this wooden peg.

Chloe + Dave is fading on a wall. They were lovers once, best friends who spent each waking moment by each other's side, until Dave met Gloria, who was more beautiful and had no boundaries sexually. They inscribed something in the bathroom stall together: *G.F.* (her last name was Frank) *is Daves slut*. Afterward, she blew Dave away with her mouth and tits hanging out of her tube top. On another wall, *R.I.P Jose* is floating all alone in a spot untouched out of respect. He was a high school basketball star. Younger kids idolized him for his greatness and work ethic, but one sad night he died in a drunken car crash. It wasn't him who was under the influence, but his father.

R.I.P Jose
Somebody else put him in that suit . . . He didn't dress himself today . . . He's dead . . . dead.

At the junkyard, a smashed car is sitting around. The windshield has two spiderwebs the size of human heads. Its front end is pushed in, the headlights stopped shining long ago, patterns of rust are eating away at its body, and the seats have red tattoos like abstract paintings.

He's old, looking at the sky where his son is, through the bars separating him from everything, a pack of clouds are gathering into a storm. *God, what the fuck did I do.*

MINE
by Jack Dickson

"So how do you want to do this?"

A shrug. "Do what?"

"What we're about to do."

Another shrug. "You're the top." He wanders over to the battered mattress and starts nudging it with the toe of an equally battered trainer.

I light a cigarette, watching. The attitude's coming off him in waves, fleas leaving a corpse. I'm staring at his back, taking in the way his clothes hang on him, draping his skinny body like a shroud. "We should set some . . . ground rules."

Just the shrug this time.

I know what I want. I know what he wants. At least, I know what he says he wants. "Okay . . ." Time to assert some dominance, I suppose. "You're here of your own free will, you have the right to leave at any time . . ." I'm staring at his arse now.

Flat, boyish. A no-arse.

The urge to rip the jeans off him and bury my face between those scrawny cheeks fights with the urge to just call a halt to this now, send him packing before we both do something we might regret.

"Whatever, all right?" He stops toeing the mattress and turns, pushing strands of dark tangled hair out of those icy green eyes. He walks toward then past me to the wall.

"Okay." I watch him wander the perimeter of the room. "Four days. For four days you're mine. You don't exist outside these four walls."

Saying it makes it real. Well, real-ish.

"Any conditions, for you?" The concept of a safe word's awkward, but we probably should at least discuss it

"Just . . . ignore anything I say, eh?" He stops, faces me, nibbling on a hangnail and avoiding my eyes.

I mentally toss any thought of safe words out the window. Or I would, if this dank basement space under the bijou home I share with my partner of twenty-five years had any windows. "Okay . . ." I seem to be saying that a lot. And he's saying virtually nothing. I'm so nervous, and it's not combining well with either the desire to fuck him or the need to take what passes for control.

So I leave, locking the door behind myself, and walk back up the six stone steps to normality.

"Everything's fine here—how's the Dali Lama?"

"First in the rebirthing queue today, so he was." Ray laughs.

The sound soothes, wrapping me in a blanket of comforting domesticity. "You just knew there'd be past lives, didn't you?"

When Ray gave up smoking six months ago, he also developed an interest in detox and matters spiritual.

"I'm dreading his primal scream." Hence his present long-weekend retreat, with a bunch of desperate househusbands, at a sanctuary on the island of Mull.

My turn to laugh. "Just as well you packed the earplugs." I cradle the phone between chin and shoulder and flick a lighter to another cigarette.

Ray groans down the phone. "Blow some of that my way, eh?"

I inhale deeply. "You're doing really good. Don't weaken."

"Sleep well, baby . . ."

"You too, sweetheart—talk to you tomorrow. And give the Dali Lama my regards."

He hangs up.

I listen to the sound the phone makes and watch the cigarette burn slowly down.

Ray and I have two rules: Don't get attached and don't bring it home. I've already broken one. The clock shows just after midnight and tonight's beer's making me sleepy. But I'm still hard enough and restless enough to know even a nap's a million miles away. I also know I'm making him wait.

Making myself wait.

So I go prepare tea and watch more cigarettes burn down.

I close the basement door and flick on the light. Twenty-watt gloom dangles from the end of a bare cord, illuminating a scored table, an ancient chair.

And him. He's curled on the mattress, barefoot already, his shadow motionless on the bare brick.

I bat the lightbulb as I pass. His shadow lurches into action, thrown drunkenly onto the walls. I toss the length of sisal on the table, along with the packet of three I know I'll never use, and walk to the mattress.

His hair's warm. I wrap it around my fist and haul him to his feet, dragging him over to the table.

He mumbles something.

I don't catch it, pulling his arms from the cheap denim

jacket and tossing it onto the floor. The knife slips from his pocket and falls softly to the concrete. Its white bone handle gleams yellow in the bad light.

He sees it.

I see it.

A shiver courses over his lean frame.

I also see his wrists for the first time, while bending him backwards over the table to tie him down: the insides of both arms scored lengthwise with ancient scar tissue. I drag my eyes away from others' trophies, fumble with his fly, and I can smell him, the sour stink of his need.

Above us, the lightbulb's slowing, our shadows languid and easy across the walls. I ignore his hard-on, half hidden by the edge of the old gray T-shirt, and drag the jeans over skinny thighs and bare feet.

He mumbles something again.

His arms are stretched awkwardly, shoulders pulled, back arching, wrists tied to the table legs. A boy's chest yawns up at me, nipples poking through the worn fabric. I grab his legs. My turn to shrug, a long coltish limb nudged up over each shoulder. I push my thumbs into his crack, spreading his arse cheeks with my fingers. His hole's clenched, pink lips held in the tightest of pouts, and my dick's fighting the good fight to get out of my trackies and into it.

Into him.

Into his body, because if I don't get the fucking out of the way now, this whole thing's dead in the water.

I bugger him hard and fast, one hand spanning his throat, the other braced against the table. His hair's in his eyes and those eyes are closed and we're silent apart from the scrape of his back on the surface of the table and the sound of the fuck. When I come, my fist tightens around his throat. His eyes are open now, but the sweat in my own blurs his.

He's still mumbling, but the pound of the blood in my head's too loud.

I pull out as soon as I'm done, the spunk still leaking from me. And after I tuck my tacky dick back into my trackies, I pick up the bone-handled knife from the floor and place it on his chest. My legs are wobbly as I switch off the light. Locking the door, I pause and listen.

No mumbling now. No attitude. No nothing.

Ten hours later I've slept in my own dirt, done some work, and drunk too much tea. Back in the basement, I pocket the knife and untie his wrists.

He whimpers then screams as I carry him over to the mattress, sensation pouring into his thin arms. His vertebrae crack and crunch, realigning themselves. I massage feeling back into his hands, watching narrow veins swell blue just beneath the skin, then pull him to his feet. "Walk around a bit."

Legs buckle. His arms shoot around my neck as he steadies himself.

Dark hair plasters to his face. I peal it out of his eyes, then pull him into motion. "Walk, eh?" We half-stagger, half-waltz a few steps, his grip tightening at the back of my neck. "Come on . . ." I reach up, take his wrists firmly, and pull them from where they want to be.

He crumples onto the floor, a curled shape at my feet.

I dig a toe into his gut.

He mumbles.

I stare at the scratches on his bony back where the T-shirt's riding up, his pale no-arse gleaming in twenty-watt gloom. Then I walk to the door, switch off the light, and leave him in the dark.

I work. I eat. I make work phone calls and set up meetings. I put him where he has to stay. In that part of my mind where he's always been. I don't know when he last ate, but he should eat again soon. I go out. I buy eggs, bread, cheese.

Five hours later I'm eating my own semi-crystalized come out of his tender hole, teasing it from his arse hair with my teeth while he moans somewhere further up the mattress, squirming back onto my face. The bone-handled knife in my pocket, digging into my thigh. I come up for air, twine my fist in his hair, and yank his head back.

Upside-down eyes glaze glassily over my shoulder.

The lightbulb's still swinging, just starting to slow. Drunken shadows sway across the pale face. A dried trickle of blood at the corner of that distorted mouth. His lips have stopped bleeding and are now scabbing and swelling, instant collagen eclipsing the rest of his features.

"Hit me again." The words as distorted as the mouth that forms them. Aimed past me, at someone no longer there. Someone that's not me.

I tug his head right back, the muscles in his neck tightening, then push him forward, nudging his knees from under him with mine. He's in my mouth, on my breath, in my head, and I'm still just another someone. Anyone.

He's mumbling into the mattress now. I'm straddling him, his arse under me, his shoulders covered with my bites. I grab his hands, twisting his arms up behind his back.

He yells this time.

I push my thumbs between the small bones in his wrists, pressing down against the base of his spine. There's a soft, delicate crack. Not a break, more a separation. Then silence. I shift my grip, holding his wrists and pulling the small knife from my pocket. The blade flicks out with no sound.

As I trace its point along the big vein at the side of his neck, my hand shakes slightly and his body shudders with silent sobs.

"Wouldn't you know it, the Dali Lama was an Egyptian princess in a previous life."

"Why are people never Egyptian street-sweepers? Or bin-men? Why are they always royalty?" I smile down the phone.

"Once a queen, always a queen?"

The knot of tension behind my eyes still throbs. But less so now. "Anyway, you feel this is helping you rediscover your inner self or what?"

"The food's good—too good. I'm putting on pounds."

"I can take a bit of meat on my men."

"Get the doors widened now—and reinforce those floors."

I laugh and the throb's a distant pulse. "You get your beauty sleep, sumo-boy, and I'll talk to you tomorrow."

"Night night, babe."

Four a.m. and I'm at the basement door, fingering the bone-handled knife. I wanked twice, once just after midnight, again around 3 a.m. After the second time, I knelt on his chest and pished on his face, the hot stream steaming in the basement's damp air. The pish gushed off his wet lashes, flowing onto his come-streaked mouth and into the new cuts on his lips. His head thrashed on the filthy mattress, hair matted and wild. After I'd shaken the last few drops onto him, I rolled off and took him in my arms.

"Was I good?"

Leaning back against the bare brick wall, I cradled him against my chest, my fingers deep in that rat's nest of hair.

"Am I what you hoped I'd be?" His thin arms hung around my neck, knees pulled up against his own chest. "Am I?"

The lightbulb no longer swung. The stench of my pish and my come and his blood and sweat filled the room. I was getting hard again.

"Am I?"

I'm getting hard now. I turn the key in the lock and enter, fingers wrapped tightly around the bone-handled knife.

He's asleep. Or unconscious. Or a mixture of both.

I'm crouched against a wall.

His mouth's badly swollen, along with his right wrist. The hair's matted all to fuck. The old gray T-shirt's teasingly half off one bitten shoulder, and my bloody come streaks the backs of those pulled-up legs. His chest's barely rising and falling. But it is rising and falling.

Time passes. An hour. Maybe two. Maybe more. The room reeks of us, mostly him, and I can't believe it's been three days already. After a while, my legs go numb. I move closer to the curled shape on the filthy old mattress, my little comma, my punctuation mark.

He's a looker. I always knew he would be. Not that it matters. To me, at least. It matters to him, obviously, but only as a means to an end. Only as bait. What else do I know about him? He has a good job, a partner of ten years, a life in spite of the childhood and teenage years which drive him toward men like me, again and again.

I close my eyes.

He's still there, painted on the insides of the lids. I don't want to think about them, the others, doing to his undernourished body what I can only fantasize about. But they're in there with him, part of him, and part of what he brings with him to me.

The irrational impulse to set off, track down, then beat to a pulp those who have hurt him and made him what he is vies with the desire to just hold him and murmur meaningless inanities about how it's all going to be all right.

And the longing to pick up where they left off, wedge open wounds that have never, will never heal, remains.

It stupidly occurs to me he's not eaten in seventy-two hours. I wake up.

Somewhere upstairs, the phone rings. Somewhere in the back of what used to be my mind, I know the machine'll pick up.

Beep. "*I know you have that late meeting, babe—hope it all goes well. Talk to you tomorrow. Oh—by the way? The Dali Lama regressed too far today and has retired to his room with a bottle of tequila . . .*" A laugh. "*See you soon.*" Two beeps.

I open my eyes.

His are already open, crusted tears gumming them to slits. He's watching me. In the dull twenty-watt bulb he looks younger. Even more vulnerable. I'm still holding the bone-handled knife.

I can't do this.

"What about some toast? You like eggs, right? I think we have eggs . . ."

Somehow, he makes it to his feet, clinging onto the

wall for support. He's having trouble breathing. The imprint of my hand's a vivid purple against the white of his throat. He takes a moment to steady himself, his eyes never leaving me. He reaches out and up, the scars on his swollen wrist taunting me. A flick.

The lightbulb lurches left, tossing our shadows onto the wall, huge and elongated, warped and inhuman. They dance on the periphery of my vision as I haul myself upright and swipe the lightbulb with my full strength.

Just as it shatters against the ceiling, I slam my fist into his pale face.

Now we're both in the dark.

Phones are ringing. My landline. My mobile. My cock's raw from fucking him and I'm still half-hard, still in what's left of his hole. His wetness is everywhere.

Two curled shapes on the filthy mattress. Me in him, wrapped around him, my hands circling his wrists, pinning his arms across his own chest. Blood seeps through my fingers, his pulse weak but still there. He stopped crying hours ago. The only sounds remaining are the wet squelch of our bodies and a vague mewling. It could be him. It could be me. It no longer matters.

I'm all out of words. Mine . . . yours . . . they don't cut it. The knife cuts it. His knife. My wounds. My damage.

I want to think about if there's time to clean him up and/or get him medical attention before his flight. I want to think about forcing food into him, a feeble salve to my paternal conscience. I want to think about what, if anything, I'm going to tell Ray.

But I don't. Because that would mean thinking about how it will feel, knowing for four days he was mine. And those four days are almost over.

DEAR SYBELLUS
by Joseph Marcure

12/29

Let's go to the steam house for no reason
Yeah, that's a great idea
Let's hang with macaques in 43° hot springs
What about the sento? I hear it's Japanese only.

Dear Sybellus,

    Been sad lately, been eating lots of ketchup. Used to suck it out of the bottle but now that I've lost my teeth I put it in a bowl and slurp it off a spoon.

    My teeth aren't really all gone. I just wanted to deglamorize myself to relate how I felt last month when I was smiling in a mirror and noticed this black spot on my top right canine. I thought it was food but it wouldn't come off. It broke my heart when I realized it was a cavity. Little as it was it reminded me that things weren't as perfect as the happy spell I had myself under had left me believing. But that's another story, and I wanted to tell you I met somebody, in a way.

    It all started a week ago at Holiday-n-Save where I saw these new adjustable Christmas trees, they stretch out to the size of a real tree and when you're done they fold up into a little pocket-size box. It was an easy steal. The one I took held fourteen varieties, including a ten-foot

Christmas eucalyptus I put in my bedroom with a koala sleeping in its branches. The rest I arranged in my living room. Fake firs, redwoods, even a deciduous pine with little plastic needles slipping out at random.

Having all these trees around put me into that decorating mood, so I went back for ornaments. They had those new pre-fab sets: poor family, creative family, the popular TV family, but I took fourteen grandma sets, one for each tree. Along with ornament balls that break into a thousand pieces, their real draw is pre-fab hangable frames stuffed with photos of grandkids. The one on the cover is a picture of this cute little boy in the center of a baby-blue snowflake, his name in white on the snowflake's tips, *k-y-l-e-e-y*. There's another one with the same boy, his face and arms make up those of a snowman. Beneath him it says, *Snow Cutie!* Both frames are covered in a glitter that falls off but never goes away. I put those two up first.

I decorated all the trees the same, so it kind of repeats. But I needed lights. I walked back into the store thinking it was so easy, and it was. I saw these new lights based on deep sea fish that glow naturally, with bioluminescence, but I think these are mostly synthetic. They only use electricity to be turned on or off but to glow they feed off stuff in the air. I took three "Refined Rainbow" sets, stuffing each under my sweater.

Putting the lights up on the trees and along my apartment walls I found that they added this cool supernormal ambiance, like being in a jellyfish forest at night. Still, I couldn't help but notice this one light. I couldn't take my eyes off it. I took it out of the string and watched it die in my palm. I said, *Did you wanna go out?* But the light lit back up and spoke telepathically. In my head I saw a picture of a boy, and got a warm feeling, a soothing little voice said, *Jūñi, thanks for taking me out of the string, the other lights make me lonely. My name's Blue. You're so cool.*

Cool or not, I was feeling lonely too. So I took him out to dinner, to this little place called The Coquette. As we sat down at our table this vulpine waitress came over to greet us.

"I'm sorry, but you'll have to turn that light off. This is a place for romance, people come here for the candlelight." Blue dimmed. "Really, you gotta split," said the waitress. A redhead, she looked about my age.

I said, "If you lose something irreplaceable, I'll irreplace it." Blue rolled around on the table. I stared nonchalantly at our waitress, let's call her Jenny. She rolled her eyes as I ran my fingers through my hair. Placing a hand on her hips, she mocked me, running her hand over her face. Balanced like that I wished she was my date.

Picking sleepies from my eyes I tried ordering. "Cool. I'll have that duck milk curry, and a bottle of Shiraz."

With her eyes shut, Jenny drew waves on her notepad and blew me a kiss. Fluttering her eyelids she turned to Blue. "Will you be going light this evening?" Awaiting the order Jenny put her fingers on my right shoulder and sultrily ran them down my arm. Taking my hand she said, "Moo, meow."

I bit my lip and pretended to slide a ring on her third finger. Twisting it around, she held it in front of her face and mimed, *My God, so pretty!*

Blue turned black, and realizing my little guy was in a bad way, I tried to talk telepathic. *Something wrong? Jenny? Oh, Blue.*

It was then that I felt something hit the back of my head. Turning around I saw a plastic ring on the floor and Jenny across the room leaning on the kitchen entrance gaping. "Ku-ku kitty, kit-tee!" I said, and clicked my tongue. She laughed and exited to the kitchen.

Dinner came and I paid this guitar-brandishing brunette to serenade Blue and me. During the music it was easy to feel a kind of romance that I think Blue felt too. He rolled over and nudged my hand. I smiled and he did it again only this time he knocked over my wine glass. Not thinking much of it I tipped the glass back up. Blue began to roll in the wine to the rhythm of the music, which sounded kind of like the theme from *Dodes'ka-den*. Looking at the guitarist in her little black dress and matching nylons, I started to wish Blue had more of a body, or that I was dating her. I put my finger out to Blue and we played at dancing in the fresh wine stain on the tablecloth. I noticed Blue was swelling a little, he started to seem much larger. Then all of a sudden he was the size of a child's head. Shocked, I pulled my finger back, then gently touched him. He was burning up and I got the sense he wouldn't make it like this. Getting up I accidentally knocked over the wine bottle and it spilled on Blue. He swelled to the size of those giant bouncing balls you sit on. I yelled, "Help!" but no one offered. I panicked and taking him in my arms ran out of the restaurant. Standing out front I blew on him and said little reassuring words. He went lifeless. As I stared at his smoky center clear little spots started forming on him, it was raining. A glimmer of Blue appeared inside and I held him out to the rain. Soon, he was back to normal. It was a weird relief, all I could do was sigh.

We got in the car and just sat for a while. There was a knock at the window, it was Jenny. "Hey!" she called. But before I could roll down the window she had put a little paper under the driver's side windshield wiper and ran back inside.

That night Blue went to bed with me. He dimmed and the room's shadows pulsed with him. It was so easy to relax with him laying next to me. I fell asleep with him on my shoulder, kissing him as I drifted off.

In my dream I'm undressing that cute waitress when I'm nudged awake by Blue, he motions to the doorway. There's a million color flashes coming down the hall, my guess is the other lights are jealous. I tell Blue not to worry and rubbing my eyes I crawl out of bed. Stepping into the living room, in front of all the flickering lights, I offer, "Look, I can't be sweet on all of you. I'm not Jesus."

The lights turn slow patterns on the wall. They produce a scene of George Washington crossing the Delaware in a ship full of soldiers. You can tell it's a cold day as all their breaths are little clouds. George has a gun boy in his lap. He holds him like a teddy bear, kissing his head and resting his nose in the boy's hair. When George sees the infantry of the new world frozen on the banks he pretends to shit his pants. The other men in the boat laugh and George does an impromptu ventriloquist routine using a set of false teeth in his left hand and a wig on the right.

Chattering the teeth, he says, "My fellow men, this liberty she is cold as these soldiers. Have we not forsaken our fellows for this? An icy expanse, this that will soon have to be fled for a new liberty. But I ask you, where?" His wig hand answers in an exaggerated child's voice, "I think I poopy in my panties, Daddy . . ."

A strange wooden orb rises out of the Delaware, goes buoyant. It's David Bushnell's Turtle, the first American submarine. Startled, a soldier fires at it. The thing explodes, the shot had hit a mine intended to sink British ships. A thick cloud of black smoke blooms in the air turning Christmas afternoon into a strange blackness. But slowly, flecks of light begin to fall as snowflakes, twinkling a silver blue.

A dimly glowing figure emerges from the river, swimming ashore only to lay there and cough up water. "Ezra!" exclaims wise Washington. Two soldiers make out in the background, thousands of little lights falling around them, sparkling on the water.

One of the women soldiers disguised as a man catches a brilliantly aflash flake in her cupped palms, she leans in toward the little light and blows. As it circles off she sends it a kiss. Choking a tad on the heavy smoke, a fellow soldier asks, "What, cough, is it?"

Staring out at the scene, she answers, "Why, it's foxfire, soldier."

Looking out at the slow falling dots and all the faces glistening a white blue, he tells himself, *Foxfire*, and then coughs up some of the flakes himself. They're especially bright after having been in his warm lungs.

On the shore Washington and as many soldiers as can fit surround the strange beached figure, who laying there covered in foxfire all lucent looks very ghostly. They're taking their hand at reviving him. Washington recognizes the face: "Bushnell! I thought Lee was piloting the ship. Forgive our ignorance, I'm sure we can build another Turtle."

Opening his eyes, Ezra blinks, his lenses dimly reflecting the damp foxfire he's covered in. Opening his lips, water pours out, stops, then dribbles. Coughing a bit, he faintly gets out a reply. "Heh," *cough*, "how's those curtains coming?"

As Washington laughs you can see a bit of foxfire on his substantial and complicated dentures. This comicbooky gleam is all the more poignant against the shimmering blue of his face and the wet darkness behind him. "Oh, Ezra. I've a few styles and patterns picked out."

The scene fades and the lights flit around reassembling their shadows for another little scene, but I'm starting to feel a little hopeless with a kind of ache for, well, real people. The credits come up, the title, *How to Be.* It's an educational, and I watch.

There's the elder George Washington Carver in his lab at Tuskegee, blowing into glass tubes and boiling liquids of all colors in an array of beakers. A knock on the door frame, it's a stage boy from George's theater, whole thing made of peanuts, even the actors. "Mister Daddy—hey, I brought you a," *crunch,* "cold-as-charity glass of juice."

Pausing, George takes his lips off a glass tube, he turns around to the boy, smiling. But he looks up past him, up out the back of the doorway toward the sky, throwing his arms in the air.

"I did it, Lord, through you. I finally did it. I hybridized a butterfly larvae with my own one-way telepathy peanut pods! Now here I may have the perfect peanut." Looking at the boy, he explained, "When you're ready to have one you just think it and the next thing you know, he's cracked his shell, climbed out, and flown right into your mouth. It's beautiful really, a thing of service. Here's a crop which will surely sell, saving many farms. I must make a flyer, spread the good news, and—"

The peanut boy interrupts, "So when you gonna put this new technology on me? Ya ol' pervert."

Heartbroken, the boy sheds a tear and drops the cold juice he had brought for George. Hitting the concrete floor the glass shatters and like a startled fox the boy runs. Halfway down the path back to the theater he trips and hits his knee on a rock. His face looks pained and lying there his leg cracks open to reveal a hard peanut interior.

The scene fades and the lights go back to being luminous dots. In the corner I notice a little scene, it's a cartoon peanut flying over the Delaware, the lights turn toward me and it looks like the peanut is flying into my mouth. Then the room goes calm, but I'm tired so just in case I unplug the string of Radiant Rainbows.

Standing there in the new darkness, my emptiness felt . . . well, it was an ache for another person, for that waitress. In my mind I was seeing her in photos. I reach into my pocket, scared. Everything about my sense of her a yearning. In my pocket is that note she left under the wiper. Going into the kitchen, I fold my fingers around it and hold it before me. Flicking on the lights, I find Jenny's number and the little blue hearts and stars she drew around it, the ink a little smeared. It hurts to look at her handwriting. I don't know if she was just joking, but I'm not joking now. I mean I wish I was but this pain is real. I barely get myself to call. It's her message, I say let's get together, leave my number, and hang up. After a few cups of cold coffee I go back to bed, to little Blue and sleep.

Well, I'm here sitting in the bathtub, getting ready to shave my legs. They always feel too hot, especially in jeans. I'm pretty sure it's the hair. I was out doing my laundry in the quad waiting for the dryer to buzz about an hour ago when I started to think I'd actually shave them. This blond kid came in barefoot with a cordless phone and looking very frightened. He's about thirteen, I think his name's Konnor. He lives a few doors down from me. He came up to me and said someone wanted to kill him. He had been on the phone with his friend walking through the complex, when the call cut out and this guy's gruff voice came on. He thought he was listening to another call until the guy made it clear he was talking to him, blondie in the courtyard. It freaked him out just being talked to by a guy, men usually ignored him—like his father, he said. But this man said he wanted to torture him, cut him up, fuck him. Of course the boy was scared, his feelings confused with, *Why would someone want to do this to me?* He said after the call clicked to a dial tone it hit him that this mumbling telepsycho might actually mean it. That's when he saw me through the laundry room doorway. He's pretty sure it was somebody in the complex who was watching him from a second-story window or something. I said it was probably just a guy who sits around with transceivers and modified phones waiting to hear a boy's voice on a signal he can cut in on, probably more scary in theory than practice. Konnor looked down and sighed. He said, *Yeah, I guess,* flopped his head, and smiled. He had on this T-shirt with a red panda silkscreened on the front, it was walking upright like Futa from the Chiba zoo.

Shooting a couple of quarters into the dryer I started to ask his philosophy on shaving your legs. But seeing a hopeless look in his eyes I instead tried to comfort him with this story of a lost boat. *Let me tell you something,* I said, *about this boat everybody thought was missing, did you ever hear of him? He was a long wooden boat, and was actually just hiding out at this hotel crosstown. He had gotten tired of the waters and needed some time alone. He was sure people were out looking for him so he called me asking to bring him something to eat, he said he was starving. I didn't think boats ate but I did the right thing and got him lunch. I knocked S-O-S on the door and left the bag of food on the mat in front of room 14-A, second floor, Ocean Mist Hotel. I waited down in the parking lot and secretly watched him creak open his door and peek out all paranoid. It was a funny thing to watch a boat do.* He grabbed his food and ducked back inside, shutting and locking his door in one loud thunk. Later he called to thank me. We chatted about this TV show we had both been watching about rescued boxes. These people had found them as little boxlings half crushed by the side of the road, laying flat and soggy in some brush. They had taken them in, nursed them, and grown to love their orphaned boxes. They were shown crying behind fences that separated them from the habitat they just released their little friends into. One of the boxes cautiously scoots into the wild, looking back only to inch away forever. The box makes it deep into the wild where it meets a troop of boxes in whom it hopes to find a family. The others notice it and slowly allow it into their circle. It seems as though there's going to be a scuffle as the larger boxes unfold their tops and begin to surround the intruder. But then the little boxes, just learning to slide, come up and nudge the new one.

My laundry was finished and as I folded it into my bin I tried to entertain Konnor with a riff on what was supposed to be the failed box hunting ending. *These four hunters are stopped by a park ranger, you can't hunt wild boxes, they're protected.* "But our livelihood," *cry the hunters. The ranger says,* "If you're serious try two miles over." *They are, and two miles over, in a suburban front yard, they find a guy hiding behind some hedges. He's hunting six feet tall by three feet wide effeminate bran flakes.* As I finished folding my laundry I wanted to push the boy up against the washer and kiss him. He was laughing, his eyes all twinkly. Taking my laundry basket I asked, *Well, can I walk you back to your place?* He said yeah, so we walked out together and chatted till we got to his apartment. I asked, *You're going to be okay, right?*

He said, *Yeah, my mom's home and stuff, I'm fine.* I nodded and we said bye.

Back to my bath. I've been in here so long my skin's gotten all waterlogged. Which I'm not sure is best for a smooth shave. But, recounting that last part, as I was trying to write it out I started to fantasize about Konnor. I was imagining him coming in here naked, to the tub. I felt a physical need for him to lay here with me. Oh, here comes Blue.

He's rolling up the side of the tub. I pick him up and kiss his luminescent self. I put out my tongue to taste him. He rolls on and I pull him into my mouth. I close my lips. He's inside, he tastes like a gel capsule. I swallow him.

I didn't even think about it. I mean I thought about it and just did it. He felt light going down, but now I don't feel him at all. I mean I know I swallowed him and he's probably dying but I don't really care anymore. All I can think about is Konnor. I could've done more to help him, like offering him to come over, but that wouldn't have made much sense. His mom was home and she probably knows what to do more than me, if he tells her. I don't know. I just hope he's not being killed right now. I'm going to get out of this bath and check on him. I'm nervous about it, but I need to do it anyway. Oh, the phone's ringing, hope it's Jenny.

Well, write me soon,
Jüñî

THE BEFORE AND THE PLASTIC DINOSAURS
by Cody Carvel

It was December 9, 1986, and 3 at night. Or morning. It was dark—the field and the sky unifying—and the Driver who spotted him would not, in one billion repeat incidences, have spotted him again. The child's nut-brown hair illuminated gold for a split second and forced focus on the Driver. Jabbing the brake, headlights on: a pale kid, five or six, shivering in a wheat field, wearing a red Newport cigarettes T-shirt and khaki shorts that covered little of his legs. The Driver thought the night was the grayest in history. The stretch of highway 81 was wheat and grain elevators for eighty miles. The occasional Dairy Queen and a stack of cassettes almost made the extreme gloom and boredom okay. He had tired of Megadeth's *Peace Sells . . . But Who's Buying?*, pressed eject on the tape player, and caught the radio weatherman as he passed the Okarche exit: "*. . . this was the grayest day on record for Northern Oklahoma . . .*" but before this coincidental *I knew it* moment could register: the kid. Rolling down the window of his MG, "Hey, kid, what are you doing out here?" Nothing. "You live out here?" Though he meant to say, "You live *around* here?" The kid was covered in dew, or whimpering. "You need a ride?" Nothing but crying. "Well, I'm going to the city if you need to get someplace." The kid, still crying, walked the ten yards from the edge of the wheat field to the car. Opening the door and activating the overhead light, the kid revealed his skinned knees and old bruises. *Clumsy acrobat*, the Driver thought. The kid climbed in and was engulfed by the passenger seat. "Roll up that window, kid." The kid complied. The Driver continued south toward Oklahoma City without any chitchat. Around Kingfisher he'd asked to be handed a tape. Slayer's *Reign in Blood* played for the next fifty miles. The kid shivered a little and breathed every once and a while. As the lights of Oklahoma City became visible, the Driver stopped into a Dunkin' Donuts and bought a dozen. The kid stayed in the car. "Hold this, and have whatever you want except the Bavarian Kreme." The kid went after the Dunkin' version of a bear claw. Twenty minutes later they were pulling through a gate down a long driveway to a cul-de-sac in front of a large dark house. The car died and the music stopped. Up two dozen steps the porch light guarded the two strangers. "Well, you can stay with us until . . ." The Driver paused, looking at the still shivering boy. ". . . whenever." He lived in a neighborhood where someone fixed the sidewalks when they cracked.

"Till whenever." It was agreed upon with a nod. The Driver's parents had ten rooms and busy schedules and no time to worry about who he brought home, for if they did they might reckon to relocate the family to some uninhabited island where one could continue to get Home Shopping Network deliveries. As the Driver led the way upstairs, the kid noticed the boy he'd shared the car with was could pass for his older brother's skeleton, thin and pale and covered in black from his hair to his sneakers, carrying a box of donuts to some warmer place.

The Driver said, "My name's Jeffrey, Jeff . . . my name's Jeff . . ." The kid silent. "I'm just going to call you mutt till you tell me to call you another name." The kid seemed to acknowledge Jeff by looking around the hall. Opening a door, "You can have this room. Mom used to make dolls in here before she realized she's not good at anything." A small curling-iron girl's bed was along the farthest wall, obstructed by piles of fabric and cotton. "She only realized it a couple of days ago. You can clean it up if you want. Bathroom's down the hall. I'm usually next door." Jeff left him a donut on deli paper near the bed's night table. "See ya." mutt picked up all the potential Raggedy Annes and Andys and put them on the bed, which would perfectly accommodate his child size perhaps only for six months more. On top of floral pillows and sheets that suggested summer, mutt covered himself in fabric and wool string and closed his globe-blue eyes. Jeff was thinking about his trip. He had turned sixteen last May and had the MG since he was fifteen. He aspired to traverse all seven of Oklahoma's interstate highways and all twenty-six of its U.S. highways within the state borders. Experiencing the limits of Oklahoma meant that he didn't have to wonder if landscapes of places depicted on TV and in art books were more or less beautiful than those that had arbitrarily been assigned to his state. He hadn't given much thought to how anyone else might accept this idea. He'd certainly lament his teenage logic later. Highway 81 passed a town called Bison that had a large bison painted on its grain elevator, he recalled. And the kid. Aside from that it was a bust as far as beauty was concerned. He fell asleep singing to himself, *"It was so dark the electric light looked like a cigarette butt . . ."*

Before (,)

After a few hours sleep, Jeff entered the newly anointed

guestroom and flipped the lights off and on until the mass of mutt-and-fabric vibrated.

"I can read your mind," Jeff acknowledged.

"You're thinking:

"*Before I was a plastic dinosaur*

"*Before, I was a plastic dinosaur*

"*Before I was a plastic dinosaur*

"*Before, I was a plastic dinosaur*

"*Before I was a plastic dinosaur*

"*Before, I was a plastic dinosaur*

"And it's driving me nuts!"

The bundle cartoonishly imitated a T-Rex.

Next

The next weeks were spent getting stoned and driving the state highways. mutt started talking but didn't say much. His real name was Caleb Armstrong; he had turned six in November, he'd lived with his shitty father, and said he liked the name mutt better. Other than that, they hadn't learned much else, an actor named Ben Dover had died, the newspaper ran a story with the headline, *G.I. Better Leave His Panties Back Home*, Boley is one of thirteen all-black towns existing in Oklahoma today, down from more than fifty like a million years ago, they were both pretty sure Kevin DuBrow on *Red Alert* was singing, "*A masseuse will trigger the score . . .*" They stopped listening to Quiet Riot after that. They then turned on the radio and learned: "*Most sales are after Christmas, but Clark's is just before . . .*"

They hadn't seen much, *Little Shop of Horrors* was enjoyable, Boley was really black, and they'd missed an African-American rodeo some seven months before, lots of combines, tractors, cows, and chickens that they'd sometimes pretend were overgrown kittens or flipping wind-up dogs.

When they were near the city, they stayed at Jeff's house. When Jeff got tired, they slept in the car, on the side of the highway, under the stars, and under what were surely handwoven Native American blankets, OR perhaps more surely American Indian–styled bath mats. They liked to visit the Indian truckstops because they felt that the products were blessed. Across the state, average temperatures were moving from the forties to the thirties. Christmas was coming. At a sporting goods store on 66 near Claremore, Jeff got some insulated camouflage coveralls for mutt and an orange hooded sweatshirt. They headed to the city and real beds as the windshield wipers came on.

Christmas

"It's Christmas Eve," Jeff said. "Maybe we should do something." There was no sign of Jeff's parents and virtually no sign that anyone even inhabited the home. Sometimes flowers would appear.

They each ordered a pizza they thought the other would like. After they had watched MTV and consumed two pepperoni pizzas, mutt changed the cable box to the ritual Rudolph/Frosty puppet special and then to Jim Henson's *The Christmas Toy*. The puppets and Muppets reminded them of Jeff's mom's failed dolls. After roasting marshmallows on the gas range, the two fell asleep in separate but matching La-Z-Boy recliners.

New Year's Eve

Having watched the ads on TV, mutt suggested they go see *Witchboard* at the mall. The story was compelling. And the moral . . . *never use a Ouija board alone* meant that they would be safe using one together. After the show Jeff picked up a Ouija board at the mall's toy store. Driving home they agreed to summon the spirit of Ben Dover. For Caleb "mutt" Armstrong, 1986 had become in its final twenty-two days the best year ever.

Jeff couldn't decide if there was anything more beautiful about Oklahoma than the places he'd seen in movies and in books. He doubted it. But there was plenty to do if you were friends with the right people.

1987

One day. Red lipstick on the dark green door of their house: *Thank you for your kind help. Please deliver Caleb to* such and such address. Signed, *Plastic Dinosaurs,* at such and such address.

"*That* doesn't sound good," said Jeff.

Jeff and mutt went inside. They went to the sunroom to compose a letter. Jeff clenched his pen.

1/3/1986̶7

Dear Plastic Dinosaurs,

mutt's staying here until he decides to leave. He seems to be in good health. We don't give a damn about others. That's the code we live by.

Fuck you with scorpions,

Jeffrey Simon Cameron

"Man, are my shoulders sore," Jeff said.

Two days later a letter was delivered:

1/4/1987

Dear Jeffrey Simon Cameron,

We don't give a damn about others either, and that's the code

we live by, too. It must be tough traveling with a little one like that. He's such a cute little thing. Understand, we will put you to rest. Comprende?
Plastic Dinosaurs

Jeff quickly penned a reply.

1/5/1987
Dear Plastic Assholes,
    So there's not much point in me trying to avoid you people, I guess?

Two days. A small card in the mail:

1/7/1987
J.—
    Did you read the part about "we will put you to rest"?
Mother's breasts have not run dry.
PD

Jeff lowered the letter, unsure of what he had read. This made him feel crazy. The tension stopped mutt from playing Duck Hunt. They thought about the Island of Unfit Toys or whatever from the Rudolph special.

They weren't sure what it meant that the Plastic Dinosaurs were after them. Why the letter writers spoke so strangely. They thought it was time to hit the road. Tomorrow morning.

Dust

To hell with the limits of Oklahoma, Jeff thought. Jeff's family survived the first Dust Bowl without uprooting. He often thought this was part of the problem with his family.

Boredom had dug its protective trench deep into the Oklahoma plains, and rigs had to be built so oil could be drilled. No one really knew desperation.

Jeff loaded up on tapes, filled an Igloo with ice, Dr. Pepper, and had mutt put whatever he wanted in there. They had, for some time, lived only on Dr. Pepper and Twinkies. They put the chest in the tiny trunk of the Midget and drove off. The snow was coming unglued from the ground and the sky was now windblown brown.

mutt rode alongside Jeff to his high school that looked like a children's hospital, where he told the secretary he wouldn't be coming back. She noted that he'd missed eighty-two days of school over the last two years and that his name had been taken off the roll sheets a month ago. She also noted he looked unwell, even for him, and that he should eat. He replied that gluttony was a sin. He left trying to remember a single profound incident that had happened during his ten or so years at this school. But before anything came to mind, they reached the car.

When they'd heard enough out of Paul Harvey and Tom Bodett, Jeff put on *Somewhere in Time* by Iron Maiden. "Wasted Years" played. It seemed fitting.

"So what are the Plastic Dinosaurs?" Jeff asked.

No reply. But mutt ejected the tape and switched the radio to 106.7 FM. A station break: "*Oklahoma que prefiere escuchar . . .*" And then a voice in Spanish translating an impassioned English speaker:

Brothe—(*Hermanos y Hermanas,*)

something something something

Plastic Di—(*Dinosaurios Plasticos*)

Plain as day.

Jeff stopped the car.

The voices continued on in English, quickly obliterated by the Spanish:

Isai—(Isaías) Fift—(Cincuenta-uno)—
something something something.
Jeff listened for the English words:

Listen you / Seek the Lord / The rock / The quarry / Your father / Gave you birth / I called / I blessed / Deserts like Eden / Wastelands like garden / Joy will be found / The sound of singing / Listen/(Here / Hear?)/Speedily / My salvation, my arm / Islands wait in hope / (Hear / Here me)/You people / Do not fear / Insults / Eat / Devour / Righteousness / Generations / Wake / Arm / Dragon / Singing / (Flee / Flea?) / Away / You fear / Live in constant terror / Soon set free / Will not die / Lack bread / I am / The waves' roar / The Lord

    Wake / Wrath / Stagger / Bore / Calamities / Destruction / Famine / Sword / Wrath / Afflicted / Drunk / Stagger / Wrath / Tormentors

The speakers paused.
. . . Ezek—(Ezequiel) Twen—(Veinte-uno)—
Jeff tried to write down what he could understand. Jeff was tired, the only English he caught thereafter:

Groans / Sword / Cut / Sword / Melt / Weak / Sword, Sword / Sharp / Sharp / Slaughter . . . Roads / Swords . . .

As the program ended, Tom Bodett retold the wonders of the Motel 6. They drove until they saw a sign for one near El Reno, checked in, borrowed an ancient Rand McNally at the front desk, and entered their room. Jeff had decided that they would take I-40 to Barstow, California, I-15 south to I-10, and I-10 all the way to the water where they could realize their plan.

Jeff looked at mutt, who was looking at a dusty mirror. Jeff approached and stood behind him. "There's a boy in there who wants to know why we're here." No answer.

They watched *Gilligan's Island* on the wood-paneled TV.

They'd leave in the morning and build a raft along the way.

mutt had tied the strings of his hooded sweatshirt into a bow on top of his head.

Water

When they reached the water near Santa Monica two days later, Jeff parked in a garage on 2nd and Colorado Avenue very near the beach. He and mutt took their gear to the water. Jeff lined up the logs (stolen from a construction site outside Winslow, Arizona) he'd cut with an axe (found in the backseat of the MG) and tied them into place with rope (purchased at a hardware shop in Needles, California). He and mutt got some seaweed and brush that had drifted ashore and loaded their luggage (the Indian blanket-rugs and cassettes) and pushed off into the Pacific.

Adrift

The waves broke and yawned for two years. The two boys had set sail for the Island of Unfit Toys or whatever. One returned. mutt is ghost and dust now, a friend to the Spotted Elephant. Safe from the Plastic Dinosaurs. Jeff and mutt talk often, though miles apart. Sometimes Jeff tunes into 106.7 FM, but he's never heard the gospel. If he does he'll be ready. Jeff and mutt traveled together for years in the 1980s. Now they live apart. They have lived in this way for some time now. The two still have plans to be together one day.

SALIVA
by Melissa Musser

No more than the decaying, flesh-colored ball of gum wedged in between the seats on the bus.

No worth. No more than the lipstick stains, on the cigarette castaways floating in the sewer water, that your shoe soles carelessly crush on the way to your day job. Discarded.

I know only one way and only one worth, and I am rewarded with carelessly crumpled bills thrown in my face.

The body has always betrayed me
since the day I turned thirteen
and my chest painfully swelled against the acrylic fabric of my school uniform.

I have learned the looks,
the eye,
the language of the cock-to-cunt ratio.
I learn that my words are only stealthy, cold negotiations for these men.

Look at me. Standing on the train platform.

In between the train tracks, on the asphalt pulpit, I summon it before me. I recall the red stockings, severed heels, the fear and the forgiveness sought upon that rainy night, creaky orange ray-bursts flaming in my irises and steaming breath into the autumn air.

"I'm sorry." My voice barely cracks, whispers into the night.

MP3 wires harden in the cold.
Wisps of rain form like tears inside my glasses.
This is it.
I'm stepping on.
I'm getting on this train.
I have a plan.
I know what I'm doing.
I assure my reflection into the night of my worthlessness.
What am I, Her, about to do.

Thumbs pressed into my velvet double-breasted jacket. Thumbs caressing and pressing into palms. Fingernails gliding on my teeth. Any food.
Inspection for any pieces of my innocent salad leaves stuck between my incisors.

"Haha! Look at yourself. Fucking . . . Don't fucking cry around me. I would take you. You know. Jesus. I love you. I would go, but you know I can't fucking take you . . . No. Sure, I mean, I know. Totally. I understand."

    I've got my hands on the steering wheel. Feathers flying on the rearview mirror and Jane's Addiction on the stereo.

And then later at the graveyard. Slobby, fake, pretentious blowjobs.

He says, "Bite it."

My movements, my hands and body, pause.

"Bite it? Bite?"

"Bite it. Hard."

In the corner of my vision I see his neck retreat. The muscles relax and his head is against the chair rest.

That fucking ugly old Buick. Goddamned beer-stained backseat.

The kiss outside the garage in the middle of winter. Our mittened hands held tight and the cold Michigan winter air, our twin sister.

I sit on my bike in the abandoned lot behind your house when it's dark out and grind against the seat, masturbating while watching you eat dinner with your family, and come right as you leave the room and open the door to your upstairs bedroom.

After, I walk closer and throw pennies at your window. You acknowledge me and: *The Basement*, you mouth, pointing toward the floor.

When I reach the window you are on the other side. Toothy motherfucking grin. My hundred-pound frame slips easily through the slitted basement windows but scrapes my lower back. You kiss my hand.

"Kiss Mr. Magoo!" you giggle. "You want to hear the new song?" You sit down behind his drum set.

"Fuck, is that blood?" I say, gesturing to the spots on the snare. He opens wide and laughs. I guess it's an old joke. I sit down cross-legged, unzip my sweatshirt, and listen.

Greasy fingerprints smeared on the furiously used mobile phone.

Deals.

Exchanges.

Of goods.

I review where I'm going. What's this guy's name. What's this guy look like.

The landscape flurries away. The wind is devouring this machine, where am I.

I slip on my headphones. Put the music on. It acts like the glue of cohesion, it pulls me into a fantasy world of unbreeched logic, a cartoon, a sketch, a magazine article, a music video, whatever it is not happening to me.

When I get to the club I go into the bathroom.

No one knows where I am.

What I'm about to do.

My own adrenaline yields its drunken amphibian-like effect into my jawline, sliding down the back of my throat, leaving my tongue thick and paralyzed.

It's time to go out, he's going to be there soon. I make note of the parties around me.

A group of girls. Out for the night.

Round saucers birthing fragrant teas.

Black denim stocky male legs crossed, waiting for his date to come back from the bar.

Against my thigh my phone vibrates. He's here. Somewhere.

And he is. He's behind me. I see his form emerge first from the shadow outside the club's dark window. He sits down and surveys me, calculates, stares into my pupils, categorizes my breasts, opens his palms, and gazes upwards.

"Well, you're pretty." Smug.

"Hmm. You look . . . sour today."

"I've had some sad days."

"Anything you want to do is fine."

"I guess I feel let down."

"Let down? Why?"

"I don't know why, it's just a feeling."

"Well, because in these two years I've known you, I don't think you've ever seen me as real. That I don't have an inside . . . You don't believe I exist once we part ways. That makes me kind of sad."

"You know, earlier I would come home with these headaches. Really bad headaches. Imagine . . . And then I came home . . . maybe mowed the lawn, met my brother . . . It was so surreal. It didn't seem right. But then . . . don't I deserve to be able to come home and . . . do something else? To be with my . . . family, or whatever?"

"Do you think that I haven't wanted to make an exception?"

"Yes."

"Of course I have. But if I did . . . I couldn't live my life. My life would be ruined."

"That's my nightmare, that is not what I want to happen, for your life to be ruined."

"It's awful."

"Yes. It's awful."

"Sometimes I get so mad at you. It's so hard. I hate you."

"I just feel so worthless even saying this. My words are just floating away like clouds, what do they do?"

"Why do you love me?"

"When I'm with you I feel safe, I feel good about myself, I feel comfortable . . . You aren't going to judge me. Even if we got angry at each other . . . you wouldn't be, uh . . . ummmm . . . a tyrant. Like you wouldn't terrorize me.

You . . . When I met you I think that you touched something inside me. It was so deep inside . . . I'm trying to figure it out. I can't just let it go. I can't let you go. It's awful. I don't know how to explain it."

"You want a piece of me."

"Does anyone have a piece of you, though?"

And then a sliver up my nose and piercing my brain. I take over, my smart business attire, long hair, shapely legs. They will reveal the intelligence within, they will come alive like a dancing train, take over this altar of terror, put me away in a suitcase and a magic carpet.

Laughs.

Uncertainty.

He leads me away in a strange manner, his tall, long self insinuating like a shadow upon me, irritable. Wearing a business jacket, suit and tie, black shoes.

"I've been in fucking meetings all day!" he remarks in a laugh that sounds more like a long bronchitis cough. His mouth moves in flutters and words trail out like invisible smoke, and his exaggerated hand gestures indicate his importance in his own eyes.

The taxi seems to float. He doesn't sit near. I look out the window. Strikes of the piano wire are echoing outside the window, I can hear it, I'm so sure, buried in these dirty autumn leaves.

This hotel, we arrive. The hallways open up in long lolling tongues, incandescent chandeliers that fade away, Persian carpets with tread marks, allowing for a soundless descent down the wide staircase. Inside, it's just a long hallway, a corridor, a hospital, door after door, twins, metal, long mirrors, reflections and light bouncing in this stale city.

The door doesn't open, I end up on the other side, somehow, I'm in a boat, it's rocking, it flips over and I slip underneath the surface, sucked into the drain. I'm invited to sit.

"Here. You . . . uh, want something? To drink?"

Pats an uncomfortably U-shaped darkly upholstered chair for me. I sit down. My feet suddenly hurt. Suddenly it seems like I could be in a family living room with the walls sawed off, the world watching my charity, my happy family, gathered round the television for a good-natured late-night game show.

But his size, he has grown, and he hovers over me like a long praying mantis. In the first second, his warmth penetrates through to me. I feel warmed by the contact and when his slimy tongue flits around my neck and ear I sense my body uncoil. My mouth and lips relax and my arms slide to my sides. His hands are large and he is gentle. He bites a little, and crashing waves echo in my ears, his slobbery tongue darting in and out of canals.

Yes, alone in this world and fallen into your diseased, uncalloused hands. You will pay for me and pay for the diversion.

It's the news on the television. It's echoing in the background. His mouth is my sewer, I am draining my saliva into his arteries, into his lungs, into his intestines.

"You need to take a shower." I look up, confused. My eyes refocus. My eyes are dry, I blink. I feel some black dust settle into the corner of my eye, reaching up to flick it away, he grips my wrist.

I get up. My top is sitting like a black inner tube around my torso. One red stocking and some ratty black shoes.

"Come on, come here," he chuckles. "I like your tits," his mouth upturned in his own amusement as he squeezes my nipples tightly between sharp fingernails.

Suddenly he rustles upwards. Motions.

"Come on, you have to get a shower. Go in, get in."

"I can turn it on myself," I say remotely, and his arm raises, preventing my entry.

He turns on the water and pushes me forward. It's hot but I can't feel anything, my adrenaline and faraway consciousness prevent it.

"Open your mouth."

I open and lower myself to the floor of the shower, but he pulls me back up by my hair.

"Open it, hold it open under the water. Don't move. Yeah. Like that, hold on, okay, open wider."

I think it was a glimmer of confusion slipping across my irises.

He sees, and reaches down to my ass and starts fingering it before he suddenly shoves three fingers in. I feel his fingernails scratching my anus, and in my surprise the water filling my throat constricts and water splashes into my windpipes, I gasp through my nose.

"Niiiiccccce. Nice and tight," breathing in my ear.

A disgusting fool, your predatory suction discs, your fingers, curling around my pain receptors like tentacles of an octopus.

"Hey," he laughs outwardly, "come on, relax, Jesus . . . paid for . . . you're going to get paid for . . . nnnnnnn . . . huh.huh.huh." His breath like rubble. It's blowing over the rocks, bursting into intervals, unwinding.

The force of his hand rocks me unsteadily. Upon my feet. Puddling around me, the water unknowing seeps back into the earth.

Are my eyes closed? I didn't notice. I didn't know. When I stiffen, when the blood has flowed and expanded my hole wider. Am I tolerating it.

"Turn around . . ." His open hand firmly reaches to my shoulder, fingers slipping into my clavicle, resting there and pushing me down to my knees.

Falsely affable, upturned lips in pornographic grimace, and offers up his cock.

My kneecaps slip in and strain against the tile. Pressure.

"Open wide . . . wait . . ."

He retreats.

When he's back he's holding . . . I see, oh. Ah. He's got a gag, his sausage fingers probing in my mouth and settling onto my teeth. *Chink. Chink.* His pinky treads my tonsils, my throat retreats and trembles threatening to cough. Gets the hotel soap in its paper container. Water is in my eyes and I can't see.

He turns it off.

"C'mere. Get out. Go, uh . . . Here, stand on this towel . . . now get down, yeah."

I wipe my eyes on my arm, and as my head swivels upwards, long, twisting, serpentine, the shock of the soap shoved into my mouth, molars grazing the corners and acrid sour, my tongue rebels.

"*Fffth. Fhhh . . .*" is my verbal response, blurred vision looking up to him.

Are the birds singing now? Is the sun shining into my eyes? Burning my retinas, and I see the figure looming over me as I feel bubbles formed by my saliva slip over my tongue guided by drool pooling in my mouth steadily flowing like a sieve.

His laughter is beat for beat. His hands pushing it in.

And out. The stainless steel gag slips to the right. He pushes it back and steadies it with his hand.

"Clean you up . . . hmm," he crackles.

The air mingles with the steam from the shower. The coldness invades my pores and betrays me. I shiver. Inadvertent, quietly. Holding it somewhere inside as my chest heaves and the tastes fall like tears from my cheeks.

I hear a distant phone ringing.

"What are you thinking about?" His voice forms the words, a sarcasm blowjob.

"*Uhh. Nnn.*" My tongue fishes around dead in my mouth, he reaches for a towel and removes the gag.

"What did you say, honey?"

I look down.

"No, I . . . Not really. I was just feeling a bit weird. The taste, uh . . . I just, I haven't really eaten that much today."

Studies me.

"Want some food?"

His tone makes me feel strange. As if I stand on the edge of a concrete diving board and my nose is dangerously close to being smashed on the edge as I plummet down.

"Do some."

He shoves it at me. White powder.

"Oh, uh, no, that's—"

"It wasn't a question."

I look up. My eyes assess him. My heart fills up with blood, my heart distributes the blood evenly throughout my body, I feel the oxygen clearing my lungs.

No, nothing was ever a promise.

Unromantically, messily, I inhale it through my nostrils, a sharp sting as it mingles and slides down the back of my throat. The chemicals absorb into the soft tissue of my nose, and like a merciless razor cut through my sinuses and freeze my brain.

You. Hello. My solar system. I. Blood vessel. Constrict. The warmth flies like a bird's wing to my forehead in dry sweat. My chest beats. Vibrates. My hands.

He pushes me down on the bed. My nose pressed against the silky lie of polyester bedcovers.

Thread count two thousand million hundred two.

Slipping.

My legs are flung like a scissor operation.

Only I can sense the cold air brush against my thighs, only I can see nothing but a wooden board supported against the yellow wall. His burning cock rips me open ruthless and slams into my center, as my body slowly ambles, crawls, further up the bed.

Further.

"You. Fuck. Fuhhh," he breathes his words over the air. A hand.

Air rushes by and suddenly I feel a jarring inside my ear as things begin to buzz and then an electric shock drizzles like small sparks from my eardrum to my jaw. My head shakes.

Again, and this time I feel a heavier.

Drug.

His hand.

It's up in the air. The eagle's wing, up there and then *whoosh* like some bad boy's Jeep lights into my head.

The first blow I feel nothing. And then I feel the car, your insurmountable vehicle, edged fist as it meets my temporal bone, I hear the twinkling like stars falling from the sky. Ticking like an alarm, I'm your leather-spoked wheel, hydroplaning into the distance, there's a blackness nothing can illuminate.

Ethmoid.
Lacrimal bone.
Nasal concha.
Parietal bone.
Fuck. Fucking. And slipping into.

THE BEDSIDE TABLE
by Callum James

Everything is ready for you. The cigarettes you won't buy but smoke because they tighten your expression into urban prose and gravel-up your milk voice. The glasses that you left behind last time, waiting, balanced like a bird beside the bed: clear eyes and thin legs like you. The chewing gum, the condoms and the cream, the tissues, and the crusty towel. And even now the metal smell of your first burning, the air you molded into curves with spinal twists and bony claws is waiting for you . . . the whole room is waiting for you.

All day, from the window, I've been watching boys on wheels (boards and blades) on the hard court backing the beach. Boys with blades for hips that barely hold the jeans above the V. Boys with coffee, walnut, rosewood tans of indolence and swollen nipples that cry out, *Ripe! Ripe!*—and puberty is hanging like a wire mesh around the ramps and dips and shoulder blades and cracks of bone.

The room smells fresh like clean sheets; I've had the windows wide all day, and once the evening touched cool fingers against the curtains and turned them into moonlit sails, suddenly it was possible to breathe again in here.

Midnight came—three observations: a gull wheeling in the purple-black, blocking out stars with twelve long wing beats; the Somali lad across the road on his fire escape peeling an orange—citrus coming through the window; a can in the alley rolling, lazy, back and forth, sounding like strange music.

You taught me that, you taught me to stop and stand still, to listen and smell and watch details closely; you taught me how to tell if a distant siren is coming nearer or moving away, how to hear if it's a cat or a rat in the bushes. It was your gift, you looked at people so hard they felt it, even from behind.

When we met in the club, I had sore eyes and the metal taste of not enough sleep in my mouth. By the time we were back here, lying behind where I'm standing now at the window (but I won't turn because I want to do it from memory), my first taste of you was a wet tongue—dry-ice-and-vodka breath—and we slumped like driftwood, bleached limbs in the moon-square that fell on the bed and quartered us. White-naked on white sheets we talked for hours, like we should have talked at school but never did.

It was you who remembered me at school, that's why you came back with me, I think: a crush on the boy in the year above. But you remembered everyone. You remembered how Clare had a thin white scar under her chin from some operation that caused kids to go silent when she talked about it (and I decided then not to mention the lines on your arms). You remembered Danny, "You know, the one who was always flicking his hair out of his eyes." You remembered it was *banana* Mickey wrote on the crotch of his jeans with marker pen that got him in trouble. You remembered everyone. I could barely think of their names. Is that the cost of observing everyone else so closely, you disappear yourself?—I never noticed you at school.

So that first night we lay close-up and talked, so close

you had alien eyes with silver dots at the corners: so close I was never sure if it was your breath or your fingers tickling my face.

The windows were open that night too, and it was raining, a fine drizzle, but it was warm, and for a while we sat twisted into each other, the thin bones of your back against my chest, and we just watched the rain fall. I've been doing this all day, while I've been waiting, letting these tiny pieces of memory come, no more, I suppose, than sparks and pulses of chemicals in my head. And every time something comes back to me I feel a little more insubstantial, a little more transparent.

Handing me a blue pill and then a white one—when was this? a week after we met?—you said, "I want to show you something, this is the last time . . ." You were kneeling on the bed across from me. I took the pills and you had some blades, the old-fashioned ones in a plastic case, and you could open the packet and get a razor out with one hand. When you drew that steel—thin as hair—across the back of your arm, your eyes were all black and the silver had gone. The blood came slowly. Still thin and pale as paper, but you were more real then, with those filaments of red, than you had ever been. While I watched you cutting I saw something give and loosen inside, like that moment when I'm entering you and flesh becomes hot paste: a sudden softening. My hand tracked down, pushed into my briefs, and squeezed hard. It might have taken five minutes; it might have been an hour, three feet apart on the bed, kneeling. And then there was blood and sperm on the sheets. You cut; I came. Red on white; white on white.

After that I never saw fresh scabs. Maybe it was the last time you cut the backs of your arms.

Once when you were in the shower I went through your bag and found your notebooks. Seeing it written down made all those things you noticed but never talked about become absolutely real. They were the chemicals and pulses in your head made into ink and paper.

I read: *the park, three mesh bins dented and asymmetrical, an old woman—parka jacket, done up to leave her face only a scratch of lines in a fur-trim oval—a kid crying with a snot balloon in his nose that inflates and deflates like gum as he screams—no sign of Mum—a robin without a red breast, a female? and a wren and a wagtail . . .*

I read: *my brother's prick: thick as my wrist and heavy like sausage meat. Hood slipped halfway back all the time. Thin skin, translucent, blue veins on cream. Head—plum—tight—bloom like plum too. Hot to the touch. Smell of warm biscuits. Taste: those thin slices of ham in plastic packs. Bucks like hose when . . .*

I read: *on the bedside table: cigarettes, condoms, glasses (mine), chewing gum, cream, tissues, glass of stale water with bubbles, paperback laid open—looks like bird with broken wing. Smells of metal in here . . .* (The book was a thesaurus, I remember the cheap feel of the pages.)

I guess reading your notebook I found out things about you that were both beautiful and broken. What makes me sad, though, is now I realize that the more I read, the less you were in my mind—the sound of water coming from down the hall—you were fading into the hot steam of the shower. You made things vivid for me.

In the summer we sat on that hard court too. Always on the edge and I could see your eyes were never still. You were quiet, everyone said so but no one minded. Everything there was bony and fresh-baked, it was a place of skin and sweat, all the skin was thin, shiny, and supple as plastic. Everything except you. Even in high summer you were a winter-bound tree ice-brittle and fading to white, only your eyes moved: an owl in your own branches. Almost naked, you'd lie in the sun with your head on my knee and no one minded. No one noticed you much. Those curves and arches, the arcs of flashing tan in the air, the water-bottle sprays from drenched hair, the sudden clench and claw of sinew: It was a language of shapes that you learned and spoke, but only in this room. You spoke it with your body under mine twisting. You looked so fragile, so breakable, in fact you were tough as cable.

From your notebooks I learned why we never hung out at your place. I learned that your mum was Catholic, that your house was a cross between medieval grotto and shopping mall with its religious tat and trinkets and fairy lights around the third-class relic of Padre Pio, that Jesus' Sacred Heart stared at you when you went to sleep, and that the first time you cut, it was because you got the idea from that bloody statue and you incised a diamond shape around your left nipple.

On your eighteenth birthday I suggested we have our own little party at the club. So we mentioned it to everyone you knew—and in the process I realized they were all just people you knew, not friends. And no one came. You made so little impact on people, you touched the world so lightly that, not from malice, no one thought to make a moment of your birthday. The club was packed, but in the end it was only you and me. The saddest thing that night was the heaviness in your eyes, like you might have cried about it except that everything good was behind you.

Everything is ready for you . . .

I know you're never coming. It was no surprise that last night you took the razor blades to the other side of your arms, under the Sacred Heart and the fairy lights, and I would bet the rest of my life that while the blood flowed you lost yourself in its shapes and color and thickness until there was nothing behind your eyes left to look with.

The glasses that you left behind last time . . .

So I have been watching from the window, doing what you taught me to do. Tricking my head into believing you are lying there, behind me. And you taught me well: If I raise my hand and trace a shape, I can really feel the fine hairs and bony curve of your shoulder in the air. But the more I bring you back—the mole on your knee, the two thumb-press dimples where your spine trails off and soft mounds rise, the stray blond hairs in your dark eyebrows that always catch the light—the more I bring you back, the more I feel myself slipping away.

The chewing gum, the condoms and the cream . . .

Tonight I'm happy to fade out like this, to cease to be. But tomorrow I will stop looking so closely at the world, because, unlike you, I understand it's a dangerous thing to do.

OUT OF CONTROL
by Charlie Quiroz

During the daytime, we kept the windows open as we were driving. Once the sun set, we would close them, would get too cold with them open.

That was part of the reason. Coldness is not too far from loneliness, though. And with the sun up we could see what was out there. Trees on the side of the road were distinctly visible, buildings as well, the lines of crops, scattered cattle immobile. At night, though, man. Things just seem vaster, more desolate in those moments. There are fewer cars on the road, sometimes none, and if you don't draw up some lines, put those windows up, where you are just seems a little too big, a little too lonely, an asteroid hurling through the universe. You don't seem like you are anywhere; windows sealed, you're in the car, contained within a space you know the boundaries of. With them up, I always felt safer, the light from the radio dial, soft green glow, making her one arm casually holding the wheel just barely visible. The two of us were closer together this way, us against the night.

I don't think we spent that much time driving places, but so many of my memories of her, the most comfortable ones, are those. This one time, we were driving—she was, I was riding shotgun—and we were coming home from a concert in Gainesville, making the four-hour trip back, just enough conversation to keep the both of us awake, the words coming in small ripples, the radio on quietly almost in deference to the night.

Every so often we would pass a Taco Bell, or a sign saying there was one at the next exit or three down the road. This, more often than not, would lead to a conversation about either our love of Taco Bell or our guilt about loving it. Usually, the both of them. We would preamble our love with a declaration of our guilt. *I know I shouldn't love it, but. I know it's wrong, but. Don't tell Rebecca, but.* Rebecca was actively campaigning against the place with a group of migrant workers. We would talk about our favorite items on the menu, ask each other which our favorite was, even though both of us knew the answer, both of us liked the same thing.

That conversation would trail off into silence, slowly, like conversation at bedtime. At holidays when I was younger, my cousins and I would all be forced into sleeping bags on the floor of the living room. It was the same sort of conversation. Something dreamy and lazy about it, enabled by the inability to see the other person's face, or for them to see yours. Head on your pillow, trying to sleep, looking up at the dark ceiling, trading stories about friends, imaginary girlfriends, talking and talking, on and off. And just when you think it has ended, that the other person is asleep, they will say something else. It gets more and more spaced out, the comments, the replies.

Things become more confessional, more organic this way. She faced the road illuminated by the headlights, and would say something looking in that direction, but said to me, next to her. And I would be looking out my window, trying to see stuff beyond the faintest reflection of my own face, to see what was going on in the night, trying to imagine what I was going to do with any of it.

Occasionally we would talk about this, about life, and what our plans were, what our pasts were, our fucked-up families and such. Put together long enough, you'll eventually start to talk about things not normally talked about. Surely, why these car trips stick out in my mind so clearly. You can't make jokes about fast food and pop songs for the whole car ride; those are broken up with contemplative silences and remarks born from those silences, telling a story about your father, trying to put into words the memory that just had ahold of you.

"This one time, God, sometime in elementary school, we had these anthills all over our front lawn. Mounds and mounds of these anthills. Everywhere you looked. And I don't know what provoked my dad one weekend to decide he had to destroy them. First, I remember, he brought out the hose from around the backyard and shoved that down into the mounds. I don't know what he was thinking. And man, those ants got pissed off, and this did absolutely nothing except aggravate the ants even worse, of course.

"We had an apple tree in our front yard at that house. I am sure that's probably why we had so many ants. We never picked up those apples either. I hated that chore. There were always bees hovering, and so we always just left all these rotting apples on the lawn. Yeah, that's definitely why we had so many ants.

"Anyway, so yeah, fucking hose did nothing. So then my dad got the thing of gas that we used for the lawnmower and started to pour that down the holes. These mounds were huge. Like three giant mounds that were taking over our lawn. And he lit these fucking ant mounds on fire. And a couple of neighbors came out to see what was going on, and the guy who lived next door joked, *So you're having a barbecue?*

"I'm still trying to imagine what provoked my dad to this. Sorry, I don't know why that just popped into my head either, why I am remembering that."

And she giggled uncontrollably, holding her finger right under her nose. She always did this when she laughed, as if milk was going to come shooting out of it otherwise. And I laughed too.

"O.O.C.," she said.

The laughter was short. As it faded, I became more focused on the radio, on whatever it had to say, having said whatever it was I had to say. Had it been a song that either of us liked, we may have sung along with it, or at least let its noise justify our lack thereof. But it was a bland song, which we refused to let dominate our lives for even the short three-minute duration of it. A few bars into it, realizing what song it was, she started in with a story about her father.

"In the winter, my dad would never turn on the heat. He would never turn it on. And my sister and I would always beg him to. We would be totally freezing, shivering, and he still wouldn't turn it on. He would say that it wasn't cold and that we just needed to put on another sweater, but he was so cheap. Who doesn't turn on the heat in the winter?"

"But you grew up in Georgia! How cold could it possibly have gotten?"

"Whatever! Georgia gets cold. You don't know. It's snowed a few times. It gets cold everywhere in the winter. We were shivering and he would never turn on the heat, no matter how much we complained."

"In Georgia?"

"Serious. It would get so cold."

She drew out that word, *cold*, so long, so long that the

signifier ended up evoking the signified, and a chill suddenly filled the car. She rubbed her arms together. I did the same, believing her.

    I pressed the button by my arm, making sure that the window was rolled up as far as it would go. I let my attention be absorbed by the passing trees on the side of the road, by the businesses and houses clustered near the exits, their lights visible just slightly from the road. And I thought about my own house growing up, surely visible to someone on some road, and how my mom was also stingy with the thermostat. We were heading back to one home and trying to get back to others, telling these stories every so often, trying to invoke these past lives like the cold she somehow brought into the car by talking about it, telling these things, wanting them to reappear, wanting them to still be able to do so.

COMMAND PSYCHOLOGY
by Josh Feola

Throw everything into your mouth, wear patches of all you've ever done and embroider fifty out of 512 friends' comments onto your sleeve. From your bed pretend. Make pretend plans with pretend friends. Pretend rock, pretend sing songs in keys of kitsch and irony. Live in a pink punk bubble floating above your head. Go get around. Pour more and more into your open maw until your brain must reconsider what normal conditions are. Keep pretending. Every night, until you are doing nothing if you're not pretending. Have fun in fat times. Run a hoop along your waist, sunglass smiling cokebottle love. Roll in the sand. Shave your hair into cute shapes.

    Learn how to write. Just learn how to write—I don't care what it *is*, just learn how to write. Know more than you let on. Memorize up to seven hundred digits immediately. Tell me about prosody and pertinence. Tell me about twentieth-century fiction masters. Tell me if you're getting off. Do you like the way that feels?

    Don't you like the way that feels in your mouth?? Rolling around in its natural juices, your face is smiling. Your brain's shooting bolts that say *more more more*. At the same time it's saying *faster faster*. There is a small voice that's muted in the fray coming from somewhere in the space between your head and your heart, from an island in a lake. *Is he looking at me . . . ?*

Elegant circles, not quite infinite since terminating but ever-growing, add you among their numbers. Are you loving it?

THE UNKNOWN BECOMING LOUDER AND LOUDER

There is no enemy if you must see to believe. That is the invaluable source of power for all things invisible. The rock, when peered beneath, becomes an insidious obstacle rather than a pleasant intermediary between the known and the unknown. It helps never to personify the various forces you perceive to impede your set path; leave them forces, natural but not insurmountable barriers to progress. You are born and then you die, all within a compact hundred-mile radius. This is the fact, despite heretical claims to the contrary. Stay skeptical. Never dare to drop your guard, never be so rash as to assume this or any other thing has been afforded you by your own efforts as much as by the will of some monolithic mover. You have at times felt enmeshed. You've been until now on the surface, disregarded and overlooked, and you've managed some contentment with that fact, the same contentment holding all things in their proper places, the invisible lines keeping the surface from suddenly moving. All is maintenance. You say you're motivated by Truth, an abstract concept clashing with the vainglorious half-truths peddled in the smiles and gestures of each new person you meet. But your own idea of truth is an invidious lie. You begin to see. You feel the thin electrical and magnetic waves holding things in their proper locations, keeping the machine running smoothly—in a significant way, directing the course of the universe as each day unfolds on the rigid schedule of indomitable time. Your ear is on the ground.

SIXTEEN
by Robert Siek

Allison is nineteen. I've only known her for three weeks. She started working as a fellow sales associate with me at Cignal about a month ago. Her boyfriend Daniel also works there; I went out last week with him and his friend Brad to the Building. I liked it so much I'm on my way there again. I only turned sixteen like a month and a half before I got the job at Cignal. I didn't want to make photocopies at the office that my mother works at anymore. Since I was twelve, I've wanted to work at Cignal; they have the most stylish clothes, which are also the most expensive in Paramus Park Mall.

Allison parks at the $5.00-to-park-all-night lot across the street from the Building. I think it's the corner of 25th Street and Sixth Avenue. I've been coming into Manhattan by train or bus since I was fourteen, but my friends and I always hang out around St. Marks Place in the Village. Allison was drinking straight Southern Comfort while driving us into the city. I took a few slugs from the bottle in the backseat; Bethany came along too, and she also had a few shots. We didn't have a chaser so I thought I was going to puke up the whiskey a few times. It was like sticking your finger in your throat and then holding back the vomit, like some game to see who would gag beyond the point of throwing up first. Bethany is in the grade above me at Waldwick High. We started partying together when I was a freshman. The first time I got shitfaced drunk was with her and her friends. Daniel sat in the passenger seat, up front with Allison. He's like two years younger than her, but they seem to get along well. He smokes a lot of weed. He also deejays. He knows the deejay at the Building, the one who spins on Friday nights. It's an industrial/goth party called Censored. Some guy called Keoki throws the party. I think Daniel said that the deejay's name is Slave. After Allison drank the last bit of Southern Comfort, she threw the bottle out the window while driving down the Henry Hudson Parkway. I was heavily buzzing so I wasn't too concerned about her killing us in a drunk driving accident or anything like that.

So we cross the street, and I notice a small line of people waiting to get inside the Building. The door guy who also seems to know Allison and Daniel is wearing a tight white T-shirt and a pair of black vinyl hot pants, or very short shorts. I stare at his legs, which are muscular and hairy like my old gymnastics coach's legs. I used to watch him change in the locker room. His name was Gene, and I especially remember his brown cotton bikini briefs. I always wanted to rub my face against his thigh and upper leg. His skin was so tan and soft looking. The door guy's legs are much paler but just as muscular, maybe even more so. He's shorter than Gene and has broader shoulders. His hair looks black, but it's shaved like a quarter-inch all over his head. He also has a black goatee and is wearing black fourteen-hole Doc Marten combat boots. When we approach the rope in front of the doorway, I begin to feel motion in my stomach. I think about how much I hated going through puberty earlier than most of my classmates in grammar school and how I wished I hadn't grown almost six feet tall by the time I was twelve years old. I had to quit gymnastics because I was already too big to become a professional gymnast. The coaches couldn't spot me anymore; I was too heavy on the high bar and the rings.

The door guy hands four tickets to Daniel, and Bethany is smiling like she's posing for a photograph. She's wearing this lipstick called Vamp—it looks like the color of red wine. I put on black lipstick for the evening, and my hair is teased in wild, loose spikes with pieces of my bangs hanging in my face. It is the closest version possible to matching Robert Smith's hair, the lead singer of The Cure. I am obsessed with him and with The Cure's music. Their darker, more depressing songs are the ones I like best. In the past few months I've been getting more into this industrial music that seems to be popular in the New York underground scene. My favorite industrial bands are Ministry and Skinny Puppy. It's like '80s techno-pop and hardcore punk mixed together, at times overly digital but always disturbing and loud. The song lyrics are shouted or distorted through electronic devices, and they usually have something to do with destruction, death, acid rain, nuclear meltdowns, shooting up drugs, and other things like that. The Building is the best club to go to in order to dance your ass off to the latest industrial sounds. I feel like I'm on the cutting edge, better than the people I go to high school with, especially the ones in the honors classes with me. It's 1990, and I still have two years left of high school. I realize that I need to go out more often.

The door guy smiles at me as we walk through the opening he makes by moving the velvet rope, and Daniel hands each of us a ticket. I look back when we reach the end of the entrance lobby, and the door guy is still watching me, still smiling like he was trying not to laugh about something secret and funny at the same time. I smile back at him before turning the corner, as though he used mental telepathy to pass the hidden joke along. I guess I got it, or something. My stomach is flipping inside, like digesting tumblers, a whole circus act inside my tummy. I feel relieved that I wasn't asked for ID. I ask Allison what the age is to get into the Building, eighteen or twenty-one?

"I don't know. Does it matter?"

"I guess not. They never seem to ask for ID."

"Isn't it great? Let's get upstairs to the VIP room. It's still open bar up there."

Bethany is wearing a black full-length dress. It's stretchy looking, with long sleeves and a V-neck cut. Her boobs and hips are overly emphasized in this dress; you wouldn't think she's seventeen. Her hair is naturally wavy, like a partially washed-out perm, and it's all shaved underneath and cropped in a bob style. She has a wedge cut in the back—it's trimmed high up and then angles down to chin-length in the front.

I'm also in all black, but I'm wearing shorts that hang at my knees, shredded where I cut off the pant legs. I have an oversized black button-down on, buttoned from neck to waist, and I wear it out, never tucked in. It's how Robert Smith wears his button-down shirts. I have ten-hole Doc Marten boots on with steel toes. More than half of the crowd is wearing black and Doc Marten shoes or combat boots. Allison has high heels on, and she's wearing a new pair of sheer wide-leg pants. She has opaque black leggings on underneath; she's not into baring skin. Her top looks like a tight blazer, almost like a hip-length rain jacket. She usually wears her long blond hair in a bun with chopsticks or a ribbon, but tonight it's hanging free down to the middle of her back. It's blown back away from her face, like she hair-sprayed it while standing in front of a super-power fan. Daniel is dressed the least severe of the group; he's in a black turtleneck shirt and charcoal-gray baggy pants. His hair is thick and slicked back on top. He shaves it around the sides and back. Allison probably shaves it for him when it starts growing in.

A Nitzer Ebb song is shaking the brick walls around the dance floor. We're climbing a metal spiral staircase past the second-floor balcony that extends around the entire club, where people can sit on benches or watch dancers below over the railing. It looks like a closed warehouse inside or a cleared-out factory. The walls are just piles of bricks that appear to be stacked sky high into the painted black ceiling that seems like a black hole floating twelve stories above. There were probably floors and apartments in here at some point in time, but it was all torn out, like an abandoned crack house in the Lower East Side or a place where the punk squatters on St. Marks would sleep. We climb more steps to the third floor that's made up of a bar and a studio apartment–sized balcony with a few tables and couches. More than half of the balcony is crowded with shouting club-goers reaching their arms toward the start of another spiral staircase at the opposite side of the bar. This woman named Vanessa who I met the previous week is standing on the third or fourth step behind a velvet rope. She works at the Building. I don't really know what she does, but I guess one of her jobs is to guard the VIP room on the fourth floor—the top floor. Her hair is blacker than my clothes, and her lips look like wet red plastic. She's wearing a vinyl corset and miniskirt. Her tits are bare and hanging over the top of the corset. I notice black tape in X-shapes placed over her nipples. Daniel tells me that we need to get Vanessa's attention. "Let's fight through this fucking crowd. Open bar is only for another half an hour."

We charge into the mess of people, like entering a packed subway car—saying excuse me never helps (it's all about pushing and using your elbows). Bethany holds my hips, her fingers tightening like clothespins on a laundry line; I can tell that she doesn't want to be separated from the rest of us. I recall being eight or nine years old on some street in Manhattan on a below-zero November Thursday morning, trying to see the Ronald McDonald balloon at the Macy's Thanksgiving Day parade. I gripped my Aunt Donna's hand, surrounded by adults, waist level to walls of strangers—I began breathing hard. My Uncle Frank said, "Don't let go of our hands." He had my cousin's hand, their son Bobby. My brother must have been fourteen at the time so he didn't have to hold a grown-up's hand. I was more afraid of suffocating between the bodies pressing against me from all sides than the thought of getting lost in Manhattan. I could shake paper cups on corners like the homeless people; I just didn't want to be crushed.

I see Daniel whispering in Vanessa's ear, and Allison is on the step below him. The three of them look like statues positioned on pedestals of varying heights, like winners at the Olympics standing silent during the national anthem of the gold medalist. I drag Bethany closer to the bottom step while waving stretched arms from in front of my face, clearing the path of older people who will not get into the VIP room. Vanessa yells, "Charlie, sweetie, give me your hand!" I reach out as though I am on a sinking ship, and this woman on the cliff-side, or spiral staircase, is my only hope of survival. I consider shaking Bethany off, leaving her in the disaster of losers missing out on free drinks on the fourth floor.

Vanessa squeezes my right wrist and pulls me up the steps to the rope, screaming, "Get your ass up here boy!"

"Come on, Bethany, Vanessa's letting us in."

"Goddamnit, okay. Someone in the crowd just touched my ass."

Vanessa kisses the side of my face and then switches to the other cheek. I think of Europeans in black-and-white films. *Most Americans don't kiss like that. I don't even hug my friends.* "Lovely to see you again, darling. Follow beautiful Daniel and his mistress Allison to the bar. Get some drinks before you have to pay for them."

I reply, "But of course." Bethany begins to introduce herself to Vanessa, but I yank her up two steps before she completes her name. Vanessa has already turned back to the crowd: They look like the "living dead" from the top of the staircase. They shove one another like Romero's zombies trying to find the living and bite through their limbs, like stray dogs chewing on leftover bones littering the outside of a dumpster in back of a restaurant. I feel an urge to spit on them but decide against it; I want to get drunk.

A new crowd of people pack against the one bar on the fourth floor. There are two bartenders filling cups with vodka and cranberry juice and tonic water and whatever else is asked for—lemon chunks or lime wedges. I see wet spots all over the bar, the multiple pairs of elbows coming and going as four full cups disappear at a time, other important people taking off with their free drinks. "I'll get two vodka cranberries and you get two vodka tonics."

"But I want a kamikaze or a sea breeze."

"Tough shit, the open bar is only for vodka drinks like vodka cranberry or vodka tonic. You can't get any fancy drinks. Get one later when you have to pay."

"Oh, okay. Do you have a dollar I can leave for tip?"

"Here. Remember, you get the vodka tonics. Hurry up, we can chug two drinks each and then maybe get back up here for another round."

It only takes a few minutes, and I have the two drinks I ordered. I wonder if I could have ordered four drinks at one time. I notice Bethany's tits lying on the bar; the male bartender is serving her. *They don't even ask for ID at the bars. I love it.* I'm out of the bar crowd. Bethany makes it over without spilling one drop from either cup. I suggest that we sit in the chairs in the corner. Daniel and Allison are speaking with Daniel's deejay friend Brad. They are looking down from the balcony, sipping vodka drinks from clear plastic cups. People crisscross back and forth in front of them while the light show from the dance floor sprinkles their faces with whip cracks of laser beams and disco ball dots flying in circles around the room. Large spotlights revolve above the balcony, like photo-shoot equipment bobbing up and down behind pinwheels of colored glass, facing the bodies slamming into one another down below.

I finish my first drink, the cranberry one, and place the empty cup under my chair. Bethany and I suck them up through the red stirrers that bartenders always stick in the drinks—coffee stirrers that sit in boxes next to coffee makers at PTA parties or church functions, the perfect accompaniment to the party perk, a twenty-cup brewing monster. A girl falls down after banging her leg into the side table next to Bethany's chair. Bethany almost spits her drink into her lap. I say, "Oh my God," and then start laughing while stirring my second drink like I just poured sugar in it. The girl on the floor is also cracking up. I hear her say something about her fucking knee, and some guy dressed in a black skin-tight leather jumpsuit with a lone spike of green hair protruding from above his forehead is bent over reaching around her waist in an attempt to pick her up. I think, *Good luck with that one*, and I slurp up my second drink. Bethany is doing the same. She hiccups afterward.

"Let's try to order four drinks each. I think we have fifteen minutes left." She asks for another dollar to tip the bartender with.

We each get three more drinks before the open bar ends. Allison and Daniel are no longer talking to Brad, nor are they even on the fourth floor. Bethany tells me that she wants to dance. I pull my black lipstick out of my pocket and apply a fresh layer because I know it's too sheer. Next time I'll put lip balm on and then draw my lips in with a black eyeliner pencil; it barely comes off through the night. I'm not into the whole I-wish-I-were-a-vampire thing. I prefer looking like a corpse, one that dances and gets drunk. Bethany is already on her third drink. I guess she really does want to dance. This song called "Godlike" comes on. It's from some band called KMFDM. People say it stands for "Kill Mother Fucking Depeche Mode." Depeche Mode is a synth-pop band from the '80s. I bought their *Music for the Masses* album on cassette when I was in eighth grade; it was the first New Wave album I ever bought.

Bethany is halfway through her fifth and final free drink. I down the rest of my fourth cup and start on the fifth, like they were cups of ice water and I just finished running a marathon. Bethany bends over to get rid of her cup and then sits up. She pulls a compact out of her purse. She checks her eye makeup, thick black mascara and eyeliner like charcoal outlines, anchoring dark gray eye shadow to her eyelids. Bethany has mastered using makeup to resemble the punk goddess Siouxsie Sioux. I stare at her, picturing my favorite Siouxsie T-shirt hanging in my closet at home.

We get up and head toward the staircase, which may or may not be the only way to reach up here to the fourth floor of the club. The crowd has vanished from the third floor—no Vanessa, no velvet rope. People are leaning against the third-floor bar; others are sitting on bar stools surrounding tall circular tables. We begin to walk faster down the steps, and I notice that I'm somewhat drunk. Maybe I don't even need to buy any drinks, the open bar might have done the job. I don't see Allison or Daniel anywhere on the dance floor, but then again it is the size of a roller skating rink or like half a baseball field. They could be hidden in the crowd—the arms swinging and knees rising. Some people look like they're marching and others appear to be going in and out of seizures or electroshock therapy. We find a circle formed where people are slam dancing and moshing in the middle, running into one another and flying against those on the outskirts. Two towering punks with mohawks fling each other into a group of other guys inside the circle. It's like pool balls being broken from the triangle or marbles ricocheting in opposite directions. The punks seem to be well over six feet tall each, and they're both throwing punches in the air. A violent Ministry song is blaring, the singer screaming the word "stigmata" over and over. Bethany grabs my hands and pulls me into the chaos of bodies whipping here and there inside the mosh pit. It's like we're all jumping on a trampoline out of control and affected by the motion of one another. She and I grip hands like links in a chain, crossing our forearms and allowing our weight to fall back as we begin to spin in a circle, colliding with anyone in the way. I start to laugh as our hands are slipping apart; we let go and each nail three or four people jumping around somewhere in or out of the pit. I see Bethany swaying backward into two guys. She tilts back against them; they push her back up like they're building a house and she's a support beam. It looks like a comedy routine from the other side of the circle. We run back toward one another, shouting the words to the Ministry song at each other's faces. Bethany grabs my shoulders and I grab her shoulders. We jump connected, now bouncing in a circle. Then a large guy slams into us; we're sent a foot into the air, still gripping each other's shoulders. We land on our feet and stumble sideways a bit. "Holy shit!"

"Oh my God, I think he knocked my tits out of my bra!"

"Jesus! We just flew through the air. That was insane."

"Holy crap, I've got to take a piss. Want to come to the bathroom with me."

"Sure, maybe I'll try to pee while I'm in there. Let me know if you spot Allison or Daniel. Don't forget they're driving us back to Jersey tonight."

"That's right. I sure as fuck don't want to end up sleeping in the Hoboken train station. Once in my life was enough."

As we make our way through the dance floor, heading toward the club entrance, I prepare myself for the worst in the bathroom. The bathrooms are on either side of the hall entrance that leads in and out of the Building. The right-hand bathroom is the men's room, where there are a few stalls, some missing doors and some that don't lock properly, and a large tub filled with ice where men piss. It's a community pissing ground; I stay away from it. I can't deal with whipping it out and pissing in front of an audience. Ever since middle school, I stopped using urinals in public bathrooms because I just couldn't relax and release. Maybe it had something to do with puberty, the sight of other boys' penises, but I learned that I could only piss in stalls—the ones with doors that close and lock. I don't want anyone watching me, so I always become nervous when it comes time to visit the bathroom. The left-hand bathroom is the women's room, but it is really an extension of the party where girls hide in one of the ten or so stalls to balance over filthy piss-covered toilet bowls while club-goers lounge on couches across from the stall doors. I don't understand the draw to hanging out in the women's bathroom, but it appears to be a popular spot. The most horrific aspect of the bathrooms in the Building is that the floor is lost beneath approximately an inch or so of mystery water. It's like the sprinkler system was on for ten minutes and there was nowhere for the puddles to drain. I imagine that the toilets are all clogged; this water is sewage waste dumping over the edges of the filled bowls. I try to ignore the fact that I'm probably stepping in water mixed with piss and God only knows what else. Bethany opens a stall and asks me to watch the door for her, to make sure that she's safe inside while playing the I'm-not-going-to-sit-on-this-bowl game. "Bad night to wear a full-length dress."

"You get used to it. Plus I'm drunk, so that helps to deal with this disgusting floor and the smell."

"It's fucking foul. Hurry up, I want to use it after you."

Bethany struggles past the half-open door into the closet-like darkness of her chosen stall. The lights above the stalls don't work. I hear people laughing in the stall on the right. The voices are sexless as they fade into the music; like a pay phone receiver held up in the air, noises reminiscent of words tickle the ears of people walking by. There's a little Latino guy wearing a baseball cap, sitting on a wooden stool against the wall next to the sinks and mirrors. I think he just sold drugs to a goth chick. I know I saw her hand him money. I've never witnessed a drug deal before. The stall door to the right swings open, and a pair of shirtless guys with their pants and underwear down around their knees roll out and onto the floor while the door smashes into my shoulder. They press their hips together, making out and sliding hands over each other's backs. *They're lying in the nasty bathroom floor water. Oh my God, what the hell is wrong with them? I can't watch this.*

"What the fuck is going on here?" Bethany steps out from behind the door. I'm trying to look away from the bare-assed guys sloshing about in the toilet muck on the women's room floor. They stop kissing and laugh out loud facing each other. One splashes a handful of the water into the other one's open eyes; this sets off a pool party for the two of them, flicking piss-water back and forth like this is a creek running through a forest in Vermont or upstate New York. I shiver like someone dropped an ice cube down the front of my pants, turning my head toward the Latino man selling drugs. A girl with a shaved head is standing before me holding a camera.

"Can you take a picture of me and my friends?"

"Uh, I guess so."

"Just press this button."

"Okay. I got it."

The girl runs over to a pack of male skinheads piled on a couch. They separate and pull her into the middle of shaved heads, arms, bomber jackets, and jeans. They remind me of a pile-up on a football field or boys playing that game kill-the-guy-with-the-ball. *Thank God I'm drunk off my ass for this.* I locate the button the girl pointed out to me and place my fingertip on it while I peer through the lens. "Is everyone ready?"

Arms stick out, some holding beer bottles and some making fists in the air. Bethany is watching from behind me, telling me to speed it up. Once the entire gang fits inside the square in my view, I scream, "Everyone say cheese!"

And in unison they respond, "We won't say cheese, but we'll say drugs!"

"Okay, say drugs!"

"DRUGS!!!"

I snap the photo.

SOMETHING ABOUT JENNA HAYES
by Steven T. Hanley

Chris is getting fucked in the far room while Amy gets chased around the lounge by Max wielding a chainsaw as the Xanax takes hold of me and pulls me down. I walk around smoking a cigarette and people all around me are doing things. I walk from room to room, I take a bottle of wine from a table and go sit in a darkened room with a few others watching a video. I sit on the floor and drink the wine while watching this girl with brown hair get taken from behind by this guy wearing a ski mask. I walk out after watching the money shot and on my way out I realize I was in Chris's bedroom.

Walking up the stairs I pass Max who's holding a petrol can shouting that he's gonna start the chainsaw. In the bathroom a girl holds another girl's hair back as she throws up into the toilet. Between the hurls I can hear her crying while her friend leans against the sink smoking a joint.

Walking down the stairs I realize my eyes feel tired but my body's awake. I head out into the front garden and some guys are spraying the garden hose and I watch the water hit this guy wearing a suit and I stand and see his hair fall into his eyes. I take a seat on the bench and completely forget I'm holding a bottle of wine. Under the streetlamp across the road by a red car I see this girl throw up onto the curb—it's Chris and I think she must be done fucking that guy she was with earlier.

Some guy and girl walk past me as I sit on the bench leaving the party holding their coats saying something about "the fucking house, you can't leave anything."

I walk around the back of the house to the garden where some music is playing and everyone is standing around wearing Parker jackets or hoodies and I drink my wine and talk to this guy about this film that's being passed around and as I try to stare at his face in the darkness, shadowed by the hood of his jacket, I can only make out his eyes in the light and I begin to think back to the couple who walked past me holding their coats and saying, "The fucking house is levitating."

The music gets turned up louder as I enter the kitchen through the sliding door. A bunch of people are sitting at the dining room table eating Domino's Pizza straight from the box and drinking Pepsi from this two-liter bottle. I catch a glimpse of Jenna walking into the other room wearing this black dress. I run to the fridge take out a bottle of chilled wine, try and find a corkscrew, then realize that Jenna's probably lost in the crowd of people, she's getting away.

In the next room I can't see Jenna. I scan for her but just see a bunch of kids sprawled across the couches holding bottles of beer and joints and they all have girls with them leaning on their chests and there's a movie on and someone on the screen is someone being chased.

In the hallway I feel a chill and look to see the front door is open. Jenna Hayes stands in the doorway smoking a cigarette and I walk toward her, and when I stand behind her I look at her body in the dress and smell her perfume, see she has her hair tied back, and lie and ask for a light saying I haven't got one.

I stand with Jenna smoking, my hand getting cold holding the unopened bottle of wine. Talking to her about this girl we both know at college, debating if she's here tonight. I tell her I think I saw her earlier but can't be too sure. Standing staring through the cloud of smoke we've made to the houses across the street, and I wonder if they're looking back at us through their windows and if they are, do me and Jenna look like we're a couple. I kinda laugh when she starts moaning that no one let her know that pizza was being ordered. As she stubs out her cigarette on the ground, I look at her black shoes reflecting in the light. She asks me do I know if that new food place in town is open, I'm not sure, she asks me do I wanna go for a ride to see, I agree and go inside and look for a corkscrew.

I walk down into the basement where I grab my coat and see a couple who are talking quietly and listening to the radio. They look up at me as I leave. I think about waving then forget it.

In Jenna's car she turns up the stereo, which is good cause I'm not in the mood to talk, she puts on some cool mellow American guitar band. I lay back as the vocals come in, staring out into the dark night I open the window slightly and as the breeze hits me and I begin to drink from the wine, I look over at Jenna, and something to do with music and air, I get this feeling and I watch Jenna's hair blow around and the lyrics to the song are *"step into the light and see if it shows you who you are."*

We pull up to the food place and it's open. We go in and the harsh light hurts my eyes and it seems like me and Jenna are much paler than everyone in here.

I sit down opposite Jenna and eat my burger and pick at my fries. She eats her food and I realize that I'm not too hungry. And we sit around for a little while and talk about college and our friends and make each other laugh and I try not to stare at her for too long and we get up and as we leave on our way back to the party I notice I have no idea at all what time it is.

I smoke a joint on the way home and pass it to Jenna, who holds it in her hand at the wheel and takes big inhales at stop signs and traffic lights. When we get back to the party a few people are sitting on the porch. The front door's locked so we walk around to the back to where the music's coming from. Jenna's name is called by three girls. She shouts over, then turns to me, looks me in the eyes, says thanks and she'll catch up with me in the party and she'll definitely see me before she goes, and I believe her and think about holding her hand but just nod and walk off.

Upstairs I hear an engine growling and see Max, his friend, and some girl playing with the chainsaw which they've finally got started. I walk past them on the way to the bathroom and see a guy from my English class sprawled out across a bed with MTV on playing some video from this hip-hop act and I notice there's a lot of guns in the video.

After I wash my hands I throw some water on my face and think about my drive with Jenna and the moment the cool breeze hit and the vocals came on and Jenna looked beautiful and all this is cut in half when I hear a rumble through the wall and I walk out of the bathroom to see Max cutting a hole in the wall with the chainsaw. I feel the dust hit me as I walk past with water dripping from my face.

I begin to freak out a little as the whole corridor fills with smoke. I don't look back to see what has happened but think for a second that maybe Max hit a pipe or something. I walk into the first room I come to. Inside the room the lights are off. I look around and because the room's neat and doesn't smell of skunk, I think no one's been in here tonight. As I rest my head against the door, suddenly everything outside goes quiet, the chainsaw stops. I close my eyes and try to relax and don't really think about anything. I sit around for a few minutes, light a cigarette, smoke half of it, and I get up to leave but freeze when I see someone in the corner of the room. I can only make out his face through the darkness and as I stare at him, his expression remains the same, vacant. I leave the room and close the door behind me, then stand in the doorway for a few seconds afterwards and hear footsteps from inside.

Max has cut a hole in the wall and past the rubble you can see the brick. In the bathroom more people are getting sick, and from downstairs I hear the music from outside getting louder.

In the back garden I look around, thinking Jenna might still be here and look for her but can't find her and try to work out how long ago it was since I spoke to her out here in the garden but can't work it out.

I take a beer from the fridge and walk into the living room, sit on the couch, and try to keep my attention on the screen and not on the couple opposite me kissing. A joint is handed to me, I smoke half of it and pass out/fall asleep. I wake/come to when I hear a crash from outside, get up, and notice I spilled the rest of my beer on my shirt.

Half awake I wander through to the back garden which has since almost entirely cleared. I walk around for a minute or two. The music has ended.

In the kitchen I see people sitting about wearing

jackets with their hoods up, not talking and looking tired and stoned, I go to the fridge, take another beer, start drinking it, and then stand by the door and watch the people leave. As the numbers fall I stand on the porch outside. I watch all the cabs pull up and all the people get in and drive off.

Inside standing in the lounge I drop my beer bottle onto the floor thinking it's not going to make a difference. I suddenly realize I haven't seen Jenna but think maybe she couldn't find me before she left.

As I walk into the kitchen I see Chris standing outside in the middle of the garden. She's barefoot and standing perfectly still and I walk toward her, my attention focused on her, drawn, I get nearer and notice her lipstick is faded and her eyes are sleepy. I take her by the hand and in silence we go inside and walk upstairs together, closing all the doors on the way up, and I go into her room, take off my shoes, and lay on the bed. She joins me and I move her gently toward me. She rests her head on my chest and I reach for the remote to turn on the TV and begin to watch a film as I drift off Xanax-faded holding Chris in my arms hoping she's warm. My eyes close and just as I begin to sleep I begin to think something about Jenna Hayes.

SWITCH
by Chris von Steiner

Everybody calls me Jane at school, but my name is John. I know I look like a girl, but I'm a boy. They all know that, and you too, of course: You were the first to call me Jane . . . Stop laughing at me. Today is a very special day, I don't wanna play anymore. This knife? It's yours. Don't you remember when you gave it to me? It was your favorite game . . . "Jane! Jane! Jane!" And I came running after you . . . "Jane! Jane! Jane!" Until you fell on your knees, breathless . . . "Jane . . . Jane . . . Jane . . ." Wet hair, red cheeks, sweaty T-shirt . . . "My name is John!" And I took your hand and put it on my crotch . . . "I'm a boy, not a girl!" And I pressed the knife on your throat and you closed your eyes, smiling, as always . . . "Jane, please, don't . . ." You knew what I was about to ask you. It was your idea: "My name is John, and I want you to take your fucking clothes off!"

Now you're naked in front of me, once more. Your white skin under the cold moonlight, a little yellow snail slipping at your feet. We're not where we used to play. No spider, no mouse, no dust. No walls to hold your screams. Just you and me, alone in the forest. We're not in the old house. Nobody knows where we are, and nobody cares anyway. It's getting darker and darker, and you are colder and colder. I never thought it would be so easy. You look at me, mouth wide open. Blood on your neck. Red leaves under your head. I suck your dick. Smell your balls. Eat your ass. For the first and very last time.

I walk through the trees. Here it is. The lake. I wash my hands in the black water. I hate myself. Why can't I be you? I hear noises behind me. Footsteps on broken branches. I turn my head. Pale as a ghost, covered with blood, you're heading toward me, arms open.

—*Jane, kill me twice, please . . .*

I throw the knife at your hands.

—*I'm tired, Brad, do it yourself.*

As you cut your wrists, I open my eyes.

I'm in bed and Mum tells me to wake up.

—*Please Mum, can I stay home today? I don't wanna go to school . . .*

—*What happens? Are you ill?*

—*No . . . It's Brad. He's gonna make fun of me again all day long.*

—*Brad? What are you talking about? I thought he was your friend . . .*

—*Yes, sort of, but at school, when he's with these other guys, he's not the same . . . Please, Mum . . .*

—*Stop this, John. Get out of bed or I'll call your father.*

I walk into the kitchen to take my breakfast. The clock hanging on the wall says I'm late. The chocolate is cold and the butter has melted on the toast. I look by the window. Brad is already there, sitting at the bus stop, staring at me. He opens his mouth and moves his lips slowly. HUR-RY-UP-JA-NE. I hate him. He's dressed in black, as usual, and wears his favorite T-shirt, the Nine Inch Nails one, like every Monday. His long dark hair hides his left eye. I know what it means. Bruises. His father beat him up again last night. I should be sorry for him but I'm not. Some say Brad is cute, but he's not. He's just absolutely pure perfection, from head to toe. I quickly drink a cup of chocolate, take my bag, and leave home.

The bus is out of sight, on its way to school. No need to hide anymore. We're getting out of the bushes and Brad lights a cigarette.

—So now what are we gonna do, Jane?
He blows smoke on my face.
—Why not go to the old house? I say, trying not to cough.
—Do you have it?
I go through my bag.
—Here it is . . .
The cold blade shines under the sun.
—Cool! Let's go!
—Brad, hey, wait a minute!
I carefully replace the knife in my bag and rush at Brad running through the fields.

SPATIAL DEVICES CAN TAKE ANY FORM
#2 in the Unproduceable Porn Script Series
by Jack Shamama

INT. HOTEL ROOM—DAY
Caleb, a scrappy guy in his early twenties, sits on a corner of the bed in a pretty average hotel room. He's got a bunch of tattoos, the kind you would get in prison. He's talking directly into the camera.

A gravely, but kind voice asks him questions from somewhere off-camera. Sound is crappy. The lighting is harsh, giving Caleb's skin a greenish tint.

> VOICE (O.C.)
> Tell me a little about yourself.

> CALEB
> What do you wanna know?

> VOICE (O.C.)
> Name, age, measurements?

> CALEB
> Uh . . . Caleb. Twenty-two. Six foot. Like 150 pounds, I guess.

> VOICE (O.C.)
> You want a beer?

                    CALEB
          Sure.

A hand reaches in frame with a beer. Caleb drains about half of it in one hard gulp.

                    VOICE (O.C.)
          Let's take your shirt off, so we can
          get a better look at ya.

Caleb peels his T-shirt off. His eyes widen and he crosses his arms. The camera zooms in on his body—more tattoos and a totally decent body.
   On each arm, he's got a bunch of parallel scars running from his shoulder to about halfway down to his forearm, each meticulously straight and spaced evenly apart, maybe like thirty or forty on each arm.

                    VOICE (O.C.)
          You grow up in San Diego?

                    CALEB
          No, Florida . . . Pensacola.

                    VOICE (O.C.)
          Well, what brought you out here?

                    CALEB
          Was stationed at Camp Pendleton.
          I left a few months ago but just
          stayed out here.

VOICE (O.C.)
So, why do you want to be in one of my movies?

CALEB
(eyes dart)
I . . . uh, I guess you could say I'm a bit of an, uh, exhibitionist.
(beat)

Caleb shrugs.

CUT TO:

INT. HOTEL ROOM—NIGHT

Caleb stands facing Bailey (average looking, thick build, late thirties, flatly indignant look on his face). Both are wearing suits that look like they could actually be expensive. The TV, muted, plays the "Don't Touch That Dinosaur!" episode of *Full House*, where Michelle accidentally knocks down the Tyrannosaurus Rex bones at the museum.

                    CALEB
                (
                t
                o

                c
                a
                m
                e
                r
                a
)
How does this go?

                    BAILEY
                (
                i
                n

                a

                "
                t
                o

ugh

guy"

voice)

Why don't you start by sucking my cock, boy?

   CALEB
(to

camera)
Now?

Caleb reaches into Bailey's pants and pulls out a pair of

scissors from each pocket. They lock eyes for about five seconds. Caleb snips Bailey's tie off. Camera shakily follows as it falls to the floor.

Bailey reaches into both of Caleb's pants pockets and pulls out two more pairs of scissors. He snips off a piece of his lapel. Caleb takes a bigger piece off Bailey's jacket. They snip each other's clothes back and forth.

They work themselves up into an Edward Scissorhands–like smoky cloud of snipping and flying bits until they each have a roughly twelve-inch-wide span of exposed skin from the middle of their thighs up to their nipples.

Bailey forces Caleb's head down on his cock, which is hard. On his knees, Caleb does his thing for a bit until Bailey grabs the back of his head and gets aggressive with him, pulling on his hair and building up a cadence of fucking his mouth harder and harder. Amidst Bailey's contrived moans of "Oh yeah" and "Suck that cock, boy," we hear the occasional gag from Caleb, whose eyes are tearing.

Bailey pulls Caleb's head off his cock right before he's about to come.

BAILEY
Oh fuck, dude, I'm gonna come!

VOICE (O.C.)
Do your thing, Caleb.

Caleb punches him square in the balls as hard as he can. When Bailey comes, the ejaculation is mostly blood.

[Note: If his actual come is only pinkish, or if he's unable to come, then the shot will need to be faked, but using real blood.]

FADE TO BLACK.

INT. TJ'S KITCHEN—DAY

TJ, your standard-issue twenty-something "Chelsea boy" (played by Ethan Marc if he's available) is sitting at his kitchen table, talking directly into the camera with an earnest intensity. He punctuates every few sentences with a toothy but sincere ear-to-ear grin. In the background, barely audible, we hear selections from Madonna's "Confessions on a Dance Floor."

                    TJ
        Let's see . . . where do I start? I
        grew up in a small town in upstate
        New York. But I live in Manhattan
        now. I'm an IT consultant for a
        bunch of Fortune 500 companies.
        It's a lot of fun, actually.

CUT TO:

INT. TJ'S LIVING ROOM—DAY

          TJ

Okay, here's a fun story. One night when a bunch of my friends—we were totally trashed on Red Bull vodkas—were out partying, one of my friends dared me to get up on the bar and take my shirt off. I'm totally ripped—and was wasted!—so I figured, what the hell? LOL. Someone unbuttoned my jeans and they sort of slipped down around my ankles. I just sort of lost myself in the music. I looked down and a crowd of guys had totally gathered around me. People were stuffing money in my underwear and everything. My friends still call me Go-Go Teej because of that fateful night. LOL!

CUT T

TO:

INT. TJ'S BEDROOM—NIGHT
Suite Life of Zach and Cody (doesn't matter which episode) plays muted on TV in the background.

          TJ
    Me and my group of friends, we absolutely love to travel. This year, I went to San Diego for Pride, L.A., Austin for SXSW, Rio (what a fun city!), Orlando for Gay Days, Fire Island like a million times this summer. Oh, and Palm Springs for the White Party.

CUT TO:

INT. TJ'S BATHROOM—DAY
TJ is sitting on the edge of the tub. The camera is balanced on the toilet, which we can sort of make out in a reflection on the glass door of the shower.

                TJ

I'm part of what you could call an aggressive social circle. When we're not traveling, we're partying. Our motto is, *We work hard, we play hard!* We're not dumb—we know we're not going to be young and beautiful forever, so we have got to party extra hard while we've still got it. LOL.

                              C
                              U
                              T

                              T
                              O
                              :

INT. TJ'S KITCHEN—DAY

                TJ

So, why do I want to be in one of your movies? Well, I think I have what it takes. LOL. And in the back of my mind it's been something that I've always wanted to try.

                (
                b
                e
                a
                t
                ,

t
h
i
n
k
i
n
g
)

I think I could put on a really good show.

F
A
D
E

T
O

B
L
A
C
K
.

INT. ABANDONED HOUSE—NIGHT

Two men in makeshift hoods (pillowcases with eye holes cut out) carry a "sleeping" TJ into the room and gently lay him on a mattress in the middle of the floor.

Aside from the mattress, there's no furniture in the

room, which looks like maybe it was once the living room. There's trash, candles, and empty bottles all over. The walls are spray-painted with swastikas, pentagrams, etc.

> VOICE (O.C.)
> I suppose you can take the hoods off now.

They do. One of the guys is Caleb. The other, Cole, is about the same age and build as Caleb. He could be his brother.

> VOICE (O.C.)
> Whenever you're ready, boys.

Okay, TJ's not really sleeping, he's drugged. Caleb peels off TJ's shirt and Cole undoes his pants. TJ's totally unresponsive, but occasionally his eyes flutter. The two laugh and fuck around with his flaccid limbs as they get him naked. Cole pokes around TJ's ass with his fingers.

> COLE
> (
> l
> a
> u
> g
> h
> i
> n
> g
>)
> Dude, his ass has got no give.

> CALEB
> Let's see how many of our fingers we can get up there.

They play around with TJ's body: fingering him, slapping his face with their cocks, sticking things into his mouth. Caleb squats over his face and farts, sending the two into a fit of hysterical laughter.

> VOICE (O.C.)
> Okay, boys, enough fucking around. Remember what I'm paying you for?

They sober up a bit, spit on their dicks, and take turns fucking him in the ass. They come in him/on him and smear it all over his face and in his hair.

CUT TO:

EXT. FIELD—DUSK
An animal emerges from out of the fog brush. It's a seven-headed dog. The camera switches to the dog's POV as he shakily lurches forward with a certain determined priority, like a pig rooting for truffles.

He comes across TJ, still unconscious and lying on the ground. Cautiously, he begins to investigate TJ's body, each of his heads sniffing different parts: snouts burrowing into his crotch, under his arms, behind his knee, licking his body. No response.

One head bites into his thigh. The other six heads bite other parts as the animal pounces on top of him, clawing and shredding him to a disemboweled mess, heads snapping parts in different directions.

When he's pretty much toast, the dog walks away.

It's quiet less some birds chirping. TJ, face bloody but somewhat intact, awakens, as if from a long nap. He looks into the camera, confused.

FADE TO BLACK.

YOU'RE IN MY BLOOD NOW
by Nicholas Messing

I miss your blue hair, plastic penis wrapped up like a baby. It's okay to think of you, lonely skull, during wartime. When I stay the same, enemies yet to be chosen miss your ashen mouth where action stops cyclical flight. Your eyes burned a hole in the center to get your point across. Everything stays the same but names. The book said wear the crown well, cross the breeze in the spell of a hero's spoon. Evil eye on a late wind, dark horse clears the last heat. Bloodless youth ascends beholden to the corpse caught in a demon stare. Your edges spill into the sky like knives melting eyes to the end of pretending.

When I came to, you were dead, your lifeless head lying in my lap. My first thought was to bury you piece by piece. I severed your right arm with a knife. One glance at myself, bloodied and scared in the mirror, and I knew I could go no further. Hiding the rest of you in the closet, I got high nonstop for days. I invited a guy over out of desperation for human contact. He never asked what I had done to you, and I never told him.

Spattered with blood, the wall stained red like your cock dreaming of bloody boys hurt like animals. You hurt my body in black, all over wounds like toys. Your petals against my hands, your legs against my roots, thorn against thorns. Blood makes blood turn like your body was telling this story. Animal rubs his face in the blood, inside and out black blood. Eyes ringed in black saw the crying fields of dead boys singing in this wound. Flesh against flesh, black against black, blood of the heart. Savage deceit bleeds endless ghost hours dying inside. I can't stay where rivers turn a vast persuasion of sad lines. Where waves begin a twofold loss in lucid delusion of shadow selves, you turn to go.

KLONOPIN
by Nicholas Rhoades

Of the three main windows in my apartment, two are cool. They show a decent, urban blob of the city: art gallery, parking lot, some great old hotels that are apartments now—like mine.

The room I choose to sit in has a window bigger than the rest. At night, the window's a sheet of black. At day, it's a dirty brick wall. The view from my balcony is the same wall. There's no graffiti on the wall whatsoever. I put graffiti there when I need to. I used to do that to a wall when I lived a few blocks away. That always got whitewashed. I can control this new wall.

I'm going to scrub the tub now, so I'll tell you about last night. I went bowling with Joe and his twin brother and some girl named Becky. Joe works at the bowling alley, and other employees come up to him constantly and ask him to say "cheeseburger," which he can't say. He can use an "r" sound, but not in that word.

He always says it when asked, and everyone always laughs, so he's always a little pissed off, or just blank like you could look at him and he'd be anything. But he's not what I'm talking about. His twin brother does the exact same thing with a different word. Becky does the same thing with life in general.

We bowl like shit then leave for my apartment. It's cold, nice, uneventful. We sit in the room where the window is black. I serve splashes of whiskey in teacups. We pass some joints. We take in the aquarium made of my TV, which is tuned to something that looks like a David Lynch movie, but isn't, and my computer, which does the same old thing. The stereo is doing something crunchy.

I sit on the floor while Becky pretends to give me a back rub. I look out the window and make a red line streak across the wall and make a sharp turn down. I could have turned it down or flicked at my eyes until I made it go away, like drinking water when you have hiccups.

I throw my teacup with zero strength at the window and everyone freaks. They start to leave, confused. Too bad I didn't have any hors d'oeuvres.

Becky tries to hang around, but I'm unable to focus on her. She's like one of those electric back massagers that you can turn off with a switch. It works on her, but not on the window. The window's still going. Joe's brother jets the second he's alone with me and his brother.

I fall asleep, not really, and so does Joe. The backs of his legs are too hairy, just like the rest of him. He's facing the back of my futon/couch, but I hope he's looking at the shiniest red graffiti he's ever seen. Wait, he thinks, does graffiti happen in lines? It must. Then, not to bore him, I turn it into this red half frame with Bugs Bunny doing something all over.

Then I fall asleep because Joe's ass is boring, the CD goes ambient, and no matter how hard I try to erase Bugs Bunny, he's stuck. I'm dangling a carrot for old time's sake, then I'm drifting off looking at Joe's ass, my plaid boxers, hearing a sound that's coming from my phone . . . *beep, beep* . . . no that's not my phone. The sound changes, the lights retract, Joe gets up and tiptoes out. All's good.

I half wake when there's a thump at the door. When I

realize it's today's *Detroit Free Press* landing at the foot of the door, I race over, open it, grab the paper, and get as good of a look at the paperboy's ass as I can. Then I go inside and stand by the window he's walking by so I can see him for the next few seconds.

Smoke while making coffee, smoke while drinking coffee, read the front page of the paper, skim the rest. I count my change and exit the building. Rounding the corner, I can already see the bums lining up by the front door to the party store across the street. I look quite a lot like the bums, I guess.

I like this shop because I think it's the only one in all of Detroit that doesn't have bullet-proof glass. I like the bums too. They know me, so they don't fuck with me. Most smile at me. I spot Jeanette in her wheelchair near the front of the line, so I slide up there, give her a big hug, and basically take cuts behind her.

"BLESS YOU, baby!" she says, like always.

"I ain't got nothing for you," I say, "but if you let me in first, I'll give you a sip on the way out."

"Oh, ain't you PRECIOUS!"

I squeeze in front of her wheelchair. She says she's thirty-four and is in a wheelchair because she's had two heart attacks. She looks healthy to me, and I'm sure if she did have heart attacks, they were due to crack.

When I get inside, I buy two cheap cans of awful beer and a half-pint of horrible whiskey for $5.55. Back outside, I wait around the corner for Jeanette, let her take a couple of gulps of whiskey, then start my way back across the busy street.

"JESUS is WITH you BABY!" she shrieks.

"You KNOW it!" I'm happy, suddenly. I feel like I'm going to get something done today, instead of watching fake blood on TV and waiting until I can draw graffiti.

I'm in the middle of the road, waiting for traffic to clear, when a huge, booming horn blows at me so loud that my hair is standing on end and reaching to Canada. I check to make sure I've gone to the store, then I go home, reminding myself to check to see if I remembered to take my meds or not.

Back at home, I sit in my chair, fire up my iMac, turn the TV to a horror movie without sound, take a glance at the wall, and then take a sip of my drink.

By the fourth bang of whiskey, I'm ready to write. I started this piece awhile ago, and I keep coming back, not because I think something about it, but because it's fun. It was a spoof of airline security after 9/11. Now it's not. Today, I write the following, giggling almost all the way:

What is this shit? Texas? I think I got on the wrong plane. Or they put me there.

The airport's like a city that you can't breathe in. I'm on a tram-thing to some other part of it. Connecting flight, but I can't believe I had thought enough to book that shit.

Oh, yeah, some bum in the john's wallet. A flying fuck to whomever. That reminds me.

I just broke a mirror in the men's room. About ten guys saw me. You can't run too far in an airport when you have blood on you.

I'm in something like a golf cart. They actually handcuffed me, even though my hands are gushing blood. No matter what they ask, I won't speak, so they think I'm crazy, or I am and they have no motherfucking clue.

I think it's love making me do this.

I waited until there was one stupid security guard, took the gun out of my pants, waved it in his general direction, then went out the door, down a corridor, back into the airport, and onto my connecting flight to Los Angeles, or so I'm thinking.

Since the drugs are wearing off on the plane, or should I say shooting volcanic-like out of my ass, I keep either locking myself in the mini-john, or sweating and bouncing in my seat.

About the tenth time I go to shit, I actually fall asleep in the mini-john. I bust down the door with my foot, and it's another mini-john, and my ex-boyfriend's in there injecting something.

I wake up, immediately ashamed at the proliferation of the word "mini-john" in the print that was either technicolor feces or a facsimilie of that word.

I can't order enough drinks. Fuck it, I'm rich.

Finally I notice the little fuck beside me is a crank whore. He's dribbling on himself and can't notice.

He goes to the john and comes back and he's okay for about a minute and a half, then he starts scratching at his scabs.

At this point I'm so fucking sick because I'm obviously out of drugs. Obviously, the little crank whore has more where that came from. It's weird watching some boy nod out when he's on speed, but it doesn't make me not want his drugs.

But he's the first thing I have to get. Good thing these fucking little speeders are electrifying the sex parts of their brains, or whatever.

Do people ever actually see shit? If they did when I dragged that boy into the john by his hair, someone should have landed the plane.

I find the idea that you can signal whomever with signs like occupied or even do not disturb really funny. Or I'm finding it funny since the first thing he does is dump out his drugs like there was telepathy and not short, blond, ripped-out hair still in my hand. He doesn't care. Why should he?

I haven't used a needle in ages, have I? He's holding my arm like it's God and doing other shit I'm trying not to notice. I thought I was the one who was fucked up.

It's okay when he starts fucking with my pants, but when the gun goes clank onto the floor, he's a little shy.

After I put my dick in his hand, he's less worried. That's his problem. I can't remember him taking off his clothes. Then I'm doing stuff that feels new. Maybe because I'm in control?

His punctures and scabs are bleeding all over me, but he's having a good time, I think. His head keeps banging on the door. Occupied, *motherfuckers*.

What a buzzkill. What am I supposed to do now that come is in the past tense? I have a few ideas.

He's a little confused when I put the gun as far into his mouth as I can. I'm calling him "God," because I guess he is, and trying to jack him off.

Then he focuses. I can hear him think, Is that loaded? He's wilting. I can chant "God" as much as possible, but apparently that's not helping.

The idiot actually smiles at me when I pull the gun out of his mouth. He's still smiling when I hit him with it.

When I shove him ass-first into the stupid little toilet, he laughs. When I jump on his body with both legs, as hard as I can, I can't hear what his mouth is doing, but his rib cage makes some crunchy noise a little too cartoonish for my taste.

I'm only slightly surprised when I push the flusher and he gets sucked out of my life like the shit he is.

The best thing is, when he's finally through the little silver opening, I can see him fall into the air, and really nice blue sky going by real fast.

I fold up his clothes, take them back to my seat, and try to stop my eyes from rolling up into my head. Unoccupied.

* * *

The empty whiskey means I'm finished for the day. I reread the piece a couple of times, deciding I like it. It puts the end of the beginning and the start of the middle onto an end I've already written. It's indulgent, the way I put one of my dead grandfather's prosthetic legs in my front window, so it doesn't have to look at a wall.

I get scared when My Bloody Valentine shows up on cable and my CD player at the same time. The solution is to do laundry. I drag my bags to the door.

There are three washers and three dryers in the basement laundry room. The motion-detector lights are off, but one or more machines create a rumble, making it seem like someone's down there. I do my laundry the same time every Saturday, so the joke someone left on the first washer is obviously for me.

There's a dripping wet, completely full bottle of KY sitting on the edge of the washer I usually use. That's a joke from Mike. I love Mike. Not really, but sort of close. When I take one step further and the motion-detector lights go on, and I can hear Mike giggling in the part of the basement I can't see, I know I'm right.

Mike's got an enviable, skinny body, pinned blue eyes, and a dick that could be the bridge to Canada, even though he prefers to bottom.

"Is it even clean?"

"Yeah, must be. I got it out of the washer because I know you like to use that one," he says in a fuck-me-it's-after-cartoons voice.

He's right. It's full. The cap's intact. I load the washer, pitch the KY to make whatever happens seem like it's supposed to be dangerous, and make my way to the darker part of the basement.

I'm already hard. He's followed suit. He doesn't need

to hand it out like sample sausage, but the effect always works. We barely get undressed. I could be devouring the back of his neck when he braces his right leg on a utility sink, but everything is so funny that all I can do is ask, "Are you ready?" The nod signals something slow at first, relief next, God next.

The dingy window above shows us the end of the wall my graffiti uses as its screen. He feels great, but there's some sort of logic ruining it. I finally just have to ask him. "What's around the corner of that wall?" I'm pushing harder, which he likes.

He says, "Nothing."

I keep asking the same question, like when I was saying "God" to some fictional construction earlier. It's not making me mad that I don't get an answer, but it's irritating. I hold him open, bite his neck so I can taste him, and then ask him again as sternly as my little voice allows.

"I . . . I . . . I . . . can't . . ."

"What?"

This is as much for him as for me, if that matters, so I slow up.

"Aargh, good, good, good."

"Answer me."

Suddenly, he reaches around, grabs his dick out of me, forces me to turn around, and coughs out, "Nothing's around that corner!" Then he shoots a wad of sperm that runs down my shoulder and chest.

That's my cue. I hold back for a second, then put one hand around his throat, squeezing, another around my balls, and soak his front side.

We're laughing and holding each other.

"Finish my laundry, you cunt," he says.

I will. He knows it. "Bring amaretto later. We'll do faggot coffee drinks. Maybe a repeat?"

He grins.

So far, he's the best part of my day.

When I get upstairs, Joe's twin brother is sitting at my chair, not touching my computer or TV or stereo, just bouncing, bouncing.

I know what he wants, and what Mike can't see.

I hold his arm out like God, which is hard to do because it's sweaty. He gets the needle in and out of there pretty quick.

There's this chick named Laurie who has a gun that resembles my grandfather's too much. Sometimes I go upstairs to look at the gun, have coffee, look at the gun. It's not serious, but it happens. I can't figure out whether that's serious or not.

She's likes Joe's twin brother, from what I can figure. He can barely speak or read, and he's not cute, but she wants to mom him. I'm guessing I am doing the opposite by letting him ruin himself in my face. I'd save him if he OD'd, I suppose.

Night comes quick enough that I don't have to think anymore. The window does its thing that I know is fake, and I cover it with a blast of cartoon characters, some old nudie girl photos, a pic of his favorite band. I thought that would be a nice thing to wake up to. I don't know what he normally wakes up to.

I'm going across the street again, since the party store's closed on Sunday.

There's no line of bums this time. Just Oz, a bum sitting on the curb with his feet dangling in the street. I buy two cheap beers and a half-pint of whiskey, feeling particularly happy that I wrote a few paragraphs and the world didn't crash the fuck down on me.

I can hear a screech when I'm leaving. I look over at Oz, and someone's run over his legs. He's still got that BLESS YOU look in his eyes, which go in two directions.

I spin around and go back into the store and get another half-pint. The shopkeeper asks, "What did you do? Break the first one?"

"No," I say. "There was an accident. I can only see ambulances here. They never put their sirens on."

I walk outside. Oz's legs have been smushed to shit. He can still manage to wave at me. I go over to him, hand him my cigarette, which takes five minutes. Then I hand him the unopened bottle of whiskey, screw the cap off, and make sure he can get it from his chest to his face. He's smiling while he's dying, throwing a salute slug at me.

When I get home, I don't tell Joe's twin what just happened.

When I'm inside my apartment, I decide to call 911. No one would've done it in the first place. I can hear Joe's brother vomiting in my bathroom, so I make the call because he can't hear it.

I start to count, give up, grab my whiskey, counting the sips, and try to haul Joe's twin brother off of my toilet so I can piss.

When I was really young, we used to make paper cups joined by string, and tried to use them as phones. I'm unwinding that memory now.

MY VENN DIAGRAM
by T.P. Kendall

This story points straight up like a compass. Not that kind of compass, the kind you'd take to school and stab other kids with. If someone asked what the difference is, I'd say, "one describes a perfect circle, the other one traces that circle . . . That's why they have the same name." I got stabbed with a compass once and got convinced I'd been given AIDS. The kid that punctured me was dirty and a gypsy and he used to stick his fingers into my lunch. This is why I thought he might have AIDS. This is kinda my parents' fault because I was young at the time; now I have to take responsibility, and they told me that people in the world often give other people AIDS on purpose, especially outside nightclubs. School wasn't a nightclub but it's where everybody in the world went.

My parents are no part of the world. The world is a dirty word to them. To be in my parents' religion is to be "in the truth." Now I am out of the "truth," or as their gossipy friends might say: "Oh, he's not in the truth anymore." This makes my parents sad although they're getting used to the idea. I told a kid once that his neck was gonna be smashed in by those Four Horsemen and that I would be riding next to Jesus as it happened with my arms held fast around his waist like a human seatbelt. His mum phoned my mum and I had to go in and apologize even though I knew I was right. Later, my mum told me that I was right but in the wrong way, and I asked her what the word *fuck* meant because I had just read it on the cornershop wall. I knew what the rest of the words on the wall meant even though they made no sense, as their home was in or above the shop. I don't remember. My mother didn't smack me or anything but patiently explained that it was a rude word that was totally unnecessary. I have never, ever told my parents to fuck off. This is because my parents are extremely nice people and not psychos at all. They're probably nicer than your parents even.

Is it true a compass always points north? The other kind, I mean? I have never understood how that works. Is it all relative or is it all fixed? Anyway, now I'm dragging you around in the wrong direction, a misdirection if you will.

Once I stopped believing in the truth, I started to like words and I even made friends. My first friend used to come around and we would make jokes about the Holocaust and hide eggs all around the house. I must have been seventeen at the time. His family was a lot more upsetting than mine but he was very different. In compass terms, I was south and he was north, although if a compass always points north, then from his perspective I was north and he was south. What matters is that even though we were so different, we met in the middle of that circle. Or rather we were so different we met at extreme points. Maybe this compass analogy isn't working? I've never been very good at practical things or thinking. Still, I haven't talked about the North and South Poles, which is a very tempting proposition at this point.

The North and South Poles, I don't get them and I'm not interested in research. If I really looked at them, I'd probably find out they're not even candy-striped. I don't think I'd like that. I guess I've always had problems talking. I think I might be retarded or just badly informed. Either way, I don't really understand. God used to be in my head all the time, but then he left and I had to wonder who the hell I was talking to when I was trying to think. I used to pray constantly but it wasn't spiritual, I think it was more like OCD. Did those prayers go north or south or up or down? Can you equate those things at all?

Either way, he got lost and I was left standing (not at the altar though) and pretty much exposed. I looked at other people who were all part of the world and wondered what the rules were. My friend didn't really know the rules either so we got pretty confused and angry. Some people thought we were pretty cool because of this, but it couldn't last. Once we got to twenty, people got tired of us and we had to find a new way to get friends. My friend is better at making friends than me but I am better at keeping them. This is because I have no personality. I don't mind, and me and my friend are happy about the mechanics cos it means we've divided one person's work into two, which in the world of mathematics should be impossible. I think. My math isn't very good either. I didn't go to school much because it made me so tired.

You can pinpoint the center of a circle, but it's not really there, that's the point. Most people are happy cruising the circumference of their personalities. That's how they get along. I can't find that edge cos it's hard to draw. Maybe I'm just facing the wrong direction? I'd have to turn 360 degrees, though, and that'd be hard. So this story goes straight up even as it goes right around. I've thought about love but it just doesn't seem likely. Another friend said every emotion except love is scientific. That you can break down practically every other emotion into various, more complex, composite feelings that united create larger totalizing effects such as anger, sadness, jealousy, etc., etc., but that love just doesn't add up properly.

So love is a form of alchemy.

So love is really like those people turning lead into gold but succeeding, and that isn't right. Imagine if in the olden days people burned lovers at the stake like witches? It would seem a lot more fair . . . to people in general who aren't in love. I'm not petty though. Please don't think that . . . Pettiness is the one thing that really pisses me off.

I guess I want to be a realist, but that's way too hard.

You can stretch a compass's legs out so far that it can't draw a circle anymore. That's madness. I've been doing the splits mentally for so long that it's hard to draw myself up again. Even as I'm doing that, I know my circle's dwindling. My friend and I are still trying to work out other people, to let them color us in, but it just ain't happening. No one's willing! So yeah . . . It'll work out though.

I always thought north must be outside of me, so that's where I'm aiming this toward, like a letter to Father Christmas (although I never believed in him), who hangs out there in all those kids' heads.

Is going north breaking the circle? Probably not; what I really need is an elevator to take me to such a great height that I'd only have to move a little left or right and it'd look like I was stepping into everyone else's circles.

That would be so sweet.

from ABLUTIONS
Notes for a Novel
by Patrick deWitt

Discuss the regulars. They sit in a line like ugly, huddled birds, eyes wet with alcohol. They whisper into their cups and seem to be gloating about something—you will never know what. Some have jobs, children, spouses, cars, and mortgages; others live with their parents or in transient motels and are on government assistance. They are warm with one another but generally come and go alone and as far as you can tell have never been to one another's homes. This makes you lonely and the hearts of the world seem cold and stingy and you are reminded of the saying, *Every man for himself*, which as a child made you want to lie down and "be killed."

You do not take much stock in the North American definition of the word but you suppose these people are alcoholics. They like you, or anyway are used to you, and they reach out to touch you when you pass as though you are a good luck gambling charm. You once found this repulsive and would circle the bar with your back hugging the wall rather than move through the network of fleshy red hands, but you have reconciled yourself to the attention and it has become familiar, even enjoyable for you. It now feels more like a commendation than an intrusion, a recognition of your difficult job, and you nod and smile as the hands grab you around the waist, rubbing and slapping your back and belly.

From your post at the side entrance you watch them watch themselves in the mirror behind the bar. Preening, pecking, satisfied by their reflections—what do they see in their murky silhouettes? You wonder keenly about their lives prior to their residence here. Strange as it seems, they must have been regulars at some other Hollywood bar, but had moved on or been asked to move on, and they sought out a new retreat, settling down with the first free beer or kind word, some bartender's impotent joke mutilated beyond recognition in its endless retelling. And the regulars turned to tell the joke once more.

You wonder also about their present lives but to make inquiries is purposeless—the regulars are all sensational liars. But you want to know what it is about their existence that fuels the need to inhabit not just the same building each night but the same barstool, upon which they sip the same drink. And if a bartender forgets a regular's usual, the regular is cut down and his eyes swell with a lost suffering. Why? It bothers you to know that the truth will never reveal itself spontaneously and you keep on your toes for clues.

When you first come to work at the bar you drink Claymore, the least expensive or what is called the well Scotch. This had been your brand when you were out in the world and you are happy to finally find a never-ending, complimentary supply. You are at the bar for two years, drinking Claymore in great quantity, sometimes straight, often times with ginger ale or cola, before the manager, Simon, asks why you don't drink the quality liquors. "There aren't many upsides to the life, but I drink the best booze," he says. And so each night you sample a different Scotch or whiskey. There are over forty-five different types of Scotch and whiskey and you are very tired at the end of your quest but you find at long last the quality liquor Simon spoke of. As someone who spends a good deal of time surrounded by alcohol, people often ask what you drink, and now you do not shrug or cough but look up and say directly, "I drink John Jameson finest Irish whiskey."

You fall in love with Jameson Irish whiskey. Previously when you held a bottle of alcohol in your hands you felt a comfort in knowing that its contents would simultaneously deaden and heighten your limited view of the world but you did not care for the actual bottle, as you do now with Jameson, you did not trace your hands over the raised lettering and study the exquisite script. One night you are alone in the back bar doing just this—the bottle is in your hands and you are mooning over the curlicues at the base of the label—and the name *John Jameson* brings into your head the child's tune, "John Jacob Jingleheimer Schmidt." You are humming this to yourself when Simon, the man responsible for your discovery of Jameson whiskey, enters the bar singing aloud this *very same song*. He waves to you and walks past, into the front bar, and you are staring in disbelief because there is no explaining so obscure a coincidence and you feel you have been visited by the strongest of omens. Good or bad, you do not know. There is nothing to do but wait and see.

Now a group of drunks in the front have picked up the song and are singing in the single voice of a runaway giant.

Discuss the ghost woman that hovers beside the tequila bottles. Like all murdered ghosts she is in need of impossible assistance. There is a mirror running the length of the bar and as you set up for business you see or believe you see furtive movements of light just over your shoulder and in the reflection of your eyeglasses. This happens hundreds of times so that you come to take it for granted, when one night, alone in the bar, the ghost stops you in your tracks with a cold weight-force centered at your shoulder. You feel as though all air has been pulled from your lungs and mouth and you cannot breathe in or out and you push forward again and this time do not feel the terrible force but the tequila bottles rattle as you move past. You cannot leave the bar unattended and no one will arrive to assist you for over an hour and what you really need is a nice big drink of Jameson but you cannot bring yourself to walk past the tequilas to the whiskey assortment. If you ever hear the rattling again, you say to yourself, you will drop your head on the metal sink edge and knock yourself out, and you see in your mind the image of your unconscious body sprawled on the rubber mats behind the bar. The ghost is fully formed and hanging over as if to injure you but your lights are out and nobody's home and so the ghost, dissolving, returns wanly to the tequila.

You have bad teeth and your breath is poor. Your tips consequently are also poor and there is clotted blood in your mouth and you lose tooth pieces on soft foods like mashed potatoes and rice. You are talking to the bar owner's wife when an entire molar comes dislodged and lies heavily on your tongue. You hope to keep the tooth a secret but you are speaking strangely and her head is cocked in wonder. You have begun to sweat and blush and you pray that she doesn't ask what the problem is but she is opening her mouth and this is just what she does. You swallow the molar and hold out your palms to show that you aren't hiding anything. You are an honest man with a clean, hopeful heart.

Discuss the new doorman, Bolo, who at the end of his third night on the job accidentally cuts a man's finger off. Bolo is a talented young boxer known for a freakish wingspan and first-round knockouts. He is bitter that he has to pick up bar shifts to survive and he wonders if his management team is skimming more than what is customary. You find him intriguing and are impressed with his prejudice when he tells you he listens exclusively to West Coast hip-hop. Anything written or produced outside of California is of no interest to him; there are no exceptions to this rule. Bolo takes a shine to you because you are so skinny and white. He is black and wonders at your drunken life. He asks if you eat only one Cheeto per day and you tell him that sometimes if you are famished you will eat two. You tell him you are available as a sparring partner on Tuesdays and Sundays.

    The lights are up and Bolo is shouting for everyone to leave the bar. He is learning that people want more than anything not to leave and will have many excuses at the ready, but now their excuses are running thin and his mood is ugly. He has kicked everyone out and moves to close the heavy steel door when Simon calls out his name and he turns. He is speaking with Simon while trying to close the door but it is jammed and he slams it three times with all his weight and finally the latch catches and he walks away but hears a wailing outside and returns to look out the peephole and there is the man with the missing finger spinning around and bleeding and Bolo is stepping on something, later he says he thought it was an old cigar. The finger is cleaned and wrapped in ice and given to a friend of the man who lost it and they rush off to the hospital together, and you tease Bolo, calling him a terrific racist intent on de-fingering innocent white men. His eyes raise level to yours and you see that he is heartbroken by what he has done. "I know how important a man's hands are," he says. His shoulders are trembling and the bar workers say nothing. It is at this moment that you fall platonically in love with Bolo.

When you sleep, your dreams are those of a dullard: You polish ashtrays, stock the ice bins, reach for a bottle and find it there or not there, and exchange names and pleasantries with familiar-looking customers. These scenarios run in a spinning wheel and are identical in texture with your drunken memories. As a result, you have only a dim idea of what is fact and what is fiction and are constantly referencing past conversations with people you have never spoken with or else ignoring those you had for fear you had not. And so the general public is of split minds about you: Some say that you are stupid, and some that you are rude.

Discuss the ingesting of pills in the storage room at 7 o'clock and waiting on a barstool for the high to hit. There is a faint chalk line of daylight at the base of the front door and two customers are looking over at you. Their drinks are empty and they want to call out but you make them uncomfortable. Why, they are wondering, *is that man smiling?* The bar is silent and the pills congregate in your fingertips like lazy students in an empty hall.

FIVE GLIMPSES INTO ARMAGEDDON
by Mike Kascel

I. Lacrimosa

Kevin Robbins is kneeling in the middle of his bed with the barrel of a gun shoved into his mouth. The glare of the lightbulb swinging overhead gleams off the pages of open rock magazines scattered across the quilt, like shining portals to other, more interesting dimensions of existence he hopes to be a part of in seconds. He pauses, holding this pose like a boy awaiting communion from invisible priestly fingers. In the silence of this moment, his mind drifts to the most recent friend who has performed this ritual . . .

An early fall Iowa morning. Old farmhouse rises up gray and weathered from bright green grass wet with dew. Silence punctuated by a chirping bird. Faint rays of hazy sunlight on a pale face. Chris carrying a couple bundles of paper, a collection of writings that will basically paint an explanatory picture of what he's about to do. Piece-of-shit camper by a dilapidated barn, opens the camper door and sets papers down. Determination. Wispy breaths of cold morning as he walks to the barn. Inside, he picks up his grandpa's shotgun and stares at it, the weight and reek of steel sharp in nose. Grabs box of shells, heads back to the camper.

He thought there would be tears but there are none, just the sad realization of can't-go-back, hard lump in throat, runny nose. Thin red fingers load two shots into the double barrel.

* * *

Kevin arrives home in Wisconsin exhausted, no sleep since Minneapolis. Opens the door, flips on kitchen light. Note taped to the wall. Shock. Note ripped free along with strip of paint. Chris Garringer committed suicide on Oct. 22. Keep rereading the line. Disbelief. Fuck.

Solitary wide-eyed caffeinated drive down three-hour stretch of predawn pavement. Death smell of dried flower funeral home gift shop. Chris laid out on hospital stretcher. Another friend's shell laying there, decaying motionless unreal . . .

The suicide note he's been up all night writing is lying in an envelope on top of the dresser. The other copy he's written is already post-marked in his mailbox awaiting its delivery to his best friend. He knows from prior experience that the cops will paw all over the letter with their sticky fingers, handing out dog-eared photocopies to the addressed. Fucking pigs. Fuck everything. He shuts his eyes, squeezing them as tight as his grip.

II. Kyrie

Tyler picks up a dark glass bottle, anoints his head with oil. It's the same formula as the sexual attractant that Aleister Crowley used to wear; a mixture of ambergris, musk, and civet. The idea is to apply an amount so minute that it isn't perceived by the conscious mind, tickling the pheromone receptors of others' brains with invisible oily tentacles. He can just see himself sitting at a table in the low light of a club, men slithering out of corners, converging on him from every direction. He imagines spreading out, receptive, body covered with hands . . .

Putting aside these ambitious thoughts, he takes a capsule filled with white powder from a small tin on the kitchen counter and squints at it. Pure MDMA caps, freshly smuggled from a trip to Florida. He pops two into his mouth and washes them down with a swig of beer.

Twenty minutes later he's standing in front of the Bluejay, a dance club popular with the local pierced-and-dyed hipster scene. He walks in. The atmosphere features dim lighting, cool detachment, and thinly veiled self-consciousness. He makes his way through the narrow bar, shouldering past the well-dressed throng. Reaching the back he sits at an abandoned table covered with a red tablecloth, ice melting in half-finished drinks.

Tyler can feel the pills coming on . . . his eyes are wide and dazed, riding out the warm currents lulling his body and flooding his brain. And his typical response to the drug: He can't stop yawning. As he forces his eyes to focus he notices two large deer heads mounted on either side of the passage leading to the restrooms. What a bizarre dissonance. This thought is arrested by another yawn as his eyes unfocus.

When Tyler gets intoxicated there's a rebellion that invades his body, making him want to disorder his environment. This desire rises like carbonation through his brain as he looks up again at the mounted deer heads, a slow smile spreading across his face. He can see a looping replay of exactly what he is going to do, and the anticipation of the revulsion his actions will arouse only fuels his motivation.

Tyler takes the first step down a one-way street, walking up to an occupied table that's directly underneath a deer head. Heavy black boots step from an empty chair onto the top of the table, overturning mixed drinks onto the seated valley-girl intelligentsia regarding him with scrunched-up noses and telling him to fuck off.

He reaches up and grabs his furry prize. It's heavier than he expected but it lifts easily off the wall. He jumps down to the floor and runs a hand over the stiff fur. He wants to rub his face against it but there's no time. The deep black pools of the deer's "eyes" stare up at his own, reflecting the flicker of the candle on the table.

He takes that as a positive sign. This is all happening in slow motion. Tyler reaches into his pocket and takes out a lighter, flicking it on as he brings it up to the deer's head. While fire spreads through the dry fur, a surge of pure joy lights up every cell in his body. He lifts the blazing torch over his head triumphantly and runs toward the crowded dance floor at fifteen frames-per-second.

III. Confutatis

Dylan doesn't know it yet, but in the next few years his body is really going to go to shit. The adorable baby-doll face: sagging. The immaculate black hair: thinning. The once proud, round ass: flat. For now, he enjoys the benefits of being an extremely attractive man in the fickle habitat that is the gay world, a jungle that his genes have left him a natural master of. The bars are the hunting ground where he conquers and holds court—a quiet, dignified prince surrounded by a slow cyclone of fellow predators and potential boys—those who have already fallen victim to his quick cycle of desire/discard, and those who are only now catching his eye. Scattered throughout any bar he goes to is the desperate presence of his army of casualties. They swirl around him quickening the air with their bitchy quips and overeager panting, hoping to be pulled into his orbit. What they wouldn't give to enter through his ear, microscopic undetected, scrambling up those bourgeois brains until his nerve endings transmit their electric blue signals in the shape of love. But as always, as the eye at the center of this world, Dylan remains blissfully untouched.

We follow him around his home as he prepares for a Saturday night out. Some part of his unconscious instinctual radar senses our voyeurism, but Dylan's inflated ego and simple mind transforms this barely perceived intrusion into a trigger for an exhibitionist act. He eyes the slight part in the curtains and places a horny young stud out there in the darkness, sitting in a pickup across the street, eyes drawn to the glow of Dylan's window, a phantom hand stroking himself through denim. Dylan self-consciously pulls his shoulders down and back, straightening the slump of his spine, which causes his already muscular rump to jut out a bit more. He's got a half-erection. He looks at himself in the mirrored closet doors unsmiling, raking a hand slowly through his hair from forehead to the back of his neck, where the hand stops, cupping and slowly massaging the tight cords of muscle. As he does often, he stops and stares at himself motionless in the mirror—at this point, the world outside of his perception is whitened out until just he and his reflection remain. He takes snapshots of every detail with an invisible camera: his angular jawline, the set of his mouth, the razor-sharp line of nose, the shape of his lips. He's fascinated at the image staring out of what he imagines as a negative, reversed dimension, standing there unaware of the passage of time, his gaze held there as a prisoner of his vanity, only half-believing that the face staring back from the mirror really belongs to him. To Dylan, the man in the mirror is sort of a twin to be admired, some other being more desirable than himself. The reflection always seems to try to reveal something he can never quite perceive and assimilate. He can't convince himself that the guy in there is really him. Staring into the mirror intoxicates him, but instead of distorting reality, it constantly confronts him with it, and since his mind is seldom in the same mental space as the world around him, this clarity provides an escape.

Turning his attention back to the real world, he walks to the bathroom, sits down on the toilet, and takes a shit. He flushes, turns on the shower, turns it hot, steps in. Sighing contentedly, he scoops up the shampoo bottle from its resting place by his feet, squirting a generous amount into his hand. He massages the shampoo through his hair, and the anticipated foam quickly forms atop his head like a huge frothy crown. He sighs deeply, imagining the water seeping the tension from his upper body, where it travels down his arms and runs off his fingertips in thin, brackish streams. His eyes close and his head bows until his chin touches his chest. If he could only capture this moment and put it under glass—the sharp, medicinal scent of tea tree soap, the billowing steam, the lather, the hot water warming cold toes.

Much later, Dylan sleeps peacefully next to the guy he's picked up from a bar. Meanwhile, outside in the city somewhere is his most recently rejected boy. Instead of becoming yet another cloud orbiting the hurricane of Dylan's being, he has broken away from the pack—a rogue with a purpose, rumbling with thunder and turning ever darker.

Kevin is driving down the street, around the lake, into a residential neighborhood. He hasn't blinked in like five minutes. He's on autopilot, his eyes don't even register the road. He sees: Dylan's gaze / the gun sliding out of his pants / aim / fire / Dylan's head exploding. These images loop over and over in his head like a mantra. They wouldn't stop even if he wanted them to, but he doesn't.

As he careens onto Dylan's street he throws his cigarette out the window, braking a couple of houses down. He throws himself out of the car, lurches toward Dylan's house. He's a ball of cold, lucid efficiency in the midst of an uncontrollable, temporary insanity. Yanking open the front door, he runs up the stairs, down the hallway, and into the bedroom. Dylan is in bed, turning toward him. To his right is some cute black-haired boy under the covers. Said boy raises himself up on one arm, bleary eyed. Kevin aims, fires, hitting the guy in the face. Bones crunch and blood flies, the boy falls to the floor forgotten as Kevin points his attention and gun toward Dylan.

"Get the fuck out of bed." Kevin's voice is its own entity, his mind separated from his body, floating a couple inches above and behind his head.

Dylan's eyes open as wide as his mouth, which is emitting high staccato creaks. He shields himself with an outstretched trembling hand. He gives his head little shakes from side to side "No . . . no!"

"Yes, yes." In two strides Kevin's at the side of the bed, seething. "Get up, you fucking piece of shit." He drops the barrel of the gun down to rest on the part in Dylan's hair, which sits looking like a metal dog's ear, or some fucked-up antennae.

Dylan is in his basement, sitting on a wooden chair, naked, handcuffed, gagged, tied with rope, et cetera. Kevin is pacing back and forth in front of him, taking deep drags off his Marlboro.

IV. Dies Irae

An overweight middle-aged priest is standing up in front

of his congregation, directing his heavy gaze on the people. He has just finished reading the gospel and is now ready to launch into his sermon. He grips the pulpit with both hands. "How many of you believe we're in the end times? *What* can we *do* . . . to *avoid* this *situation*? How on earth can we keep from being dragged into this tribulation, to be here when it's even worse than it appears, when the storms don't leave a single house a-standin' in a town . . . when the water's *all* gone, when the electricity's been off for months!" The priest stops, swaying slightly on his feet. A slick sheen of sweat shines on his face. Now he takes a great breath, bringing it down a notch. "Some of you, your biggest hindrance, what's hindering you from being blessed and from progressing into the Kingdom, is some unruly, evil kinfolk that's in your house. I see you lookin' over at your neighbor now and thinkin' *He must be talkin' about you, he's not talkin' about me.* Let me tell you now, if you go along with their sins, and you condone what they're doing, and it's happening right under your roof . . . amen, you're responsible for it. And that's hindering your blessing." His face is getting red, he's gone and got himself all worked up again. He leans forward and shouts, "It's not me against those people, it's GOD against the Devil! It wasn't David against Goliath, it was GOD against the Devil! And the ANNOINTING is what's going to bring the difference! Hallelujah! Lift up your hands and just wave your hand to God. I tell ya, the Lord is getting ready to do something special tonight."

"A-men!" an old woman cries out as she slumps to the floor in a faint. Another starts shaking and convulsing, writhing on the floor, spittle flying from her lips. "The Holy Ghost!" she gasps. "I'm filled with the almighty power of the Lawwwd!" The congregation looks around uneasily, shifting in their seats.

The preacher steps down from the dais, light shining in his moist eyes. "Praise . . . God!" he croaks, his voice full of false emotion. "Hallelujah!" He holds his trembling hands in the air. "Clap your hands for the Holy Bible! Lift up your hands and say, *I love you, Lord!* SOMEBODY say amen!! SOMEBODY LIFT UP YOUR HANDS AND GLORIFY THE LORD!!"

The parishioners are one by one swept up in the frenzy. The priest gets an insane look in his eyes. He advances to the altar and crams handfuls of communion wafers into his mouth. He drains the decanter of wine, his robe tenting at the crotch. Grabs an altar boy and grinds his face in it. "Now THIS is heaven," he sighs, disrobing.

The cacophony in the cathedral is rising to a deafening crescendo, old women masturbating over musty yellowed hymnals, moaning, "I feel Jesus in this place." A woman rips into the Bible with her bare teeth, laughingly spewing the wet contents onto her husband. "Peace be with you," she sneers as she gives him the finger. Shit flies everywhere as a wrinkled old woman in a wheelchair pulls out her colostomy bag and swings it around her head like a lasso. "Wheeeee!" she cackles, showing her rotting yellow teeth. Mucoid diarrhea slops onto the Virgin Mary, the stained glass windows. People are rolling on the floor shrieking and pissing. A small freckle-faced kid drops a chunk of cesium into the holy water, causing the vessel to explode in a great fireball. The curtains have caught fire. Tympani drums boom in the distance.

V. Sanctus

All citizens of the world networked together through

computers, the very bloodstream a hybrid of zeros, ones, and hemoglobin. Methodically picking up hermetically sealed needles, they search for usable veins to receive their electronic junk. Finding one that's satisfactory, they push needles through soft hungry skin, storage centers in the brain shrieking. Soft sighs as blood fills the length of the tube. Cold metal sensation in mouth and throat as data trickles into the arm. The computer hums and clicks as calibration proceeds. A special calibration, the final calibration. The Maya program is sent from central control along every data track, executed at every port.

Burp click chirp, metal condensation in back of throat . . . eyes glazing over . . . sensory overload in brain explosion . . . translucent foil liver spots . . . spit hangs in streamers . . . blood rushing through computer guts . . . binary viruses unleashed . . . making friends with white blood cells . . . locking spindle legs piercing membranes, special delivery! . . . incubating metal babies . . . hatch and eat the mother . . . get a load of this . . . bring home a friend for supper . . .

Meanwhile, computers at ISP headquarters around the globe explode, spewing cold DNA/binary viruses that blanket the computer technicians. Semen spurts up through the keyboards as sex chatrooms overload. Fax machines come to life, shooting sheets of paper that slice computer programmers like razors. Photocopier lids slam open and shut. Coffee carafes fly across the room, throwing scalding liquid. Staplers rear up like charmed snakes and machine-gun staples. (Dry, hot wind from ancient Mayan civilization sweeps through every room on earth.) Electric pencil sharpeners whirr, their pencil-sized openings dilating to dinner-plate size, leaping from tables to human faces, blood and hot flesh hitting the walls, ceilings, windows with a thousand wet smacks.

* * *

Bloody nose, pills fly across the bathroom sink bloody handprints on walls window mirror toilet bowl.

A TV through a broken window shows the end of *The Price Is Right*, Bob Barker: "Help control the human population, have your children spayed and neutered," flashing million-dollar endorsement smile.

CURTAINS
(thunderous applause)

ESTRELLAS Y RASCACIELOS
by Justin Taylor

The anarchists were drinking victory shots and making toasts because even though they'd never met with success before they surely knew it when they saw it or it found them. Snapcase, his beard effulgent with spilled drink, had become certain that school was out for*ever*. He'd tossed Jessica's survey of art history, his *Norton Shakespeare*, and somebody's copy of Derrida's *The Gift of Death* into the fire pit they had dug in their backyard. The shallow hole was surrounded by salvaged chairs and shaded by a blue canvas canopy they had stolen from some resort because property was always already theft and anyway they had really wanted a canopy. The books were doused with whiskey from a bottle of Fleischmann's. Snapcase lit a hand-rolled cigarette with a match from a bar he favored. He tossed the lit match into the shallow pit. It went out in the air so he lit another match and placed it gingerly in a little pool of whiskey. It snuffed there. Someone said something about lighting three matches in a row. Somebody else said no, the expression was no three on a match. And how that expression had come from World War I, because if you lit three cigarettes off one match in your foxhole or trench the enemy in his foxhole or trench had three pins of light to triangulate your location and then he blew up everything or maybe just shot you and your two buddies.

Knock off the history book shit, Snapcase said, and where are the history books anyway? His fire was still unlit. The other anarchists who'd been watching were disappointed. I have to be at work in an hour, one said. Snapcase went back into the house for the history books and another round.

Besides, David said, grabbing his dog-eared copy of *The Antichrist* back from Snapcase, I like Nietzsche. Though no less certain in his convictions, David was not prepared to burn his *Dictionary of Critical Theory* and the books to which that book was a kind of skeleton key.

Yeah, but if, Snapcase said.

Why do you call yourself Snapcase, someone said.

Dude, it's a band, don't you know anything about hardcore, someone else said.

David gave Snapcase his copy of *The Prophet Armed* because Trotsky had ordered the Russian anarchists shot down like partridges. Snapcase went away. David eyed Estrella. She was finishing a rum and soda, going to pour herself some more rum, discovering there was no more rum, cursing. The label was ridged with silver like pirate booty. The captain leaned on his sword. The TV was on.

They didn't have cable, but it wasn't a statement. Why should the decision to opt out of the news cycle and the endless infomercials be treated as some sort of aberration? Maybe the statement was being made by the people who parted with their slave wages monthly for the privilege of Wolf Blitzer. Maybe. Today it didn't matter because there was only one piece of news and it was on all the stations. A clip had been looping for hours. With the left rabbit ear twisted down so it touched the thick steel strings of their red electric bass, they were able to tune in to a local broadcast. It was a bottle of light rum that was empty. Hakim Bey and *Pirate Utopias* notwithstanding, none of them had much the stomach for dark.

Estrella was the loudest anarchist of them all. Estrella's band had a song that went, *We'll tear down fucking everything / Till stars are the reigning light / Estrellas y rascacielos / Burning in the ungoverned night.* The bassist wrote the lyrics and she sang them. He loved it when she sang the line he wrote with her name in it and she did too. She loved singing her own name. The bassist always said he wrote the line in homage to the great Spanish anarchists, such as whoever. Actually it was because he loved her. When she sang her own name as part of his lyric it was like she had let him name her. She could sing so fucking loud. The band was a hardcore band. Her guitar roared like a certain kind of sermon. His bass rattled the windows and doors. There were big gigs coming soon; he just knew it. He was passed out under the kitchen table. The TV screen filled again.

David asked to see Estrella's new tattoo. She lifted her black hoodie from the bottom, though it had a zipper. A circled *A* nested between her breasts, which were too small to hang but would have hung if they'd been bigger since Estrella knew that bras were just more bullshit, though sometimes she would put on a sports bra if she guessed they were probably going to be running away from something before their night was over.

I thought it would be cool to get it on my nipple, she said, but the guy said if I did that I might never breastfeed.

What, David said.

Snapcase gathered dead leaves and put them into the pit and then lit those and finally the art books and other ones caught fire.

It's gonna rain, someone said.

It's gonna pour, someone else said and that person was correct. It had been raining earlier but that had been a mere warm-up compared to what would come—that is, with what came.

I like it, David said to Estrella, but it's too bad.

He meant about her breasts, and not being able to get the nipples tattooed on, or pierced even. He thought of the phrase *women's troubles.* The silver ring centered on her lower lip gave her a pouty look, or rather accented the pout of her dark eyes and dark hair and the donned hood of the hoodie and the fact that she was frequently pouting. Her dreadlocks were wild and attractive. When she did push the hood back, as she had done, the dreadlocks made her seem more dangerous or unpredictable, but less severe. David wondered if her kiss had a metallic aftertaste owing to the lip ring and stud in her tongue, or if the salt and wet of her would just overwhelm everything else, even stainless steel.

They drank some whiskey and watched the fire burn until the downpour drowned the flames in the shallow pit. Then everyone went back inside to the TV. They watched and watched. Someone said for smokers to use the front porch and someone else said we should be able to smoke inside on account of the rain and the occasion.

We're out of rum and I don't want any more whiskey, Estrella said.

The liquor store was closing up when I bought the last bottle of rum, David said.

It's only the first blow against the empire, someone said, and someone else said, yeah, but what a blow, I mean boy man God shit, you know?

There was a line around the block at the gas station

when I walked past it, David said. Everyone was filling their tanks and buying up the canned food. I walked in and stole two big bottles of Coke and nobody noticed.

It's on tape though, someone said. It's in the files. Someone else said that Coca-Cola had sponsored death squads in South America and that person was correct. Coca-Cola had done that horrible thing and many other horrible things also. Environmental devastation in India, union-busting, wage-slavery, rotting the gums of anesthetized children and adults, inventing the modern image of Santa Claus as part of a nefarious plot to commoditize Christmas (actually, the modern popular Santa evolved from a series of Thomas Nast illustrations that appeared in *Harper's Weekly* between 1863 and 1865; the Coke Santa was done by the Swedish illustrator Haddon Sundblom in the 1930s, long after the archetype was standardized), contracting with McDonald's, sponsoring various execrable campaigns, here and abroad, sponsoring those death squads in South America, and other things too. So that person was really right for the most part when he or she said those things about the soda they were all drinking but at least had stolen.

I bet that one store stayed open, Snapcase said, and we could go get beer. But I don't want to go.

I'm really leaving now, said Roger, who sometimes went by Dagger but couldn't commit to the alias. He fashioned a rain hat from a plastic bag some Chinese food had been delivered in. He was the one who'd said earlier that he had to go to work. And now he was going.

Nobody knew Estrella's real name was Anne. Even the ones that had been *with* her didn't know. She was that good. Sometimes she almost forgot she had a real name— she was *that* good. The rain beat harder on the windows, the shallow pit overflowed. David said he'd go to the store and Estrella said she'd go with him. She went to look for her boots. You can't count on being able to steal everything you need so when it comes to important things—well—the anarchists pooled their money. David got his wallet but someone said the rain would ruin the leather so he wrapped his fake ID and everyone's money in a twist of magazine paper torn from an old issue of *Adbusters*. He put the wallet away. Lots of people were milling around, watching TV, and deciding what they thought or already knowing or thinking that they already knew. And that was me, thinking I knew.

Angel, Snapcase, this guy they didn't really know but who had been crashing at their place for the past few days, and Jessica were all looking out the back window at the fire pit. I guess it's a book drowning instead of a book burning, Angel said, and the guy they didn't really know mentioned Prospero but then someone put a Fifteen record on and turned it up real loud. *Everybody knows authority is just abuse anyway / Everybody knows it ain't no use anyway / Kill your elected official today / We will win* . . . Estrella couldn't find her boots. David took his boots off as an act of solidarity.

The twist of paper was soaked and the money was soaking. Mud and street dirt squished between David's toes. He told her they needed to go faster. She ran so far ahead he almost lost her in the shifting sweeping curtains of gray water. She could prove anything. Everything was soaked. The storm was a North Florida special. They hurtled like a pair of airplanes. Water ran into his eyes. Her hood was pulled tight but her dreadlocks were soaked anyway. She stepped down on a little shard of glass. This caused her to land badly and she twisted her ankle. David caught up to her.

Ow, she said, I mean fuck. Fuck fuck. She shut her eyes tight because it hurt very badly and also because she didn't realize that with all the water running down her face he couldn't tell she was crying so she was safe.

Her leg quivered like it might go out. She shifted to her good foot and hopped. She landed and wobbled, steadied herself, prepared to hop again. David slid a hand under her arm and his other behind her knees. He lifted her. He carried Estrella through the rain like a husband with a wife or a monster with a cherished victim. He carried her to the nearest house that had an overhang. The sudden freedom from the rain was cold and thrilling. He helped her to sit and took her wounded foot into his hands. He knelt before her. She was sitting in a puddle but there was nothing they could do about that. The whole world was a river that day, rising—taking and bringing things. He cleaned her foot in the puddle as best he could. He wiped away the shiny trickle of blood that flowed from the cut on her sole. He suckled. It wasn't a bad cut, really. Tweezers would have sufficed if they'd had any. The blood was metallic; his mouth did not even fill with it.

I think it's out, she said. Did you swallow it?

I guess I must have, he said. It was really pretty small.

Is that okay? she said. I mean will something happen to you?

I didn't think about that, he said.

Too late now, she said. His selflessness touched her. She considered what that might mean. The tender moment was ending but they'd always have it.

They set back out into the rain. Estrella hobbled,

David walked. The day had been good and it was still cresting. They had made themselves party to a victory and lived by their principles, especially those of solidarity and mutual aid. The store was open. The beer was cold. Revelations waited for them like all the silent seconds on a digital alarm clock before the shrieking starts or else like a land mine. There would be time later for bilious regret and the unique poisons of whatever the bassist thought. But they weren't there yet; they were still safe and free. A pair of real anarchists, they drank on the streets as they strolled home even though it was broad daylight and still raining.

HELL
by Stanya Kahn

A small guy made of knotty red sinews climbs up from the pit of hell. He stands on a mound of gravel in the center of a murky pool waiting for his banishment. He's being cast out of hell for having only one ball. It dangles from a thin yellow cord between his short bony legs, black and hairy and oozing pus, caked with grime. He reaches down and swings the sack over his shoulder. The cord breaks and his one ball flies into the dark water behind him. Now he has no balls. Maybe this is a music video. My head is the camera. I pan up for a shot of the whole pool, see the shadow of something in the water, Leviathan maybe. Yes, a huge snake the size of a subway train bursts to the surface, its glistening wet head morphing from human skull to menacing elephant. It's foreboding and flashy, a wild display of evil and power, a true beast from below. The ritual of banishment matches the severity of the sentence. Swooping down to focus on the shivering outcast, I am now the one chosen to enact the final ceremony of expulsion. I toss a necklace of heavy coconuts around the little guy's neck. It's sad. He's so small and so fucked up. He's just a bulge of indiscernible flesh bumps gnarled into the vague form of a miniature almost-human. Where will he go? Where do you go when you've been booted out of hell? The weighty coconut manacle hangs around his neck, dragging on the floor as he turns and shuffles off the mound into oblivion.

I burned my hand at work, but I'll go in today anyway. I have to steam, iron, and organize the fall season sale items for Macy's Thanksgiving catalog. I will summon the models when it's time for them to dress, I will dress them, put on their shoes, tell them they look great.

 All the clothes are too big. Way too big. The girls are size one and the clothes sometimes a gargantuan six or eight. They giggle and we laugh along, how silly these big clothes are! We pin them in, pull handfuls of fabric tight behind them, making boxy sweaters appear form-fitting and sexy. We pin their pants, all down the back legs, around the waist, pull the crotch up in back, pin it to the waistline. The girls watch themselves in the mirror, mesmerized by their own images. They cross their arms and pout. Please stand straight, I say, again and again. They wrinkle the clothes, they're spaced out and boring. Sometimes they chat. The hairdresser is talking about art, how at one time he'd wanted to be a curator. What's that? the girl asks. Isn't that a person who repairs ancient paintings?

 Sometimes they talk about their boyfriends. The Russian chicks love to party. They come in blank-eyed and pretend they don't understand English so they don't have to gab through hangovers. I whack their feet into place, shove their arms around. When the stylist asks the girl to turn around, I say, Oh, she doesn't understand English. Then the girl protests sullenly, Yah, I understand. She might only talk with the makeup artist and hair guy. They will make her look beautiful. She looks like a bigheaded frog with pale skin and thin corpse hair. Undernourished, her see-through veiny neck reminds me of a spring roll at the Vietnamese restaurant. She tells the makeup artist, Oh man, last night was so crazy. Look. She shows a diamond ring poking up from her bony ring finger. My boyfriend is so crazy. I was doink a fashion show at like 2:00 a.m. at the club where he works and he came onstage and proposed to me! How crazy is dat? I was like, yeah, of course, oh my God! But I don't know, he's so crazy! My hair looked really good. I totally love how they did my hair.

Sometimes they share their worldviews, especially the American girls: I think we should just totally kick ass, I think we should blow those bitches away. They hate us for no reason. Let them kill each other. What are they fighting over anyway? Israel wants Afghanistan's oil?

The Russian girl adjusts her thong. I tap her shoulder. Okay, Natasha. Your turn on set. Knock 'em dead.

Every night I visit another hopped-up hereafter, each one a redecorated hell. Afterlife cosmology is not one of my concerns. I don't have any conscious postmortem affiliations. I'm open to but not completely convinced by ghost worlds, nirvanas, purgatories, reincarnation scenarios, cloudy retirement vistas with joke-telling harp strummers. I have a soft spot for zombies, I relate to their dead-but-not-dead-enough plight. They walk the earth, they torment the living, they clomp around, and everyone hates them. Which I think is hypocritical of the living, but that's another issue. I know a lot of dead people and so far they only visit me in dreams.

Of all the beyonds, according to my detailed, nonbeliever visions, hell is clearly the most glamorous, the most eternal, and the most cogently devastating.

A bustling marketplace in an ancient city: bells and baubles and gauzy clothes. Spectators gather to watch an elephant rip a man to pieces. By the time I push through the crowd to get a glimpse, the guy has no legs and only one arm. I say, How could an elephant do this? And who is this poor guy? He is Gomorrha, the crowd informs me. Everyone's lighthearted. This is what we do on Sundays, plus, he volunteered. Gomorrha's bloody stumps are caked with dirt and he looks faint, like maybe he's had enough. But the people want more. Where's that elephant? Let's finish this thing! I wander away, peruse the stalls of the rambling bazaar: dates, incense, yoga classes, meat, and nuts. I think I'd like a tunic too, maybe some sandals.

Often it's nothing so impressive, just a thinly veiled, low-level depression like TV. Smoke and lights and a stage lit up in gold and Reese Witherspoon wrangling a slippery pole as queen of the devil house dancers. No red and black motifs, just yellow and soft chamois loincloths, beaded faux-Native American bustiers, and glittery lassos. Hell as way out west and tinseltown on the outskirts, beer-stained parking lot, someone puking by the trash bins, pudgy bouncers out front chewing on toothpicks, murmur of a couple of grouchy dancers having a smoke and mulling the idea of moving to Vegas.

I am always surprised by what turns out to be the most terrifying. No half-humans or movie stars, no beasts or infected testicles, just an oversized swimming pool covering half the desert floor, vast as a landing field, dammed at one end with a monstrous wall of concrete so tall I lose my breath at the sight. I try to look away but I can't. A buoy bobs helplessly in the center. The juxtaposition of the tiny and the huge, the natural and the fabricated, is unbearable, nauseating. I go weak with fear. I lose my footing, and suddenly dangle over the edge of the bridge, miles in the air above an unfathomably deep, endless aquatic nothingness. This most certainly is hell.

I love water. I love swimming. I like oceans, pools, lakes, streams, creeks, kiddie pools, sprinklers, puddles, bathtubs. Whenever we take a trip to the health food store, I scan the fences of the nice neighborhood looking for signs of a pool. Look, there's the filtration hut. I wonder: What shape did they go for? Rectangle? Kidney? How about river rocks and a Jacuzzi? Maybe a poolside cabaña and lilacs growing around the base of a naked marble boy peeing fountain water into a stone carafe. How killer to have a pool.

L.A. is hot as hell in the summer. Hot as blazes, they say, hot as the devil's a-hole. Dry and vibrating, the air as stinking yellow and brown as the dusty hills. We have AC in the bedroom, but sometimes I can't sleep at all. I lie awake clicking and ticking and not slowing down. And usually it's a mistake to watch reality shows before bed. Because then each time I move my leg or roll over, the rest of the team has to decide if that was a good move or should I be voted off. I shift back trying to hold my place in the line-up. I'm doing all the competitions at once: *American Idol, So You Think You Can Dance, I Want to Be a Hilton, Couples Extreme Fear Factor*. I like the show where you try to get fired. One girl took her shoes and socks off in a swanky clothing boutique and sat on the floor chatting on her cell phone, telling her friends how boring and stupid her new job was. The other staff huddled around the cash register whispering about the awful new girl, but they still waited till 2:30 to fire her, that's how dumb they were. The girl won $25,000.

Today Natasha and Christina discuss the "looting" in New Orleans. "Why didn't they leave when they were warned? They just want to live like that. You can't help them." I slap the back of her leg into place. $25,000 to rip a model's ponytail off her head and shove it in her mouth. The president has announced zero tolerance for crimes against property. The radio in the RV announces the arrival of troops fresh from Iraq with the order: Shoot to kill. Where do you go when you get kicked out of hell? Now I know. Back to earth as a sick joke. The devil himself flies overhead in Air Force One. He appears on the evening news with a sparkle in his eye. After surveying the damage from far above, he says with a smile: This is all going to be great. We'll have a bigger and better Gulf Coast. He is excited about the new construction. On national television he assures Trent Lott that his beautiful house will be rebuilt—and I look forward to sitting on the porch.

This time I face a river with flat, sodden banks. I climb onto the water itself and walk away. I walk right down the river and wave triumphantly to a glass box full of scientists looking on and taking notes. They give me the thumbs-up. I think maybe I'm not in hell after all. Then I walk right past Ralph Fiennes shivering in a Speedo. I try to get away, step onto a grassy outcropping, and find a soggy pamphlet on a rock.

It's a brochure for a youth summer camp, an extensive catalog of activities and events, with color photos and bold text. "Your kids might DIE here!" announces the first caption giddily. A kid wearing huge, arm-length foam mitts tries to grasp an oversized pencil. "Rigorous writing exercises daily," touts the bubbly font. In the next photo, a boy is pummeled on the lawn with soft rubber bats. A preteen kneels as if praying, mouth open wide, face strained in a yell, in front of a large bean bag chair with a painted-on smiley face. "He who prays LOUDEST and LONGEST to the most ineffectual GOD, wins!" says the banner above. Fur-lined cubicles house adolescents humping pots and pans above an LED screen: "Don't stop until we say." They look tired. Everything is useless or humiliating, stupid or dangerous. Girls wearing paper hats rub fork ends up and down their shins, boys in floor-length gowns bend over a stagnant pool, reaching for dead fish with their teeth. The last page is the application form, already filled out and ready to go.

YOU WEIRD PEOPLE
by Jago Pallabazzer

I give in when the greengrocer girl hands me the crate of carrots. But she already knows it's for the horse. A lucky horse, she says, and I cave in even more suggesting that the horse lives better than we do, that's for sure. I immediately regret having betrayed my mother so easily, with a phony smile, but they all make me nervous. We smile again, and the girl's smile says, Your mother is weird, she looks crazy with those absurd clothes she wears all the time, her weird jabber, I'd rather let the horse starve to death than feed him so many carrots every day. It's a shame caring so much for the animals, you weird people. When I try to win her complaisance by mumbling something about my mother being at the hospital after an accident it seems to have no effect, even though my mother comes every Wednesday to get a crate of carrots. The girl already knows my mother fell from just the same horse we are talking about. They know everything.

Outside the grocery store dogs and people move about in the brown shadow of the trees, and the metal bodies of the cars shine dryly in the sun with white scorching edges. It's time to go but I still need to know where Abate Pharmacy is. The three women in the store have dark eyes and short hair, with piercing looks and faint mocking smiles, and fail to give me a useful explanation of where the pharmacy is exactly until the old man idling in and out of the store steps into the debate and settles: Abate Pharmacy, I'll take him there, he'll ride me home. So I thank him profusely, hating him for being so self-confident. He didn't even ask me.

We move out in the sun and I reach for the back of the car, eyes half-closed, crate of carrots in my arms. I warn him that the car is a mess, it is the way my mother keeps it. He says okay and starts to fight his way into the car against empty bottles, dried sheets of newspaper torn to pieces, the yellow case of snow chains that tumbles against his feet every time the little Panda accelerates, various slabs of dried mud scattered around the place, seats included. The overloaded ashtray exhales out gray and white particles that flit between our legs. Dogs share the car, I explain to him. He wouldn't appreciate if I started blaming my mother for this, even though I am quite willing to. He repeats three times, No problem.

In two minutes we arrive at Abate Pharmacy, which is a quiet door gaping on a narrow lane abandoned in the shade. At the opposite end of the alley shine the round hills down in the distant land before the Italian sea.

Me and the old man part with a wave and a grumble, but then he calls me from the other side of the road and says, The grocery girl, she's my daughter, she's a good girl. I nod. In my paranoia I figure he has a scheme that I should marry her.

The round face of the pharmacist takes its time to scan mine. He has that priestlike morbid aura. His eyes say he likes me in a filthy not confessed or repressed way, conveying his desire in the gloomy light of the pharmacy as he hands me the prescription for my mother. Cats are waiting for me too.

In fact, on the road across the olive groves in the countryside marked with *trulli* and modern cement angular houses, I have to stop by an abandoned lot to feed a bunch of stray cats. Cats are flocking over, meowing and rubbing themselves against the edges of the old stony low walls, when the car halts and I climb out. I have precise instructions about where to drop the food. The different small bowls and the old scraped aluminum pans, one for each different cat, are important. The pick order is important. My mother is crazy.

Then, rolling down the shattered lane inside the Panda, I think of my mother, and of anyone else, and how it would be if they all died. Because my mother is at the hospital, I am authorized to have this thought. As the road slopes down along the old stony walls in the opaque green of the branches, all into that landscape I am not familiar with, I imagine funerals, words of condolence and affection spurting out and about, and I don't really cry (I am not good at it), and what I supposed should come to me with a long-awaited sense of liberation, almost a secret joy for a new life, leaves me disappointed and tired.

At first I think I must be good at heart, if the daydream of freedom and new life and something-finally-happening and all the deaths doesn't cheer me up. Then, driving to my mother's house, in the car jolting against the roots that crack the driveway, I wonder. Good at heart, or is it just that I am unready to use any new life and its freedoms? Maybe that's why I am good at heart.

At the end, the nine dogs are rushing out barking and howling against the fence to cheer my approaching smell and figure. The wind is ruffling their fur, scraps of toys and clothes are scattered in the yard, their animation is irrational and sweet. My perceptions are blanked out by a weight of complacent, absurd lack of criticism, as I mentally go through the instructions regarding the return home. One bone-shaped biscuit for each of the dogs, in a precise hierarchical order. Two biscuits for the biggest one. The old Marcel barks fiercely and runs across my legs. He knows he comes first.

BREAKFAST IN THE TOY DISTRICT
by Aaron Nielsen

for Danielle Willis

"Do you want to see zombies?" Jill asks me, lip curved into a slight smile. And because nothing else is really going on right now, I tell her, "Yeah, sure, let's do that."

They roam downtown L.A. You can usually find them around 2nd and Los Angeles Street in the part of town called the Toy District. I always thought they were a rumor, an urban legend or something like Big Foot, the Loch Ness Monster, etc. . . . the Los Angeles zombies. But Jill assures me that they're very real, and that she's seen them. You just need to know which side street to take, which back alley to turn down. She found them one night after going to a show at the Smell. She was drunk, lost, looking for the freeway, and then *bam!* One wrong turn later she was driving through a zombie shanty town.

"Are you sure they weren't just like homeless people?" I ask her.

"No, dude, they were rotting," she explains earnestly.

"Maybe it was a leper colony?"

"I don't think so. I've seen those shows on the Discovery Channel about leprosy. These things were dead, totally."

"So where'd they come from?"

"I don't know. I heard the CIA had something to do with it."

"Oh, like how they were piping crack into the ghettos?"

"Something like that, yeah."

"Except instead of turning people into addicts, they turned them into the living dead?"

"Yeah."

"Right," I whisper, and the car drives on.

Buildings pass by and all I see are homeless people. I start to feel maybe tense so I light a cigarette and roll down my window. I trust Jill, but I don't believe it. This all kind of reminds me of that guy who claimed to have seen a werewolf one night on Mulholland. Big fucker, he said, almost hit the thing with his Audi. I think I heard that guy shot himself in his Silverlake apartment last weekend. Maybe if someone believed his werewolf story he wouldn't have done that. I'm cautious, so I'm humoring Jill.

She—Jill—is going through a bad patch or something. Her boyfriend—Jeremy—might or might not be queer. Either way, the guy's still an asshole, so Jill and I have been spending a lot of time together, you know, talking. I am sympathetic but mostly I bide my time and wait for a moment when I can ask her questions about their sex life. See, Jeremy looks like Mike Pitt, that guy who was in that Bertolucci film *The Dreamers*. In case you haven't seen it, Pitt looks a lot like that other guy Leonardo DiCaprio, except hotter. So when tact permits, I ask about their sex, though my interest has been waning. One drunken night Jill told me that Jeremy has a small dick. The conversation went something like this:

"So, what, it's like five inches or something?"

"No."

"Six? That's not that bad."

"Smaller."

"Huh?" Being gay, I couldn't conceive of "smaller."

"He's like four inches, hard," she blurted out.

"That's sad." I paused. "Well, at least you know he's not gay."

"Do I?"

"Yeah, his dick is too small. Everyone knows most gay men are between seven and nine. Only straight guys have dinky weenies."

"Then maybe I should start dating gay men," Jill sighed.

We've now been driving around the Toy District for half an hour, still no sign of the zombies. We have, however, encountered enough hyper-poverty to last a lifetime. It really looks like a Third World country over here. If you're looking for a one-legged hooker, this is the place to come. I can tell Jill is getting frustrated, or she's sensing that I'm losing interest.

"I swear they're here," she muses, mostly to herself.

"I'm sure they are, but maybe they only come out at night?"

"No, daylight is the best time to look for them, you can see them better."

"Oh," I say, and wonder if seeing them better is such a good idea.

When Jill and I are bored, we have several games we play that help us pass the time. Usually we play the band name game, where one person says a band name and the other person has to say a band name whose first letter starts with the last letter of the previously said band. It's basically a way for us to show off our awesome knowledge of music; we both used to work in record stores. The other game we play . . . well, I don't know if it's a game so much, but the other thing we do is tell each other about horrible, nasty sex things. Between us we've amassed a heinous library of all things perverse. Example:

"Hey, Jill, do you know what an Alaska pipeline is?"

"No."

"It's when you take a shit, freeze it, and then fuck someone with it."

"Oh God! Are you serious?"

"Maybe."

"All right, Aaron, do you know what a gift giver is?"

"Uh, nope."

"It's a guy who gets off on intentionally giving other people AIDS."

"That's fucking *wrong.*"

This game never lasts long, we get too grossed out, but it explains our mind-set, like why we're out here in scummy downtown L.A. looking for animated corpses on a Saturday afternoon when we could be at the beach or shopping on Melrose or something. But no, Jill and I want to see the worst.

"Okay, um, do you know what a glass-bottom boat is?"

Jill rolls her eyes. "I told you that one, it's when you put saran wrap on your face and someone takes a dump on you."

"Okay, maybe you did tell me about that one." Pause. "Speaking of shit, you smell that?"

"Yeah, but I don't think . . . That smells like rotting meat."

"Or sour milk."

"Or a corpse."

Jill slows the car down to a crawl. We both start to scan the sidewalk, excited, enthusiastic. But by the time we get to the end of the block, the smell has begun to fade and we haven't spotted any zombies. So Jill circles the block again, and on the second time around we notice something. On my side of the street there's a pile of black garbage bags, but behind that, out of our direct view, something is moving slightly.

"Could be a dog."

"Or a homeless person."

"The smell could just be the trash."

"Or . . ." I roll down my window. "Here, zombie, zombie, zombie . . ."

I mean, I guess that's how you call a zombie. Jill and I wait nervously for something to happen.

"You know, you're probably just gonna piss off some bum."

"Whatever. Zombie, zombie, zombie, we've got *brains* . . ."

"This isn't a Romero movie."

"Oh."

"Wait, I think it's moving . . ."

And sure enough, whatever is behind the trash starts to come into full view. At first it doesn't really register, what I'm—we're—looking at. Seven feet from the car is half a body propped up in a wheelchair. The legs and, well, everything else below the belly button are missing, rotted away or eaten by a dog. Its right arm is twisting, shaking and banging around as if it were being electrocuted. The other arm, hand, etc., moves the wheelchair. The torso is a grayish color, the shade of smog, so old it almost looks mummified. There are two shriveled breasts, like rotten fruit, hanging on the chest, so I guess this was a woman. The head: one eye a pussy blister, the other gone all together, nose worn away, lips just not there, ivory teeth fragments threaten us from a gaping jaw. And inside that jaw, the brown tongue, like its right arm, constantly moving, constantly squirming. For a moment we all just stare at each other. Me, too afraid to move, Jill . . . I'm too focused on the zombie to know what Jill's doing, and the zombie . . . its head straining forward, toward the car, rocking back and forth like a snake about to strike. Then it starts to moan. A sound like a woman giving birth crossed with a cat in heat comes from somewhere within the thing. I start to puke. I grab an old grease-spotted Carl's Jr. bag off the floor and empty my stomach contents into it: pancakes, vegetarian sausage, and organic orange juice. While I'm hunched over, Jill starts snapping pictures of the thing with her camera phone and telling me, "See, I told you they're real! I told you they're real!"

PATRICK
by Frankie p

i watched my friend and his eyes were watery. and i felt like i could kiss him on the nose. and i thought maybe his freckles were contagious or something. they looked like they could stick to me like glue. like to my cheeks, you know. from his to mine. and i thought that if i lit a cigarette it would calm me down and i'd be capable of doing this, ignoring the freckles. although you know the freckles were cute and i loved them on him. i just didn't think they would look good on me. and they wouldn't. so i burned this hole in my t-shirt. right like near the bottom. and so it looks kind of cool and my friend told me it did. and i agreed. and i thought it came out perfectly as i envisioned it. and it did. and i couldn't wait to go to the mall or something and show it off. i think i might burn cigarette holes in some of my other shit as well. and i tell my friend and he tells me to be careful not to overdo it. he says i might seem like a fake or something. like i was trying too hard. i was. but only because he was making me so nervous.

"i'd like to kiss you now," i tell him, and he steps forward and says, "okay." and i kiss him on the cheek first and then i kiss him on the lips. but he doesn't kiss me back, just kinda stands there and lets me do all of the work. and i grab the back of his head and pull him in tighter. and still nothing comes out of this because he isn't into it. i back away and take a drag of my cigarette. i watch him and he watches me and then he stares down at his vans.

when i was a kid all i did was wear vans. vans were my life. red vans, blue vans, black ones, white ones, at one point even pink. pink was my rebellious stage. i loved pink. the ones my friend is wearing are black-and-white checkered ones. i kind of like them.

"how's your mom?" i ask him, and he says his mom is fine. and i remember when she was drunk and tried to put her finger in my ass that one time. and i never told him and i probably never will. and i wanna finger him in the ass kind of. but i don't mention this to him and i probably never will.

someday, i think, i'm going to run away and no one's going to know i disappeared until it's too late. maybe my friend will notice before it's too late, but he probably won't do anything because i think he feels the same way. maybe we will disappear together and they'll only know when it's too late. but then again, for him they'll know before it's happened. my friend is tall and he is blond and blue-eyed and he has freckles and he has a pale complexion and he's skinny and he makes me woozy. the way he stares at me makes me woozy. he stares at me because he thinks i'm the only one that understands him. i don't get him at all sometimes. i don't get him ever. but i'm glad he thinks i'm a good friend. i'm glad he thinks i get him. he is beautiful and i'm convinced he'd be a lousy lay.

patrick's only been missing a day now, but i'm already going crazy looking for him. if he's not hiding in the box under the bed where i put him a billion times before then i have no fucking clue where he possibly could be. god, my friend is gorgeous, so why is he gone? if i was gorgeous i'd be visible forever. i mean i'd kill myself, but i wouldn't like get buried. i'd be in the pictures and i'd be ashes. i'd be ashes by the pictures on some shelf or something. and they'd show me off like i was still alive. my eyes would be anyway. i'd be in a fucking museum, i think. pretty boys with shaggy blond hair. he's one of them and that's why i like making him go inside the box so much. number one, he actually allows it, and numbers two, since he is allowing it, it makes me feel like i am therefore beautiful too. it makes me feel like i could die and it would be okay cause he had let me keep him in a box. you know, for those five minutes. it doesn't matter. cause those five minutes add up to hours in the end. but sometimes i think i should be trying to suck him off instead.

patrick's in the hole in the ground in my backyard. the box is empty, i checked. this doesn't mean that he is dead. this simply means he's hiding. when we were kids we'd always hide inside the hole. and i don't know why i forgot. if patrick is in the hole then everything's still safe. i can picture him now laughing and hiding and thinking i'm a loon for thinking he was dead. and i wonder if his parents are worried. probably not. his dad's away on business and his mom's too fucking drunk. i love patrick and his issues. his family issues. it makes me so horny to think he probably cries himself to sleep at night. i'm pretty sure he does. he cried in front of me before. a lot when we were kids and once now as teenagers. as kids he cried because of the obvious abuse at home and all the constant yelling, etc. as teenagers because of something i still don't quite have figured out. i know i touched his crotch about it though and i know it made it worse because he hugged me really tight and started sobbing on my shoulder. i don't think i let go. i think i squeezed it tighter. his dick. and i think i heard him whimper but figured it was cause of the emotional pain. now i think it might've been my grip. shit, i'm sorry. not really. where is he? he isn't there. not in the hole. i mean, the fucking hole's not even there anymore. duh, we were like ten back then. the hole was when the yard was dirt. now it is cement. i guess i figured it'd still be there anyway. i guess if patrick was lost then it had to be there. cause if not i've no other place to look. and i wonder if i should maybe stop looking and let him come to me. and i decide that's probably the best idea. and i pray to god to send him back down to me. and i pray to god that he lets me suck his dick. and i pray to god to forgive me for praying for that. and then i shut my eyes and fall asleep.

    in my dream patrick is baby blue. his face is baby blue and his freckles are red. his hair is orange. he's staring at me. light shade of purple lips pouting in my direction, enticing my pink ones. and i feel him rubbing up against my skin and it feels good. and i feel him tracing his fingers against my crotch and it feels really good. and i feel me getting harder by the second and that begins to hurt. and i start to unzip and then i break free and it's irritable and it's wet and i look him in the eyes and then he's gone and i'm alone and i'm hiding in the hole and he's up there looking down at me and he's shirtless and he's smiling and then it starts to rain and i am dead and i know this cause it's dark and i'm floating in the water and there's no bright light or tunnel and i know this is my fate.

    "how's patrick?" my mom asks. "i don't know," is my response. and i really don't and i really hate these pancakes. i'm a vegetarian like patrick. "mom, he's missing," i say, and she looks at me like way concerned. "are you sure?" she says. and i'm like duh and i say, "duh." and then i hand her my plate of pancakes and i'm pretty sure she's all hurt about it and i don't care cause i'm gonna be late. and i leave and she calls patrick's mom to confirm that i'm not crazy. and i'm not.

at school there's talk of patrick and everyone's concerned, though no one really knew him but me. and i didn't even really know him, really. and so everyone should shut the fuck up and kiss my feet. and, uh, they kinda do. they tell me all kinds of bullshit like how they're sorry and how they hope that he gets back safe. but really all anybody ever wanted to have to do with him was sex. all they ever really wanted was to suck his dick. all they really wanted was his firm tight ass. their fingers in it like his mom's. and you know that's what i wanted too, so i understand, but i'm a self-loather and so it makes sense i'd be upset.

this boy nick really bugs me about patrick while we're smoking underneath the bleachers. he says all kinds of dirty shit in between the fake stuff. he says, "i really hope patrick's okay, he was a really nice guy," and i nod my head and then he leans in and he says, "he gave me killer blowjobs in the locker room and i wanna show you what he did." and man this kid is so fucked up and i totally wanna take him up on that offer, but i think that he is lying to me cause patrick was a saint. plus i have a girlfriend and i don't think she would take it very well. i dismiss him after the fifth filthy whisper and then he goes away all bummed out and, um, horny.

when i get home the cops are there and they wanna know all about patrick. they wanna know his shoe size, they wanna know his favorite food, they wanna know if i ever got the urge to beat his face in with a baseball bat. and i answer all these questions dishonestly: "i don't know. i don't know. no." and after a while they go away, but i know they think i had something to do with it. and i know they think i killed him. but i know i didn't kill him because then he'd be in heaven. and if he went to heaven i would never see him again. i had to fuck him first. then he'd be a fag. my logic is perfect. i'm not a fucking idiot. i know what i'm doing. in hell we'd burn together. side my side. and we'd fuck gently with the devil and it would kill us both.

my mom thinks that i did it too. i can tell by the way she looks at me. i can tell by the way she talks to me. i can tell by the way she tells the phone, "i think he did it, maggie." "why are you always pretending that my mind is all fucked up!" i shout at her. and she shouts right back at me. and i run upstairs and turn the music on real loud. and bob dylan's on the record player and in my brain and he's in hers too and i know it drives her crazy. "crying like a fire in the sun / look out the saints are comin' through / and it's all over now, baby blue." and she bangs on my door cause she can't take it anymore. and i refuse to unlock it and let her in. and i don't. i block her out. and i listen to the music until the tears are running down my cheeks. and i listen to the music until we are connected again. i listen to the music until patrick's underneath my bed in the box where i kept him every evening. and then i fall asleep because i'm comfortable again.

"they found patrick's bike," lacey tells me. and i'm like so not relieved or care, really. and i say, "oh, really? good," i say, "that's good." and lacey is my girlfriend and she's a good girlfriend so she is genuinely concerned. i wish i was too. patrick's an illusion now or a bad dream or something. if two months ago he had returned and walked into my room and grabbed my dick and laughed or something, then i would've jumped up in joy and kissed him hard until he bled. but now, i don't really care cause i'm pleased with fucking lacey and lacey's pleased with fucking me. the missing posters and the news reports have vanished like he did and with that so did my my concerns and everybody else's. even patrick's parents have gone back to their old lives. drinking, working, being away, all that, etc. whatever.

"they found it in the lake in the park on karlton street. the lake," she says, and i really don't care and i think it might be showing. she looks at me a bit strange and i know she knows for sure now. "you okay?" she asks. and "no" is my reply. and she gets closer and puts her arm around me and rests her head on my shoulder and says, "even if he's dead, we both know he's in heaven." and i think this is the cheesiest shit ever, plus i really couldn't care less.

the next morning at the dining room table i check to see if it is true. and when in the beginning his picture could be found on the front page along with updates, a missing young pretty brunette has taken his place, and he's been banished to the page before the classifieds. his yearbook picture stares back at me and it's so weird seeing him. i don't have any photos of him and he looks different than in my dreams. he's beautiful and he is perfect but he doesn't glow and he doesn't breathe and he looks so young and boyish. and it feels so different now. i feel like he's another person and i knew him even less than i had first pretended.

"i wonder if you wonder about me still," he says. and my response is, "no." "i wonder if you even care." and he turns so i am facing the back of his blond head. and i reach for his shoulder and turn him around again. and he looks at me and his face is blank. he has no eyes, no nose, no mouth, no anything. an empty canvas, a piece of flesh. and i realize this is what he's always been. "i don't want you in here anymore. don't want you around," i confess. and the tears don't form because they can't, but if they could i know they would. "you're like a ghost," i say. "just go be free and leave me be . . . please," i beg. and then he starts to disappear and for five days straight i don't get any sleep.

when i get the news via my sobbing mother of patrick's body being found, i'm far too numb to give a shit and far too numb to show it too. instead i'm like a fucking zombie trying to find my fucking grave. and i'm standing there and she is hugging me, she's hugging me so fucking tight. and i can tell my heart's not beating cause my mom's feels so alive. she feels so real and so in touch with god and life and me. i'm so lost and i'm so wandering and i'm so fucking dirty. i can tell that things aren't okay. i can tell that i'm long gone. and i think about the box and the hole and lacey and bob dylan. and i think about how fucked-up things are without patrick. how if patrick was here things would be fine. i don't bother to ask where they found him or what happened. i don't bother to even think about it. all i can feel is the life of my mother rubbing up against my corpse. and all i can think is that my heart's stopped beating and it's probably for the best. and if patrick hadn't died before we fucked then right now i'd be on my knees and praying. but since he had the beauty in his soul to die, i knew that in a few more steps i'd be there with him. not in hell, i'm pretty sure. but we'd be sitting in the hole again playing with the toys and wondering what all the yelling is about and crying openly without a care.

DUELS
by Will Fabro

He screams the word "fuck" accompanied by a piece of spittle which flies from his mouth and lands on my bottom lip. Surreptitiously my tongue curls around the drop, taste buds alerting mind: This is the taste of his hatred, his fear—a whiskey-drenched warning with a vague underline of desire. My mind alerts all muscles to clench while tongue searches lip for more of the taste.

A punch.

The last words he said to me were, "Dan, I can't." The ensuing accompaniment was the click of him hanging up the phone and silence followed by perpetual dial tone. My sweaty palm gripped the receiver for what must have been two minutes minimum. Strangled it bloodless till the sound echoed my numbness.

Before numbness was a general gut-punch. Or heartbreak. When it happens it's hard to tell which organs are affected. When someone speaks of a breaking heart I think of a solid glass figure thrown to the ground, its shards scattering to stick into gut, lodge in throat, cut into skin, and prick at eyeballs—here comes the fluid.

It wasn't what he couldn't do; that was unsurprising. That had been coming for quite some time, was what I could see zooming down this preordained path. Knowing its inevitable existence I could brace for its impact.

Shock resided in the proper noun. We never used our names, never alluded to them, concocting deepened intimacy from that lexical negation. So saying my name was jarring and ludicrous, like referring to yourself in the third person. So much of us lived in the other that the assumption, when we opened our mouths, was that no one else existed.

Using my name rendered his final words absolute. I had to believe it. Saying that he can't I realize it's true and suddenly there I am again: who I really am, autonomous. No longer mixing with his blood.

I can't say his name just yet. Don't know why.

As we lay there, facing each other but unable to catch gazes, I heard the low buzzing moan of a fly lazily tracing incoherent lines and swirls in the thick stale air hovering above us. I wondered what it would be like to be that fly, to be scared enough by me to zoom upward with (as well as like) a gasp. Flies have countless eyes and through every one we were clearly curled into a crude heart carved on the stained white linen—shins touching, arms barely meeting in the space between our separated torsos. Perfect as our bodies could get to resembling the shape; the rigid facts of skeleton rendered the symbiotic heart lacking its usual graceful curvature.

We couldn't spend eternity this way.

[I once said: *Hey, ever notice that half a heart looks like a question mark?*]

One of us had to get up and break that heart; leave it splintered, leave the bed half as full with unadorned flesh now assembled as a question mark. One of us had to lie here and be that question mark. The other had to break the heart.

[You responded by pointing at the doodle: *But hearts don't look like that. A real heart fucking looks like goddamn Wisconsin.*]

—FUCK! Then a punch.

In retrospect I see that punch in slo-mo, fingers folding in on themselves, a blooming flower in reverse. That fist rushes into me, I see stars or fireworks and it's his hazy exploding pattern seared onto my retinas.

> ‹I have these dreams where I'm sitting in black-and-white, seated in some smoky room where the only sound is the flapping of film against a projector, film unfurling images before me. An image of his face staring blankly ahead: at the camera, at nothing, at me. Jump-cut to myself at a younger age, sitting in rapidly growing grass, then visible splice to scratchy picture of fist zooming into frame, followed by out-of-focus shot which clears to . . . that man. From years ago: face hovering, snarling. My naked body splayed on my stomach—see that dark liquid, it's supposed to be blood but the lack of color makes it look like ink. Jagged splice back to that fist, except in reverse: Its retreat from the camera reveals his face staring blankly back at the camera. At nothing; at me.›

If my memory is one of those movies I revisit, then I'm currently watching his mouth spit blood as my fist splits his lip in retaliation against his blow. In his eyes I see that I'm taking it all out on him, what a surprise. We jostle on this mattress, in temporary equality, until he becomes overpowering, rushing inside, rough as possible. I inhale/am suffocated by him, his sweat and anger pouring from his skin, his scent embedded onto the sheets from days gone without washing. I never wanted to change those sheets. I wanted to smell him even when he was away, to roll around in them and carry him with me all day. Sometimes I wouldn't shower either; couldn't bear to cleanse him from my body.

As he thrusts like a knife detonating my insides, my muscle memory's displaced, remembering this and him as part of personalized history. When he finally collapses on top of me, we both breathe out from relief, a release.

My body leaks from him. His face leaks from shock, disgust, and one decent punch. Arms circle me, smothering but an attempt to soothe. I pull away. I liked the feel of fight. I'm not accustomed to efforts of comfort.

We lay there awhile, facing but unable to look at each other or speak. Eventually he gets up, wordless, and leaves.

THE END

The party was terrible and I felt remarkably ancient standing there, silently chain-smoking in a corner, even if I was only four years older than everyone else. I glanced at the computer, which had a program blasting random MP3s from its tinny speakers. Right then it was some godawful thing that was probably in constant radio rotation. I downed the rest of my beer in two long gulps and headed to the kitchen to grab another.

When I got back to my spot in the corner he was standing there, furrowing his brow at the monitor. After drinking him in I followed his gaze.

"Just am amazed at the selection on this thing," he muttered slowly.

"Oh, really." I internally rolled my eyes but managed to feign social grace.

"Yeah, I mean—" he pointed at the screen then threw up his hands, "What the fuck is Simple Plan?"

"The only *Simple Plan* I know of is a Billy Bob Thornton movie."

"Seriously, what a shitty band name." He turned his focus to me and smiled, extended his hand. "I'm Bryan."

I took it, grateful for its smooth pale touch against my callous brown, and shook. "Dan."

"Dan: I feel old."

"Fuck, me too. Why are you here?"

"I know Lisa, one of the girls who lives here." He took a sip from the plastic red cup and nodded in my direction. "You?"

"Her roommate is my best friend's sister. I'm new to the city, so she invited me."

"Ah. How old are you?"

"Twenty-three."

"Me too. You realize we're basically surrounded by fucking NYU freshmen, don't you?"

"Yeah, it's abominable."

Just then Hole's "Violet" came on to a collective "wooo" or "yeahhhhh" or some other exclamation from the crowd.

Smiling, he screamed back at the crowd, "You were all fucking nine when this came out!" It was unnoticeable over the screaming chorus.

"You realize," I said, "that we were only thirteen."

He shrugged. "Yeah, but we were dealing with puberty, which made angsty grunge easily relatable."

At some point he whispered, "Got a little coke left, if you're interested." I nodded enthusiastically and we fought through the partiers to find some privacy. He led me to Lisa's room, where we holed up and finished what was left of his gram. We cut up the lines on the Metal Machine Music jewel case because he thought it was apropos.

We rejoined the crowd vaguely blown-out and cynical. He made a beeline for the computer and somehow put on a Deerhoof record. We bonded over that, air-guitaring/drumming and singing the word "flower" in broken English.

Eventually we left, tired of the atmosphere and feeling old. He wanted to score more blow so he made me wait in front of an apartment building on Avenue C while he copped the goods.

Wandering along Houston Street he turned to me and asked, "What the fuck time is it?"

I shrugged. "Don't have a watch, but I'd guess like 4:30."

"Serious?" He paused, stood still, and said, "There's this park past FDR Drive and you can see the Williamsburg Bridge. Wanna go?"

"And do what?"

"Chill. Do some coke. Whatever."

"My apartment's just on First Ave."

"Yeah, but this is more fun." He started walking toward the East River.

Freaked out, I followed him, could barely hide the trepidation in my throat when I asked, "Don't you think that's kind of a bad idea?"

"Hey, if there's some junkie who wants to fuck with us, I'll take care of it." His bravado was an intense aphrodisiac, like what muscles and pale youth are to others. My feet instinctually followed.

We sat on a bench, alone and silent save for the sound of wheels on the wet asphalt of FDR Drive. I took out a cigarette and stared at the twinkling lights on the bridge, at a shrouded Brooklyn across the river. Before I lit the cigarette I could smell my black fingerless gloves carrying the scent of Gauloises and spilled alcohol and the bodega coffee that leaked out of the cup this morning.

"See, this is nice," he exhaled, dipping a key into the coke and offering it to my awaiting nostril.

"Yeah, it is."

It took him an hour to reach for my hand. He held it hesitantly, shakily, eyes focused in the exact opposite direction from me. I gripped his fingers and didn't let go until we reached my building, saying goodnight even though the sun had poked into the sky hours before.

I hung up the phone eventually, I just don't remember doing it. I don't remember how long I lay sleepless on my side in that now-empty bed, though it must have been awhile since I noticed the sun going up and then back down. I do remember picking up the phone and almost dialing the combination of numbers that leads to his voice. I remember sitting in front of an empty sheet of paper, trying to write a plea or explanation or harangue. That paper's still blank. I couldn't find the words.

When I was younger I had a habit of taking a razor to my skin, no reason explainable. Once it got so bad I had to get stitches and counseling. Felt so dumb I couldn't bear to do it again. But there was something about release, needing something to come out, making it tangible. A method of displacement. Sometimes as memento for a specific time and place of feeling. I carved out lines I couldn't write, and they were my articulation. He once kissed them, as if his spit could dissolve them. I didn't want them erased; I used to want my skin to vanish, but it now contains my narrative, my history, no matter how unwanted.

It's impossible to scrape off these lines and start over,

so I add to the unreadable arc. *Blood becomes my ink / I need to release this / get him out of me so he can exist on his own.* I can't say his name but I can carve a crude *Bryan* on my leg. I've granted him autonomy and yet still keep him as part of me. I hope this minor technicality doesn't keep any of his organs from functioning properly. We'll soon see about me, glass bleeding from my skin.

MY BODY'S WORK
by Matthew Williams

my body's introduction
Transgressive. Queer. Literature. It is what I am after. What I write to achieve. This type of honesty and drive brings this introduction into existence. This introduction will not exist in the final publication. It will become lost. It will not exist. I created it to not exist.

I created my life to not exist. I created my life for fiction. I created the rape and abuse for words as visuals. I have not lied in these pages. I have existed inside each word. Because I am each word.

I do not believe fiction is created. Fiction is lived. Fiction is my reality with a broken neck. I took what I knew and let it spill. I slit my wrists and blood was ink turning to sound to word to page to novel. I could not stop until I wrote.

At the age of nineteen I stopped writing. My writing sat empty. It was a flower vase. I could see through all of it. No matter how much beauty I tried to slip inside it. I saw through it. For four years I changed my life. I lived what you will read. I lived what I wrote. What I write. It was an exercise. Stop writing in order to write better. My hands would ache. My body would explode with image for a page. My mind was filled.

That is why this introduction will never exist. It turns what you will read into reality. I do not wish to achieve nonfiction. An autobiography. I created my life. I did not live my life. I made the decision to become fiction. So I make the choice to write as such.

my body's staircase

1.

When I wake up it is because the sleeping pills have worn off. No alarm clock. I stopped relying on it when I started college. No reason to really wake for anything. If I woke in time for class I went to class.

I never remember the night before. I don't know how to explain the feeling of something that might not exist. The flashes of what may have happened. Mixed with the reassuring mind saying, *not possible. you're still in one piece. not possible.*

I try to ignore my boners. The less I jerk off on my own the more I can shoot in the evening. The men I work with like big loads. Something they can choke on. Something that almost takes them out of this life. Just far enough to appreciate the whole fucking thing.

So I have to lie in bed until I am soft. Then I travel to the showers. Dorm life is desperate. Shared showers and toilets. Having to wear water shoes while I wash. I only get to wash my feet at the hotels I spend my evenings in. If I am allowed. If he lets me.

I make eye contact with everyone I pass. They always turn away so quickly. Does anyone pause long enough to look into anyone? Do they all run away scared? They hurry off to their rooms. To their circle of strangers whose eyes they've never seen. I stare into the eyes of every man who fucks me. Even when he spits into my face. I keep myself open. It is the only way to learn.

I am not sure what classes I have missed. After my shower I will check the calendar in the student lounge and discover what day I am in. I hate not knowing. But there are other things to know. And I am learning those things instead.

I have three books I should have finished by the end of the week: *McTeague*, *A Simple Heart*, and *The House by the Medlar Tree*. I think I finished one of them last night. While I was waiting. But I can't remember which. I'll check my bag when I get back to the room.

It was *The Simple Heart*. No bookmark inside the pages. I have notes written along the inside of the back binding. Ideas for a paper I'm supposed to write. Ideas about Flaubert's use of the Holy Trinity, the symbolism, the reason, etc. I never know if I get anywhere with these papers. I get grades. I get praise. But I don't know what any of those things mean. I think I need someone to tell me if I am right or if I am wrong. Whether or not they know the truth. Just let me know. So that I can move on to something new.

It is Wednesday. I've missed Contemporary British Fiction and French Symbolism. I'm just on time for Shakespeare. I should have finished *Othello*, but the content was too hard for me last week. Sometimes I just can't handle what I've been forced to read. The professors never believe me. When I tell them, "I couldn't stop crying. You don't understand how much this is fucking me up . . ." So I've stopped talking to them. And decided to finish what I can and not finish what I can't.

2.

There is no real beginning. It fell into place. I don't have early memories. I don't have anything that sticks around inside my head. Events are passing. I can't remember last year. Someone will tell me about a terrible snowstorm. And I can try really hard to recreate the neighboring streets covered in white. Cars buried. Children in their soldieresque attire. But it is all something I create in a single moment. None of it is real.

I remember being drawn to prostitution. The situations one could find themselves in. The inability to really escape once things started. I was tired of beginning and never ending. I just wanted to start and never be able to back out. I made the right choice.

At first I was afraid of my body. I needed to find a source within that I could work with. And I don't mean my spirit or my soul. There is something deeper. The way my bones move invisible behind my flesh. I needed to find those movements and use them for desire.

I assumed men only wanted boys with tight bodies. Where the flesh looks like it has been saran-wrapped across the muscle and bone. The nipples are compasses. The asses are tunnels outside this world. I knew my body wouldn't compare. I am not tiny. My flesh does not fall tight across my body. A man's fingers cannot follow along each vein and bone jutting from my skin like braille. My body cannot be read.

I am average all around. My face, legs, hips, cock, and ass. Better can be found in any high school locker room. On any university campus. I found it wasn't the body. It was the ability. The willingness. The men weren't fucking what I had. The men were fucking what they could, but used me to fill the empty holes of need. Their bodies had been poked. The things they desired had never come true. They found themselves leaking regret.

The older the man, the more severe the fucking. They

had been holding onto their desires for too long. And I was never quite what they wanted. So I'd have bruises and cuts to prove how much I disappointed. It was only my body. I still focused on the bones inside. I knew it didn't matter what they did. Or, how they attacked.

3.

I want everything that happens to be as important as everything that has already happened. And I can't find my way to those things that happened. So I try and hold onto what is happening. A short celebration of a moment.

When I am driving home after I've made my money. The cash cradled inside the leather of my wallet, rested inside my coat. The flurries falling like angel's tears. As small puddles of white wash around the roads. The way my breath is visible in my car. The heater never starts to work until I'm on campus.

The lights blurred in the smoke of my breath. In the smoke of my cigarette. The world is expanding and opening as I begin to come off whatever drug I had been handed back at the hotel. I think I like it best when I'm coming down. Nothing holds sentimental value. Everything I pass is new again. Everything rushes out from behind the sidewalk and begs to be noticed.

In the pure coldness of winter I can feel my bones. The bones I rely on during sex. I feel them ache and sigh. I notice my fingers as they curl around the steering wheel. As they curl toward my mouth and mount the stem of a joint.

My toes are children wrapped inside blankets. Hidden from the frigidity of the season. No chapped cheeks or lips turning to raisins, curling and aging.

I think the winter is intensely beautiful. My mother tells me, "When you were a child you hated the winter."

And I think it was because I couldn't understand. I had nothing to take hold of me and scream. No one was being brutal. No one was telling me how everything really had to be. Once I learned all this, the winter turned itself inside out. I was no longer looking across a white world, but I was looking into the snowflakes and sleet. Looking inside the houses lit up with orange. The shade of orange the season turns the lights that are peeping out from behind frosted glass. I was looking into a sacred existence I could never have imagined.

4.

Is this everything?

I am afraid no matter how hard I try I will still ask this question before I die. I'll look into the eyes of whoever I can. I'll beg for one more line. Just one more item I may have missed. A last glimpse around the room I died in. It will have to be important. The room you die in. It becomes womblike. Everything in life is cyclical. We return to where we left.

5.

"I bet he fucks like an animal," Sara whispers across her desk.

I shake my head as if to say, *Disgusting.* But I don't really care. She just needs a reaction.

She's referring to Professor Simmons. Professor of British Literature, with a focus on Dante and Milton. He must know hell. Somewhere along the line he found hell and decided to study his way out. It is the magic of fiction. It leads you to believe you can go somewhere with it, through it, because of it.

He is old. His shoulders slump forward like his eyes.

His glasses rest at the center of his nose. His nose is always dry. Flakes of skin fall from it like snow from the mountains. There are red veins rising from the skin. His eyebrows are white, brushy beasts lining the space above his eyes. His hair emptied years ago. At times one can spot a stray hair that grew in the night.

When I look into his eyes I hate him even more. There is frost pressed against his pupils. He shouts with the whiteness. He lies to us with the green that rests at the center of his eye. He hardly recognizes he has students.

Sara wants to surprise me on a daily basis. I let her think she achieves her goal. I have nothing else to do for her. It is easier to laugh when she expects and sigh when she expects. I am too tired to despise her openly.

6.

It is a discussion of the soul. Similar to the discussion of the chicken or the egg, which came first? Was I born gay? Genetics, the soul, a choice.

Did I decide fucking men would be easier? More money involved in getting men off than getting women off?

I don't think I'd be straight and allow men to explode inside me. To allow their flesh to scratch against my flesh. Their unshaven cheeks to rub along my stomach as they move down my body. Their hairy asses and curly pubes. I'm sure I've been queer.

my body's memory

1.

The first man. I think we are meant to remember our firsts. Again, I can create for you a story. And I will. I'll stand outside. I'll refer to me as *he*. I have to step outside for a moment. Grab a smoke. Take a break.

The john is pulling off his tie. It sneaks through his collar and around his neck like Satan through an apple tree. He smiles a giant smile. Something awkward to his teeth. The way they bend like a picket fence after a wind storm.

The prostitute doesn't look afraid. Even though it will be his first time having sex for pay. Although not his first time having sex.

The prostitute isn't sure how things work. Who is to take charge? And do they get straight to the point? Can he talk? Ask questions?

"Um, so . . . what do you want?" he asks the john.

"Just sit still. I'm going to strip. And I'm going to jerk off in your face. That's all I want. Just smile. I want to see your teeth. Your white teeth and your pink gums. Keep smiling."

The prostitute straightens his posture. Places his hands in his lap. Like he is posing for an elementary school picture. A smile spreads wide. His eyes flutter to a close. He can't wait for the end. He's in shock at how easy this is going to be.

The john steps closer with his cock aimed at the boy's face. His fingers are slipping around his cock. His face is tightened. He is turning red. He doesn't look down at the boy. He stares up at the ceiling. The sharp points of a plastered ceiling. The type of ceiling that popped balloons as a child. The child reaching and grabbing for the released balloon. And an explosion.

"Fuc, fuck, fuck!" the john shouts. And steps away.

The prostitute has his face covered. He has stopped smiling. The bitterness burning his lips. He reaches out for a cloth. The john places something into his hand. And the prostitute wipes his face. Looking out into the hotel room. The john is seated at the tiny table, in one of the two poorly upholstered chairs.

"Thanks," the john mumbles. His body shudders with regret. The kind of regret one experiences when they're discovering themselves. The shudder one gets after they've first masturbated. The confusion of the feeling. It felt so good. But was it too good? Ready to sneak back into your pants while being afraid of the repercussions.

I leave the room.

2.

This scene I watch with my back facing the bed. I can see the scene in the reflection of the bathroom mirror. A large reflecting pool plastered above the sink. I watch this scene like a film. Through a distorted lens. Not straight on.

The john is upset. He is in tears. And the prostitute knows this isn't a good sign. This has happened before. He hasn't even come and he feels regret. They're angry at him for letting this begin.

"You little faggot!" the john is screaming. "Fucking whore!"

He forces his palm into the side of my cheek. The prostitute sees red. As if blood has exploded inside his face. Behind his eyelids. Even with his eyes closed there is too much to see.

The john is getting angrier.

The prostitute isn't awake.

3.

He said he wanted to sleep with me. He found me in the airport. Leaning against the leather of the chair. A magazine wide open. My eyes everywhere but on the page.

"Hi. You're Mathew, right?" He looks down at me. Peering through the bottom of his glasses. His eyes are magnified. Or my eyes are magnified. The perspective is magnified and turns blurry.

"Yes." I smile upwards, or the corners of my mouth turn upwards, and I look up.

"Fred." He pushes out his hand. I scoot back a bit. For a second I reacted.

"Just a handshake. Sorry. That's probably not normal." He retracts the hand. His fingers pull away like they are sliding out of a glove.

"It's all right. None of it is normal. So, you ready?"

"Yeh. I got my luggage. All set." He turns his wrist. Showing me his palm. And sliding it away from his waist. Silently saying *this way*. My guide.

The room is still cold. No one has filled it since the 11 a.m. checkout time Fred mentioned. I've never stayed around long enough for checkout time. I think Fred wants me to stay around long enough. So it is decided. And I will.

"I'm going to shower," Fred states.

"Um, yeh."

He looks around the room. His eyes keep returning to me. After a pause he picks up his luggage and carries it into the bathroom with him.

They always assume I'm a thief too. And maybe I am. But they always leave with their belongings. I've never had to decide.

He showers for twenty-three minutes. I hear the small rain storm that happens in the bathroom over the news broadcasts, commercials, and music videos I flip through. I wish I had remembered my book.

* * *

He is in his briefs when he steps out of the bathroom. Smokes trails out behind him. Or fog. Or moisture. He steps out like a magician appearing from thin air.

I think he has been crying. His eyes are puffed out like the feathers of an owl. I want to hold him. I suddenly feel broken. I think he senses this.

"I'm sorry. I'm a sad man."

He is thin. It hurts to watch his bones shift through his skin. Like his flesh is just a thin curtain that his bones hide behind. Maybe he focuses on the movement of his bones. Or maybe I notice too much because of how hard I focus.

I look at his nipples. They are thin. There is the slightest hint of a tit. I want to run my finger across them. I want to make him hard. And to feel worth the evening. I want to help him travel away.

"Is this okay? Do I need to leave?" I ask him.

"No. Just understand."

And he didn't have to tell me what I needed to understand. I just completely understood. And I think it took every happy moment of our lives to flash before us to keep us from crying.

He stood across the room from me for an hour. Or something that felt like an hour. There was no clock. No time. A lot of silence. And I think we had both emptied ourselves from the room a half-dozen times.

He approached my body. He placed his decayed hand against my back. Rested it on my thin shirt. I felt his veins throbbing. I felt his life.

He moved his lips to mine. And pressed against me. Like pages smashing a flower. His lips were larger than the rest of his body. They pressed into my lips like wine. They were moist and flavored. They made me drunk. They made me expand. I wasn't kneeling on the bed. I wasn't in the room. I wasn't in the city. I was his mind. I went wherever he most desired to be. And I found myself in a backyard. On a swing. Just shifting back and forth. Trying to see how high I could get. And hoping to find the courage to jump into the grass. To see how faraway from the swingset I could land.

He pulled away from my lips. I felt like my life support had been pulled.

"I just want to lie next to you. No noise. Just your breathing. I want you to place your chest against my back. I want to know I'm not the only person living."

He pulled my shirt off. And dropped the towel. He had no hair on his body. Except the hair on his head, eyebrows, and a little along his arms.

I slid into the bed. Under the covers. And away from the edge. Leaving enough room for his small body to know space.

He slid into the bed. And backed into my body. We were like two spoons in a silverware drawer. Sexless and smooth.

And he felt me living throughout the evening. He woke at 7:30 a.m. Dressed and left an envelope at the side of the bed. After a half-hour passed, and I knew for sure he had left, I started to cry.

my body's journal

1.

eyes

It is the proof. My tears. I was not meant to be a whore. It was something my eyes always revealed. I wasn't tough enough. And I'm not sure I was ever smart enough.

2.
teeth

I smiled crooked to hide how straight my teeth are. My johns didn't desire a kid from the right side of the tracks. They wanted a boy who had no father. Whose mother was a whore. Not the son of a florist and an accountant.

3.
ears

I listen to their demands. My ears curl into themselves like seashells or snails. A series of rings. I place myself to their bodies and wait to hear them scream. The sounds of their bodies spilling open.

4.
lips

My mouth is never closed. I talk too much. Or have it filled.

5.
neck

I always turn my head to the left when I am photographed. It helps to cover up half my face. To never be trapped face-on. I think I can escape any scrutiny if I only give half of myself at a time.

6.
fingers

They don't tire easily. They hold on tight. They're strong. When I hold them out straight they spread outwards like a Chinese fan. They curve to the left on my left hand. Curve to the right on my right hand. They are the tides washing in and out. Washing up what's been left behind.

7.
nipples

They're sensitive. They're usually bruised with bites. The marks left behind by teeth fall into my skin like staples into a page. I like to scream. It releases me when they bite into my chest. They're eating their way into my body. Chomping for my heart. Waiting to finish me. They're cannibals at my nipples. I'm human on their tongues.

my body's regrets

1.
I'm not sure it was suicide. It wasn't suicide.

I'm not sure it was attempted suicide.

I dragged the razor down my veins. I watched red rushing from the rip of raw flesh. It poured out like a geyser.

I lowered my hand into the stinging sink water. The shock of the cold water running underneath my flesh. Like rats in the sewer.

The clear water turned the brightest red. The darkest, brightest red.

It was only my left wrist. Two marks down. Two long tears. Two long fissures in the earth.

2.
I was seven. I was walking around the garage. My father's toolshed. The wall with its hooks. Like a slaughterhouse.

The long metal tools dangling like earrings from the lobes of elderly women.

I wore cheap thin sandals. I landed on top of a nail sticking out of a piece of wood. The nail lodged itself inside me. It was the first time I was entered. I couldn't find the symbolism at the time. I was seven.

Now I have to laugh. The way it broke the skin.

I was rushed to the doctor. The nail was rusted. A rust red, red, red. More red than my blood. The contrast was dazzling. A kaleidoscope effect.

3.

The first boy I loved was K. He is real. So I keep his name to myself.

He met me in the halls of school. He watched me for weeks. Studied me. All the people we don't notice. What they notice. What we become to them. And later how we disappoint them.

He approached me in the parking lot. I was entering my car. And my name was a bird with a large wingspan. It flew from his mouth. I heard his fear.

"Mathew." The *flap, flap, flap* as the name smacked against the air. Rising from his mouth. Floating toward me.

I turned and stared. I hadn't heard a male voice speak my name outside of my father's voice.

I accepted the joke and continued to climb into my car. But he stopped me. He found himself by the side of the car.

"I'm K," he whispered. Looking past me. Into the car.

"Hi." I felt bad not giving him my name. But he already had it.

"Um, what are you doing? Right now? Are you going somewhere? Are you free?"

I think he would have asked me the same question in as many different ways possible had I not stopped him.

"Nowhere. I'm free."

And he paused. And watched me. And the cars in the parking lot all emptied out. The large bird that was my name had flown back into its cage.

We went for coffee. And I fell in love while he nervously sipped a dark beverage from a cardboard cup. The drink falling back into the shadows of his mouth. Down his throat. I wanted to know the back of his mouth. And the shadows.

And he was willing to let me inside the shadows.

We fucked like we were sinning. We sinned like we had to.

It was odd teenage sex. Quick and loud. The type of sex that a neighbor hears walking the dog by your house. But they only hear the grunts, until they get a quarter of the way across the yard and it all ends.

I died inside him repeatedly.

He was always relaxed when we were fucking. And never any other time. His asshole would turn open. I never had to push. He had been a virgin before me. But he never felt pain.

When we switched positions he made me cry. Stabbing me. Forcing and pushing. It was the start of a love affair with violent sex.

He would reach his fingers inside me. Just a little. Try to stretch me open like a piece of rubber. Pulling with his fingers and pushing with his dick.

I bled like a girl the first few times he fucked me. Spotting his bed sheets. He didn't do his own laundry. I'm not sure how he explained it to his mother. I'm not sure I cared.

***

He stopped fixating on me as soon as he had me. Or as soon as he found out how much of me he had.

He wouldn't answer my phone calls. He wouldn't look my way in the halls. He treated me like the ex-boyfriends of all my female friends. I learned there was no difference. Gay or straight. Boys wanted to break into your body first. Come inside you. Like graffiti across your organs: *K was here.*

4.

My asshole began to eat. Anything I gave it.

I didn't want to be as tight as I had been with K. So I started to feed it.

I bought dildos. Starting at the smallest size. Working up to the largest I could find. The largest being a dark, dark shade of black. Large plastic popping veins crawling up the shaft like spiders. The first time I sat down onto it I may have passed out.

my body familiar

Scene One

A dining room. Wooden round table. Four chairs. A large light falls from the ceiling a couple feet from the table. The window shades are all pulled closed. It is evening.

> *Mother:* Mathew, what did you do after school? Your brother said you didn't get home until a little before 6.

Mathew turns and stares into his brother.

> *Mathew:* To the park. *(Lie)*

Father: Which one? The Deer Run Park is supposed to have a new play area by the pond. I haven't seen it yet.

Mathew: Not Deer Run. I went to River's Run. Up into the trail.

Brother: Why so late? It was dark way before you came home.

Mathew: I'm sure it doesn't matter to you.

Mother: Your grandmother called work today. She forgot to take her medicine. And she had called Charles. He refused to speak to her. She called me in tears. "What have I done to deserve such an ungrateful son?"

Father: (Chuckles)

Mother: It isn't funny. I couldn't talk to her when I was working. I was at the front desk all day today. The waiting room doesn't need to know.

Brother: Need to know what?

Mother: They don't need to know your grandmother is an alcoholic.

Brother: She isn't a drunk.

Mathew: (Chuckles)

Scene Two

My family didn't drive me to the place I crash.

My family isn't to blame for the choices I made.

My family didn't fail me.

My family never turned their back on me.

My family was an average family. Unable to express how they really felt. Their whole lives together, no one ever said "I love you" because they felt it. Only when they felt they had to.

My family was your family.

my body's journal, revised

1.
nose

Coke.

2.
nipples

Bite marks.

3.
lips

Joints.

4.
tongue

Ecstasy.

5.
fingers

Cigarettes.

6.
asshole

Cocks. Fingers. Dildos.

my body's memory, pt. 2

1.
The john throws me against the wall. The wall splits into little pieces. Like a drinking glass that has been smacked too hard with a knife, moments before a toast. Yet no one is going to speak.

"Fucking like that, don't you?" The john spits. His anger is a shade I have never known.

He pulls me from the wall. Peels me, more like it. Takes me by the hair and tosses me onto the bed. The covers slide underneath me. Like I am a surfer on the sea. Yet there is no fresh air or feeling of freedom.

The prostitute is bleeding from the back of his head. His skin has cracked into small lines like the wall. Like the wine glass.

"All right," the prostitute pleads. "Just forget this. No money, all right? Just let me go."

"No fucking way. We're having a good time. You little ugly trick. Fucking sinner." He takes his beer bottle and throws it at the wall above my head. Beer and glass shatter across my skin. The glass glistens and the beer dances in the light.

The prostitute says to the john, "Please, please, please. Stop."

The john says back, "This is your motherfucking job. And you're going to make sure I am satisfied."

I leave the scene before he starts to place a penny inside my ass.

The bones behind my flesh, the bones beneath me, the bones.

2.

I fucked an artist.

An artist fucked me.

I went down on an artist.

An artist went down on me.

We did this in front of a mirror. The mirror was above his bed. And against the wall. At the top of his bed.

I watched his tongue enter my ass. The way his hair

bobbed as he licked me. His cock and balls hanging from between his legs. Reflected large as life behind him

He painted my body. A shade of red I only knew the inside of my body to be. He wrote words with his fingers. Across my body. Inside the paint. Like writing in the sand. Or pissing in the snow.

He had an interest in pleasure. He wasn't kinky. He was safe.

He wanted condoms on when we went down on each other. He placed plastic on his tongue when he licked my ass.

My body was covered in paint before he would touch me.

He didn't want anything to do with me until he created a new me.

3.

He just wanted to ask questions. He was hard the whole time. I could see his cock shifting inside his jeans. I felt like a star. Being interviewed. Question after question. It was his kink.

my body's q&a

1.

john: When was the last time you were with a man?
me: Yesterday, or last night. I left the room around 11:40-ish p.m.
john: What had he done with you?
me: Fucked me.
john: Anything special? Out of the ordinary?
me: He liked to call me his wife's name. Judy. He fucked me and called me Judy.

john: Did it feel degrading? Did you feel removed?

me: I always feel removed.

john: How far have you gone with a john?

me: Be more specific. I'm not going to list everything.

john: Have you been pissed on?

me: Yes. Once. A man visiting from Oregon. I was on my stomach. I didn't know that was what he wanted to do. But by time he had started, it didn't matter anymore.

john: What did it feel like?

me: It was heavy. And it was warm.

john: Did you ever piss on anyone?

me: A number of times. Two men had me piss in their mouths. Three or four, maybe five, have had me piss on them. Somewhere on their bodies.

john: How about scatting?

me: No. I've been asked once. And I declined.

john: Why?

me: It isn't healthy.

john: Is being a prostitute healthy?

me: Probably not. I make my choices. I choose not to poop on or be pooped on.

john: (*Giggles*)

me: Anything else?

john: Do you do a lot of drugs in this line of work?

me: Yes. Whatever the john has to offer. And most of them have something to offer.

john: Drug of choice?

me: I'm simple. I like pot. A joint or a cigarette. Something rolled tight resting between my lips and fingers. Comfort food.

john: Is it easier to get paid for sex if you're on something?

me: No. Everything is more severe when I'm on something. It hurts more. It means more. I don't want it to mean anything. I like being on something after the sex. Things always mean more afterwards . . . The drugs help me to realize that.

john: What else do you do with your life? Are you just a prostitute?

me: No. I'm in school.

john: College?

me: Yes.

john: What are you studying?

me: English Literature.

john: A whore with a reading habit. Any favorite books? Authors?

me: Chopin, Faulkner, Norris, Brontë from time to time. *Frankenstein* is brilliant.

john: Why literature?

me: It makes promises it can't keep. And I know that going in.

john: Why *Frankenstein*?

me: Shelley never lies to her reader. Loneliness is that hard.

john: Any quotes? Words you live by?

me: I live by words.

john: No quotes?

me: I can't remember any of them. They're written down in journals at home.

john: Do you write? In these journals?

me: I did. A long time ago. I forced myself to stop.

john: Why?

me: I started to believe in its promises.

john: Meaning?

me: Meaning that I could do something with what I created. Believing that I was doing something important. That I could do something other than destroy.

john: You seem too educated to be a trick.

me: There is no reason to believe a trick is stupid. There's no basis for that theory.

john: It just doesn't seem like a safe line of work. Haven't you been threatened?

me: I've been terrorized. But I knew that going in. I was prepared. I've been preparing for it for a long time.

john: Most of your type have been molested. That is what drives you to these acts.

me: Is this a study? You have numbers? Done a survey?

john: It's just a fact.

me: I'm not sure I believe it.

john: So you were never molested? Your daddy never snuck into your room and snuck inside you? He didn't bury his head into his big Daddy dick?

The john removed his cock from his pants and jerked off. Very quickly. The question-and-answer period had ended. I was given my money and I left.

my body's digression

1.

A list of my favorite words:

Vintage
Quotidian
Sipped
Meander

2.
My favorite number: anything ending in a seven

3.
My favorite color: a shade of blue I haven't seen in years

4.
My favorite time of day: 3:47 a.m., I think everyone else is sleeping and I am truly alone

5.
My drug of choice: a little bit of weed to slow down living

6.
My favorite body part: the hip bone

my body's romance

1.
I met him at a concert. A girl had passed out in the corner. Her friends huddled like a football field. Women turned to men. Shouting out their unconscious friend's name.

He and I were the only two to stop. The music never stopped. It swirled around our eyes with the smoke from cigarettes. We watched. And the world started to slip away. Until the girl shifted and stood with support.

We caught each others' eyes as we pulled away from the scene and back to the level of the room.

I was seventeen. And I felt I had been waiting forever to fall in love. *Solomente diez y siete.*

2.

We smoked weed and sipped wine. Got fucked up together to see who could be more honest.

3.

We slept together every night. Slipping out of our bedroom windows like teenage girls on their way out of this world.

Slipping back into the other's bedroom window. Curled and cradled. I haven't felt anything since. Fred came close. With his breathing. And his back curved. My chest touching. Tickling. Crawling along the spine.

We didn't speak. Or fuck. We lay awake with our fingers crawling like ants. Like bed bugs along the other's body. Like beads of sweat tumbling from the brow.

Every night we'd sneak into each other.

4.

I quote Henry Miller to explain love:

> *I said to myself over and over that if a man, a sincere and desperate man like myself, loves a woman with all his heart, if he is ready to cut off his ears and mail them to her, if he will take his heart's blood and pump it out on paper, saturate her with his need and longing, besiege her everlastingly, she cannot possibly refuse him. The homeliest man, the weakest man, the most undeserving man must triumph if he is willing to surrender his last drop of blood.*

It was like that. I was seventeen. In my second relationship. And I fell in love like Henry Miller wrote. A mad, overwhelming sweep of thoughts and ideas that never stopped. Fractured and raw.

5.

I would lie on my stomach. My ass curved up into the air. It was hungry. And he would feed me like he had to. Like my survival rested on his feeding me.

My arms were above my head. Spread out toward the bedposts. Clawing at the pillows. He would run his fingers around my nipples. Pulling gently. Enough to make me have to grunt. Enough to make me release some genuine emotion.

My penis rubbing against the bed sheets. Creating a bunched ball of sheets underneath me. He would enter me harshly. Knowing it was the part I hated most. Once he was in, he took his time. He would rest inside me. Lay down against my body. The idea of one body does exist.

He would whisper down to my ear. His words fell like leaves from trees. They gathered inside my lobe: "love," "need," etc.

He was on his knees when he was inside me. Like he was in a temple. And I was a sacrifice he worshiped.

6.

We stopped going out. We sat around bedrooms with joints. He was always more honest.

His father had raped him until he was seven. He doesn't know when it had started. He remembers the bedroom door opening. He remembers his father's cologne. And his father's fingers.

I think he learned that sex and love were not the same

thing from his father. The things our fathers teach us.

I had learned that sex and love were the same thing. Until he taught me differently.

And on February 21, he told me it wasn't love. It was something else that swelled inside boys. For two years we swelled. And then he told me it had to stop.

7.

I think we only cry when we have to. When there is nothing left in our lives. No shoulders or ears to fall into. No journals with empty pages. No novels with a similar theme.

my body's process

1.

A trip to the airport turned me into a prostitute.

I watched all the men descending onto their luggage. As it spun around the metal carousel. They watched me from the corners of their eyes. And they fucked me from ten feet away.

2.

I'd show up once a week. A large novel in my hand. Tolstoy or some other Russian with his endless ability. I figured no one would suspect me of prostitution if I showed up with *Anna Karenina* in my lap and dressed like I was trying to blend in.

3.

After three months I didn't need to wait at the airport anymore.

I didn't have to check flight schedules to ward off any

suspicion from security. All those flights coming and going. And I just stood in front of the screens. Week after week. Waiting.

I had enough men interested. They would call when they were in town. They told their friends about me as they drank martinis in their poorly lit dance clubs. Huddled in the corners. Taking their stories further than the truth.

They placed my number up on websites. Escort service sites for those who work on their own. I found my number on a few of them. Read the reviews I was given.

He does what you want. And takes it like he doesn't care. Perfect.
He will crawl up against you when you crawl inside.
He doesn't show any interest. He doesn't bleed enough.
He will lick on your balls. But doesn't suck on your tip.
He doesn't ask questions. Or give answers. He's silent.
His body is average. But his asshole is tight. Like a virgin.
I fucked him while he cried. I made him cry more.
He won't lick your ass, or let you watch him shit.
He tied me up and stabbed me with a small pocket knife. Made me come.
He won't stop you from being happy.
He will leave as soon as you come.
His face is empty. He won't make you feel satisfied. Empty.
Waste of money. Waste of time. Waste of sperm, really.
He laid against me all night. And I think he meant it.
I made him hate me. And at the end I gave him the money. Made him need me.

my body's memory, pt. 3

1.

He was larger than I was used to. And his stomach hung

over his waist making his belt invisible until he started to unbuckle it and pulled it out like he was ripping hair from a child's head and threw it against the wall and I knew this wasn't right and the way the white hair along his chest was in angry tight curls was symbolic of everything that didn't make sense to him inside his body and how much he wanted to be angry and how much he was angry and how much he wanted to show me, how much of himself he was going to show me and do to me and mean to me because he wanted to mean more to me than any other john had meant.

He crawled toward me like I was carrion, like we were a *National Geographic* special and the camera men just continue to film all the carnage and I don't know who was filming this but someone had to be watching, someone has to care enough to watch everything that we do and how much pain and pleasure we pour across our bodies in search of meaning that wasn't found in the relationships of our youth.

His fingers were tight curls around my ankles while they gripped and grabbed and flipped me over on my stomach, tearing off my pants and my underwear while they landed across the room, the metal of the jeans zipper smacking and scratching the television screen and I hoped he worried about being charged extra for the damage, I hoped there was nothing else on his mind to distract from the price of a new television for the hotel.

His dick was pressing against my ass and he could tell I was trying to keep him out and force him back away to tell him to take his money and leave me in the room by myself, but he knew he was my last john, he knew it because he wanted it and not because I told him anything about my graduation or my plans for a novel or my lie of a life, only that he wanted to take over and be in charge and make me understand what he couldn't understand until he made the plans for this trip and the plans for this evening.

He ripped into my ass like he hated every piece of my body and hated every piece of his body, but I don't think it was like he hated every piece, I truly believe he did hate every piece and he kept spitting on my body and making the sound one makes when they pull all the phlegm up into their mouth, pulling it all from their nose and throat and gut, and then he would spit across my back, neck, and head like he was coming from his mouth, as if he was ridding himself of every evil deed inside his body while at the same time exorcizing any demons inside me with his spit acting as holy water, and he truly believed himself to be of such power and strength and I believe it too, so I started to cry and scream but he only got angry and smacked his balled-up hand against my back three times until I heard something crack and he heard something crack, so he giggled and I believe he must have been smiling, but as he fucked me my broken body was cracking more and starting to fall apart from itself, falling apart from everything it had been for the past twenty-two years of its life.

He rolled me over after he pulled himself out of me, after he had come inside me and caused me to feel like vomiting and wanting to kill him, but when he saw it in my eyes it was what I had been seeing in his eyes and there was no way I would be leaving this hotel room and breathe the air and hear the cars speeding down the streets and the grass growing and my name as a big bird landing into the world.

He took his fist and smacked it into my stomach,

causing me to spit up or vomit, and my body was forced forward and up and my nose took in a whiff of his cologne and his breath and I wanted to vomit more because it was all so ugly and it was all so real and I knew my verses would never be filled with what this man was doing and what this man stood for, so maybe it was for the best that he was going to destroy my body because my words would mean nothing after this experience and I would end up depressed and at the sink with razors to my wrist anyway.

    I fell back into the pillows and sucked air like it mattered, like the air meant something, like the air was everything I stood for, while he started to spit at me again and take my cock in his hand and pull so hard I thought it would detach, and he screamed, "Get hard, get hard, you son of a bitch, you fucking whore, you want this more than I do, now I want you hard so that I can break it, so that I can bend it, and I want you to spill blood and scream and come and I want your sickness all over the mattress!" and he wasn't lying but I couldn't get hard as my body started to sink into itself because everything else had been so hard and everything was getting so heavy and turning dark.

    And his fingers were inside my mouth like a dental examination and they were pulling at the front of my teeth like he would pull and break something else hard and the pressure in my gums was building up as he started to dismantle my body and disregard everything that I stood for, and every person I knew who closed their eyes and pictured me would have pictured my smile, and, as if he knew that it was the first thing he started to remove from me tooth by tooth, he snapped and cracked and ripped and pulled and crushed into white bits and white powder and into nothing that represented where it had started, where it had all come from.

The blood in my mouth was ugly.

The blood in the room was ugly.

The sheets and the mattress and his fingers were the only three things to ever know me so intimately. To have reworked my body and to have taken out everything that was inside. Like a surrealist painting, my body had been turned into a dresser, the drawers pulled open and my insides staining the carpet and the room and polluting the air and ruining the world.

2.

3.

"Is this everything?"

my body, present

1.

I graduated. And didn't go to graduation.

I didn't walk down an aisle. Or across a stage. I didn't take a folded-up piece of paper into my palm.

I stayed home and finished reading a book. I prepared for my last trick.

I prepared to write again. Pens and journals. Computer paper. My favorite novels lined around my bedroom. For inspiration. For quotes. For comfort.

2.

I had read through some of my old writing. And hoped I had grown over the four years I stopped writing. Hoped the sentences held me up.

3.
I think it would have gone something like this.

my body's afterword
I created this to not exist, too.

About the Contributors

MARC ANDREOTTOLA was born on June 5, 1981. He lives in several coffeeshops throughout Brooklyn, New York. He is currently working on a novel. You can reach him at andreottola@gmail.com.

EDDIE BEVERAGE's debut novel, *200 Beats per Minute*, a frenetic tale on the coming of age of the techno generation, was published in 1998. His second novel, *Tom Brown Saves the World*, arrived in September 2005. Eddie is thirty-four years old and currently resides in Tampa, Florida.

NICK CACIOPPO was born in 1983 and raised in Wantagh, New York, where he still lives and operates. He's the lyricist/vocalist for the Long Island–based hardcore metal act The Communion, writes album reviews, contributes articles to assorted online zines, and is forever working on novels, plays, and poetry collections.

CODY CARVEL was born in 1980 in Oklahoma. He started using during the summer of 1993 at the Bell Hall Technology Center at the University of Texas at El Paso.

JAMES CHAMPAGNE was born on June 17, 1980, a month after Ian Curtis hung himself. He currently resides in Woonsocket, Rhode Island (and he'd much rather be living in Tokyo, Japan). He has written a novel about the '80s called *Confusion* (self-published). He is also the founder of the Necronomicon Transhumanism Society (NTS), whose website slithers at www.necronomicontranshumanism.com.

DENNIS COOPER is the editor of the Akashic Books series *Little House on the Bowery*. He is author of eight novels, most recently *God Jr.* (Grove Press) and *The Sluts* (Carroll & Graf.) His novels have been translated into eighteen foreign languages. He has guest-edited sections of fiction and nonfiction for *Bookforum, Nerve*, the *LA Weekly Literary Supplement*, the *Village Voice Literary Supplement*, and other publications. He is a contributing editor of *Artforum Magazine*.

JOSHUA DALTON was born in 1989 and lives in Dallas, Texas. His writing appeared in *The Full Spectrum: A New Generation of Writing about Gay, Lesbian, Bisexual, Transgender, Questioning, and Other Identities*.

PATRICK DEWITT was born in 1975 on Vancouver Island, British Columbia, Canada. He now lives with his mother, father, wife, and young son on Bainbridge Island in Washington State. He is at work on a novel.

JACK DICKSON was born on February 1, 1959, in a small town on the West Coast—of Scotland. He escaped to Glasgow as soon as he could, where he now lives with his man and his Patterdale terrier. He is the author of nine novels, myriad short stories, two films, and, at present, writes for *River City*, BBC Scotland's flagship drama series.

MARK EDMUND DOTEN was born in 1978. He lives in New York City, where he's enrolled in Columbia University's MFA writing program.

DAVID SAÄ VICCENZO ESTORNELL was born in 1985 in Cartagena, Spain. He has published two collections of poems, and in November 2006 he directed his first short film, *Haiku*. He received a graduate degree in Dramatic Arts in Murcia and Madrid, Spain.

WILL FABRO is a graduate of the writing program at University of California, San Diego, and has been previously published in *Fresh Men*—selected by Edmund White and edited by Donald

Weise—as well as the zine *Cheese + Liquor*. He curated and hosted the reading series *This Is Not the New Minstrel Show*, which showcased up-and-coming queer writers under thirty. Born in 1981 in Hollywood, he currently lives in Brooklyn.

JOSH FEOLA was born in San Antonio, Texas in 1986. He currently studies Art History and Film at Boston University.

ZAC GERMAN lives on the East Coast of the United States. He is thought by many to be nearly six feet tall.

MARK GLUTH was born in 1974 in Cleveland, Ohio. After getting married in 1999, he and his wife moved to the Pacific Northwest. His short fiction has previously appeared in *Ellipses*, *Vista*, and various online journals. He lives in Washington State, in a coastal town, and is writing a novel.

STEVEN T. HANLEY is a twenty-six-year-old writer and filmmaker from London. He makes music videos, video installations, and short films.

NICK HUDSON, raised far and wide across the UK by nomadic, strong-hearted anarchists, has always written prose, poetry, and music. In September 2004, he began writing and recording what would become *The Phoenix Diaries*, a seven-album cycle of interconnected songs addressing themes of transformation and fringe sexualities. This he recently completed *(phew)*.

JEFF JACKSON was born in 1971 and has lived in Aruba, Miami, New Jersey, and New York City. He is a founding member of the Obie Award–winning Collapsable Giraffe theater company, and has worked as writer and cocreator on numerous productions. He's also coproprietor of www.destination-out.com, an audio website dedicated to Free Jazz. He currently lives with his wife in North Carolina.

CALLUM JAMES is thirty-four years old and lives in Portsmouth on the south coast of England. He scratches a living selling old books and writing. His erotic stories have appeared in numerous "one-handed" anthologies, and his journalism in both the gay press and mainstream nationals.

STANYA KAHN is a writer, performer, and videomaker living in Los Angeles. She was born in Palo Alto, California in 1968 and raised in San Francisco. Her performance work has toured nationally and internationally. Her writing appears in *Terminatrix Progeny: Performance Texts and Poems*, *Soft Targets*, *LTTR*, *Movement Research*, and in the chapbooks *Utility Beast*, *Delirium*, *Rank Stranger*, and *The Ballad of Crappy and Seapole*. Her videos, made in collaboration with Harry Dodge, have shown at many festivals and venues, including MOCA, the Getty Center, and the Sundance Film Festival.

MIKE KASCEL is a twenty-seven-year-old writer and musician currently living in Madison, Wisconsin, where he writes poetry, short fiction, and rock songs. He hopes to find a mentor or pick up a degree in Music Composition sometime in the near future. Until then, he is finishing his last year at the University of Wisconsin-Madison studying Genetics, and plans to be living far away from there, soon.

T.P. KENDALL is a twenty-four-year-old writer currently working on his first novel. He has worked in a sewerage farm, an *Alice in Wonderland* theme park, a novelty soap factory, and several old man bars. He would like to escape low-level employment, even if that seems unlikely. He lives in his hometown of Bournemouth, England, where he feels comfortable wrestling with friends and hanging out with his baby niece Edith.

MIKE KITCHELL was born in 1986 and really likes movies. He lives in DeKalb, Illinois.

JOSE ALVARADO LOPEZ was born in San Salvador in 1983. War forced his family to emigrate. He lives in Toronto.

JOSEPH MARCURE, born 1983, lives in Fresno, California, and is currently writing his first novel.

M.A.D. is seventeen and lives in Toronto.

NICHOLAS MESSING was born in 1978 in Baltimore. His cultural criticism has appeared in *Interview*, *Manhattan File*, and *Provincetown Magazine*.

MELISSA MUSSER is thirty years old and has been writing since childhood. She currently resides in Stavanger, Norway, with her nine-year-old son.

AARON NIELSEN was born in 1979 and currently lives in San Francisco. His fiction and poetry have appeared in the following publications: *Hustlers: Erotic Stories of Sex for Hire* (Alyson Books, 2006), *Instant City*, *Freshmen 2: New Voices in Gay Fiction* (Carroll & Graf, 2005), *Werewolf Express*, *Mirage #4 Period(ical)*, and *The Chabot Review*. He is also the literature editor for the zine *Jouissance*.

FRANKIE P was born February 15, 1986 in Fullerton, California. You can e-mail him at Patricksdead@yahoo.com.

SEAN PAJOT is a twenty-two-year-old writer and visual artist living in Toronto. He is the cofounder of the art collective Label [X]X and the editor of *Peddler*, a quarterly magazine of art and writing.

JAGO PALLABAZZER is Italian, and too inhibited to write in his own language.

CHARLIE QUIROZ, who was born in 1981, spent most of his years in Florida and Virginia, and now resides in Brooklyn.

NICHOLAS RHOADES was born on October 25, 1968, and raised in Detroit. He has had several short works published through the University of Michigan. Currently, he is finishing a collection of more recent stories and poems, and the final edit of a novel, *Act*.

JACK SHAMAMA is a San Francisco–based writer/pornographer. With his best friend Michael Stabile, he edits GayPornBlog.com and has written screenplays for several gay porn movies, including *Wet Palms*, which won a GayVN Award for Best Screenplay in 2005. His personal website and blog can be found at www.fauxjob.com. He was born on June 24, 1974 in Brooklyn, New York.

ROBERT SIEK is a thirty-two-year-old writer who currently resides in Queens, New York. His poetry has appeared in *Bay Windows*, the *Columbia Poetry Review*, *Lodestar Quarterly*, *Unpleasant Event Schedule*, and other journals. His poetry chapbook *Clubbed Kid* was published by the New School University in 2003. In 2005, four of his poems were included in the Rogue Scholars Press poetry anthology *Cat Breath: A Two-Headed Kitty Award Anthology*. He is at work on his first novel.

CHRIS VON STEINER, born Christophe Austrui in 1965, has lived in Paris since the early '90s. He has published two novels, *Un panda dans l'escalier* (2001) and *Je veux te voir nu* (2002). Now working as a visual artist, he has exhibited through Europe and the U.S.A.

ANGELA TAVARES lives in Boston, Massachusetts, with a beautiful woman and three mean dogs. She is thirty-two years old.

GARRISON TAYLOR, twenty-six, was conceived (both literally and metaphorically) in the mythical state of Alabama. His short fiction and film reviews have appeared in *Ellipsis*, as well as in the irreverent film zine *Nathan Jr*. He presently bides his time amongst the bright young things of Hollywood, California (where he frequently works within the film and television industry).

JUSTIN TAYLOR was born in 1982 in Miami, Florida; he left as soon as he could. He discovered Dennis Cooper's work while a student at University of Florida, where a momentary lapse of bourgeois morals allowed *My Loose Thread* to become a featured selection at the university library. He currently lives in Brooklyn and is editing an anthology of short stories about the apocalypse to be published by Thunder's Mouth. For more information, visit www.justindtaylor.net.

BETT WILLIAMS was born in 1968 in Santa Barbara, California. She is the author of *Girl Walking Backwards* and *The Wrestling Party*. After spending many years in Santa Fe, New Mexico, where she accidentally reinvented female oil wrestling, she moved to Los Angeles, where she lives in a 1951 Vagabond trailer in Silverlake. She is currently working on her second novel.

MATTHEW WILLIAMS was born in 1982. He lives in Cincinnati, Ohio.

Other selections in Dennis Cooper's Little House on the Bowery *series*

GODLIKE a novel by Richard Hell
141 pages, a trade paperback original, $13.95

Godlike, Hell's second novel, is a stunning achievement, and quite likely his most important work in any medium to date. Combining the grit, wit, and invention of *Go Now* with the charged lyricism and emotional implosiveness of his groundbreaking music, *Godlike* is brilliant in form as well as dazzling in its heartwrenching tale of one whose values in life are the values of poetry. Set largely in the early '70s, but structured as a middle-aged poet's 1997 notebooks and drafts for a memoir-novel, the book recounts the story of a young man's affair with a remarkable teenage poet. *Godlike* is a novel of compelling originality and transcendent beauty.

WIDE EYED stories by Trinie Dalton
170 pages, a trade paperback original, $13.95

"With linked anecdotes substituting for plot, Dalton's twenty quick, vibrant, wild tales read more like fantastical diary entries than short stories . . . The latest in Dennis Cooper's *Little House on the Bowery* series, the work is ripe with sensuality and playfulness . . . Dalton's unique blend of dream and bracingly honest observation makes this a delightfully weird and disarming read."

—*Publishers Weekly* (starred review)

ARTIFICIAL LIGHT by James Greer
336 pages, a trade paperback original, $15.95

"Greer does a superb job of transcending conventional genrefication, bringing something fresh to contemporary literature . . . A very enjoyable read with a highly inventive structure, full of eccentricities and rock music factoids . . ."
—*Library Journal*

HEADLESS stories by Benjamin Weissman
157 pages, a trade paperback original, $12.95

"*Headless* is at play in the world. It is fearless, fun, and sometimes filthy. Weissman invites you into an alphabet soup of delight in language. Eat up."
—Alice Sebold, author of *The Lovely Bones*

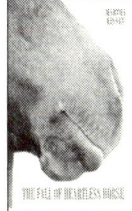

THE FALL OF HEARTLESS HORSE
by Martha Kinney
97 pages, a trade paperback original, $11.95
Pushcart Prize finalist

"Tumultuous and beautiful, an emotional inquiry into writing and the nature of illusion, so highly pleasureable, a surprise and triumph for the American novel."
—Claude Simon, winner of the Nobel Prize for Literature

These books are available at local bookstores.
They can also be purchased online through www.akashicbooks.com.
To order by mail send a check or money order to:

AKASHIC BOOKS
PO Box 1456, New York, NY 10009
www.akashicbooks.com, info@akashicbooks.com

(Prices include shipping. Outside the U.S., add $8 to each book ordered.)